Revolution

Jakob Ejersbo

REVOLUTION

BOOK TWO OF
The Africa Trilogy

Translated from the Danish by
Mette Petersen

MACLEHOSE PRESS
QUERCUS . LONDON

First published in Denmark as *Revolution*
by Gyldendal, Copenhagen, 2009
First published in Great Britain in 2012 by

MacLehose Press
an imprint of Quercus
55 Baker Street
7th Floor, South Block
London W1U 8EW

The publication of Jakob Ejersbo in English is sponsored
by the Danish Arts Agency

A CIP catalogue record for this book is available
from the British Library

ISBN 978 0 85705 108 0

10 9 8 7 6 5 4 3 2 1

Designed and typeset in Collis and Quadraat Sans by Libanus Press
Printed and bound in Great Britain by Clays Ltd, St Ives plc

A big thank you is due to my first reader Christian Kirk Muff for stoking the fire and kicking my arse to bits. Thanks are also due to Ole Christian Madsen for tune-ups. And to Morten Alsinger for a thousand coffee breaks.

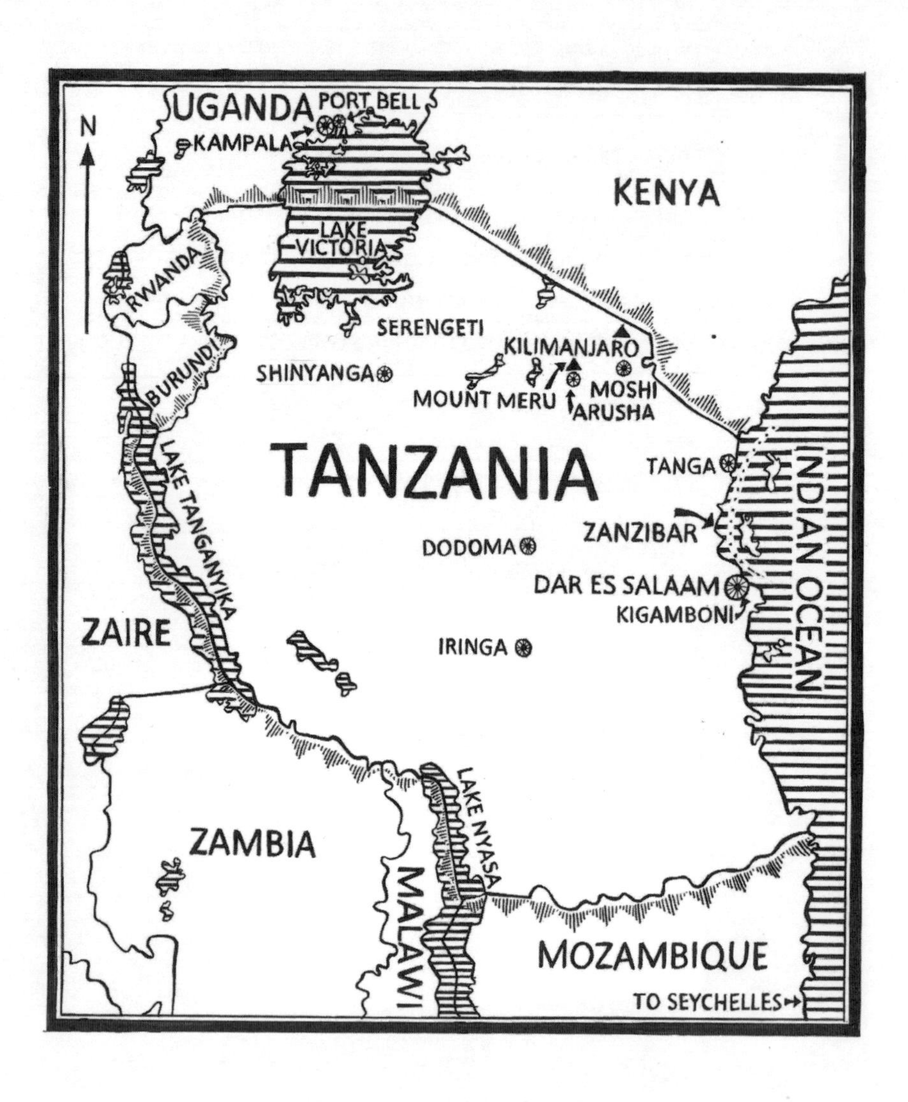
N
UGANDA
PORT BELL
KAMPALA
KENYA
LAKE VICTORIA
RWANDA
BURUNDI
SERENGETI
KILIMANJARO
SHINYANGA
MOUNT MERU
MOSHI
ARUSHA
TANZANIA
TANGA
LAKE TANGANYIKA
INDIAN OCEAN
ZANZIBAR
DODOMA
DAR ES SALAAM
KIGAMBONI
ZAIRE
IRINGA
LAKE NYASA
ZAMBIA
MALAWI
MOZAMBIQUE
TO SEYCHELLES

CONTENTS

Punk Afrique

Greenland

It's all in my horoscope: I'm going to hate Danish hippies, fall head over heels in love with a French fakir, be Agent 007 in Morocco, starve in Sudan, smuggle gold in my cunt, be robbed by Idi Amin and carry six different kinds of worm around in my intestine, the sixth of which is very special indeed.

My name is Sofie Naasunnguaq Petersen and I was born in Upernavik, northern Greenland, in 1955. My mum is a Greenlander and my dad is Danish. We live as Danes do and speak Danish at home. Our house is a good one – it's got central heating and electricity and several rooms. Greenlanders live in small wooden houses built especially for them. They all live in one room and everyone sleeps in the same bed, and they have an unbelievable number of children. Lots of people live truly execrable lives. Their alcohol consumption is staggering. There's no shortage of poverty and misery. But we're the upper class. My dad oversees all the utilities in our town: electricity and water plants, and the shipping yard and stone quarry. He's got a lot of people under him, and they report to work at random intervals. And then there are the other Danes – the ones that make our community work: the doctor, the teachers, the postmaster. The Greenlanders are almost all of them whalers and sealers, nomadic people with nowhere to go. They sew kayaks and hunt seals.

My mother has a lot of Greenlandic friends, and they're forever popping round. But they always sit in the kitchen, because they don't like it in our sitting room. Not that there's anything fancy about it – we just have an ordinary sitting room where we sit and snuggle on the sofa, listening to the radio. But when there are Greenlanders here, they always sit in the kitchen and have Greenlandic food. My dad doesn't want Greenlandic food in the sitting room – he says it stinks to high heaven – it smells of whale oil. We kids have Greenlandic food as well – my mum makes it for us. My dad is an avid hunter and fishes in his spare time. He's a boy scout if there ever was one. He catches wild birds. He once caught a seal that my mum then cleaned on the kitchen floor. But he won't eat blubber.

I don't speak any Greenlandic. At first I pick up a little, but by the time I start school that's already stopped. The Greenlandic children speak enough Danish to allow us to play. When the grown-ups start speaking fast in Greenlandic, I understand precisely nothing at all. I think I do though, and then when I answer a question they laugh at me because I'm on about something different altogether. So in the end I stop trying, and my dad and I get even closer.

The all-Danish families have nothing to do with the Greenlanders after working hours. The Danes and the Greenlanders never visit each other's houses. But many of the Danes have a *kifak* – a Greenlandic daily – who comes round to scrub the floors and do the washing and that sort of heavy-duty housework.

I start school in 1962. The school has a couple of Greenlandic teachers, but we are all taught in Danish. All the other teachers are from Denmark. I'm in the all-Danish class – we are taught in one classroom, regardless of our age or year. The Greenlandic children are taught separately – and teaching them takes forever because they don't speak much Danish. It's not till Year Four that the Danish and Greenlandic children are taught together. I don't do well at school. I daydream. I sit there and stare out of the window. My dad thinks that teachers are spawn of the devil. My mum only went to school for four years. How is an education going to be of any use to a daughter of hers? After all, she's done alright for herself.

As long as someone is going to marry us, what's the problem?

I've got a friend called Uvalu who comes round to play in the afternoons. One day my dad swings by in the afternoon. Normally he doesn't come home until quite late – right before dinner. He opens the door to my room and sees Uvalu.

"Err . . . hello," he says. I can see the jolt he gives. It makes me nervous; what's going on?

"Hello, Mr Petersen," Uvalu says.

"Hi, Dad," I say.

"You two girls have fun now," he says and smiles, closing the door. What did we do? Later we go outside to play, and I forget about it until that night when we've had dinner and my dad is sitting on the sofa and says:

"Sofie – come here for a sec." I go over and sit down next to him, and he puts his arm around my shoulder. "Sofie, you mustn't bring the Greenlandic children home," he says.

But I am a Greenlander, because of my mum.

"Why not?" I ask.

"It's not good for them to have to see how nice our house is," he says. "It'll upset them."

"Why will it upset them?" I ask.

"Because we have such a nice home, and they live in such small, uncomfortable houses," my dad says. I don't say anything, but I think it's odd. Maybe he doesn't think they're nice enough.

My parents met on board a ship in 1950 when my dad was on his way to Greenland. There was a piano on board, and my dad had brought his guitar. My mum played the piano. Isn't music the food of love? She had been in Denmark training to be a bookbinder, and now she was on her way home to see her family. She was apprenticed to someone who bound teeny-weeny Hans Christian Andersen books, one fairy tale per book. She was never to work as a bookbinder. There's no such thing as bookbinding in Greenland. They were married and had my two big sisters, and then they had me.

It says something about how Greenlandic my mum is that neither of her parents speak anything but Greenlandic. But there was a Norwegian in my granddad's family and a German in my granny's. My mother's family can trace Danish blood back to 1775. And actually my granddad has blue eyes, and my granny has curly hair – Greenlanders don't, so there has to have been quite a bit of white blood in the family.

When my mum was a girl, her dad was a catechist – a curate – and then he was a teacher. He was actually paid in money. That was when most people only had whatever they caught and whatever money they could make from selling what they had caught, which never amounted to much. So you could say that my mum was from an affluent family, even though it was a family of sixteen children – my granddad had four children from his previous marriage and he went on to have twelve children with my granny. They're very old now. They still live in the little grey house behind the old church in Nuuk – sitting room, kitchen and two bedrooms upstairs.

My granddad says that my mum was always upwardly mobile. She most certainly wasn't going to be an impoverished Greenlander with an alcoholic husband. And she really does call the shots at home. We have to sit nicely with our knees together and become good housewives – at least my older sisters do. I get off a lot easier, because I'm the youngest and the apple of my dad's eye. My older sisters have jobs to do around the house, including some of the heavier work. They have to help out with the washing, which is done by hand in great wooden tubs, and all our clothes must be wrung by hand. But then my mum gets a wringing machine and a washing machine – the first in our village, because, after all, my dad has been trained as a machinist and he is the manager of the town's electricity plant and knows about technical stuff.

In 1964 we move to Holsteinsborg on Greenland's west coast. My parents play in a dance band and there is a dance every Friday and Saturday in the town hall, where there is a piano. I'm not old enough to go, but my sisters take me and let me watch through the window. The room is packed. My mum and dad play polka on guitar and piano, and a Danish man plays the drums, and everyone is dancing and laughing. As we walk home, we hear a man being sick. My sisters just keep walking.

"We have to help him – he's not well," I say. They laugh, and there are dogs running towards the sound.

"He's just drunk," my oldest sister says. "Now the dogs are going to run over and eat his sick."

We have a piano at home as well, and the band comes over for practice; my mum and dad and some Danish men who know how to play the drums and the bass. My oldest sister gets to sing "The Girl from Ipanema" with them.

Every summer the town's population is doubled by the builders from Denmark who come to slap up five blocks of flats in no time. Tiny wooden terraces for the Greenlanders to move in to. None of the Greenlanders are involved in construction. The Danes work in shifts around the clock, because it's light all the time, so it's all hands on deck while the ground is unfrozen. Most of the men are single. On the weekend they go mad. The builders drink like sponges and behave like wild beasts. And the Greenlandic girls throng around them, because the builders have money and men with money means free drinks. The girls are going to get laid, and then they can have a warm bed to sleep in and maybe even a free meal afterwards. There are the prefab girls and the harbour girls. The young men from town are ticked off, which means that Saturday-night dances are full of fights. Some of the Danish men stay on for years and marry the girls, or they take their missus back to Denmark. Those are the decent ones. The others, and that's most of them, simply get the girls up the duff and leave town.

I long for civilization. Every year some of the older boys are sent off to technical schools in Denmark and they return two years later. They're the most exciting thing – flashy modern clothes and new haircuts. They move in a different way, speak in a different way and have a new side to them which gives them an air of something altogether different. You don't recognize them straight off. I'm standing with my classmate Malo, watching them at a distance.

"I think that one's Anton," Malo says.

"Anton? Nooo, really?" I say.

"I'm not sure," Malo says.

"He is one hot number," I say.

"Yes," Malo says. And we are afraid to even speak to the guy, that's how hot he is.

I see a lot of pictures in my mum's magazines, the ones she has sent up every week from Denmark – pictures of hippies, blokes with long hair, flower children. Something new is coming. I want to be a part of it. The Anton effect wears off. The new clothes get less new with time, and some of it is stolen by family members, and then he's back to being execrable and worn again.

Denmark

I've finished Year Six in Holsteinsborg. I'm twelve years old, and we sail to Denmark for a six-month holiday before my dad starts his next contract. We stay with my dad's sister and in a rented holiday cottage. It's my thirteenth birthday – they take me to Sejrgårdskolen in Tølløse just a day or two before they're due to fly back.

"Bye for now," I tell them and give a quick wave. Now's my time to shine. I'm diving into my new life head first. But nothing's prepared me for the Danes.

"My, my, you must have had all the blubber you could eat back in your settlement," one of the older pupils tells me, pinching my cheek, laughing. I get flustered and frightened. I go to the toilet and cry, staring in the mirror. I'm a half-Greenlander with plump cheeks and straight black hair. But I speak Danish and have lived like a Dane in Greenland. Only here, Danish is somehow foreign and different. Danes are harsh with each other. My grandmother has told me that the first Greenlanders who came to Denmark in the 1700s died from the shock. There are other half-Greenlanders at the school – we're all outsiders. I try to connect with a Danish girl.

"You smell of piss," she says.

"What do you mean?" I say.

"You Greenlander-slags all wash your hair in piss – you're just rank." She turns her back on me and walks off. I've never heard anything like it.

The only thing I recognize at school is the piano in the assembly hall, so for the first year I go over and play it whenever I get the chance. It's my way of hiding in plain sight.

After some time I come out of isolation. I've come up with a way of defending myself – extreme arrogance: I carry myself with dignity – coldness, my back as straight as a rod, my head held high. Friendly and to the point, but aloof. Don't get clever with me. Don't even think about it.

Luckily there are lots of ex-pats at school – their parents are ambassadors in countries like India and Malaysia, and there are several D.A.N.I.D.A. children whose parents are working in Africa on various aid projects. We've got something in common because we've grown up outside Denmark even though we're really Danish. Most of the pupils come from Copenhagen and Frederiksberg, but especially from the well-to-do areas north of the capital. Their parents are company directors with little or no time for kids: Daddy's busy with his career, and Mummy's got a facial mask slapped on and is having her nails done – that is, if she's not out shopping. We don't talk about our parents, but when the others return from weekends with their folks, they have loads of new clothes, and their parents drive flashy cars and look like the right sort of people.

In the summer I fly home to visit, and suddenly it's me who's interesting and strange. I stuff myself with my mum's cooking and get drunk with my old friends in front of the bonfires we light at night. I lose my virginity to Anton in a field of summer flowers.

After four years at the boarding school in Tølløse I've finished my final exams and am moving to Copenhagen; my dad has got me a job at the Greenland Office as a trainee clerical assistant, starting in January 1973. I'm going to work at the Greenland Technical Organization, which is a subdivision of the Greenland Office on Hauser Plads, just round the corner from Kultorvet.

The average age at the Greenland Office is sixty, and I'm the only trainee. I don't make any friends at work, but they're as sweet as anything. A great bunch. O.K., to be honest there are women in the office who are terrible prudes – native Danes who've never been to Greenland. But almost everyone else is an old hand who has worked on Greenland for years – they're as tolerant as can be and crack jokes all the time, so the atmosphere is really good. But there aren't any Greenlanders – I'm as close as it gets to that.

I'm a little hippie and swan about in flowery dresses with my John Lennon glasses and wooden-soled boots, but it's fine – there's no strict dress code at the Greenland Office. I take evening classes at a commercial school while I work my way through the different departments and offices at the Ministry: the typing pool, the copy room, mail room, archive and accounts, where I don't do too well. I learn to type and become quite good at being organized and an ace at prepping the mail. I even get a short period on the telex, sitting and writing directly to Greenland.

I am eighteen years old and in Copenhagen where I don't know a living soul. A lot of the people I met at boarding school were expats and have moved back to the places where their parents live, and a few have gone on to Herlufsholm. But I'm not doing *gymnasiet*, because I have no interest whatsoever in academic education; I despise it.

My parents haven't prepared me for life or done anything to help me get ahead. My dad got me the trainee job and from there on I'm on my own. Luckily one of the former pupils from the boarding school has told me you have to read the classified ads when you're looking for a room, because obviously I have no idea how to do these things. And I don't want to ask my big sisters. The older one has married a bricklayer and is planning to have children and fry meatballs all day. And the younger never has any time for me, so I've given up on her – she's gone all snooty and thinks that my being a hippie is reprehensible.

The first room I apply for is in a large flat on Frederiksberg. I arrive at the door, which is opened by a cross-looking old hag. She looks at me with blatant suspicion.

"Now then, where are you from?" she asks.

"Me? I'm a Dane from Tølløse," I say. Which, I suppose, I sort of am, even though my mother is a Greenlander. But during the first month I get several letters from Greenland, and that makes the crone even more suspicious.

"Are you a Greenlander?" she asks.

"No, but my parents both work on Greenland," I say. A couple of days later there's a knock on my door. I open.

"I want you out by the end of the month," the crone says.

"Why?" I ask.

"You don't tidy the kitchen when you've used it," she says.

"I'll do better, I promise," I say.

"And, you're a liar," she says. "That's what you're all like."

"What do you mean?"

"You told me you were Danish. But you look funny. You're not a proper Dane."

"So what if I'm not?" I ask.

"I don't want you here. I want you out by the end of the month," she says and leaves. Mercifully, by then I've found out how it's done. I go to *Use It* at Huset in Magstræde, where they've got a locations office, and they get me another room on Frederiksberg, in an attic under the roof of the oldest house in the area. It's got central heating – there's a giant radiator there. But the room is just wooden boards, and the wind whips in through every crack. I get a terrible cold. And I can't be bothered to cook. I never learned how at home, and at long last I can decide when I want to eat – I've never been that hot on food. It's all the time and then some. And then I sort of forget, or I just don't bother, and at one point I simply collapse because I haven't eaten for so long, and I'm almost in shock because I'm so lonely. It's utter, wretched misery those first six months in Copenhagen. When I'm not at work, I just sleep.

One day it's snowing, and I suddenly think of my oldest sister in Brønshøj – that I really want to see her. I take the bus there, and the first thing she tells me is that I can get myself a fella at Søpavillionen or Damhuskroen.

"That's what I did – there's no shortage of builders," she says.

"Who says I want to go out with a builder?" I say.

"I'm just trying to help," she says. I drain my coffee cup, say goodbye and go and put my coat on. As I walk out of the drive, I meet her bricklayer.

"Have you got yourself a boyfriend yet?" he asks straight off. Apparently that's the plan.

"No," I say.

"I know an electrician who might be interested in a little hippie-chick like yourself."

"Oh," I say.

"That electrician . . . he used to work in Greenland," the bricklayer says. "He likes Greenlandic girls."

"Oh," I say.

"Are you as good a cook as your sister?" he asks.

"I don't cook at all," I say.

"Oh," he says.

"Ta-ta," I say and stomp off through the snow.

Hippies

Then suddenly spring is upon us, and the city opens its arms to me. I have been trudging along like a zombie around the office all winter and have slept so much you wouldn't believe it. Now I stroll along Strøget. There are all sorts of goings-on, with street vendors, illusionists and buskers. I'm staring at one man's guitar

"You like my guitar?" he asks, and I say yes and ask if I can have a try, surprising him by playing a Danish folksong my dad taught me to play.

"Dulcimer Chuck from San Francisco," he says, shaking my hand.

"Sofie from Greenland," I say. He's also got a four-stringed instrument from the Appalachians called a dulcimer. We head down to Huset, and later we go to Sofies Kælder to drink beer and chat, and the next day we meet again, and not long after we're in my bed.

Chuck tells me he grew up in West Tennessee. He's of Georgian decent and has an eighth indigenous blood, because his great-grandfather was a horse thief and married a Cherokee woman.

I tell him I'm a Greenlander mixed with whalers, sailors, explorers, merchants and missionaries. And he doesn't act funny when I tell him.

"Blood travels the world to find new blood to mix with," Chuck says and grabs on to me. And then we're shagging again. It's fantastic.

Through Chuck I get to know all the other buskers. Most of them are foreigners: Americans, French, Germans, Italians and all sorts of others. It cheers me up no end. I have friends again. It's fun, hippie-homely. I buy a second-hand guitar and start remembering the songs my dad taught me as a child. My relationship with Chuck is soon over, but we're still friends, and now at least I've got started and there are loads of hippies, and of course loads of Danes as well. There's nothing homely about that, however. The Danish hippies give me the greatest disappointment of my life. I have dreamt of meeting them ever since I saw the first pictures of flower children in my mum's magazines in Greenland. At school I comforted myself with the thought that only the petit-bourgeois brats were stupid and prejudiced. But the hippies are exactly the same. I can be sitting at the bar in Sofies Kælder, chatting away with a Danish hippie in his Afghan fur coat and homemade Icelandic sweater, plenty of jewellery and hair down to here. For hours we can be talking, totally open-minded. Intimacy is flowering; we both believe in Utopia, no borders and the free mixing of races, humanity as one big happy family building a big happy world together – where everyone is equal and equally happy. The bloke will have his hand on my thigh and he'll be leaning forwards:

"Where are you from, Sofie?" he'll whisper.

"Upernavik," I'll whisper back. "Greenland." And that'll be the end of it. The tree-hugger will turn his back on me and chat to someone else.

"Hey there," I'll say. No reaction. "What happened?" I'll say. "We were just talking." And he'll get up and leave. That bloody hurts. Greenlanders have a reputation for being drunks, and the women are flee-ridden, dirty whores. I can feel tears stinging in my eyes, so I'll hurry outside and walk home with my hands balled into fists. All the hippies attend university and are sickos. They're mad about India, and spirituality, and African independence, and cross-cultural whatnot, and isn't it just frightful how the negroes were treated in the colonial times, and all sorts of bollocks. The hippies lap it up unreservedly, but in their heads they still have a ruthless opinion of Greenlanders. They can't see that there's a human being inside me when I come from Greenland.

I go over and talk to Chuck.

"If I tell them I'm from Greenland, the Danes just sit there, staring at me whenever I lift a beer bottle as if they think I am going to spew curses, syphilis and sick."

Chuck shakes his head.

"The hippies think they've shed all their middle-class values. But underneath the surface they still believe everything their parents taught them: they're as prissy and puritan as hell. All hippies talk of new ideas – how they'd like things to be. But they can't live it. They don't know how to get started. They're middle class, middle-of-the-road to their core."

"But why do the hippies hate me just because I'm from Greenland?" I ask.

"They're the same with the Native Americans in the States," he says. "The hippies wear native get-ups even though they hate the Native Americans."

"I don't understand," I say. Chuck laughs:

"The hippies feel that the Native Americans are *born* real – in harmony with Mother Nature – while the hippies themselves are just trying to *become* real. And deep down they know they don't stand a chance because they're so irreparably corrupted by their middle-class backgrounds."

Chuck and me get it together for old time's sake, but he's seeing someone else, so I keep going to Sofie Kælder. But it keeps happening. Damned Danes. I'm from the colony, and apparently the colonial overlord needs to perceive me as second-class human because that shields him from perceiving himself as an abuser.

The hypocrisy of Danish hippies disgusts me so much that I start to visit ordinary pubs when I want a beer. But the builders really aren't any better. Kurt, a drunken carpenter, starts flirting with me, but the result is the same when I tell him where I was born:

"You're a Greenlander?" he says.

"Yes. Is that a problem?" I ask.

"Niggers the lot of you," he says.

"Why would you say that?" his mate who has been eyeing me up asks him.

"I've worked there, remember?" Kurt says. "It's rubbish."

"But you hooked up with a Greenlander-girl, didn't you?" his mate asks.

"The girls know how to fuck, I'll give them that. And they're keen. Just give them a couple of pints and they'll shag you silly. And they'll shag any foreigner who drops by to get some fresh blood into their inbred tribe," Kurt says. "But you've got to be careful or they'll give you the clap."

"That's no way to talk about people," his mate says, casting a shy look at me.

"I'm not making it up. It's a fact. It's rotten. They're completely clueless. They drink. They don't understand the concept of keeping appointments, and they know bugger all about anything whatever. All the things that matter in Greenland are done by Danes who have been trained in Denmark, because otherwise Greenland would just fall apart. Mooching is the only thing they do well. It's our tax money paying for it all. We don't get anything in return. You can't get Greenlanders into the system. They don't want it. They just want to fanny about being Greenlanders."

"But still, you're going back next summer, aren't you?" his mate says.

"Yes," Kurt says. "Yes. I'm going. The money's good."

They just don't get it. Greenland is a sealer–whaler society. The climate is beastly. It's nigh on impossible to get around the country, and it's unbelievably hard to live there. It's primitive to be sure, of course it is. All those Danes with shit for brains have 1500 years of development that Greenland hasn't had. If we had, we bloody well wouldn't have let the colonialists in, would we?

Soon I start sorting people into groups: the ones who can handle the fact that I come from Greenland and the ones who can't: the Danes. Foreigners don't have screwed-up preconceptions of Greenland, so to them I'm just another foreigner.

Walking down Strøget one day I meet a bloke called Gene who has a country band, and I make friends with his girlfriend, Dorthe; my first Danish friend in Copenhagen. Dorthe is a 29-year-old seamstress – that's more than ten years older than me, and I think she's ancient. To her I'm an innocent – even though I may not be as innocent as all that – who comes to visit a bit too often in their Fredericiagade flat. But she's kind to me and teaches me how to knit, and sew, and crochet. I start going out with a busker, and when he leaves I start seeing another busker.

Everyone is teaching everyone else songs. There are always a couple of guitars on the go when people meet. Soon I am on Strøget myself, passing round the hat, and before long I'm even playing.

The streets are full of people of only one colour: dishwater blond. There are a few immigrants from Turkey, but you never see them walking about anywhere. There aren't any negroes in Copenhagen, unless you go to jazz concerts.

"It's just terrible," Dorthe says. She is reading some books about the Danish slave trade between the Danish colonies in Guinea and the Danish West Indies in the years 1673–1803 – tens of thousands of negroes were shipped to the islands for slave labour on sugarcane plantations. But Denmark sold the islands to the U.S. in 1917. "The islands are full of black people," Dorthe says. "Imagine if we had kept them. Then there would have been loads of black Danes. How great would that have been!" She's dying to shag a black man.

Our gang listens to an insane amount of music. We busk on Strøget, and I get on stage with them when Gene's country band is playing. There are parties every day of the week. And then I'm off to the office – often straight from the pub. And I don't have access to a bathroom and don't often get to the public baths; mostly I just manage to give myself a bit of a splash with some water from a bucket in my windswept room. So *eeeeew* . . . I'm sure sorting mail with me in the Greenland Office is great fun!

Fakir

A bunch of us are meeting at Gene and Dorthe's. There are a few of the band members and their girlfriends and some other musicians and buskers and their friends. There's probably ten or fifteen of us who meet up at weekends and a few times during the week. One evening, when we're together and have had a bite to eat, we're sitting there, smoking and drinking, having an all-round good time. We always speak English when we're together because everyone understands that. Often there'll be someone who isn't a regular member of the group – a guest or visitor. And tonight there's a bloke who looks *quite* unlike the rest of us. We're all hippies after all; the guys have hair as long as the girls' and are really hip. It's changed now from flower-power get-ups to jeans and denim. But this bloke is sitting in gabardine woven slacks and a slimline shirt with a huge collar, and enormous sideburns and a moustache – *yuck!* He's a proper porn stud; gold chain around his neck with a lion's claw pendant and gold rings on his fingers. A different sort of bloke. What on earth is he doing here? But he's good-looking; a large man with a hairy chest and muscles. The beatniks all wear oversized shirts and sweaters because they have no body to speak of. This porn-stud chap is sitting there chatting away about languages, and national character, and war, and diving, and philosophy, and evolution, and . . . it seems there's nothing he doesn't have an opinion on. I'm not actually eyeing him up – I've just noticed that he's there and that it's weird. Then Gene says:

"Hey, Jacques, do that thing you do with the needles, won't you? Just show them, yeah?"

"Nah, not today," Jacques says. But Gene keeps at it, and everyone looks at Jacques and asks him what they're talking about. And then Jacques tells Dorthe to bring him all her darning needles and safety pins. And he asks Gene for a thin guitar string. Dorthe brings him everything he's asked for, and everyone sits there there yakking away about what he might need it for until, suddenly, he sticks a large darning needle through his tongue and two large needles out through his cheeks and closes his mouth with five large safety pins through his lips and puts seven large safety pins through the skin by his Adam's apple. He's a fakir – there's not one drop of blood. And then he takes the thin guitar string and weaves it between the bones in the palm of his hand; he sticks it in, through, up and down, out and back in. And then he's sitting there, smoking cigarettes and drinking beer, with all that stuff in his face and his hand. *Wow* – that's my man right there. I've got to have him. He's amazing. But not long after he takes it all out and leaves with a Polish Jew – they've got some business to attend to. The next few nights he doesn't show, and I go about thinking of nothing but him.

The next week I'm in luck. I live some way outside the city centre, all the way out by Nordre Fasanvej, and I haven't started biking yet because I never learnt how to in Greenland, so I always get bus no.2, which goes down Godthåbsvej. And there he is: on the bus. And I'm so on it. Over to him, going: "*Heeeey you!*" with my eyes as wide as saucers.

"My, my, my. Who is this gorgeous little thing?" he says in Danish with a French accent. And I bat my eyes, and he stares at me as if I were a juicy joint of lamb. In ten seconds flat I'm on his lap, purring contentedly, and he's caressing my thighs, telling me how beautiful my eyes are. A real French charmer. I'm heading in to see Gene and Dorthe, and he was heading home to the bedsit on Amager he shares with the Polish Jew. But we end up in a pub in central Copenhagen, chatting and drinking. I ask him how he did that thing with the needles.

"I'll tell you sometime when we've got to know each other better," he tells me, his hands already on me underneath the table.

"But you didn't bleed at all," I say.

"I can cut myself," he says. "When I was a soldier, I discovered that."

"A soldier?" I say.

"In Algeria. I was on guard duty outside the village while the others were out looking for the rebels. I was sitting there, bored out of my mind, thinking about women. And I suddenly remembered having heard that Jews last longer when making love to a woman because they are circumcized. I wanted that for myself, so I start sharpening my knife on a stone until it's razor sharp. And then I sit myself down and masturbate." Jacques is gesticulating.

"Why?"

"I wanted to be stiff, so that it would be easier to control the cut. And then I cut off the foreskin and wrap a handkerchief around it, and then the others came back, and we went out on a very long march."

"What about the pain?"

"You're two people who want to control that process. The body says no, don't. But the body is just flesh. I don't care about the cries of the flesh."

"Did it work, then?"

"Yes, I marched for hours.

"No . . . do you last longer now – like the Jews?" I ask.

"Yes," Jacques says, and then we go home to mine, and he eats lamb minge, and he has a really big tool to do the job.

He-man

Jacques is thirty-five, teaches French at Berlitz and looks just like Sean Connery. He has tried all sorts of things in his life. Right now he shares a bedsit with the Polish Jew so he can save up for a trip around the world. He knows how to dive because he was taught in the army, and now he wants to go somewhere tropical to set up home. We meet out at night and at mine when he's got the time, but most days it's not easy – he works at night when I'm off work, and during the day I'm at the office. And I start dreaming. I'm nineteen years old and, really, I'm bored out of my head working in that office, and all my friends have been all over the world, busking and trying out stuff, and it simply sounds so exciting and I want to try it too. I have no idea how I'd get the money together or how to even go about this sort of thing. And Jacques is just one big James Bond-esque he-man. A grown man who has the know-how and can come up with a plan, and who's got a huge cock. He hasn't got an Icelandic sweater or hippie hair – he's got a past. As a soldier.

Jacques entered the army when he was eighteen, and he was tall by French standards – six foot one. The average height for a Frenchman is five foot nine. And he's of a really sturdy build, so he was sent straight on to the Special Forces. They were trained just outside Nice, in a fort where they were almost tortured if they didn't do exactly as they were told. One of the punishments they encountered was a three foot by three foot cell with a leaking water tank on the roof; you'd be stuck there – lying or sitting huddled up in whatever way you could devise – for up to a fortnight, at the end of which you'd emerge a total wreck. Jacques has been through all that – mad is what it is. And forced marches with full kit – but instead of real backpacks they had cords that could really cut into their skin. All of it done to heighten their pain threshold. And he was thrown out of a helicopter in full kit and then he'd better land right or he'd do his ankles in.

Jacques was sent to war in Algiers back in the day when Algeria was trying to achieve independence from France in the late 1950s. The advance guard was sent in to locate the rebels and torture information out of them. They did it with electrodes – they shocked the rebels, beat them, did all sorts of nasty things to them. He says it was such an intense feeling. It was being alive, it was living. When he returned from the war, he couldn't feel anything – everything felt dead and flat. It took years and years before he started being just a little bit human again. At first he drove dangerously. Whenever he was in a car, he would drive on the wrong side of the road, straight at the oncoming traffic until the very last moment. How stupid is that? Childish. But then he was only a baby of twenty-three when he left the army.

After his stint in the army, he went to Paris and read Literature at the Sorbonne. Then for a while he wrote pulp novels. "Any idiot can write those," he says. And he lived on that for a bit. But France was no good. He's from Salzburg and has a deep-seated hatred of his family; his dad's a drunk, and his mum is the regional witch. And his brother and sister – both much older than him – are proper bourgeois, and he despises them both deeply and intensely. I've never met anyone like him when it came to badmouthing his family. Then he learnt that there was money to be made from working as a tourist guide in Italy.

"Do you speak Italian?" I ask.

"Italian, French, Danish, German, English and Spanish," he says. "I was married to a Spaniard. And a little Arabic."

"You were married?" I ask.

"Yes. Back when I was living in Nice, I met a Spanish woman whom I married and had a child with – a daughter. That was when I had my nose done as well."

"Your nose?" I say, looking at it. It's a straight nose with a small *schwung* to it. And Jacques gets out his wallet and pulls out a picture of himself. In the picture he has a gorgeous beak.

"How *could* you?" I say, because I simply love beaks like that, but this one has gone.

"It didn't look good," he says and tells me that he met a female plastic surgeon.

"The Spanish lady?"

"No, someone else – she was just someone I met," he says. Jacques tells me that the woman doctor made him a special offer. I'm thinking that he probably gave her a good rogering with that big cock of his to get a reduction on the price. "She told me that the most expensive part of the procedure was the anaesthetic, and so I said, 'O.K. then, let's dispense with that,' because that way I could afford to have it done." The plastic surgeon put a device up his nose and turned on a screw to dilate the nostril. And then she made a small incision in his nasal septum and separated the bone from the flesh. Using a hammer and a chisel, she worked away at the root of his nose, making a thin crack. And then she broke off the bone, right between his eyes. He describes hearing all the sounds *incredibly* loudly inside his skull. How it went *DONG, DONG, DONG* inside his head every time she used the hammer. And the sound of the crunch when she broke the bone. And then she used a small whetting thingy to smooth down the bone where she'd broken it, and then she sutured the whole thing back together and put on a huge bandage with great big tampons in his nostril to hold the thing in shape. You really can't see it today. How insane is that.

"But are you still married?" I ask. "To that Spanish lady?"

"No, no, no – that was years ago."

Fidelity

The first three months we see each other a few times a week. We have a lovely time together up in my windswept attic. We both want to travel. Jacques comes up with the idea that we should look for somewhere where he can teach diving. We could have a small beach bar where I could serve piña coladas. It's our dream, and it's not necessarily a terribly expensive one. After all, Jacques know how cheap it is out there once you get going – provided you live as the locals do. But you do of course need cash to get started. We haven't agreed on anything, but we are talking about it. Dreaming about it.

At night when we've made love, he asks me about my sexual fantasies – what I'd like. I tell him that I frequently fantasize about bondage and sadomasochism.

"Really?" he says.

"It's just a fantasy," I say.

"But do you want me to tie you up?" he asks.

"I suppose we could do that some time," I say. He's lying next me, smoking.

"Have you been with many men before me?" he asks.

"How many is many?" I ask.

"I mean, when did you start . . . ?"

"Anton on Greenland – when I was fourteen.

"Fourteen?" Jacques says. "And then who?" he asks and gets me to list them all. It makes for quite a long recital, and with each name he gets more upset. Chuck, and Mike, and Roberto, and Gene, and Carl, and Heinz, and . . .

"That many?" he says.

"Yes," I say.

"But you're only nineteen," Jacques says. I sing a line to him:

"'Have you ever been experienced?'" because he's always listening to Jimmi Hendrix's "Electric Ladyland".

"But . . ." he says.

"You were married," I say.

"Don't tell me that was Dorthe's Gene you slept with?" he asks.

"It was."

"Before he met Dorthe?"

"No."

"While he was seeing Dorthe?"

"Yes," I say, and Jacques leaps out of bed and stands on the floor completely naked.

"That's just not on."

"Why not?"

"She's your best friend, and you're shagging her boyfriend," Jacques says.

"Jacques," I say. "She was the one who asked me to – as a personal favour."

"She asked you to?" he says.

"Yes," I say. "She went for a walk while we did it."

"But . . . why?"

"Because Gene thinks I'm lush."

"But you're . . . perverts," Jacques says.

"They're into free love, Jacques – it's not just something they say," I say.

"I don't want you doing that while you're with me," he says.

"Then you can't either," I say.

At one point he's gone for a week to see his Spanish daughter and visit his mother, but soon after he's back in my bed.

One night we're going to a party in a large commune on Oehlenschlægergade. Gene and Dorthe and all the other buskers are there, but

Jacques is late. I'm sitting there, having a great time until Gene asks:

"How about Jacques' wife – how do you feel about that, really?

"The Spaniard? Oh, they were divorced years ago," I say.

"No, not the Spaniard," Gene says. "His wife in Tårnby – the flight attendant."

"What wife?" I say, and my face goes funny. Gene on the other hand goes pale:

"Oops," he says. "Me and my big mouth." I look at Dorthe who gives me a blank look. It's awful.

"But . . ." I say to her and stop.

"He's married to a Danish flight attendant who lives in Tårnby," she says.

"But he's living with that Polack," I say.

"No," Dorthe says. "He's living with his wife." It's just . . . if he . . . that's so abusive. A flight attendant – she's been able to get him cheap flights, like that time when he said he was going to see his Spanish daughter. And he told me he was sharing that bedsit with the Polack, so we couldn't go there, because . . . so I wouldn't know about his wife. And he was teaching nights and had private pupils, so it was hard to find the time for us to see each other. My arse. All lies – to her and me both.

I'm more than a little huffy when he shows up. He goes a little pale when he sees me, and I walk straight past him and out of the room, saying: "Liar." I disappear out into the hall, and he comes after me and gives me explanations and reasons, graphs and pie charts, and cutting a long story short: he and the flight attendant who appears to be called Mette are over, really they are. "Then how can you be living with her?" I shriek and start wailing like a baby.

"But you see, I can't really move away from Mette when you and I don't have a place to live," he says. And it's not like I'm not head over heels in love with the man, and I don't want to back away from what we have.

"But . . ." I say.

"That's how it is," he says. "We're not together anymore – me and my wife. I sleep on the sofa, and most of the time she's out flying anyway." I'm just standing there in the hall, and he starts touching me, and I think that I'm just a little girlie with perky tits, and more than likely both younger and juicier than his flight-attendant wife, so I can win him away from her even though I don't believe for a second that he's sleeping on the sofa if there's a bed around.

"Mette is addicted to feeling safe, and I'm divorcing her so that I can live with you and then we can go travelling together," he says.

Needless to say it's not long before there's a knock on my attic door, and there's a flight attendant in an S.A.S. uniform outside who says her name is Mette.

"I'm shagging him," I say. "I've been shagging him for a long time while you've been out flying."

"I haven't been out flying," she says. "I've worked in the airport these last four months."

"Oh," I say.

"And shagged him."

"Yes, but you're just an old, neurotic safety addict," I say and slam the door in her face.

My mum and dad come to Denmark on holiday and buy a summer cottage near Silkeborg. From now on they plan to come down every summer – that's a new thing. When I was little, we'd stay on Greenland for two and a half years at a time and then spend six months in Denmark. But now they've changed things so that they get a shorter vacation every year – due to the cheaper flights. I leave Jacques behind in Copenhagen when I go to visit. We have a lovely time. My oldest sister and the bricklayer from Brønshøj have had a baby and we have the christening when my middle sister gets married to a lawyer from Hellerup.

Middle class

Back in Copenhagen I'm asked if I want a two-bedroom flat, because Chuck and his girlfriend want to move to Canada. Eighty square metres in Baggesensgade by the inner-city lakes. Jacques is absolutely up for it. In no time at all he has moved in with me and gets a separation from flight-attendant Mette – there'll be a one-year trial separation and after that they'll be divorced. And I know he's serious about me, because I want to travel and explore the world, and I'm not a safety addict; I don't mind if it's really tough and that, hell or high water just throw it at me. He thinks that's really cool. And he's genuinely fond of me.

I'm as beatnik as they come when we move in together, because I just don't like rules, but as it happens . . . the second we move in together, Jacques starts thinking I should stop being a beatnik and become more middle class. He starts by filing down my teeth, which have tiny jagged points on the bite rim because I had rickets as a girl – vitamin D deficiency when my teeth were coming through. Long term that means you can't absorb calcium properly, so my front teeth have serrated jags of half a millimetre or so, and Jacques thinks it's hideous. He takes one of those whetting stones you use for sharpening knives and he uses it on my teeth until the serrated bits have gone. I look in the mirror. My teeth look shorter. Like an old Eskimo hag who has been chewing skins for years to make them soft enough to turn into clothes. I miss my jags. And Jacques buys me new clothes and make-up and shows me how to use it – I'm clueless. I've never used that stuff before. I mean, of course I have friends who use a black line to frame their eyes; it's alright as long as it's real Indian kohl. Eyeliner is a no-go – that's middle class. And lipstick is out of the question – that's suppression of women.

Personally I like to look a bit rugged. I'll wear striped dungarees, and grandfather shirts, and shaggy furs. And I've got a weak spot for flowery frocks from the 1940s – it makes for a strange look when mixed with my John Lennon glasses and my clogs. And I've worked out how to walk bow-legged, because if I do, I look rugged. Sort of like a bricklayer. I don't tell Jacques that, but I grumble when he tries to get me into gabardine slacks and ladylike blouses from Magasin.

"I thought the plan was for us to save up," I say.

"But, darling – some of the places we're travelling to won't let you in if you're a beatnik. And we're going everywhere. We won't let something like clothes stop us, will we?" When he isn't dressing me, I still go about looking like a rugged John Lennon bricklayer.

While all this is going on, Jacques stops shaving and grows his hair long like a beatnik although he still wears jewellery and slimline shirts. I don't get it at all, but I make no comment, because he's as vain as a peacock. He tells me we need to go and get passports done so that we're ready to go, even though we don't have nearly enough money yet. As soon as the passports are done, he cuts his hair and shaves and is my old porn stud once more, while I still have my long ponytail.

"You need to practise using that make-up," Jacques says when we're back in our flat.

"But I don't want to look like that," I say and go over to the sitting-room window to look at the sky.

"It's important to be able to come across in different ways," he says.

"Not to me it isn't," I say. Jacques goes out into the kitchen. Then he returns with a pair of scissors in his hand and gets behind me and gestures with them.

"I'm going to cut off your ponytail," he says.

"Yes, right, if you say so," I say. *Riiiiittzz . . .* "*What are you doing!?*" I yell, touching my hair with my hands – it's gone, it's short. "*No – my long hair,*" I sob.

"You need to try it," he says and takes me to the hairdressers' and they dye my hair, and I get one of those standard haircuts which everyone has, and I think it's the ugliest thing ever. He pays and we leave.

"You've made me look like an ABBA girl, only nicer. I can't bear it," I say.

"It looks lovely – you're very beautiful now," he says.

"I'm a beatnik," I say. "And you've made me look middle class. You've got appalling taste," I say.

"It's not middle class," Jacques says – slightly put out. The man claims to hate the middle classes, but really he is the epitome of petit-bourgeois.

"You're just a repressed old parson," I tell him right there on the pavement, and he shoves his index finger into my face and yells:

"*Don't you ever call me that again.*" Then he turns and stalks off.

"*Old parson,*" I yell at him. But he's got all sorts of other talents – he can shag like nobody's business. And a roll in the hay is all it takes to put a smile back on his face.

We talk about travelling down through Europe and on to Africa.

"We need to report our passports missing," he says.

"Why?" I say.

"It's important to have more than one passport when you travel in Africa," he says. "Some countries won't let us in if we have stamps in our passports from countries they consider their enemies." So I willingly hop along and have another passport made – we need to be able to travel where we want to.

Jacques thinks I ought to give up my job as a trainee at the Greenland Office:

"What you need to do is get out there and make some real money, so we can get out and see the world," he says. "It's not like you're ever going to need that training once we've started travelling."

"You're right," I say. Because I've already failed my shorthand exam twice, and I'll never be able to pass it. I pack in my traineeship a couple of months early and sign up with ManPower, a temp agency that mostly sends me to various large companies: Hellesens, B. & W., Ø.K. – mostly typing or phone-minding jobs. My dad is disappointed, but that can't be helped.

We both work two jobs and spend no money on anything and save like crazy – I work as a secretary during the day and a cleaner at night. For a year and a half – really just working flat out, just working. And eating the cheapest food – we live as cheaply as can be and don't shop for clothes or anything. We spend no money at all and stop going out for meals or to the cinema and all the things that I had got used to.

Smuggling hash

After a year and a half of working two jobs each we've still only managed to save up 25,000 kroner, and Jacques doesn't think that will do us.

"We'll go on a package holiday to Morocco and pick up some hash," he says. He's found a Danish wholesale dealer with the requisite connections who can shift a shipment for us in just two days.

I'm packing.

"I want you to bring these," Jacques says, handing me the gabardine slacks, the tailored shirts and high-heeled shoes. And some make-up.

"Do you want me to wear that in Morocco?" I ask

"No, just bring them," he says and walks around the flat, thinking so loudly that I swear I can hear it.

We're flying to Tangier on a Spies flight and get off the plane without telling anyone. We rent a pale blue Renault and drive south, dressed as hippies – Jacques has stopped shaving and is sweating in a strange woollen poncho. But in the boot are his slimline shirts and my middle-class get-up. Jacques stops in all the villages and chats to people. He finds a shed we can rent somewhere in the countryside by a mountain just outside a city called Ksar el Kebir. It's completely isolated, and Jacques dashes off every day to hook up with the right people. I just sit there smoking cigarettes, until Jacques returns with some very good hash. He's found the right man at last, but seems increasingly on edge. The deal is approaching. We drive into town in our pale blue Renault and buy two large and deep suitcases, and he keeps making calculations and is becoming greedy. "No, that's not enough at all. Not enough at all," he mutters and walks out the door.

"Where are you going?" I call to him, but he's already left. That night he cuts my hair and dyes it again, so I look like the picture in my middle-class passport.

"I want you to keep your hippie clothes on and put a scarf over your hair, so no-one sees your new haircut," he says. In two days we're due to leave on a flight from Casablanca. Jacques is up early the next morning.

"What are you doing?" I ask.

"I need to get us another car," he says.

"Why?" I ask.

"When we leave here this afternoon – that's when it might get dangerous," he says.

"But why do we need another car?" I ask. Jacques stops in the door and turns around – slowly and with a fake calm he explains it to me as if I were a slow-witted child: there's a risk that the chap he is buying from is in league with the police. He'll get his money, and then we'll be arrested with all the hash, which will then be confiscated and can be sold again. And then we'll be sent off to a Moroccan prison, which is tantamount to a death sentence. That's why Jacques has done something to the car's engine which means that it doesn't drive well, and he's got the car rental place in town to get him one exactly like it – exactly the same colour. "I told him that my young little wife only wanted that same pale blue, so the man has got one for us for today."

"Yes but why?"

"Because then it'll have a different number plate, and when that hash dealer brings the goods, he won't notice that the registration number is different because it'll be the same make and colour. And then the police will be looking for a car with two hippies and a different number plate altogether." Jacques turns and walks out the door. A couple of hours later he returns with the new pale blue Renault, and a little later the dealer shows up. The curtains are drawn, and they're sitting on the floor, packing the suitcases. It's utterly absurd; eleven kilos worth of hash. Jacques has got a good price and has got greedy. The hash takes up so much room that any idiot can see that there just aren't enough clothes in there. It's early afternoon. The dealer gets his money and splits. Jacques rushes into the bathroom, yelling at me to get into the middle-class clothes and put on the make-up and touch up my hair. Not long after he comes out, freshly shaved and wearing a slimline shirt. He carries the suitcases to the car, and we take a detour down some dirt tracks to the main road – a very posh, decent-looking couple – and we drive towards Casablanca where we've got a flight to Zűrich.

"Are we going to use the other passports at the airport?" I ask.

"No, no," he says. "Same passports as when we entered the country." I don't say anything else. We're dressed as middle-class people but are meant to use our hippie passports – I don't get it. I'm just oddly numb. Jacques is sitting tapping the dashboard and keeps asking me what time it is. It's terrible about those suitcases. Jacques drives slowly even though there's no traffic to speak of, and he keeps asking what the time is. The flight is due to leave soon.

"Why don't you go faster?" I ask.

"Be quiet," he says.

I starting worrying that we'll miss the plane – it's all I can think about. We arrive at the airport at the very last minute. Jacques rushes in ahead of me carrying the suitcases, and I trot along in my high heels. Jacques roars:

"Really, I do apologize. Well, there was a traffic jam. We have to be on that plane. I have an important meeting in Zűrich before we fly on to Frankfurt."

Through the terminal windows I can see the final passengers climbing a flight of steps – a tractor is standing by, ready to pull away the steps, while a man is loading their suitcases onto the baggage tray that will carry them to the plane's cargo hold. But Jacques talks them into rushing our suitcases out to the plane without checking them – just like that, *zooooom* – and the two of us take a car that rushes us to the plane; we leap up the steps and we're off. They almost didn't have time to look at our passports, where we look like a pair of doped-up hippies. I feel like I'm in a James Bond film: Sofie – Agent 007.

In Zürich we're transiting, so our suitcases don't go anywhere – they're taken straight from the plane to our new flight. We've got four hours, and the flight attendants have told us that the airport has a shuttle into Zürich and back so that people in transit can get in to look at the sights. We go. When we return to the airport, Jacques gets our new posh passports out.

"Would you stamp these for us, please?" he tells the customs officer, with an arm around my shoulder. He smiles at me before adding: "It's our first holiday together." And I smile back like a good little girlfriend. We get stamps from Zürich in our middle-class passports, which of course don't have any stamps from Morocco – those are in our hippie passports. We fly to Frankfurt and get our suitcases out through customs in Germany, where our passports show us to have been on a scheduled flight from Zürich – which is not particularly incriminating: to tell the truth we're not even searched. And then we get a train to Copenhagen.

"But why didn't we just take a flight from Frankfurt to Copenhagen instead?" I ask. Jacques shakes his head and whispers into my ear:

"The Danish hash-hounds are very good." I fall asleep on the train and when I wake up we're almost at Fredericia: Jacques has shown our middle-class passports to the customs officer: We're a young couple who have been on a trip to Zürich and Frankfurt – no problems. And there are no problems in Copenhagen either. Jacques' dealer arrives and puts down a deposit and sells the whole thing in forty-eight hours and gives us the money as agreed. Jacques flits about shopping for gear for our trip: tent, sleeping bags, backpacks, spirit stoves, flashlights – all sorts of things. We've got the money, and we're leaving in a few weeks.

I don't tell him, but I do wonder: why didn't he explain all that stuff about different passports to me, instead of going to all that hullabaloo with cutting off my hair and using make-up and shit? Sometimes he really is odd.

Power balance

"We're getting married," Jacques tells me.

"It hardly matters," I say. "As long as we're together."

"For the purpose of our travels," he says. "It's important to be married. There are so many countries where you can't share a hotel room if you're not married."

My parents are in Denmark in their summer cottage in Silkeborg, so we borrow the Polack's car and drive over and are married at the town hall. Goodbye Sofie Petersen, hello Sofie Rouvre – which is French for summer rain. We have a large family dinner in the garden. Everyone's talking and drinking and having a lovely time. Jacques is going on about his personal philosophy, and at one point I notice that my father's face is getting increasingly clenched up, and suddenly he snaps: "*But you're a complete antisocial!*" And I think: Is he? I suppose so. But we're going travelling. That's what we're going to do. Later Jacques gets incredibly drunk and starts badmouthing my sisters:

"There should be a law against being so middle class and having such large arses," he says. I'm pissed off because I won't have him speaking like that about my family.

"I won't have you talk like that," I tell him, getting up from my chair. "There'll be no lamb's minge on this wedding night. You can sleep in the car." And I go inside and lock the door. And they're not even that large, my sisters' arses.

Back in Copenhagen we rush about trying to get everything sorted before leaving – we're going to be gone for several years, after all, maybe even forever. One night when we're both doped-up, Jacques gets out some electric wires and starts tying me up. He gropes me and licks me roughly, then suddenly gets up, grabs a wire and starts whipping me. I don't know how to react at all. Then he sits his bare arse on my face and pounds me with his big cock and shafts me and . . . all of it without me being really a part of it. As if he were punishing me for . . . having been with so many men before him. Men are allowed to – girls aren't. He's utterly hypocritical about things: he still retains old-fashioned morals about sex and yet wants free love a-plenty. When he's done, he unties me and goes to sleep. I'm sobbing quietly, because I don't actually want him to wake up – I feel utterly humiliated. And he just sleeps. I don't feel like I can live past this. I go out to the kitchen where we have some sleeping pills – then I swallow all the pills in the glass and get into bed next to him. He'll wake up tomorrow morning. *And then I'll be dead – BASTARD!*

Drunk out of my head, I wake up late the next morning. I am *furious* to wake up by myself; I wanted Jacques to find me dead and resuscitate me and be terribly upset and penitent. But Jacques isn't even in the flat. "DAMMIT!" I say loudly. I am totally angry, and furious, and fully conscious, and stoned out of my head. "WRRAAUWRRR – WHERE ARE YOU?" I roar as I tilt out of bed, get dressed and go out. I reel drunkenly down the street – I almost can't stay on my feet. I have a notion of where he might be – at his friend's, the Polish Jew. Slimy bugger. Cunning bastard. Always a trick up his sleeve – dodgy mates. The Polack is staying at the Y.M.C.A. & W. in Kannikestræde, and I totter right in.

"You twisted bastard! What do you think you're playing at? Do you think I'll stand for it? You hitting and whipping me? Putting your dirty, great arse on my face? You twisted, old middle-class psycho-parson you." I almost start laughing because Jacques is scared witless of me. And I realize that I am yelling at him like a madwoman – proper Greenlander-mad; I've never done that before.

"I'm so sorry," he says cowering. "I won't ever do it again."

“If you ever so much as *think* of doing it again, I’ll bite off your cock.”

“I’m so, so sorry,” Jacques says. The Polack is sitting there, a slimy grin on his face, so I go over and slap him. That wipes the grin off his face – now it’s me who’s smiling.

“Off you go,” I tell Jacques and point at the door. And he gets up like a good little boy and trots off. And as I stagger after him I can feel it – the shift in the balance of power between us; I can get my own way. He’s afraid I will call off our trip because he’s gone too far. That I will want my share of the money and call the whole thing off. I don’t even have to threaten him with doing it because he’s so cowed.

But I’m close to thinking we will have to postpone our travels. We’ve bought the tickets, but Jacques comes down with something. He seems odd and walks about holding his stomach, saying it hurts. He hasn’t washed for days and hasn’t shaved either.

“But do you want me to change our tickets?” I ask him.

“No, no, I’ll be fine,” he says and waves dismissively, before dashing off to the shared toilet on the landing. I’m packing our bags – we leave the following day – and listen to Jacques being sick.

“Are you O.K.?” I ask when he returns.

“Yes, yes, but I’m going to have to go over to Mette’s tomorrow morning,” he says. “I need to say goodbye to her properly and give her that present.” He’s bought a very expensive lamp for her. We arrange it so that he’ll get a taxi to Mette’s, and I’ll get the bus to Kastrup Airport, and we’ll meet in the terminal.

He arrives as agreed, and we check in, board the plane and sit there – next stop Paris – and Jacques opens his shirt; taped to his abdomen is a fat wad of thousand-kroner notes.

“*Whaaaat!* What a lot of money,” I say, laughing, and he laughs, and we kiss. We’ve done well, we’ve got loads of cash, and we’re off.

Heading south

In Paris we check into a niceish hotel and roll about on the bed, throwing the hundred and twenty thousand-kroner notes around. Jacques shows me Paris. We buy nice clothes and put them on, then rent a car and drive to Geneva and open an account in a very nice bank and deposit the money and have it set up so that we can both draw travel cheques from the account. The banker takes a very polite leave of us, and I leave hand in hand with Jacques, who says:

"He can't be sure we're not future major clients." James Bond all over again.

We drive down to Nice and visit Jacques' daughter, Carmen, who is twelve years old. And his ex, who is staggeringly beautiful. From there we head towards Greece via Italy, where we're really supposed to leave our rented car – we're not allowed to bring it into Yugoslavia.

"It's no big deal," Jacques says. "I'll send them the key."

"Alright then," I say, and we cross the border and decide that we're going to try to get into Albania to see what it's like. On the way to the Albanian border we pick up a strange hitchhiker. He's wearing white-and-turquoise checked acrylic trousers, and a turquoise V-neck acrylic T-shirt; a total square. And he's high on pep pills. He's got two weeks in Europe and has some serious border-hopping planned. Two weeks of getting European stamps in his passport so he can show all his friends in New York that he's been absolutely everywhere; he doesn't see anything but motorways. But he's completely keyed up when he learns that we're heading to Albania – I don't think he even knows what Albania really is. It seems he's just heard that that it's completely impossible for Americans to enter the country.

We arrive at the border control on the Yugoslavian side, and there's no-one there. Jacques honks his horn, and nothing happens. Oh well, in that case we'll just drive on. We drive through no-man's-land and arrive at Albanian border control, where a very military-looking chap with a star on his beret is making signs at us with his fists. He's very friendly and explains that we can't enter the country, and that if we want to, we must go to Beograd and have visas issued. But just then our friend from New York starts making a fuss in the backseat:

"*IS THIS ALBANIA?*" he shrieks. And then he pushes my seat forward so that I'm squashed against the front window. He flings open the door and leaps from the car and walks around with an odd spring in his step, as if to make sure he is really setting foot there, while his elbows are up really high and eyes have a mad glare: "*IS THIS ALBANIA?*" And he walks towards the soldier, who is standing there as stiff as a statue with his machine-gun in his hands. Jacques gets out of the car, and the soldier points his gun at Mr New York, and Jacques holds his hands up while the soldier walks slowly backwards and Mr New York keeps walking towards him, shouting about Albania, until Jacques steps up to him and grabs him from behind and, lugging him back to the car, dumps him on the backseat, and we turn around and drive back. But now the Yugoslavian border control is suddenly manned, and they say:

"Where have you been? What is your business? No, you can't enter the country."

We're dragged into their office and show our passports, which they study with all the scepticism they can muster while Jacques does some serious explaining. They're not impressed:

"See, you could have gone to pick up some spy or other from Albania – like that one," he says, pointing at Mr New York, who is standing in a corner, hopping and shaking in his amphetamine high. But in the end it doesn't really seem very likely. He just doesn't seem all that Albanian. After an hour or so they let us go, and we have to drive around Albania. We drive across some incredibly green mountains where we pass horse-drawn gypsy wagons – two bears in flower-embroidered harnesses lumber after one of them, tied to the back of it. It's too much for Mr New York to deal with:

"*Oh no. Oh no. This is . . . this is wild,*" he mutters. This has got to be the furthest he's ever been from a skyscraper. We have to cross the mountain, and the road gets increasingly impassable with gravel and steep rocks and bottomless ravines, and in the evening it gets terribly foggy. I realize that our passenger hasn't said anything for a long time, and I turn around; he's simply pulled his T-shirt up over his head, so he can't see out.

"New York?" I say.

"Oh no, ohhh noooo," he mutters from inside his top. "Do you think we'll ever make it back to civilization?"

"No," I say.

"*Ohhh no,*" he says inside his T-shirt – mad as a hatter. We're across the peak; Greece is not far away – we've been on the road for twenty-four hours nonstop and are very tired. Jacques slows down.

"We're going into this hotel for a kip," he tells New York. "Are you coming?" New York pops his head out of the T-shirt:

"What!? You're stopping? But I have to get to Greece now. Let me out!" He's not tired at all, he doesn't have time to sleep. We pull over, and he leaps out onto the road, thumb at the ready, and we take a room and collapse.

We continue down through Greece and leave the car in Athens. Jacques sends the car keys back to Avis in Italy with details of where it's parked.

"What about the bill?" I ask.

"I'm sure Avis will survive without us paying," he says. "It's only when we leave Europe that that sort of thing becomes too dangerous." We sail to a Greek island. A fisherman carries us across to a Turkish island where we get a ferry to the Turkish mainland and have a lovely time for a month and a half. We discover a couple of small deserted fishing shacks on the beach and stay in those. It's as primitive as can be. Jacques teaches me how to dive. He catches fish using a harpoon. We spend almost no money and eat fish. Behind the beach there's a fig plantation, where I go to pick figs.

Later we sail to Cyprus and swim some more, but by now we really need to cut loose and see the world. We get on the ferry to Alexandria and on the ferry we meet other backpackers who are also travelling about the world on the cheap. Alexandria has a different sort of architecture from elsewhere on the Mediterranean; more of a stately British style with large mansions dating from when it was a colony.

Turkey and Egypt, there's not a lot of difference really. The Egyptians are slightly bigger arseholes. Bloody Muslims. For some reason they think they have to fuck over any and all Europeans – it appears to be a national pastime. But Jacques has been to war in a north-African country, so he hates the lot of them. Even though he also seems to hate the French government for having sent him there in the first place. As a soldier Jacques was required to torture information out of Algerian rebels – he must have had to teach himself to hate them in order to do it.

In Alexandria we're stoned by a group of kids. We've strayed into a slum, looking for some catacombs. Tourists normally travel in packs, led by a guide. We just plod along the two of us, and suddenly we're surrounded by a bunch of street urchins: wretched, rag-clad kids hurling rocks the size of tennis balls at us. We make a run for it. I constantly have a strange feeling – the Arabs always look angry, and I don't understand the language. It sounds quite off-putting – all those hawking sounds. I constantly feel like they must be saying bad things about me as I walk down the street. But I don't know. Maybe they're just saying: "*Good morning to you, madam. Don't you look pretty. Would you like to buy a cucumber?*"

I buy myself a *djelleba* and wear a scarf – I go the whole hog. O.K., I don't cover my face, but then the local women don't either – except for the religiously fanatical ones. But people can tell that I'm white – which is so annoying. In Cairo I have a bloke simply groping me in the middle of the street. I get so insulted that I spit in his face. You're not allowed to, because that makes him unclean and then he can't go to the mosque for another twenty-four hours. It makes him as mad as anything – he flails his arms and everything – I think he's about to bash me up. But then I just call my big, strong hubby. Jacques is just round the corner, having a piss. He comes at once and saves me.

Africa

We try to get visas for Libya, because Jacques wants to see it. But we simply can't get into the Libyan embassy; there's a constant throng of Egyptians crowding the entrance because Libya is one of the few places they can go to get jobs. Jacques ends up scampering over the embassy walls and climbing through a window. Once he's got in with our passports, he's told that we can only get a visa if we have an Arabic translation in our passports. He returns, and I go straight to the Danish embassy, where they stamp my passport with a standard translation into Arabic, and then they fill in my name in Arabic characters. But at the French embassy – oh no. They don't do these things, so we have to give up on seeing Libya. We don't have a route planned – we're on the road, plain and simple, and we go wherever we can. We learn that we can get into Sudan – the borders are open and getting in poses no political problem. We get our permits and sail down the Nile until we reach Luxor. When we arrive, we're told that the Sudanese border has been shut. There's just been an attempted *coup d'état* in Khartoum. Christ on a bike. Africa. It's been like that ever since.

We stay in Luxor for three weeks, the last fortnight of which I refuse to leave the hotel room – I can't stand the sight of another Egyptian. I am furious at the way I'm treated.

Finally the border is opened, and we get on board the boat and sail south and cross Lake Nasser in twelve hours, and then it's on towards the Sudanese border. We sleep on the deck with all the other travellers. We're about fifteen white people on board – some of them are people we met on the ferry from Cyprus. We land on a sandy beach in the middle of the desert. There's nothing but sand and the little wooden shacks where the locals sell tea. We sit down on chairs by low tables and order some tea, and a man comes to serve us and . . . nothing. No pissing about, no messing, no fuss, no attempts at conning us. Just friendly service and nice people. No-one giving me the evil eye. When we want to pay, they won't let us:

"No, no, no, the man over there has already paid for you," the waiter says, pointing at one of the locals. Our eyes go as wide as saucers, and our jaws drop.

"What?" I say to Jacques. "And he hasn't even come over and he doesn't want anything from us or . . . ?" And there's one of those tiny choo-choo trains which are really quite sweet that they've bought in Hungary. I don't know why it's so small; I don't know if people in Hungary are that petite. The seats are just tiny – everything is eensy and made of plastic. The train leaves from the dock, and we have a thirty-six-hour journey ahead of us, between Lake Nasser and Khartoum.

I need to pee and am going towards the corridor where the toilets are. And there he is: a naked man, black as tar, with a filthy cloth tied in a knot around his shoulders and a long spear. He's just standing there, like a statue, looking out of the window. I stop. He's got a row of warts across his forehead – tribal tattoos of a sort. I'm slightly taken aback and a little scared of him – just stand there gawping at my first tribal man, and no doubt my mouth is hanging open. He turns his head ever so slowly and looks me straight in the eye, and then he just *smiles*, a big wide smile, and suddenly I am head over heels in love with Africa. *That* is a real man. It bloody well is, dammit – this is as different from Egypt as chalk from cheese. He is simple and straightforward. He doesn't need anything from me. I love that.

We get off at a station and go out to Port Sudan on the Red Sea and down to Suakin, which used to be a bustling Arab port until it was abandoned thirty years ago. The city's completely empty now and there's almost nothing left, only the foundations and a few ruins. Everything has been washed away by the wind and weather. That's the sort of thing

Jacques wants to see. Things that are broken. It was the same when we were diving in the Mediterranean: he wanted us to look for underwater ruins. I don't know – I suppose it's O.K., but I don't really think it's all that interesting. We go for a walk in the desert behind Suakin and all of a sudden there's a sort of circular wall. In the middle of absolutely nowhere – it makes no sense. Jacques lifts me so I can look over the wall. A sea of camel faces looking straight at me. They don't say anything. There are hundreds of them. They have such darling eyes and cute-as-button faces when you see them straight on. I don't see any people. I see them later, because all of Sudan's desert north of Ethiopia is camel country – the camels of the whole Arabic world are bred here, and the camel drivers are a tribe with a distinct look of their own. I've started to work it out; in Africa everyone belongs to a tribe, and they all have some very strong and very important characteristics. In some tribes people are short and squat, in others they are slender, and then they have a certain hairstyle or other distinguishing feature. The camel drivers are a sort of little, fair-skinned Arabic type – not negroid at all. Little dried-up men with dreadlock-like, bob-cut hair. They wear a dusty white cloth draped around their hips – on their upper bodies they wear short vests and they have turbans on their heads; Arabian Nights all over. And then they all carry a large sword and a large whip. Many of them also have ammunition belts slung over their shoulders and a long carbine.

Famine

From Port Sudan we head to Khartoum, where we get stuck. There's Green Monkey Disease in southern Sudan, and the area is quarantined. Some scientists have dissected green monkeys in the Ruwenzori region of Zaire. The virus was found in the monkeys' kidneys. Three hundred and eighty-five people died in just two weeks, and the disease has spread rapidly to Uganda and southern Sudan. The virus has flu-like symptoms, people shit and vomit blood. On the outside you can't see anything's wrong. After twenty-four hours they die of internal haemorrhaging.

After about a month the disease seems to have done away with itself, the quarantine is lifted and we can get back on the road. In order to get to southern Sudan we must sail down the White Nile on an old ramshackle paddle steamer with five barges tied to it, a veritable floating island. There are first, second, third, fourth and fifth classes. We're travelling on the cheap, so we get fifth-class tickets, and it's pretty grim. Among our travelling companions are a herd of shrieking goats. But still we get bunks, even though it's just a shelf which you can only worm into if you are on the skinny side – pot bellies are a no-go. And if you need to scratch your nose, you have to move your arm sideways out of the bunk and up along the side. They've made sure to fix up mosquito netting of course, but it's full of holes. And needless to say there's mosquitoes a-plenty on the boat, because there's all sorts of goodies for them on board. The toilet facilities amount to a heap of shit on the deck – apparently no-one's smart enough to stick their arse over the railing before they take a dump. You go on the deck in a large communal pile. And yes, people have intestinal worms and things, so there are bloody lumps and *eeeeeww*. The pile of shit isn't shielded in any way, but still, it has been put in a corner. Next to it is a mother, cooking a meal on a coal fire. She's put down her baby on the deck just two feet from the shit heap.

I send Jacques down to speak to the captain about moving us up to first or second class, but it's sold out. We get to go to the restaurant for a meal only once on our voyage. The entire journey to Juba, which is Sudan's southernmost city, is going to take us six days. After three days we can't take it any longer and get off when the barge docks in Malakal, which is a sort of small town on the Nile – but at least it's a town of some kind. We head towards the city centre.

"What is this place?" I ask.

"Damned if I know," Jacques says. Men are walking around naked as Adam in the streets, looking starved. Jacques tries talking to some of the people wearing clothes, but they have strangely vacant stares and seem disoriented. The shops are all closed.

"They're starving," I say.

"They are," Jacques says, and we hurry back to the quay, but the ship has already left. An angry man accosts us and says we have to report at the police station to be registered. We go there with our passports and are listed in a grubby notebook. We ask the policeman for advice. Where can we buy food? Where can we stay the night? He wouldn't know. His job is to register us, nothing more. There's no food to be had, but they stay on top of the red tape. We plod about town for hours trying to hear about transport out, but there isn't any. There's nothing but famine. There's no diesel and no jet fuel, even though there's an airport and loads of trucks. We simply can't leave. It turns out to be a town on the border between rivalling tribes, a place no-one really wants anything to do with, so the rejects from all the tribes end up here. They hadn't warned us about that on the boat – that was our business. But then, we didn't ask, did we? We just wanted off. We find a mission house where they let us camp on their porch; they won't have us indoors. And they won't share their food with us either; our hunger is our own business. We then find a shelter where they sell tins from aid packages at crazy prices; there are porridge oats and there are sardines. And they have tinned corned beef, but it's best not to read the sell-by date – they're old American military rations from the 1960s, irradiated to a point where they can last till the end of time. And that's it. That's what we live on: water from the Nile, porridge oats, sardines and irradiated beef. It's so gross. Luckily we've brought iodine tablets, so the water doesn't make us ill. The town is plagued by dysentery and hepatitis. I start thinking about how my mother used to be in her kitchen, teaching my sisters to make large warm meals – me, who never cared about food and never eats anything but cheese sandwiches and apples. Out of the blue I suddenly remember recipes for strange and wonderful things like ham with creamed spinach and caramelized potatoes. I dream about Coca-Cola, which I never used to like. We yearn for a simple cup of tea. One day we hear a rumour of there being bread for sale. We dash off at once, but no-one wants to tell us where the bakery is, so by the time we get there, it's all sold out. It's horrible. Every day Jacques goes into town to look for transport. But nothing.

Finally – after a fortnight – we're told that there's jet fuel again. We fly out. It's amazing. We arrive in Juba in southern Sudan, not far from the Ugandan border. In Juba there's misery as well. It's a city of huts spread across the plain. But there's a police station where we go to be registered. They don't mind us starving to death so long they know where we are while we do it.

From Juba we find that we can't get into Kenya. They won't let us in because we come from an infected area – the green monkeys. Again we locate the mission house. It looks like we'll be starving on Christmas Eve. We're stuck for another fortnight while Jacques dashes around trying to sort something out for us. In the end we manage to get a private plane, a small Cessna, from Juba to Nairobi, the capital of Kenya. Jacques has paid through his nose, and it's all a bit dodgy; we fly out in the grey dawn, and we don't check out of Sudan officially with passports and stuff, we just get on board and take off. At last.

Bountyland

We land in a real airport with actual passport control. Nairobi is a proper city with skyscrapers and civilization. It's Christmas; we go to a restaurant and have steaks. It's such a luxury, it's amazing. There are great nightclubs here and beautiful hotels. Quite a bit of poverty around, but also a staunch middle class.

We're staying with the locals at a little hotel called Almansura. It has an external gallery around a quad, and in the yard the women sit and cook dinner on coal fires. The rooms are very dirty, the beds shoddy and there are cockroaches everywhere. But people are very, very kind. The women in the yard wave at me.

"Can we do your hair?" one of them asks.

"Yes," I say, and they all laugh and come over and do my hair in little cornrows across my scalp. The white skin between the plaits burns, so I take the cornrows out the next day; now I'm a Greenlander with an afro, and everyone smiles at me.

The hotel charges us seven kroner a day, and food sets us back another fourteen kroner. So cheap.

We don't stay long in Nairobi. We catch a train to the coast; Mombasa – the most beautiful place. Those houses, in the Arabian style with carved woodwork, and that glorious sandy beach with coral reefs and clear water and loads of brilliant pot. We're staying in a great hotel where the first two floors are made of stone, reception and restaurant areas and some of the rooms too. The top floor is a huge terrace with a large wooden shed where we stay in a room that sleeps five with locals and other travellers. Such a lovely time. We go to the beach to dive. Jacques harpoons moraine eels. They have firm white flesh like monkfish. I fry them up for us in a little olive oil with a sprinkling of herbs and salt – *yummy!* We go out sometimes as well – restaurants and bars. We don't really do nightclubs – Jacques isn't into that sort of thing. He talks and talks to everyone he meets to find out where they've been to and what's going on. And he goes on and on about his own views about anything and everything, and people listen to him because he's so overpowering. I don't listen anymore, but I bask in his aura. He's my man.

From Mombasa we travel north along the coast to Lamu Island. It's an old Arabian colony from where they used to ship slaves off to the Arabian Peninsula. It's a gem of an island, not much more than a sandbar but with a jewel of a village in the perfect Swahili style. Narrow alleys between the houses, which have beautifully carved doors leading on to courtyards, and stairs going up on the outside, and roof terraces, and roofs made of palm fronds.

It's while we're on Lamu Island that Jacques learns that there's cheap gold to be had in Zaire.

"Those guys come out of the jungle where they've been washing gold themselves. They don't know the world market prices. So if we exchange dollars on the black market, we can make a fortune," he says. He also looks into the possibility of buying diamonds from the mines in southern Zaire close to Zambia, but it's too dangerous – capture means execution on the spot. Gold carries a pretty heavy punishment as well, but the chances of survival are better.

"When are we leaving?" I ask.

"I need to read up on this first," Jacques says. "If there's gold, there's bound to be swindlers as well who will sell you something that looks like gold. So I have to know exactly how to be sure it's the real deal."

Back in Nairobi Jacques gets hold of some nitric acid, which is the only thing that can corrode gold. And he gets himself a test tube and some weights. It's something to do with dividing the weight by the cubic content which should give you a number called the unit weight, which is different depending on which metal you're dealing with. Something like that.

It's not like we're running out of money, but Jacques is afraid that we're squandering it. "Money needs to multiply," he keeps saying. "If it doesn't, we'll end up running out." And we can't have that. He doesn't want a regular job. And we'll only set up the diving business once we really settle down. First we must travel the whole world. We want to have something to choose from. Apparently Mombasa isn't an option, even though I think it's lovely. But he feels that Africa is too tumultuous. He went to the Seychelles with his flight-attendant wife once, and he thought it was the coolest place ever. "But it's too small," he says.

"Too small how?" I ask.

"Too cramped, too much of a squeeze – everyone knows everyone," he says and shivers like a man who feels suddenly cold. No, I don't suppose you could scam anyone in a place like that for long before you were caught. "But we're not settling down yet anyway," he says. "We have to go to India and Asia and Australia first." Jacques has given that gold some thought. Who's going to take it off his hands? The Indians, of course. But not in Kenya – in India. There's no gold to be dug for in India, so the Indians are all dying to put their fortunes into gold. "They all do it, because it's safer than leaving the money in the bank," he says.

L'or vivant

The goldmines are in the Kivu district in Zaire, close to the borders of Uganda and Rwanda. We have tickets for a train from Nairobi to Kampala – Uganda's capital, where Idi Amin is in charge. There are stories about him in the Kenyan newspapers every day. They write that he's a late-stage syphilitic, that he eats his wives and that he's mad. He doesn't distinguish between blacks and whites – he kills everyone he cares to. He has done away with 100,000 people. He's a veritable devil. We exchange dollars for Ugandan shillings on the black market in Nairobi and get them back at five times the official exchange rate. Everyone does it.

In Uganda we find a super-swanky lodge in a wildlife park, where we shack up for ten days. We're driven around and look at the animals – hippos and antelopes and three hundred elephants who are spread across the landscape, feeding. Wow. We eat scrumptious food, cosy up and have a lovely time while the local population is being butchered.

From there we continue inland by *matatu* – the small local buses – towards the western border and into Kivu from the north. It's the highland part of Zaire, which is so beautiful: Tarzan country. Lake Kivu, Goma, Mountains of the Moon, Staircase of Venus – this is where people used to look for the Queen of Sheba's Mines and the source of the Nile. Zaire is a former colony – once known as Belgian Congo. As uncivilized as can be. We arrive during the long rains, and it's high above sea level, so it's actually cold. There are almost no hotels, only rotten guesthouses. There's nothing to be had here, only some strange deep-fried greasy dumplings. Dough in hot fat – that's what we have. In Zaire there aren't as many *matatu*, so we go by lorry and sit on the back with the locals – we get the best view ever, driving up the road on the fringes of the Congo basin. There's a view that stretches forever, across treetops and more mountains. The atmosphere is different from that of East Africa. Everything seems shoddier. The houses look European – tiny little ugly brick buildings: a single room with a window and a door and a metal roof. And it's always pitch black over the window and the door because they cook over coal fires inside. People do seem a bit oppressed, but maybe that's just the rain.

Every time we stop in a village, Jacques goes over and talks to people, because he has to find out where the gold is. We drive for five days along that route, down towards the borders with Uganda and Rwanda. We reach the final village in the highlands, right by a steep slope down towards the savannah-rich valley where Nyirangongo lies – a giant volcano, almost three and a half kilometres high. In that village Jacques finally meets a little pygmy-like fellow who nods in recognition when we ask him about gold. He comes over to our room at the hotel and gets out his things. They're wrapped in a piece of plastic. Jacques opens it, and the yellow lumps of metal make an odd, clanging sort of sound. Me and Jacques look at each other, because gold shouldn't really sound like that, should it? Jacques sits on the edge of the bed and throws a lump of gold from one hand to the other and knocks two together. *Clang clang*, they say. He gets out his weights and measures and weighs the lumps and looks up at the pygmy. "This isn't gold," Jacques says, and the pygmy looks really scared and quickly picks up his things and leaves. Jacques is pissed off because that was the first person he's been in touch with. "Dammit, it was probably just a story. Maybe we've been sent on a wild goose chase," he says.

But the next the day Jacques runs in to another bloke who's got a lot of it. He too carries it wrapped in a plastic bag, but he's got a proper chunk of it, about the size of an egg and with stones in it. It looks completely different – it doesn't say *clang*, it says *donk*. I bite it and it feels sort of soft – I can't actually bite into it, but it does feel like it yields a bit. Jacques measures and weighs, and it has the right unit weight. They start bargaining, and it turns out that the bloke actually does know that world market price.

"How could he know?" Jacques says, flabbergasted. "He's just come in from the jungle, hasn't he?"

But of course the villages have a radio connection to the surrounding world and there are short-wave receivers tuned to the B.B.C. World Service, so they're not really living in darkest Africa after all. The guy wants a proper price, and Jacques had banked on making a huge profit, and now there isn't really that much to be made. But he buys the gold anyway because he's had a word with the Indians in Nairobi and knows that he can shift a load quickly. The Indians are interested in gold as a sort of start-up capital in case they need to leave Africa. Idi Amin has kicked all the Indians out of Uganda, so the ones in East Africa are worried about their fate at the hands of the negroes and are trying to escape to the U.K., or the U.S. or Canada.

We end up with a kilo of gold, but a kilo doesn't actually take up much space; it's only about half the size of an average erect cock. I'm allowed to say as much because Jacques is standing there wrapping it up in two condoms. He hands it to me:

"Try popping it up," he says.

"You carry it. This is your idea," I say.

"Where would you have me put it?" he says.

"You've got an arsehole – I know that much."

"Don't be funny," he says.

From the village we head across the plain, past the Nyiragongo volcano, which had erupted a month earlier. There's solid lava everywhere. They've already sent bulldozers across it and made roads. During the eruption the volcano sent a number of offshoots down its slopes, and we head out to see them. We walk for eight hours through the jungle, and it pissing well pisses down. Everything is absolutely sodden. And then we get to a place where glowing lava and stone spew out of the ground. The dried-up volcanic stone-desert has strands of bubbling lava woven through it. We hang our clothes to dry on some shrubs and settle down by a crack and toast bread and roast sausages, and all our things are dry in half an hour flat.

We're going back to Kenya, and the nearest airport with scheduled flights is Kigali in Rwanda. The landscape is totally stunning. We have our gold, but nobody knows. We're just tourists. The airport terminal is thankfully perfectly basic – they have no metal detectors or screening devices, so our baggage is searched by hand. I stew a little as I walk through customs, across the tarmac and up the steps to the aircraft; the gold is heavy and I have to tighten my cunt all I can. The gold stays put. I nod off on the plane, and by the time we reach Nairobi it's not looking good. Jacques is standing there, lifting out our bags from the overhead compartments.

"I can't hold it in," I whisper to him, as I get up to walk down the aisle.

"Just clench your cunt then," he says.

"It's slipping out," I say, sitting down again.

"You usually know how to give a good clench," he says.

"Yes, well, unfortunately I don't normally have a kilo's worth up there," I say. He looks at me.

"Tear a hole in your pocket and keep it in," he says and walks towards the exit. Bastard. I turn my pocket inside out, rip it and get my hand down there – luckily I'm wearing wide khaki trousers, so I can thrust my hand down my pocket and hold onto the golden cock without it looking like I'm plodding about scratching my own groin.

That night Jacques is standing as naked as Adam in our hotel room with a stiffy, wanting to give me "*l'or vivant*" – the living gold.

"You're an idiot," I say. "My cunt hurts."

"Oh come on," he says. I turn to the wall and pull the blanket over my head.

*

We find a guesthouse some ten or fifteen kilometres north of Mombasa; Pole-pole House – that means *take it easy* in Swahili. It overlooks the beach – there are two railway rails with steps leading down to the sand. Originally there were probably twenty-five steps, now there's nine left. You can scamper down, and there are reefs some way out and a lagoon with loads of fish and corals. We go scuba-diving every day – the water is 25–27° C. I run ten kilometres on the beach every morning and carry out a full exercise routine and a full yoga routine, and then I smoke a ton of pot. I'm in Nirvana – I can't feel my body at all.

And Jacques thinks so hard, I swear I can hear it. We still have the gold – he didn't sell it in Nairobi. He wants to take it to India. How we're going to pull that off, I have no idea. He doesn't have the least scrap of paper to imply that it's legally his. The international airports have metal detectors and screening machines. Golden cock in a honey pot; it can't be done. But I don't say anything. I've stopped asking questions altogether.

Jacques wants some more gold. And he is not happy about investing more money without knowing what will come of it. He comes up with a plan: he wants us to cash some traveller's cheques and then the cheques will be stolen, and we'll get some new ones. He means to use the "stolen" cheques as payment in Zaire where he'll exchange traveller's cheques for Congolese francs on the black market. After our last trip he has a connection – a white guy – who is willing to help us.

"But there are always lists of cheques that have been reported stolen," I say.

"They don't have those lists in the jungle," Jacques says.

No, of course they don't. Just like they don't know the world market price. I don't ask what it is that Jacques has told the black-marketeer we need all that Zairian money for. It's quite a lot of money.

Our second trip: We fly directly to Kigali and go on to Goma in Zaire.

Jacques has arranged with the white guy to meet at a bar. We check into our hotel, and Jacques has a strange plan: once we've exchanged our money, we must hide our Zairian money in some packages with washing detergent because he's worried about the police. To be honest he's afraid that the black-marketeer is in league with the police. It's that old trick: the police show up as soon as you've made the exchange and say: "What? Where does all this money come from? Can we see your bank receipt? Oh you don't have one! Well then, in that case we'll confiscate the money and we'll fine you." That's how you're meant to treat tourists after all. And we've got all that bloody washing detergent in our hotel room. There's a knock on the door. It's the police. Jacques hasn't had time to make the exchange yet, and all they want is to see our passports. But we've already been to the police station to be registered, because you have to whenever you get to a new city. And yet here they are, wanting to see our passports. My heart is pounding away. The plan is that we head off as soon as we've made the exchange from traveller's cheques to Zairian money. Fly in to buy some gold and then out of there, back to Nairobi and on to India.

As soon as the police leave, we're out of there, because there's a decided whiff of danger about this. Something must have happened. Most likely that black-marketeer has paid the police to check us out and perhaps give us a bit of a scare to see if we are what we claim to be. He's running a risk as well – he could lose his money. And as we're not anything like what we claim to be, we run hell for leather. Back to Kenya with all our useless traveller's cheques that we can't use now because they've been reported stolen.

Conman

We're stranded at the Pole-pole House on the beach, and I have such a hard time being around Jacques. Because he's *thinking*. And he's keeping me in mind in everything he's thinking, and it's no good.

"Jacques, I think we should take a break," I say.

"A break!" he says. "That's the same as saying it's over." I tell him that

I've had it up to here with his mania. His death wish. Then he starts telling me about the time we went to Morocco to pick up hash.

After handing over the first shipment of dope to the Danish wholesale dealer, Jacques had told the bloke that there would be another shipment in a week. Jacques had only been paid in full for that first shipment after forty-eight hours when the dealer had shifted all the hash. But this time Jacques knew that the dealer had made lots of money on those first eleven kilos and consequently had lots of cash. Jacques had explained to the dealer that the next shipment was to be paid in full on delivery, otherwise Jacques would find someone else to take it off him, because he simply couldn't be bothered with all this mucking about. And seeing as it was really good hash, the dealer agreed to it. Jacques tells me about his little charade before we left for that flight to Paris, when he had those terrible stomach aches and told me he had to go and see his ex – flight-attendant Mette – and give her a present, and then we would meet at the airport. But really it was on purpose, going about pretending to be ill and not shaving – to convince himself that he was ill, so he could convince others as well. Then he had called the hash dealer and told him that he was ill and feeling poorly – that he'd had the runs all night and been sick. Could the dealer come to Jacques' instead and pick up the hash? Sure he could – they were mates. And the dealer gets there, and Jacques acts like he's done for. I believed the act, so I know. He's got a talent for projecting things, like a swarm of bees that pulls you in and makes you succumb to him, arch-manipulator that he is. Jacques had let the dealer in and had said: "Oh hello there, no really, I'm not feeling too hot, it's errr . . . that bloody Arabian food in Morocco . . . ugh-err, it's . . . oh, I errr . . . it's over there in that drawer, errr let me have the money, errr . . . oh you go and have a look at it, I'll just . . . I just really need to go and take a dump." And we had a bog on the backstairs landing, and Jacques had fitted the outside of the kitchen door with a hasp for a padlock. So out he went onto the landing, closed the door, popped in the padlock, locked it and leapt down the stairs and into the taxi he had arranged to have waiting. The dealer thought that Jacques was taking a dump, so he went over to look at the dope. And it was one of those plank-bed drawers, and Jacques had made sure that it would jam. So when Jacques had got a few steps down the stairs, he heard an almighty crash as the dealer finally managed to get the drawer open. And inside the drawer were lots of packages looking like they might be just the thing – that's how elaborate the hoax was. Jacques must have already been in the taxi going to the airport before the dealer discovered just how badly he'd been shafted.

I shiver. All that planning ahead he's been doing. All the things that could have gone wrong if he hadn't convinced him. Just think what would have happened if that dealer had insisted on seeing the goods before he handed over the money? Yes, well . . . and that time we were flying out of Casablanca with those suitcases with the fake bottoms, and Jacques made sure we arrived at the last minute. It could easily have gone wrong so many times over.

And of course Jacques knows that I would think it was out of order to trick that poor dealer. And by now I can't even work out if it's the truth he's telling me. Maybe it's just some story he's worked out in that twisted brain of his to make me too scared to go home. Because there's nothing he hasn't thought about. He knew that I would tire of him eventually. Because he's the limit. And now I can expect to be held accountable for his shit if I return to Copenhagen.

"Then you didn't go out to Mette?" I ask.

"No," he says.

"Then what about that lamp you bought for her?"

"I got a taxi to take that out to her," he says. It's so lame. Maybe it's true, I don't know. He's so warped.

"That's a bit much," I say.

"And, you know, all that stuff we've got – all the stuff I bought for our trip, right before we left," he says.

"Yes?" I say.

"Tent, sleeping bags, back packs," he says.

"Yes?"

"I bought that on tick with our Magasin account card," he says.

"I don't have a Magasin account card," I say.

"Yes, you do. I had it set up so that both me and my charming little wifey could use it."

"You conman," I say. He just laughs.

I collapse on my run and can't move – it's as if all strength in my body is drained from me, but it doesn't actually hurt. I get back up quickly enough, and can't feel anything wrong. I don't tell Jacques about it, I just stop running. And I smoke insane amounts of pot to stand being around him. But the pot turns against me. I can sense his thoughts like a physical presence in the room – I feel quashed. Jacques is pacing like a lion in a cage. Something has to be done about those traveller's cheques, before it's too late. He's banking on there not being new lists of stolen cheques if he heads far enough into the jungle. Christ, an ado for a teensy profit – instead of getting an honest job. Suddenly I collapse again with terrible abdominal pains.

"You'd better see a doctor," Jacques says. I locate a doctor in Mombasa, and he gets more and more agitated as he examines me:

"You get a taxi right now and go *straight* to the hospital. You don't stop and call anyone. I'll call them and tell them you're coming. You're going *straight* there. *NOW!*"

The doctor thinks I have an ectopic pregnancy. He's sending his secretary down to the street to get me into a taxi, and he promises to send word to Jacques. At the hospital they send me straight on to the operating table. It's as surreal as anything. When I wake up, they tell me that I've had a gargantuan cyst on my ovary – like a big pouch of infection that had been contained within itself. And that pouch had exploded – most likely during my run a week ago. And there's pus all over my abdominal cavity, so the apexes of my lungs, and my liver and my kidneys are all inflamed. They've had to remove my ovary. At the same time they tell me I have five different kinds of intestinal worm.

The hospital itself is top of the trees. I relax completely. Jacques doesn't come to visit – it's lovely. I try to think; what am I to do? First I need to recuperate. For ten days I'm in bed. When I leave the hospital, I'm skin and bones – completely drained. I'm almost afraid to step onto the kerb. I've left my safe hospital environment with its kindly nurses and come straight back to the lion's den. He thinks and thinks and thinks. I've been gone for ten days, and still he's thinking. The air disappears around me. He tells me he's hatched a plan, but he doesn't tell me what it is. Not that I want to know. It's probably something even more shady than usual. Luckily he doesn't say much, but he keeps going around with this really dodgy chap from Switzerland called Florian. After a week they leave together. Destination: Zaire via Uganda.

"If you haven't heard from me at the end of a month, you must look for me and have me reported missing," he says.

"O.K.," I say. He leaves the stolen cheques with me. He probably thinks they're no longer valid – it's been too long. In reality they're stolen goods and prove that I'm a fraudster, so the first thing I do is to burn them.

A month passes. I don't hear anything. I go to Nairobi and have the French embassy call their French embassy in Kampala to check if they've heard anything about a Jacques Rouvre. They haven't, and I get the distinct impression that they're not bothered. The Danish embassy isn't really bothered either, because we're talking about a French citizen.

Search

I've got my strength back. I meet a lot of backpackers and go to nightclubs every night. I shag my first negro. Black men work. And just one more to be absolutely sure. He puts on all the light and studies every inch of my body in a way that makes my skin quiver. I'm his first white woman. I tell him about the long winter nights in Greenland. He laughs, but I don't think he believes me.

It's lovely being alone, but I have to go and look for Jacques. I'm afraid to travel into Uganda, and I don't want to travel on my own, so I hook up with two Swiss travellers and an American, and we fly to Kigali in Rwanda. They come with me into Zaire through Goma and up to the village at the top of the ridge. I walk around and ask at the hotels and at the police station to see if Jacques has been registered there. He hasn't. I feel silly. As far as I can make out Jacques never showed up in Zaire. And before leaving he said that their plan was to go through Uganda. That's where the trail ends. I refuse to go to Kampala to check up on it, because Kampala is where Idi Amin lives.

Me and my travel companions decide to move on. I have three blokes courting me – it's fun and I have lovely time of it. I'm living in a film. We're looking at gorillas, and we camp, and smoke a lot of pot. We go south to the capital of Burundi, Bujumbura, and we're sitting on the roof terrace of some hotel – drinking gin and tonics while looking at the divine view across Lake Tanganyika – when I suddenly hear a Jewish-looking woman speaking in Danish to her blond children. Her name is Anne, she's a psychologist and tells me that she's here to treat the victims of the 1972 massacre, when a Tutsi-dominated army killed upwards of 15,000 Hutus on the president's orders. Wow – you can't see it in people's faces at all even though it's only been five years.

Back in Nairobi I go round the embassies again, and the French embassy refer me to the local police in Nairobi. They are incredibly helpful. The policeman says: "That Ugandan business, it's just terrible." It seems like they're really trying to look into it, but no-one seems to have heard anything – the French embassy in Kampala haven't heard from him either. At the same time I'm worried that they might hear too much;

find out what we've been up to. So I don't press too hard for answers. I'm slightly concerned for my own skin.

I don't have very much money left in valid cheques, because Jacques took most of it when he went off. Of course I have access to the Swiss account, so I check the balance, and there's only 10,000 kroner left after our two years on the go. I take it out. I have no idea how much we've spent. I just let him handle the finances and went along for the ride. It's entirely possible that he's taken out half or the lion's share and just left a drop for me. And then I have to sort out the business with the gold, which I still have. Before he left, he told me where to sell it in case he didn't come back. And what I could expect to be paid for it. And I did tell him I wanted a break. So maybe he's just . . . gone. I mean, because of course he has to be the one who leaves. I can't be the one who says: That's it. I just can't be bothered any longer. It has to be him binning me, because he's a proud warrior sort of chap, and a big man, and all that crap. So that's what I think some of the time: Maybe he's just left me.

I have enough money to give me another six months in Kenya and a ticket home. And I have the gold. I go out to Lamu Island again and to Twiga Beach in Mombasa. Every time I go somewhere I'm terrified that I'll see Jacques on the veranda with a beer in his hand. I'm afraid that he's dead, but I'm also afraid that he'll show up again because now I've got my freedom I really like it. I really open up and meet my own sort of people. Jacques always met dodgy people, and I meet people who are sort of creative, and fun, and who want to play all night long and sit beneath the palm trees with a late-night joint and watch the sun rise over the ocean.

I meet a Dutch couple – Mariann and Ruben – who have a safari company and arrange trips on motorbikes for European tourists. But President Jomo Kenyatta has thrown a shadow over their lives – his nephew has taken a shine to their company and wants it for his own. So Mariann and Ruben lose their residence permits and are forced to sell the company cheaply to the president's nephew. They arrange a going-away trip for their friends and ask me along. We walk through the landscape by the Rift Valley, and we have a Land Rover full of our tents, and chilled foods, and wine, and beer, and pot; pot in Africa is just fantastic – it's all that sunshine. We are treated to the extensive French-African cuisine every night, and when we run out of tea, we simply chuck half an arm's worth of pot down the kettle – we're close to hallucinating. There's jungle here, and open bush-land, and rock formations and ravines. The country is full of antelopes and boars and monkeys. Early one morning a lion makes a kill somewhere close to the camp – I hear the roar and a reedbuck shrieking, and hyenas that approach wailing their *mpwouuwiiiip, mpwouuwiiiip*. The others scurry out of their tents to see what's happened, but I climb further down into my sleeping bag – not for me, thanks very much. A couple of hours later I'm no longer afraid to come out. I go over to look at the place, and the entire area reeks of lion – the smell of predator. The buck has been eaten. All that's left is a few scraps of skin and a bit of bone. Fifty metres from my tent; it sends shivers up my spine.

Apprentice

In Nairobi I sell the gold to the people Jacques put me on to. It's almost dull; a couple of overweight Indians sitting in a drab office. I bring the goods, and they already know how much there's going to be – maybe they've already seen it. But still they weigh it and point at the numbers on the scale and present me with their calculations. Jacques has told me how much I could expect to be paid, and it's true, that's what I get. They pay me in Kenyan shillings, and then I do my own little scam.

It's time to go home because the kitty's almost empty. I need a little to get me started when I get back to Copenhagen. The money for the gold amounts to about 8,000 kroner, and I want to buy traveller's cheques with every last shilling so I can take it home with me, because you can't use Kenyan shillings anywhere but Kenya. I go into a bank and walk towards the counter with big teary eyes, looking completely . . . disconsolate.

Kenya doesn't let foreigners go to the bank with Kenyan shillings and exchange them for Western currencies or traveller's cheques. The cashier is a small, well-groomed negro lady.

"I hope you can help me," I snivel, and she gets up and helps me to a chair. And I patter out my story: my husband and I have been here for a while, and we had planned to go to the Seychelles, and we had taken out all this Kenyan money to buy the tickets. "But now, my husband's met someone else and he's left me, and I just want to go home," I say and wail in earnest – I've managed to convince myself. And the negro lady is really nice.

"Ohh, missus. I'm so sorry. Oh, I'm so sorry for you."

"I'm sorry too," I sob. And she gets up and goes over and talks to her boss for a bit. And I sit there, crying and snivelling. She returns and tells me consolingly:

"It's alright – it's going to be alright, you know." I get my traveller's cheques, buy myself a ticket and save the rest. If nothing else my wretched teacher taught me that much.

The second to last day I'm sitting at the Norfolk Hotel's terrace where Baroness Blixen used to have gin and tonics with Denys Finch Hatton. The place is swarming with fat old Americans, but a young man sits down across from me. His name is Pierre; he's half German and half English-Austrian. His family owns Kahawa Mountain Lodge in Arusha in Tanzania and deals in high-end safaris. He asks me out for dinner, we dance on the dance floor, and then we dance some more in his bed – so much so that the condom breaks. He asks me if I'll come to Tanzania with him, but my plane is leaving the next day.

"If you're ever in Tanzania, do drop by," he says and gives me the address of the Lodge.

At the airport I have phantom pains in my cunt as I walk past the customs officers and the armed policemen. I fly to Crete. I don't want to arrive home too soon. I get the Magic Bus from Athens to Amsterdam – it's a dirt-cheap hippie bus that goes back and forth all over Europe. I get incredibly travel sick and throw up the whole way. And then I spend some time in Amsterdam before getting the train to Copenhagen. I'm a bit nervous because of that stunt Jacques pulled on the hash dealer and that account card with Magasin, and the fact that we did a bit of tax evasion before we went off while we were busy getting money together. So I'm a bit apprehensive about the whole thing, but there's nothing to be done. I go to Use It in Huset, rent a flat and report at Folkeregisteret. Nothing happens. Right up until the point when I am summoned to the police station to be questioned about that Jacques Rouvre character because someone has reported him for the theft of some pieces of jewellery. And of course it's that hash dealer. He wanted the police to stop Jacques at Kastrup Airport back when we left, but he could hardly say it was about hash.

"I don't know anything about it," I tell the policeman. "I've never heard anything about any bits of jewellery. And as it happens, my husband has gone missing." The policeman isn't particularly persistent. It turns out that the hash dealer is in prison, and the police have little confidence in his tales. So I don't have to worry about him.

I haven't reported Jacques missing anywhere. To whom should I report it? In the end I call the Foreign Office and am put through to twelve different people before I get a man on the line who says:

"Uganda? That's ominous."

"But what about my husband?" I ask.

"Yes, but you see, he's not a Danish citizen," the official says. "But I'll write it down, and I promise to be in touch if we hear anything."

I feel funny in my tummy. Maybe I've carted a load of intestinal worm home, so I go to the doctor.

"You're pregnant," he says. Oh. I write to Pierre in Tanzania and ask him if he really meant it when he said that I should drop by. I don't say anything about my tummy. Apparently the postal services are a bit ramshackle, because I get no reply. Or else he simply didn't mean what he said.

Idi sends his love

I work as an usher at Grand Teatret. Copenhagen has changed – there aren't that many buskers anymore. Being married to Jacques feels odd – whether he's dead or not – when Pierre's baby is growing inside me.

I decide to get a divorce or find out if I'm a widow or how I'm meant to deal with the situation. I talk to a man at the chief administrative authority who says: "We'll put in notice for him in the official gazette and grant you your divorce in absentia." When he doesn't show up, we just move things along and pretend that Jacques has consented to the divorce. Because there's no final proof of his death. I'm sitting there with my baby bump at the chief administrative authority, and the man asks me if I want to revert to my maiden name.

"Heavens no. I'd like to go on being a Rouvre," I say.

"Understood," he says. "Much more fun than Petersen." The man is looking at my tummy.

"No, it isn't his," I say. The man smiles and points at my hand.

"Are you keeping your wedding ring on?" he asks.

"I don't know if he's dead. Maybe I really am a widow," I say.

"You could move your ring to your left hand," he says.

"Why?"

"That way potential suitors can tell that you're widowed."

I cross Rådhuspladsen and there's Jacques, sleeping on a bench. It freaks me out. And I go up close, eyes as wide as saucers, shaking with nerves. I'm just completely . . . *oh no – it's him*. And at the same time, jubilant on the inside; Christ, if it is him, then he hasn't been murdered. And yet: *Oh no, then what? No more being the widow Rouvre.* Of course it isn't him. But not knowing what really happened is gnawing away at me.

I find a new place to live where my child can be warm and dry, and keep working at Grand Teatret until my waters break and I give birth to a boy with the exact same shape of head as Pierre. In the newspaper I read that Idi Amin has attacked Tanzania, who have sent their army into Uganda to try to remove him from power.

I have to go down to social services and sign a piece of paper saying that I don't know the identity of the father in order to have a little money to live on. It's not much fun being twenty-three years old and a single mum. But the boy is gorgeous. I name him Anton.

When Anton is six months old, I get a letter from the Foreign Office about an English professor who wants to get in touch with me. I write to the man, and he answers: he's a professor of history and was sent to Kampala after Idi Amin's fall from power to go over the archives of the Ugandan secret police. In the archives he'd found a letter from Jacques Rouvre addressed to Idi Amin himself where Jacques explains that he and Florian have been interned in the Ministry of Information and have been there for thirty-seven days at the time of writing. Jacques tells all sorts of tales about his little wifey who is waiting for him in Kenya with bated breath, and claims that he has a heart condition – and doesn't have his medicine. All lies, of course. And that Florian is on familiar terms with the Austrian president Kurt Waldheim, and that things will look pretty bleak for Idi Amin if Waldheim hears about this. The English professor seems to think that that letter was their death warrant. They never should have made Idi Amin aware of their existence, because Idi didn't bloody care about Kurt Waldheim, and he certainly wasn't going to stand for anyone threatening him. The professor thinks they must have been executed not long after. In his letter to Idi, Jacques claims that he and Florian had been in Kampala, and the weather had been so lovely that they'd gone down to Lake Victoria for a dip and a laugh, and then they'd fallen asleep on the beach, and the sun had set and of course there was a curfew after 8.00, and they'd gone up to the road to hitch a ride back into town and had been picked up by some officers who had locked them up for breaking the curfew. And since then they'd been locked up in a cell at the Ministry of Information. Just think, if they been more careful and had walked into town instead, and maybe even had snuck a bit behind trees and shrubs – I mean, if they had actually realized how dangerous it was. But Jacques . . . I think, when I was with him, I was more careful about the two of us, because I was so scared. But he had his death wish and at the same time he'd be damned if he let anyone tell him what he could and couldn't do.

I have constant fantasies of Jacques having that letter planted with the Ugandan secret police, because that's what he's like. He's so utterly manipulative. Maybe it's his little revenge on me or something – having me think that he's dead so that I'd love him even more or something. His entire way of thinking was so utterly twisted and far-fetched that anything can be true.

One Tuesday I get a crumpled letter from Tanzania, full of crossed-out addresses and stickers. It was sent from Tanzania eight months ago. Pierre. I have moved twice since writing to him, and his letter has been stranded more than once. And I can tell that it's not his first letter to me. He doesn't understand why I don't answer. I look down on Anton sucking at my nipple. I'll give Pierre his answer. I sell all my stuff and get all my money together. Then I go down and buy a ticket to Tanzania. Anton gets to come for free.

Baby Naseen

"Come on, baby, you have to eat," Mum says. She's standing at the cooker with her back to me, deep-frying cakes in a saucepan full of boiling oil. The kitchen smells of cloves and cardamom. I peck at my food and look at her back, which the sari half reveals: rolls of fat hanging in drapes – her spine is the parting of two sickening curtains which look like well-proved dough. She eats cakes and deep-fried foods. She says that thing she says, and then she says it again: "Don't be cheeky, Naseen. Speak nicely, sit up straight, smile. Try to be a bit more like your older sister. And eat, baby, eat."

Eating means eating more. I'm skinny. "It's all that running about," Mum says, shaking her head. We have games in the afternoon at the international school – it's compulsory. She thinks that's why I'm skinny.

We show up to tennis in our saris and high heels. Tubby Sally from America is our teacher.

"Come on, girls," she says.

We don't move.

"Where are your tennis shoes?" she asks.

"We don't have any," Parminder says.

"Why not?" Sally asks.

"We're not tennis players," Parminder says. Sally doesn't say anything. She goes over to pick up the rackets. Parminder is the most beautiful girl at school. She's a Sikh and tells all the Indian girls what to do, even though most of us are Hindus. We don't want games; we're not meant to want them. We're ladies. If a tennis ball hits your hand, your nails might break.

We're standing in the shade of a tree. I look up at an aeroplane passing over the peak of Kilimanjaro, flying north – maybe to England, which is where I ought to be. Sally comes over and hands us each a racket. She teams us up with a partner. I'm unlucky and get the white girl, Samantha, who is two years above me. Samantha hits the ball every time – she hits hard and aims high, so that it flies over the fence and across the games fields and lands between the trees. She drops her racket, making it fall with a *clang-clonk* onto the tarmac on the court, and then she saunters over to the opening in the fence and walks out slowly to pick up the ball, wearing only the tightest T-shirt and no bra, and shorts so short that it's positively revolting. High heels, sari, tennis racket. That's not going to make anyone skinny; it won't make anyone anything but annoyed. We're Hindus and vegetarians. Vegetables can be boiled, fried or baked in oil. I'm skinny because Mum makes me nervous. Dad makes me nervous, school makes me nervous, the blacks, the economy, the future – everything makes me nervous.

And Sabita, my eldest sister, she makes me nervous too. Sabita will finish school in a few months, and every day when we return, she calls to Mum: "Has Dad been to the post office? Has it come yet?" It's the Wedding File from Kenya she's waiting for, filled with pictures and information about potential husbands who are Hindus, of our caste and preferably relatives however distant a cousin they may be. It's better that way, because it's a guarantee of sorts of their treating the woman well. But the File hasn't arrived yet.

Photographs of Sabita have been circulating in Tanzania for almost six months already with information about her family, education and interests. The photographs were taken by an Indian photographer in Moshi who has done some careful shading so you don't see any acne or the little hairs that we aren't allowed to remove until after we're married. There have been suitors from our community in Tanzania because Sabita is very beautiful. But my parents weren't satisfied with what they had to offer, so now we're waiting for Kenya.

We live in a flat on Rindi Lane, which is the nice part of central Moshi. Dad is a developer and took over my granddad's firm when he died. Dad is always busy, because it's hard to make money in Tanzania. And we girls have to be home all the time because a good Hindu girl doesn't walk about freely.

I'm the youngest – fourteen years old – and the family call me Baby. The oldest are my two sisters, Sabita who is nineteen and Padma who is seventeen. Next in line is my older brother Badri, who is fifteen and the apple of my father's eye. In our culture people want sons because only a son will continue a father's line. A daughter's children belong to the family she marries into. Sabita claims Dad almost had a heart attack when I was born – yet another girl:

"You came out, and then Mum started crying, and Dad was called in, and he looked at you once and left without saying anything, and returned two days later, reeking and in filthy clothes."

I don't believe that Sabita remembers anything – she was only five at the time.

My older sisters' dowries are going to drain Dad dry. There's not likely to be much left for me. Maybe they'll let me get an education. I'd like that. I want to go to the West – away from here. Or if not that – they'll marry me to some scummy man who doesn't care about a dowry, but who just wants a machine for making sons and cooking food.

Mum knows that she won't have another baby, even though she would love an afterthought. "He never touches me," she whimpers on the phone to her younger sister in Canada while I sit, quiet as a mouse, on the balcony, listening. "You know, I think he might be seeing . . ." Mum stops talking and starts crying and sobbing – she can't make herself say it out loud. "I feel so terrible," Mum sobs down the phone.

"There are more girls than boys inside your mother," Dad tells Badri. "But you have to find yourself a wife who will give you male children," Dad says. Badri nods and munches away at his cake. Mum spoils him. He is fat and a nuisance, never does his homework and gets terrible grades. But then he's a son, so he'll inherit the property company no matter what – he's got nothing to worry about.

"You – maid," Badri yells in Swahili from his room. "Where's my shirt?" The maid irons a fresh shirt for Badri every afternoon so he can look his best when he goes out at night with his friends. Mum leaps from her chair in the sitting room, because the maid is out running an errand. God forbid Badri should have to do something himself.

"I'll bring it in, darling," Mum says. Badri opens his door and takes it from her.

"And my shoes," he says. "They're supposed to be in my wardrobe once they've been polished."

"I'll get them for you," Mum says and runs off to locate the shoes, which have been polished by the driver so that they're ready for *babu* Badri – the young master.

Sons are always spoiled, because looking after the parents in their retirement is the job of the sons, whereas girls are simply an expense.

Dad looked after his mother in her retirement. When Granddad died of a brain haemorrhage, Granny moved in with us. She followed Mum around and never stopped talking:

"You can't let your daughters wear those clothes – no man will ever want to marry them. You have been incredibly fortunate to marry a man as good as my son, but when you have such a lot of daughters, you must make sure to rear them right, or they'll cost a fortune to be rid off. And don't cook the peas for so long. My son won't like it – they'll be inedible."

I think Mum was relieved when Granny died of a heart attack.

And now, here's Mum spoiling Badri rotten. Lord have mercy on Badri's poor future wife, who'll have Mum plodding about at her heels with her incessant reminders of how Badri prefers his cakes, and his morning tea, and his freshly ironed shirts sprinkled with rose water.

I don't want to live with a mean mother-in-law. I have to have a husband who has so many older brothers that my mother-in-law can live with them or be shared between them.

Tennis. Samantha threatens me:

"If you don't at least try, I'll aim the ball straight at you."

"But you can't do that," I say, looking at Sally, who is even fatter than Mum. Sally breathes so heavily that she can't hear a thing.

"Watch me," Samantha says and hits a ball right past my face. I turn around and leave.

"Where are you going?" Sally asks.

"She's shooting at me," I say. Samantha shouts:

"And the next time, bring a pair of tennis shoes – this isn't a bloody ballroom, you know."

"Samantha!" Sally says.

"What?" Samantha says. "I've come to play tennis, not to be made a fool of." She leaves the fenced area. Panos, the mulatto, and a white boy are sitting in the shade, waiting for her

"Where do you think you're going?" Sally asks.

"Anywhere that isn't here," Samantha says and leaves with the two boys in the direction of the fields behind the school. What is she doing, one girl with those two boys? What are they up to? Sally is standing there, shaking her head. The rest of us have gathered in the shade of the tree.

"Samantha's a dirty tart," Parminder says. The rest of us nod. The other white girls opt for volleyball, but Samantha needs must disrupt our tennis.

Parminder tells us how to behave at school:

"Don't talk to the white boys, because then the Indian boys will speak ill of you, and you'll get a bad reputation." Parminder doesn't tell us not to speak to the black boys – we know that of course.

*

The international school is very expensive, but an education will ensure a good marriage. The better we do at English, the better we'll be able to help a husband who is in business. The woman is supposed to look after the family and be good at planning social events, and she's supposed to be able to mingle with all sorts of business associates of her husband's, even though she's never met them before.

Badri always shouts at us girls. Right after the last lesson of the day, you'll see him out in the car park where we're picked up:

"Hurry up, will you. We have to get going." He wants to go home and eat. The driver is sitting ready at the wheel. But Badri wants to drive the car.

"I'm the driver," the driver says.

"Get in the back," Badri says in Swahili.

"No," the driver says.

"I'll tell my mother that you're leering at my sisters," Badri says. The driver laughs. "What?" Badri says.

"You've obviously never met my wife. Your sisters can't make me hungry – *tsk*," the driver says.

"Watch it," Badri says. The driver starts the engine:

"You'll drive the car when your father says you can. Not a moment sooner," he says. Badri gets into the passenger seat. The driver drives. We girls smile at each other.

"Don't get above yourselves," Badri says sullenly. Sabita doesn't say anything, even though she is the eldest.

"You're not even allowed to drive the car," Padma tells Badri in Gujarati, so the driver won't understand.

"Don't even think about telling," Badri says, raising an admonishing index finger.

"I don't know – I might," Padma says.

"Then I'll tell them you're running about with white boys at school," Badri says.

"That's not true!" Padma says and stares sullenly out of window.

"Driver, would you please slow down?" I say as saccharinely as I can as we fly over the dirt road. He doesn't care what I say – he's black and I'm just a girl.

After school I must stay in. Mum is always busy teaching me about housekeeping, so I can become a good wife.

"It's very hard to teach negro girls how to cook good Indian food," Mum says. "You have to watch them constantly."

Some afternoons I do homework at one of my friends' – all of whom belong to our community. Or they're driven to ours by a driver who sits in the car and waits until we're done. He's not allowed in for a cup of tea, poured by the cook, because the car could be stolen while he's inside. And he'd interrupt our cook in her work, because all the blacks ever think about is wickedness. We do our prep and talk about love; about the heroes in the Bollywood films we see at ABC Theatre and Plaza. I'm in love with Savio, who is one of the oldest pupils at school. But he's from Goa and a Catholic, so I wouldn't dare tell anyone. Savio's big, strong arms. That black stubble grating against my cheek. The rumble of his voice in his chest when he speaks to me gently and lifts me onto the bed to caress me everywhere. *Oohhh*, that's the sweetest dream of all.

I see Savio at a Cultural Day at school where we're performing in Karibu Hall. A lot of parents have come – Mum and Dad included. We Indian girls have rehearsed an Indian dance – inspired by a Bollywood film – where we use thin sticks to move thin veils about in the air. We're wearing sequinned saris and flower garlands around our necks, and have henna tattoos on our palms, and polished nails, and clanging bracelets. I watch Savio as we perform, but he's wearing sunglasses, so I can't actually see his eyes and whether he's looking at me.

The black girls are up next; bare feet, kangas wrapped around their naked bodies and everything rocking. Badri is sitting gawping at them hungrily. The white girls perform a play – I don't think they know any traditional European dances – they only know how to writhe to disco music.

The phone rings in the sitting room. Dad picks up, hangs up and groans:

"Everybody's out to steal my money. What have I done to deserve these trials?" He looks at Mum, who looks away and says nothing.

Yes, he must pay the taxman, the Party office-holder, the union man, the local official of building regulations; he must buy beers for the regional commissioner every time they meet at Moshi Club. Everything is an expense. And Dad can't be too successful, because then everyone will want an even bigger slice of the cake – if he lets them down, they might even nationalize his company and give him some sort of hopeless compensation.

The company does well enough, but we live in a flat because the villas in Shanty Town almost all belong to the state and if we build a house ourselves, the blacks will claim that the Indians live posh lives. And what are the Indians really doing here? We're in Africa – India is across the ocean. We shouldn't even be here. It's my granddad's fault. He brought his family here to work as subcontractors when the Germans built the railway. Many of the Indian workers stayed on and set up companies in Tanzania since it was easier to get by here than in India. But when the blacks had their independence and the Brits left, we should have left as well. The Brits gave all the Indians colonial passports, because everyone was worried what might happen when the blacks came to power. Colonial passports didn't give us the right to settle down in England or Canada, but people did it anyway. A great many Indians left East Africa around the time I was born.

The next day Mum is hysterical when Dad returns for his supper. She's read in the *Daily News* that the authorities have arrested seven Indians for black-marketeering in Dodoma:

"It'll be like it was in Uganda. The blacks will confiscate everything we own and kick us out of the country. We'll have only the clothes we wear," Mum says shrilly.

"Calm down," Dad says bleakly. Mum keeps going:

"My own little sister had to leave her home in Kampala with only bundles and a single suitcase. Idi Amin took everything she had. Fifty thousand Indians he got rid of. Do you think it'll be any different here?" she shrieks. Dad raises his voice:

"Be quiet, woman. I'll hear no more of that talk." Mum snivels and mutters as she goes into the kitchen:

"My own sister. And you think this Nyerere is any better than Amin? You'll see soon enough. All blacks are the same. Barbarians. We should have left when we had the chance."

I look at Dad. He's hidden behind his newspaper. My aunt was kicked out of Uganda in 1972. Back then my grandfather decided that he and his family would stay in Tanzania because things were safe there. When Africa became more affluent, he and my father would make fortunes while all those jittery Indians would be walking around England shivering with the cold. But Tanzania never did become affluent – it became bad and corrupt. And now they're cracking down on the Indians and their black market, which is the only market in this country which actually works.

"Why did Granddad come here?" I ask. Dad lowers his newspaper and looks at me.

"India was a hard and unstable place back then," he says. "You couldn't rise above the position society thought you'd been born into, but you could always sink to a lower one." My father was sent to a boarding school in India for two years before he joined my grandfather's company. I've never been to India, but we stay in touch with my father's cousins, who are poorer than us. Dad winks at me: "We can get you to India easily enough, baby. All my cousins dream of having their sons marry my beautiful daughters." My father smiles at me. My mother appears at the door.

"Over my dead body," she says firmly.

"What are you saying?" Dad asks, looking at her. Mum huffs and puffs:

"Must we teach your poor relatives to live in Africa when there are plenty of competent Hindus who will be interested in our beautiful daughters, and who have received international educations, and will give us beautiful grandchildren whom we can visit in Kenya while we enjoy retirement and live in peace and quiet with Badri here in Moshi?"

"Our daughters might go to India," Dad says.

"India?" Mum says. "If my daughters ever leave, it'll be to go to England or Canada. Never to India.

"What's wrong with India?" Dad says loudly and gets up with the newspaper rattling in his hand.

"I don't want my daughters living there and being treated badly because they were born in Africa," Mum says.

"Serve me my dinner, woman, and let me have some quiet," Dad says and falls back into his chair with a sigh. Mum turns around and goes back out towards the kitchen, muttering:

"India? I never heard anything like it." She was born there herself, and two of her older brothers were killed in the uprisings when Pakistan was separated from British India in 1947. My mother's little sister lives in Vancouver, Canada, which Mum thinks is the best country in the world.

Dad goes to Moshi Club; at least that's what he says. Badri also goes out at night – he's allowed to because he's a boy. Padma says he lends the black boys money and makes a huge profit in interest and has a bad guy to get his money back if there's any trouble. Mum almost only leaves the house to go shopping. The cook walks behind her through the market, carrying the baskets, and Mum scolds the sellers for trying to trick her.

Now Mum is in the kitchen, crying.

"What's wrong?" I ask.

"Nothing," she says.

"Tell me what's wrong," I say. Mum sobs so hard the fat rolls on her back shake.

"I've given your father too many daughters – it's very hard on him," she says.

The next day it happens:

"The File has arrived from Kenya," Mum says when we come through the door after school. Sabita shrieks. We rush into the sitting room to look, but Mum shoos me and Padma out. "Leave your sister be," she says. Not long after we're all at the dining table. Sabita has a rapt, crazy look in her eyes. No-one says anything while we eat. Dad alone speaks:

"How am I ever going to manage?" he says, shaking his head. "They're stealing everything away." Is it the blacks he's talking about? Or his daughters?

After lunch Sabita sits down in the sitting room with Mum. The rest of us are to keep away. Padma and I mope in our room. There must be a way for us to get decent husbands. We have expressive eyes – alluring, teasing; luscious laughter and smooth limbs. We can dance like the stars in Bollywood films. We must make men uneasy.

"You'll have a good husband someday," Padma says.

"I'm the youngest," I say. "I'll marry some useless husband – maybe even an old one. Because Dad will have to spend his entire fortune on your dowries. What can I hope for?"

I want to own a shop one day. I don't just want to be a wife and a mother. I'm good at Maths, and Physics, and English. I think glasses are cool. My dream is to own an optician's shop with lenses that refract light so the world appears in focus. But where? Our relatives in India live poor lives. But why did Granddad bring us to Africa without taking us away again when the British left? We're stranded in the most dangerous world, surrounded by blacks who despise us and covet our wealth.

We snooze for a bit and wake up and do our prep. We're not allowed to disturb Sabita in the sitting room. Mum calls for me. I'm supposed to help her make supper so I can learn how to touch a man through his stomach. "Food is the way to a man's heart," Mum says.

"I prefer skinny men," I say.

"Shush," she says. "Don't say that. A skinny man is a skittish man. You have to fill out a bit too, Baby."

No, I don't.

Dad and Badri come home for their supper. Afterwards we all sit in the sitting room, sipping tea, and we girls leaf through Indian magazines while Mum and Sabita are infuriatingly secretive and the Wedding File is kept out of sight.

Dad gets up and gets his car keys.

"Going out tonight as well?" I ask sweetly. But Mum hears the edge in my question nonetheless.

"*Shush*," she says as soon as he's left. "Let your father have his recreation with his friends at the club." But I don't think Dad's going to the club. I think he goes out for a different sort of recreation altogether. Because Dad has stopped touching Mum's rolls of fat. Maybe he's running about town like an old tomcat, squandering our dowries on the female barbarians.

"Can we please have a look at the Wedding File, Mummy?" Padma asks.

"No," she says. "Not before it's your turn." Sabita looks scornfully at us. She's not nervous. There must be some interesting men in that file.

It takes me a long time to fall asleep that night. I think of how I may need to get up and use the bathroom during a lesson, and as I am headed back through the empty corridors, Savio comes out of a classroom and speaks to me, he says my name, how beautiful he thinks I am, and he takes my hand, he caresses my cheek . . . I am woken by loud noises. Dad has returned from his club, humming and slamming doors. Not long after he's snoring in their bedroom, so loudly that the walls are shaking. I go out for a pee. He drowns his sorrows – the hall reeks of beer and whisky and cigarettes.

The next afternoon Sabita is driven to school after lunch – the oldest years have lessons in the afternoons as well. Padma and I badger Mum until she lets us look in the Wedding File.

We sit leafing through it. Our husbands must be found in one of our ex-pat communities in East Africa. Because we don't have much contact with the West. And a man from India wouldn't be much use here, because he'd first have to learn from scratch about Africa and how black people . . . how that all works. My future husband must be oriented towards the West – a country that offers us more security; it could be England or Canada, America or even Australia. The white countries.

"There aren't any good men in here," I say.

"Lots of them are good men. What's wrong with them?" Padma asks.

"They're completely settled in Kenya. I want to be able to travel," I say.

"Where do you want to travel to? What do you want to do?" Padma asks.

"I want to do well at school, so I can get a scholarship."

"Don't you go anywhere far – how would you cope? You have to stay with us. We'll find you a good husband. Don't worry," Padma says. She sounds exactly like Mum. I do worry.

That night at supper Dad tells us that they've found a nice young man in the Wedding File who is from a nice, well-off family in Nairobi, related to us via some great-uncle or other. Sabita shows us his picture. I don't think he's anything special, but I pretend I think he's amazing.

The next day Dad gets in touch with his family, and Mum and Sabita go visit a newly-wed girl from our community. Sabita wants to hear all the dirt on how it's all done when you meet a young man for the first time and must talk and work out whether or not to get engaged.

*

At tennis Samantha scares me, every lesson. I complain about it to Mum.

"It's the limit, you girls having to put up with that sort of thing," Mum says. "Games are for boys." She gets our doctor to sign a note – I am to be permanently excused due to a crooked spine. Mr Owen reads it and looks at my feet.

"If you have back problems, it's probably not a good idea to wear high heels," he says.

"The doctor says I can wear them," I say.

"Hmmm," Owen says and looks at his desk. I stay where I am. He shuffles some piles about. He looks up.

"O.K., that's alright then," he says, nodding once, and waves me out.

"Goodbye, Mr Owen," I say.

"Goodbye, Naseen."

The next week I pass Samantha at break.

"Why don't you come to tennis anymore?" she asks.

"I'm not a tennis player," I say and walk on.

"You bet you are," she says to my back. That girl, she's a mystery to me.

Two weeks later the family from Kenya arrives– they must have greased some official's palm to be allowed to cross the border, as it's officially closed at the moment. The young man is wearing a new suit and polished shoes. He looks nice enough but isn't particularly masculine. He and Sabita sit in the sitting room across from each other, sending each other shy looks, while their mothers speak of food and their fathers hum at each other.

"Without us Tanzania would collapse," Dad says.

"The blacks are ruining business," the other dad says.

Sabita gets up and hands round cakes and tea.

"Yes, Sabita made all the cakes," Mum says even though it isn't strictly true. Finally the young man asks Sabita if she would like to go for a short stroll? She would like that very much, and me and Padma go to watch them from our bedroom window. Who knows what sort of a man he might be? Is he decent, and will he support Sabita through her life? But his family have the money required. We're immigrants. We must stick together. The Africans hate us because we're successful. We're afraid of them. I know I am.

I go out into the kitchen and start working, so our guests will taste that the daughters of this household are good cooks. I boss the cook about.

"Enough!" I say. "Don't put so much oil in." The young man's mother comes to the door. She's got a son at home in Nairobi – in the Wedding File it says that Sabita's suitor has a younger brother.

"What are your dreams, then, Naseen?" she asks.

"I'd like to own an optician's," I say.

"And where would you like to own it – here in Moshi?" she asks.

"In Canada," I say and start giggling. I stop and then add: "Yes, well, that's my dream, because my aunt lives there."

"My younger son asked me to see if there were any more good girls to be had in Moshi," she says, smiling.

"Is he getting married then as well?" I ask.

"No, he's only seventeen. First he wants to go abroad and study to be an engineer. He might even go to Canada," she says and smiles at me. Once you've gone abroad to study, you stay abroad – everyone knows that. But maybe you want a beautiful girl to come with you – especially if she's also your sister-in-law's little sister.

"Studying is important," I say and nod gravely. This mother seems really nice, and maybe she'll want to grow old with her oldest son who might be marrying Sabita. Then I can marry his little brother and we can live in Canada and be free.

"And what sorts of interests do you have, Naseen?" she asks.

"I like Physics, Maths and English," I tell her. "And then I like cooking, and I love children."

"Food without much oil – you follow the fashions of the young people," the lady – who is almost as fat as my mother – says. "My son wears glasses," she says.

"Does he? Then he can come to my shop in Canada and try on a new pair," I say smiling. "If he's in Canada, that is," I add. She doesn't say anything. "And if I am in Canada . . . by then," I say and look at the pots, because I don't know what else to say.

"And my son is very fond of tennis. Do you play tennis?" she asks.

"I'm learning at school," I say.

"Then you can play each other when we meet at the engagement party," she says.

"Are they getting engaged?" I ask, and my eyes are as wide as saucers. She smiles.

"It looks like it," she says.

"Oh, that's such lovely news," I say, kissing her cheeks and running in to Mum and throwing my arms around her neck. Then I'll meet the youngest son at the engagement party and later at the wedding and again if I go to see Sabita in Kenya.

School. Masuma is in the library. She's an Indian but a Muslim, and she doesn't follow Parminder's rules like the rest of us. Masuma is skinny and bony, and the best badminton player at school – she can beat any and all of the boys. She plays in white plimsolls, long white trousers and a white long-sleeved T-shirt, with her long hair in a ponytail. I ask her where she buys her clothes. She is friendly and gives me the name of her tailor. I lie to Mum:

"I need proper clothes for tennis," I tell her. "If I wear a sari just one more time, they'll give me a detention."

"But what about your bad back?" Mum asks.

"My back has sorted itself out," I say.

"But you don't have to play," Mum says.

"Mum. I want to learn how to play tennis," I say.

"Tennis," Mum says and, shaking her head, goes to get her purse. "That school is no good for a good Hindu girl."

We go to the tailor and make an order for the clothes and then find a shoe shop that carries expensive white plimsolls from China.

I go alone to the girls' changing rooms by the pool and get changed. I feel strange in those full-length trousers as I cross the playing fields on the way to the tennis courts.

"What are you doing?" Parminder asks, standing in the shade of the tree.

"Practising tennis," I say.

"But, we're not playing tennis, are we?" Parminder – with the polished nails, the gold bangles, the orange sari, the high-heeled sandals and the long plait down her back – says.

"I am," I say and go out on the court. Samantha is on the other side of the net.

"I told you so," she says.

"You told me what?" I say.

"You're a tennis player," Samantha says and hits the ball, and I break a nail, and my arm twitches when I hit it, and the ball goes flying. Maybe it'll fly all the way to Canada.

Uhuru Peak

I take a *matatu* out to Himo, and then up towards Marangu. The road rises before me. The farmers are growing banana plants, coffee, sweetcorn, beans, all sorts of veg. There are mango trees here and well-fed cattle. I walk the final five kilometres up to Kilimanjaro National Park, where coolies and carriers throng at the gates, looking for work.

"You must have a guide," the park warden in the office says.

"But I know the way," I tell him in Swahili.

"It says so in the rules," he says.

"Righto, I'll get one then," I say.

"He has to be certified," the warden says.

"I'll see you later," I say and walk back towards the gates. Damn. That path is so trodden and trampled that a child could find its way. When I was on the school football team, we used to do practice runs up to the first hut and back without stopping. For most of the boys it was no problem, but I was fat. I've been as far as Gilman's Point with the school as well. I was sick as a dog all the way from the third hut and couldn't face going on to Uhuru Peak, which is the highest point. These days I run sixty kilometres a week. I'm just going up and down. I walk back towards Marangu town and am accosted by a friendly person with dreads.

"I'm Eddy," he says.

"Panos," I say.

"I can come with you and carry your things."

"Are you certified?" I ask. Eddy shrugs.

"No," he says apologetically. "But I'd like to carry stuff for you."

"I can carry things myself."

"Do you have a cigarette?" he asks.

"Yes." We sit down by the roadside. Smoke. I ask after a cheap guest-house. He recommends one. I ask about it on the street. I find a guide – Samueli – and tell him my plan:

"This is how we'll do it. Tomorrow we'll walk up to the second hut, sleep there, walk up to the top and back down to the second hut, sleep a bit and then back down to the gate. Do you have that in you?" I ask.

"No problem," Samueli says. Of course he's fit. Walking to the top is how he earns his living. Alright then.

I find somewhere to eat and put away a large meal. I have to be in Kilimanjaro Airport in less than five days and catch my flight back to exile in England.

These last few days I've been with my parents in Arusha because I can't visit them at home in Iringa. I could be killed. Stefano and his family still live there, and his father might hire someone to do for me – it wouldn't cost much. Stefano's sense of balance is ruined and his face destroyed. Just over a year ago I beat him to a pulp because he didn't stop Baltazar raping Samantha. And now Samantha's dead. That's why I'm going to the top. No-one really knows what happened, but she mixed with the wrong sort of people in Dar es Salaam – too many drugs, Mick says.

I go to bed. Sleep for as long as I can and have a large breakfast. Samueli comes to fetch me, and we walk up towards the gates. I have my rice, onions, carrots and tinned beans. I buy bananas by the roadside and peanuts in a paper cone. I have my water bottles, trainers on my feet, my winter coat, sleeping bag, a saucepan with a lid. Everything in a tiny backpack. No gas ring or anything. I have a spliff with me and my candle. I'm bringing the candle with me to Uhuru Peak. That's the mission – apart from enjoying the trip.

We reach the gates and the office. It's the same park warden as yesterday. I hand him Mick's passport, which I've borrowed; it has a stamp on it with Mick's residence permit, and with it I can get in at the local rate rather than pay in foreign currency. The warden looks at the passport and then at my face. Mick is white. I'm a mulatto – one quarter *hehe*. My mother is the great-great-granddaughter of Chief Mkwawa, who fought the Germans and had his head lopped off in 1898.

"This isn't your passport," the warden says.

"I've got a tan," I say.

"This isn't your passport," he says.

"Let me see that," I say. He hands it to me. I open it, put some one-dollar bills inside it and hand it back. He opens it and takes the banknotes.

"Alright then," he says, and I pay for myself and my guide in shillings.

I walk ahead of Samueli at a steady pace. The jungle tumbles into your eyeballs until they grow weary of the sight. Big, gnarly trees crawling with vines and creepers – so dense that it's murky at ground level, even though there isn't a cloud in sight. High above us a herd of black-and-white colobus monkeys skip from branch to branch.

The tourists spend three days getting to the third hut. And the fourth day they get up just after midnight and start walking in the dark so that they can reach Gilman's Point and enjoy the sunrise – it's slightly easier walking uphill over the volcanic gravel when it's frozen. Some of them continue upwards to Uhuru Peak, which is the highest point at 5,895 metres above sea level – making Kilimanjaro the world's highest free-standing mountain. Afterwards they go down to the second hut and spend the night before finally returning to Marangu on the fifth day. Some people add a day of simply resting at the second or third hut to get their bodies used to the altitude, the thin air.

We pass the first hut, an old rickety brick building with a tin roof. Next to it are nice-looking wooden huts – a present from Norway to Tanzania in the late 1970s. The tourists go about having a lovely time of it. This morning they've ambled up here in four hours with carriers lugging all their stuff. Now they're chilling on the patio, admiring the view or lounging about in the sun, drinking Safari beer – you can get to the first hut in a Land Rover, and there's a fridge here full of drinks. Not long after the hut we leave the jungle and enter a heath-like area with clear views of Mawenzi's ragged points. We walk on at a steady pace and reach the second hut at around 5.30 – giving me enough time to get my bearings, get some water and chat to some guides and carriers.

"Can I use your bonfire?" I ask them.

"Yes, of course," they say. I have my saucepan, onions, carrots, tinned beans and rice. I chop the veg with my Swiss Army knife and chuck them into the pan. I've cut a stick to stir with and am about to put the saucepan over the fire.

"*Tia mafuta*," one of the blokes says – put some oil it that.

"*Hamna*," I say, because I haven't got any oil. He hands me a bottle.

"*Karibu*," he says. I thank him, put a bit of oil in the pan, fry off my veg, pour it out onto my plate, pop rice in my pan, add water, cook it until ready and flip the fried veg and tinned beans in, mixing it all around and letting it warm over the cinders. The guides and carriers look at me. I know what they're thinking: That mulatto doesn't know how to cook. No, I went to a boarding school, and when I was at home, there were always servants and my mother.

"*Wewe unatoka wapi?*" the man with the oil asks. I answer that I'm from Iringa.

"I am *hehe*," I say.

"But you're very fair-skinned," he says.

"Mixed with *mzungu*," I say, explaining that my father is white and my mother is half white, half black – half Tanzania, half England. My grandmother was *hehe* and my grandfather was English and ran the Tanzania Tobacco Company plant in Morogoro. He died of black malaria before I was born, but he made sure my mother had an English passport, and so do I. My mother married my father, who is Greek and runs a large tobacco plantation outside Iringa with some Indians. Mum has a good education and works as a schoolteacher. She is very proud of being related to Chief Mkwawa.

"Were they warriors, *wahehe*?" Samueli asks.

"They were the only ones who really resisted the German colonization of Tanganyika almost a hundred years ago," I say and throw back my head as I shriek: "*Heh-heh* – the name comes from the warrior's war cry."

"But the Germans beat them," Samueli says.

"No," I say. "The Germans attacked with African troops, burning the villages down to the ground, shooting the chief's emissaries. The name of the chief was Mkwawa, and he took it as a declaration of war and set a trap for them at Lugalo – three thousand *wahehe* warriors attacked and butchered most of the Germans and took their weapons as spoils of war."

"*Eeehhh*," one of the carriers says. "But the Germans came back."

"Yes. They attacked the *hehe* warriors' fort, but Chief Mkwawa managed to escape and launched a guerrilla war. The Germans couldn't catch him for the next seven years, even though they put a bounty on his head," I say.

"A great chief," the carrier says.

"But in the end they did get him," I say.

"What happened?" Samueli asks. I stir the saucepan.

"1898," I say, getting up. "The Germans were lucky and surrounded the area where Mkwawa was hiding. They closed in on him from all sides." I go over and grab another log and put it on the fire. "When the chief realized that he couldn't escape, he built a bonfire and took his rifle." I take another stick and hold it up like a rifle pointing it at myself. I'm standing with my back to the fire. "And he shot himself so that his body fell into the flames – *PAH!*" I allow myself to fall down by the edge of the bonfire. They all look at me. "He did it to prevent the Germans from catching him, even in death. And a German sergeant came over and dragged his body from the fire and shot him through the head and cut off the head and brought it to Iringa."

"Barbarians," the carrier says.

"Yes," I say. "The head was sent to Germany and exhibited in a museum so the *wahehe* had to make do with burying their chief's body."

"Those were bad *wazungu*," the carrier says.

"But then the British took Tanganyika off the Germans in a big war where the *hehe* people helped the British. And by way of a thank-you they got the chief's skull back and gave it to Mkwawa's grandchild."

"That is good," the carrier says.

I eat my food by the fire and smoke a cigarette before I get up, say goodnight, take my half-empty saucepan with me and walk up towards the large cabin where the tourists sleep – walking this far has made me tired after all.

Inside, the German and French tourists are sitting at a dining table laid with china, cutlery and wine glasses – white tourists from Hotel Marangu on an outing. Everything has been carried here. There's a tablecloth on the table, and wine and a waiter in his uniform, while outside the cooks are frying up the meat, preparing the chips and mixing the salad.

I tuck my saucepan away by my sleeping berth, go outside and talk the cooks into giving me a cup of tea – I chat to them and smoke the final cigarette of the day while the posh people eat. Then I go and lie down. Not far from me is a French couple – they're being loud. It sounds like a single woman in the middle of some intense masturbation, because the man makes no sound.

In a few days I'm going back to England. I'm at an agricultural school so I can come down and run a tobacco farm like my dad. But I don't know. Learning about soil conditions and chemistry is all very well, but they don't teach us about Tanzanian soil, and at school they don't allow us to get our hands dirty. I work at a petrol station in the afternoons and evenings. But I can't make ends meet, so the last few months I've worked nights at Heathrow chucking luggage about. Maybe I should give up school and just work – get money. You could build a business in Tanzania – maybe a safari camp for affluent tourists on the outskirts of Ruaha National Park – but you have to have start-up capital. My brother is a great white huntsman – the only problem is that he's a mulatto. He's explained it to me over the phone:

"We negotiate the hunt via fax and on the phone, and I don't tell the white people that I am coloured. When they see me, they get nervous. They're going hunting in the bush with some half-black man who happens to be armed. But by then they've travelled this far to hunt with the Greek, Mr Kloukinas. Can you be a barbarian when your name is Kloukinas, even if you are a mulatto?"

This week he couldn't come to Arusha and meet me, because he's got some Americans out hunting in the Tsavo area.

The tourists' pumping continues two metres from where I'm lying, but I'm tired. I set my mental alarm clock and fall asleep sometime around 21.00.

The next morning: *Bing* – wide awake at 5.00 before anyone else in the cabin. The cooks are at it outside. My guide is waiting, we get ourselves some sugary, milk-laden tea – Tanzanian style. I offer them cigarettes. In return I get more sugary tea in one of my Thermoses. And then we're off as soon as it begins to dawn. 5.45 – still a bit murky. You just have to get on with it. At "Last Water" after the second hut we fill our water bottles. We walk on, fast, towards the third hut. On the way we meet a patient transport: two men – fit as fiddles – running downwards with an altitude-sick man on a special stretcher that has been mounted on a bicycle wheel with added suspension. Samueli tells me that the men have some basic paramedic training. They run from Marangu up to the third hut, pick up the patient and run down again. They're on form.

I look up towards the glaciers of Kibo – thick white frosting on black volcanic gravel – they've become smaller since I was a child. The logging on the slopes of Kilimanjaro has been intense. Before the white people came, people believed that Kibo's icecap was made of silver and that anyone who attempted to go there would be frozen to death by evil spirits.

After the second hut, the heath is covered in grass, moss and flowers and clumps of heather standing as high as man, covered in hanging lichen. There are gargantuan lobelias here, several metres tall.

We reach the third hut before 10.00. Sit down for a bit, grab a bite to eat. Yes, I have a bit more of my stew. I had a large plateful yesterday. Now that it's cold it tastes like shit. But I know it needs to be eaten. I drink the cold tea, which tastes wonderful – an energy injection. I light a cigarette, smoke for a bit. There are loads of tourists here, spending a day getting used to the altitude before continuing to the peak. A lot of them sit down, working on their tans, wearing full mountain get-up – the carriers wear rags and sandals made from car tyres, balancing fifty kilos worth of goods on their heads as they walk up the mountain – that's a nifty trick.

"We have to leave now," Samueli says.

"O.K., fine," I say. And we trudge upwards through the barren landscape towards Gilman's Point on the edge of the crater. I don't need the European winter jacket I'm carrying with me – it's warm and sunny, and there's no wind. On our way up we meet tourists who have slept at the third hut, have been to the top and are now going down to the second hut.

"You're late," one of the guides says to us.

"We left the second hut this morning," Samueli says. A guide comes down towards me, arm in arm with an American lady who suddenly had trouble breathing at the top. The lady is fat; I hope he won't have to carry her.

It's heavy going – volcanic gravel; you take two steps forwards and slide one step back, but we keep at it until we're at Gilman's Point, looking out over the lowlands. The last time I was here I had sick on my chin. I feel fine. We're all alone up here – the others have gone down long ago.

"Alright then," Samueli says. "That's enough, we're at the top now."

"No, we're not at the top," I say, pointing. "Uhuru Peak is over there – you know that. I've been here before."

"Yes, but we're not going over there this time of day," he says.

"Yes, we are. Come on, let's get going – it's not far."

"No, no, we're going back now."

"We're going over there – that's what we agreed."

"But it's too late, if we're to get back to the second hut before dark," he says. He should go with me, because he's the guide and not supposed to let me go alone. But I'd like to go alone.

"Oh well, I'm going now," I say.

"You're mad," he says. "I'm not coming."

"I'll see you at the third hut then," I say and set off at full speed – it takes me just twenty minutes along the edge of the crater – staggeringly beautiful, the weather is amazing. The clouds are gathering below Kibo by the time I get there. There's a cairn with a flag on it and a box with a book where you write your name. I don't care about the name thing. I'm alone on the roof of Africa, and get out my candle and the spliff. My plan was to light the candle for Sam and smoke the spliff, but . . . I have a hard day behind me and more ahead. The spliff I'll save for later, and lighting the candle – it's just symbolism, like the book of names. We don't need these things. I don't have to prove all that or show off. She knows I'm here. Samantha. *Sam the Man*. She's here, I'm here; that's the point – simple, really. Thank you. I miss you. Bye now. The view is amazing. The clouds have gathered below me in a ring all the way around Kibo, and on the other side of them I see the airport and Nyumba ya Mungu and Lake Jipe – everything. The only living person at the top of Africa. And Sam is here as well, riding piggyback. A bit heavy, yes, but there we are. And I have to go now. Back to Gilman's Point, which I put behind me soon enough – I slide the first stretch in the volcanic gravel. Then I sit down. O.K., just a moment's peace – just me. I sit in the gravel and light a cigarette, smoking it slowly. Smokers have an easier time scaling Kilimanjaro – they're used to not getting enough oxygen. My big brother says so. Hopefully I'll see him soon; according to my dad there's a good chance that Stefano's family will move back to Italy, and then I can return.

Outdone by the flesh; the cigarette tastes nice, but I can't smoke it. I put it out, put the butt in my pocket. I'm cold – have to put my jacket on. I totter on with shaking knees. I want to sit down, lie back, rest – but I mustn't. I can feel that the cigarette has made me ill somehow – it's taken something out of me. I get short of breath and feel dizzy; my head aches. Mild altitude sickness – I'd better get down soon. I force myself on to the third hut. Samueli is waiting for me.

"Good," he says, handing me a large mug of tea. I sit down and drink.

"Cheers," I say. I try to regain my equilibrium. Samueli is ready, but I need to sit for half an hour. He was right, from his point of view, we are late. But I had urgent business up there. My face is swollen from the sun and my lips are chapped.

"We had better get going," he says.

"Yes." I get up. It's four in the afternoon, and we have to reach the second hut before nightfall. I can go on. I think my discomfort was due to the cigarette. Maybe I'm a bit dehydrated as well. We sort of run down. The air becomes richer, and the oxygen helps me. It starts to get dark. At "Last Water" we fill up and Samueli turns on his torch. But he knows the path very well. We go straight to the guides' and carriers' area. I sit down by their bonfire. Someone's frying onion, cooking *ugali*. The smell of it – my mouth waters. Every cell in my body is screaming for food. I could eat stale bread. Rasta Eddy is here – the bloke who wanted to carry stuff for me but who wasn't a licensed guide.

"You made it," Eddy says.

"Uhuru Peak," I say. "It was lovely."

"You're a fast man," he says.

"Yes, but I'm really tired now," I say. Samueli comes over to us.

"I can get us some food," he says. "Do you want some?"

"I'd love some," I say. "Thanks." He returns with a plate. The most brilliant meal I've had. *Ugali na maharage* – a stodgy corn porridge with a bean sauce. Yes, it's standard fare, but these guys know how to cook it. The consistency of the corn porridge is perfect. And the bean sauce is masterly – they've used onions and tomatoes, and there's salt and pepper in it. It gives me something to work with – much more than rice, potatoes or pasta. Ask the mamas across the nation who work the fields: if you have a choice between rice or potatoes or *ugali*, which will you have? They'll tell you: if I'm working the next day – *ugali*.

"Thank you," I say.

"Do you want some more?" the cook asks – he's a man named Daniel.

"I'm full. That was wonderful," I say. Daniel laughs:

"*Wewe unasema kama wahehe,*" he says – I talk like a *wahehe*; Iringa dialect.

"I am *hehe*," I tell him. "But I'm also three-quarters *mzungu*, from England and Greece."

"*Eeehhhh,*" he says and nods in the glow of the flames.

"So there are *mwafrika* who say that I'm market dust, and *wazungu* who think that I'm just a mess. But this," I say and lick my arm, "tastes like milk chocolate." They laugh. I light the last cigarette of the day and stare into the flames. Not white, not black – just Panos.

With the logical sense and work ethic of a white man, you can go far in Africa. Planning doesn't come easily to black people, because tomorrow will be nothing like what you planned anyway; it may as well be a dream. It's not laziness. White people plant things in order to harvest their fruits later. Black people know that Africa can eat everything you sow and leave you naked to the bone. You're here to wait for your own death or harvest your brothers' blood. You're born black on the earth under the scorching sun. Nothing is preordained. Nothing written in stone. No-one can answer your questions. You till the soil, you plant a seed, you hope for rain. Maybe the rain will wash everything away. Maybe malaria will strike you to the ground while pests ravage your fields. Can you fight the power that is Africa when you yourself are Africa? Only a sick man fights himself. The authorities say that they are helping you. But how? Nothing happens. As a white man you can exploit that helplessness – you can harvest the black blood and live a great life. Yes, it's cruel; it's the human way.

I slip into my sleeping bag under the open sky; the stars hug me from all sides. I fall asleep at once.

I get up with the sun. My sleeping bag is covered with dew. I find Samueli. Buy tea from a cook at the large cabin with all the tourists. No breakfast – in Tanzania it's normal to only have one meal a day. We run down. We move quickly – really. It doesn't take a lot, but it's hard on your knees. The path is rough, uneven. We reach the gates, and that makes it exactly forty-eight hours, because we started out at noon and return at noon. Somehow the story has travelled. I hear other guides ask Samueli.

"Did you make it?"

"Yes," he says.

"Really?" they say. They're impressed. They don't talk to me – my colour is just too odd. But I hear them. I go over to the office so they can register my leaving the national park.

"You'll have to wait for your certificate," they tell me.

"I don't need a certificate," I say. Everything's fine. I go back to settle with Samueli.

"I've had a hard time on this trip," he says. It's true. It was hard. He does this for a living – runs up and down the mountain. Anything I can spare is welcome. Not to mention having to listen to my bullshit at Gilman's Point. What must he have thought? I give him a nice bit of change on top of his fee, certainly compared to what I have.

"That's as much as I can spare," I say.

"Thanks," he says. "That's fine." O.K. then, we agree. I go down the road to Marangu town, get on a *matatu* to Moshi and on to Arusha by bus. Peaceful. My country. When I'm ready, I'm coming home.

Hostess

1.

On my first day in Moshi I walk with Auntie through the Majengo suburb, and she points out the bars with a curt nod:

"Don't go to these places, Rachel, or talk to those girls – they are wicked and godless." I look towards the bars: the girls who sit at the tables under the awnings – they have nice clothes, polished nails, their hair has been done by a hairdresser. "Don't look at them," Auntie says and pulls at my arm.

Auntie Esther met me at the bus station. She is my mother's older sister. My mother died many years ago. Now my stepbrother in Arusha has died as well, so I have to come and live with Auntie. She lives with her daughter Anna in a small room in Majengo.

Anna is twenty years old – four years older than me. She explains that Majengo is the part of Moshi where all the dirty bars are. And we live in that worst end of the poor part of town, where you can't go alone at night without losing everything. I'm afraid to ask Auntie about her husband, who she has divorced, so instead I ask Anna:

"Where is your father?"

"He has a new wife in another town," she says.

"Do you miss him?" I ask.

"It's a good thing he left – he drank a lot, and he beat my mother," Anna says. "He was nothing but trouble."

I too am glad that he's gone. I know what it's like from back when I lived in the village. A man who drinks thinks about drinking before he thinks about food for his family. My father drank a lot from the time my mother died until he married my stepmother.

Auntie's room is a small brick house with a concrete floor and a roof made of sheet metal. Like servants' quarters hidden behind the owner's house, which does its best to look like a villa – but that's not easy in Majengo, with open sewers and filthy children in rags and chickens everywhere, scraping through the dust.

I have to be careful not to cry, because life at my stepbrother's was better. This place is bad. There are two rooms in Auntie's small house, and then there's the garage, which has been turned into a room as well. Auntie has one of the actual rooms. You enter from the back of the house, where there's a roofed niche of perhaps four or five square metres. At the gable end of the house is the door to the shower, and next to the shower is the hole. But there's rarely water for more than three showers a day; this house isn't plugged into the water supply in the owner's large house – instead there are tubs of water by the shower. Next to the entrance to the shower and the hole, there's a small niche in the wall with a tap where you can wash your dishes or your clothes. The roof extends a bit so you can do your cooking in a pan over a coal fire there when it's raining.

Three families share everything – fourteen people in all. I will have to pay a third of the rent for the room once I find myself a job.

Anna works as a maid in a hotel, and Auntie sells dried fish just outside the market. I start out by helping Auntie. The market is in *mtaa chini* – the bad part of the inner city where all the *waswahili* live – like me, many of them are poor immigrants from the coastal regions; but *mtaa chini* is still better than Majengo. Auntie doesn't have a stall at the market itself, so the police can come at any time and chase us off or demand a present.

I know the dried fish from my childhood in Galambo on the coast, not far from Tanga. The fresh fish are split open and spread on a trellis over a faintly smouldering fire where they're smoked while they dry in the sun. After two days they're ready for the transport. The head has to be attached because people here won't buy fish without the head – what sort of fish would that be? And you can't preserve the fish using salt, because salt is far too expensive. The smallest fish are dried whole and spread out on burlap in the sun. There was once an Indian in Tanga who tried freezing fish and driving it to town in refrigerated lorries, but the cars broke down and the fish rotted. Auntie does poor business with her dried fish, because these days you can get frozen giant bass from Lake Victoria. Transporting them works quite well now that Europe has made a present in the form of refrigerated lorries.

We share our spot on the roadside with poor women from the surrounding villages who sell a few vegetables and some fruit – it's all piled up on burlap in front of them. On the other side of the road, tailors are sitting outside their shops, sewing in the shade provided by the awnings. Their needles and the drive belts make a singing sound when they press the pedal down quickly.

"Maybe I can find work with a tailor," I say, because I sew quite well – my stepbrother Edward in Arusha taught me before he died.

"No," Auntie says. "Only a man can be a tailor."

"But maybe I could work in a nice clothes shop in *mtaa juu* when the dress and trousers need to be fitted?"

"You'd need your own sewing machine," Auntie says.

"It's the only thing I know how to do," I say.

"I'll talk to my friends at church – we'll find you some work," Auntie says. She always goes to church, and at church they help each other against the godless. And she finds me a job with a *mama mtilie* who has a kitchen on Rengua Road in *mtaa juu* where the offices, the banks and the rich people's shops are. Her eatery is behind a shop in a former garage. There's an open space and a tall roof covering a large area with an oil-stained concrete floor. Under the roof are tables and chairs. At one end there's a partition made of wooden boards; behind it are the women who work at the pots and pans. The men stop by during their lunch hour and look across the partition to see what's on offer. Once they've made their order, they sit down, and I have to serve them.

2.

"Come, sister," the men call. And I go to their table. The fattest man takes my hand. And I let him hold it, and smile without saying anything. "Where do you live?" he asks.

"With my aunt in Majengo," I say.

"Are you coming to the disco at Moshi Hotel on Saturday?"

"No, I can't," I say. Because I haven't got enough money to pay for the entrance.

"I could come pick you up in Majengo – you'd be with me," he says. And *mama mtilie* shouts:

"Rachel, come here."

"Coming," I call back.

"We need some salt," another man says.

"Yes," I say.

"And some of that sugar of yours," the fat man says, and the other men laugh loudly. I go over to the mama.

"You must be good," she says quickly and in a low voice, so only I can hear. "Don't play up to the men. That kind of man is bad news, they'll only use you."

"I'm not playing up," I say. "It was you who said to be friendly and ask them what they wanted."

"Yes, but don't give them everything they want," *mama* says.

I bring the men salt and water and *pili-pili*. Serve them their food in the covered area while I smile on the outside and think: Are these fat men the kind of godless *wabwana wakubwa* who buy girls?

But it's not only fat, old men who come here. Faizal, who's a disc jockey at Moshi Hotel, does too. Nice sunglasses, smart T-shirt, large gold watch. Faizal is the most fascinating man I have ever met. I can't take my mind off him. And at night when I'm dreaming: Faizal, Faizal, Faizal.

"Thanks a lot, beautiful girl," he says when I serve him his food. And he looks at me at lot, but I pretend I haven't noticed.

3.

I work from 7.30 to 16.00. First I must sweep the area clean of leaves and twigs and fetch water from the tap by the toilets in the corner. I must wipe the tables and chairs clean of the dust that settles everywhere in the dry season. Then shop for groceries with *mama* and clean and chop them. And then take orders, serve, tidy dirty plates away, wash up. When the lunchtime rush dies down, we sit down on wooden crates behind the partition and eat whatever food wasn't sold. Afterwards it's time to tidy up, do the dishes and sort things out.

The job's bad because the pay is bad. But the place is nice. The area is owned by the municipality of Moshi, and *mama mtilie* has had it put at her disposal for free. They've done that all over town to eradicate the street cuisine problem – women bringing food in buckets to serve it under shady trees on the pavement. How can you wash your hands without running water? A lot of people get cholera that way. The street cuisine is still there, and the food is cheaper than ever, but these days the women who run the stalls have to grease the policeman's palm to avoid being fined

At *mama*'s the food is good; the rice isn't sticky – it's high quality basmati rice, cooked in the juice of a coconut; she serves lovely chapattis, as light as air because the oil she uses is good and the dough has been properly kneaded so the chapatti flakes just so. And her meat stew is good as well. The food here is more expensive than on the street, so it is *wabwana wakubwa* who eat here.

Rengua Road is a nice place. The electricity company Tanesco has its headquarters here. The cinema ABC Theatre is here as well, but it's closed now. On the other hand, these days there's Roots Rock, which is a recording shop run by Marcus; he can record and sell cassettes with reggae and disco and Zaire Rock, and his wife Claire sells clothes from a wooden clothes rack on the street. Next to their shop is Stereo Bar, where a lot of important people go. Rengua Road has shops, and hairdressers', and coffee parlours. It's the good part of Moshi where the *chaggas* and the Indians live.

4.

Since I'm a waitress, it's important that I'm presentable, so Saturday after work I go to the market in Moshi and buy second-hand clothes.

"These clothes don't fit well," I say while I help Auntie clean the house.

"We can talk to my friend at church tomorrow – she has a sewing machine." Auntie and her daughter are Lutherans like *mama mtilie,* so now I have to spend all my time at church. After the service we go home and cook and eat together – far too much of the fish Auntie hasn't sold. Later me and Anna plait each other's hair and I meet her friends, who are good girls, or very nearly good girls.

But this Sunday I go home with Auntie's friend from church, and I work on my clothes; the shirt and the skirt I reduce at the sides so you can see my curves. The tips are better when the clothes are tight-fitting. Anna says so. The clothes turn out well enough. I put them on and put my church clothes in the plastic bag. On my way back I stop at a small kiosk in Majengo. I can't sit down on the bench in front of the shop because I can't afford a fizzy drink. But the radio is playing Zaire Rock, and I need some music. My stepbrother had a radio, but at Auntie's there's nothing to listen to but talk of God's Will. There are two girls – one of them short and plump, the other very tall and good-looking. She wears her hair down and is wearing red lipstick, high-heeled sandals, tight jeans from America and a T-shirt with very short sleeves. Are they wicked and godless like Auntie says? I don't know where to look. Then the plump, short one leaves.

"You there," the good-looking one says, smiling. "Come on over here, will you?" She pats the bench next to her. I think she's a couple of years older than me. "I'm Salama," she says, extending her hand.

"Rachel," I say, sitting down.

"That's a very nice skirt," she says.

"Thanks," I say. "I like your trousers."

"What's in the bag?" she asks.

"My other clothes, the ones I wore to church."

"But you've changed. Are you going to the bar?"

"No," I say and giggle. "I don't go to bars. I've just been at a lady's house, making a few adjustments with a sewing machine."

"You know how to sew?" Salama says.

"Yes – my stepbrother taught me."

"You there – are you buying anything?"

"*Tsk*," Salama says and turns to face him. "Enough!" She shakes her head at him. I am ready to get up. "No, no," Salama says. "Just stay where you are. Do you want anything?"

"I haven't got any money," I say.

"Would you like a Coke?"

"But I haven't got any money."

"I do. *Bring out a Coke then*," she shouts. And he brings it out.

"Thank you," I say. It's cold and sweet. How can she have money for a Coke? She must have a good job or a wealthy family.

"Do you work in an office?" I ask, because her nails are long and perfectly polished.

"No, I'm a hostess at a restaurant in Shanty Town," she says. I don't know what a hostess is.

"Do you . . . serve food?" I ask. Salama laughs.

"The waiters do that. I greet them, show them to their table, tell them about the menu, take their order. And I manage the waiters and make sure the guests have a nice time."

"That sounds lovely," I say. "How do you get a job like that?"

"It's very difficult," Salama says, and even though I try to ask her, I can tell that she isn't going to tell me any more about it.

"How old are you?" she asks.

"I've just turned sixteen," I say.

"That's old enough," Salama says.

"Old enough for what?"

"Anything," she says and laughs. "I haven't seen you before. Where are you from?"

"Galambo," I say.

"Where's that?"

"On the coast, near Tanga." I tell her about it, because talking to her is easy. Salama listens with interest. I tell her my village is quite big. My father's a farmer, his land belongs to my grandfather. My mother died when I was little, and my father married a woman who has two little daughters and a big son – Edward, six years my senior – from a previous relationship. I started school when I was eleven in 1979 and went for three years; that's how long my father could afford to send me for, because it takes money for school uniforms and materials, and you have to grease the headmaster's palm just a little. And if you go to school, you can't really help out at home. "If you can't continue at school for many years, then school is just going to be a waste of time for you." That's what my father said. I can read and write and do calculus – well, almost.

I stayed in my family's home until I was fourteen.

My stepbrother had been taught how to sew by a tailor from his family and had gone to Arusha with his wife and two young children. He worked for a safari company owned by some Germans; he made the uniforms for their drivers, guards and guides; he did repairs on tents and sewed bedding for their beds, and he made covers for the car seats and that sort of thing. And if there was no more sewing to be done, he worked as a driver in a uniform he had made for himself.

My father would have liked to keep me at home, but he didn't have the money to help me learn a trade, and there was no work to be had for a young girl in the village, so I went to Arusha to find a better life.

"You'll come home to us again when you've learned how to be a good woman around the house. Then we'll find you a good husband," my father said. Families will often have their daughters sent off to stay with relatives in the big city before they marry a man from the village. Back then Tanga was the only real city I had ever been to; very lively, and rich, and exciting. I already knew that after Arusha I'd never return to the village.

I stayed with Edward and his family for two years and helped around the house, and he taught me how to sew all kinds of clothes. But then he caught some sort of violent disease that the doctors didn't understand. He died not long after, and his wife had to move home to her relatives in Tongoni, to the south of Tanga. And I went to my Auntie in Majengo in Moshi to start my life over again. Life isn't good yet, but my job with *mama mtilie* gives me options.

5.

Every afternoon I go to the shop and buy milk – our little luxury for next morning's tea – along with cane sugar, because we can't afford the white stuff. Every morning: tea and bread and fruit – mango, papaya or banana which Auntie has traded at the market in return for some of the fish she hasn't sold. But luckily I get proper food at *mama mtilie*'s, so I don't have to eat so much corn porridge and fish at night.

I have bought the milk and am walking down the street. Salama steps out of a nice car with a young man. She is wearing good clothes from Zanzibar – a dress and nice high-heeled shoes. With shoes like that you have to have a good car, because you can't walk through the mud and muck of Majengo in them. She sees me.

"Rachel," she says. "Come and meet my friend – his name is Alwyn." I go over and greet him politely. Salama says:

"Alwyn has a nice souvenir shop in Boma Road."

"Do you live here?" I ask her.

"Yes, that's my room over there," she says, pointing to a door in a good house – the best end of Majengo. "You can have a look," she says and walks towards the door. And it's so nice. She has a room all to herself – properly painted as well. Bed, chairs, table with a tablecloth, a radio with a tape recorder, curtains, everything.

"*Ahhh*, this is very nice."

"Thank you," she says. "I have to get dressed now and go to work."

"O.K.," I say. "Bye then."

"See you," she says, and I make to leave. Alwyn has sat down on the bench in front of the kiosk.

"Come here," he calls. I go over to him. "Sit down," he says.

"I have to go home," I say, because I don't want to sit here and talk to Salama's friend. I'd like to be her friend, so I don't want to make her cross with me.

"Sit down, will you, just for a minute." He turns and calls to the owner of the kiosk. "Bring a Coke for my friend here." So I sit down.

"What do you do?" he asks.

"I'm a waitress at *mama mtilie*'s behind the shop on Rengua Road." He asks where I live and who with.

"Waitress – that's not a good job," he says.

"No, but I'd like to learn how to speak English, because then I could get a job like Salama's."

"A job like Salama's? If you learn to speak English?" Alwyn says.

"Yes, then I could be a hostess at a restaurant that tourists go to, or work in a nice café."

Alwyn laughs.

"Why do you laugh?" I ask him shyly.

"That's a good idea," he says, shaking his head. Salama comes out of her room and crosses the street – very tight trousers, nice high-heeled sandals with pearl embroidery, tight-fitting top

"What are you talking about?" she asks. Alwyn is still laughing:

"Your friend wants a nice job like yours. She wants to be a hostess at a restaurant, but she says she doesn't know the language."

"That's no job for her. Let's get going," Salama says. Maybe she's cross with me for talking to Alwyn.

"Be well," I say. Alwyn gets up.

"Maybe I could help her learn the language," he says to Salama.

"*Tsk* – you're always in a hurry."

They walk to the car, get in and drive off.

6.

At work I am very attentive. I try to understand who it is who comes to have their lunch here. Who has what job? Who is decent? The shopkeeper employs a girl to go into the courtyard at lunchtime – she's supposed to go and ask the men if they want to buy a drink from the shopkeeper's fridge. But she's a lazy Moshi girl – she likes nothing better than lounging about in the shade; being a waitress is beneath her dignity. The shopkeeper, he sees me – I work diligently under his watchful eye. When he eats at *mama*'s I make sure he gets his things quickly and neatly, and he gets salt and water and *pili-pili*.

"Would you like me to fetch you something cold to drink?" I ask. He looks towards the Moshi girl who stands, hanging about the back door of his shop – in the shade.

"*Tsk*," he says quietly, shaking his head. Then he looks at me. "You're from the coast," he says.

"Yes," I say, standing there nicely, waiting for his words like I would on a command. I am lucky to come from Tanga region. In both Arusha and Moshi they say that village girls from Tanga are the best sort of girls because they are well behaved and work hard. City girls are too lazy and always grumble as they try to get out of doing any work.

"Rachel," *mama* calls.

"Go on," the shopkeeper says and waves me off. "*There! Come*," he shouts at the girl in the door. Using her hip she lazily pushes her body off the door frame and starts sloping across the yard. That girl must be an absolute idiot. "Quick, quick now," the shopkeeper says angrily as she comes closer. "You must be attentive to the customers here."

"I am attentive," she says, looking at the ground.

"You must ask them if they want to buy something to drink."

"I see if they want something – if they do, they signal," she says, looking away from him.

"You must go and ask them," the shopkeeper says.

"Yes," she says. But I can tell that she finds it humiliating to go over and ask.

"Fetch me a Fanta," he says.

O.K.," she says and moves sluggishly across the yard like a city girl – her entire brain is in her bottom and works only at finding the perfect swing. But that bottom won't quench the thirst like a Fanta would. The shopkeeper shakes his head.

Two weeks later he offers me a job, and it's a much better job than with the mama, because the shopkeeper pays more.

"I have to ask *mama*," I say, because Auntie Esther asked her to give me that job.

"I've talked to *mama* about it," the shopkeeper says. "She doesn't mind."

"In that case I'd like to work for you."

"It's important that you be well dressed every day when you're selling fizzy drinks to the customers," he says.

"That won't be a problem," I say.

7.

The new job is very different from the old one. Every morning I get up at 6.00 and wash. Then I get a *matatu* into town. I work six days a week from 8.00 until 21.00 or 21.30, except on Saturdays when I get off early because the offices close at noon and almost everyone goes home to have their lunch. And I work every third or fourth Sunday. After work I get a *matatu* home. The shopkeeper pays for my transport – if he didn't, I'd walk like I used to. But you can't walk to Majengo after dark, because you'd get in trouble. The shopkeeper is a good man. We get breakfast and lunch at work. And frequently I get dinner as well, but then it's because there are customers in *mama*'s yard who buy me something because I've been nice, or because they'd like company while they eat. But otherwise I have dinner at home, because Auntie comes home earlier and prepares a meal.

The work isn't hard. I sell fizzy drinks from the Coca-Cola fridge, which is on the pavement beside two benches that have been placed beneath the trees so people can enjoy their drinks in the shade. And of course I must make sure the fridge is stocked, and that the empty crates are ready when the Coca-Cola lorry comes in the afternoon. When I become more familiar with the job, I'm supposed to help tally up and keep account of things. But there's plenty of time to talk to people.

At lunchtime I'm supposed to stay by the shop's back door. When there are customers at *mama mtilie*'s I go over and ask them if they would like to buy something to drink. I take their order, fetch the fizzy drink from the fridge and a clean glass, serve it to them and receive payment, which I give to the cashier who then gives me change to give to the men. I have to make sure glasses and bottles are returned, and that the glasses are washed up. The lunch guests don't tip me much. Why would they? They're going back to their offices straight away. But sometimes I get lucky if someone thinks I'm nice. Lunch is from noon until 14.00. After that I'm back at the fridge on the pavement. Later I'll be working at the till as well, I think.

But I never have any time off.

"That's good," Auntie says. "Then you have no time for being wicked."

In the afternoon the shopkeeper opens a bar in the yard where you can buy beer. There's also a *bwana nyama choma*, a local entrepreneur who barbecues whatever meat you want in the afternoon and evening. There's a grown-up lady who minds the bar. I serve the beers at the tables.

"You can have a beer as well," the men say. "It's on us."

"No thanks," I say. The lady behind the bar says yes please, but she isn't offered all that many.

"Have a fizzy drink instead," the men say.

"Thanks," I say. I don't drink beer. I don't smoke cigarettes either – it's too expensive.

8.

There aren't as many tourists here as in Arusha. Nonetheless, Moshi has quite a few *wazungu* who work on aid projects. Some of them come here to eat with their *waafrika* business partners or drink beer. And there are many *wazungu* children who go to the international school up in Shanty Town. Some of them are older than me. On Saturdays they come into town, and they all have good tennis shoes and nice sandals, and jeans and money. The older boys come into the yard and drink beer; I don't think they're allowed to, but white children have no manners. They look at me a lot, and talk to each other and laugh.

"Those *wazungu* boys think you're very good-looking," the bar mama says and smiles at me.

"They're just children," I say. Yes, they've got money for beer and they've got good clothes, but they're not independent, because it's their parents who pay for it all.

I find Moshi fascinating. In Arusha I almost always had to be at home to mind the children, clean, cook or sew. My sister-in-law went out alone when she went shopping. And whenever I did get out, I went with Edward. At least now I'm seeing more of the world.

The pay here is so good I can afford to save. I'd like to learn how to speak English so I can get a job somewhere better where you have to be able to speak to tourists. A hotel or a bar or a café where the *wazungu* go; they pay well in places like that, the tips are better as well, and you meet a better class of people. My dream is to own a shop selling ladies' wear or to run a café.

"I need to have my hair done," I tell the lady at the till when there aren't any customers. It's always under a scarf because I'm always working –

there isn't time anymore for Anna and me to do each other's hair.

"You can go to the hairdresser's if you like," she says.

"During work hours?"

"Yes, just ask him." So I ask the shopkeeper.

"Yes," he says. *Eeehhh*, he wants me to be a beauty in the eyes of the customers.

"Can I go for a stroll around town as well, because I need to get some new clothes? I can't wear the same thing day in and day out." He says I can. So I go around all the nice shops in *mtaa juu* where they sell clothes from Zanzibar. But it's all too expensive, and at the market in *mtaa chini* there's only junk.

9.

That night I walk past Salama's place, but there's no-one home. The next day she is there.

"Would you like a Coke?" I ask, because now I have money to buy her one. We go to the kiosk and sit down. Then that little plump girl Salama knows comes over. Her name is Deborah.

"Where can you buy nice clothes that aren't too expensive?" I ask.

"At the market in Kiborloni," Deborah says. "They get all the nice clothes straight from Europe – barely used."

"There isn't anything at Kiborloni," Salama says.

"Yes," Deborah says. "They got in a new shipment yesterday."

"How do you know?" Salama asks.

"I was with the lorry driver last night who drove the stuff from Dar es Salaam." Deborah is one of the wicked girls. Why does Salama want to be her friend?

"We'll go there on Saturday when you get off from the shop," Salama says and tells Deborah that I am very good at sewing clothes to make them fit perfectly.

I talk Anna into coming with me, even though she thinks Auntie won't approve of us being friendly with those two. But Anna needs new clothes as well.

Saturday we get a *matatu* out of Moshi, heading east, and soon reach Kiborloni, which has a huge open-air market. There are rows and rows of wooden tables with all sorts of clothes. And it's true. Much of it is nice and hardly worn at all and still cheap. Salama looks at children's clothes.

"Who is that for?" I ask.

"My son," Salama says and smiles.

"You have a son?" I ask.

"Yes, but he lives with my mother."

"What about his father?"

"He's dead," Salama says.

"Oh, I'm sorry."

"Never mind. It was a traffic accident a long time ago."

Sunday Anna tells Auntie that we both have our moon blood and are in pain. Auntie huffs and puffs, but we manage to stay home from church and rent a sewing machine from a local tailor's in Majengo, because I don't want to bring Deborah and Salama to Auntie's friend – she would tell Auntie that I am going about with wicked girls. We're not allowed to move the sewing machine, so we have to work in the tailor's room while he goes to the local bar and buys *mbege* with our money.

I measure and unstitch, drawing lines with chalk and putting in needles like Edward showed me.

"Yes, sister," Salama says, and she twists into her T-shirt. "Sew it so tight I'm like naked." We laugh.

"Now I'm going to catch me a fat fish tonight," Deborah says – she has made me sew her top so tight that everything on her body juts right out into your eyes.

I put my new clothes in a bag and put my everyday clothes back on, but Anna doesn't want to get changed – she's really pleased with her new skirt and her V-neck top. We go home to Auntie.

"What's that you're wearing?" she asks surprised.

"My new clothes," Anna says, smiling, doing a twirl, smoothing her hands over her hips. "Rachel has fitted them for me."

"God doesn't like your wearing such tight clothes."

"*Tsk*," Anna says. "My clothes are fine."

"Your clothes show off too much of your body," Auntie says.

"God has made my body – he's happy when I show it off," Anna says.

"Don't talk about God like that. He has made your body to be shown to your husband only. Not so that you can show it off on the street like a *malaya*."

"You don't know what God likes," Anna says. Auntie looks at me.

"*Tsk*," she says. "You, Rachel, you're doing the devil's work when you're at the sewing machine. Now you've made my daughter so that only bad men will look at her." I don't say anything. Anna is cross with her mother:

"You've lived with a bad man yourself – was that God's will?" Anna asks. Auntie looks away – she doesn't say anything else. Auntie couldn't hang on to her husband because she put God first. And because she suffers for God, she wants us to suffer as well.

10.

A couple of days later I run into Salama at the kiosk late in the day; she is dressed up to the nines. We talk for a little while, but then Alwyn shows up in his car. He honks his horn.

"Do you want to come?" Salama asks.

"Where are you going?" I ask.

"Just a little drive." I think about it for a bit:

"O.K.," I say. We go over to the car.

"Rachel can't come. You're going to work now," Alwyn says.

"Don't worry about it," I say.

"But we can give her a lift home, can't we?" Salama says.

"O.K.," Alwyn says. "Jump in." And then I'm in the car, and we're off. It has a tape recorder – that's nice Zaire Rock they're playing. I leap out of the car at our house and go into the yard. Auntie's cooking dinner. Anna comes home not long after me. We all eat. Auntie goes over to talk to a neighbour about some chickens.

"I saw you with Salama and Alwyn," Anna says.

"Yes, they gave me a lift home in his car," I say.

"Salama is a very wicked girl – people say that."

"She's Alwyn's friend," I say. "She's not wicked."

"Where do you think she gets all that money from?"

"She works as a hostess at a restaurant," I say.

"Don't believe everything she says – Alwyn lets *wabwana wakubwa* pump her for money."

"You're mad," I say.

"That's what I've heard," Anna says. I can't believe it.

"You're just jealous," I say.

11.

At work I see more people in the second-hand clothes from Europe. The tailors at the market are busy altering it. Many people have bought clothes and want them to fit their figure. The fat ladies in their shops are crying, because they have bought pretty clothes from the dressmakers in Zanzibar, but now the stock is collecting dust on the shelves and the fat ladies are losing their entire investment. The clothes from Europe win the day; they're better, smarter, cheaper.

"My, my, my, you're looking pretty today, Rachel," the young men say, lounging about on the pavement, talking while they drink their soft drinks because they're not allowed to leave with the bottle – bottles are very expensive and hard to get hold of. Rogarth is the cheekiest of the lot. Little by little I get to know him. He went to the international school with the *wazungu* kids, but now he's poor because his father was sent to

Karanga Prison for having cheated too much at the sugar plantation T.P.C. I like Rogarth.

"Has some backstreet *wabwana wakubwa* tried to make you do wicked things?" he says with a naughty grin.

"No," I say.

"Don't they all try to buy you beer?"

"Yes, but I don't drink beer."

"That's good," Rogarth says.

"Why?"

"If you accept their beer, then you can leave work in the evening and find four men who feel you owe them a big serving of sweet, sweet fruit because you've had two beers that they've paid for."

"*Tsk*, you're being silly."

"Try it if you like," Rogarth says. When I ask him what he does, he doesn't really answer; he just says that he's in business. It can't be a very good sort of business, because his clothes are worn and his shoes scuffed.

"No, I don't want a fizzy drink today," he says. I fetch him a glass of water.

"There you are," I say.

"Thank you," Rogarth says and empties the glass in one. "You know how to quench a man's thirst," he says, winking at me. "Do you never go to the disco at Moshi Hotel?" he asks. "Very important people go – people with lots of money. Not riff-raff like in Majengo."

"I don't have the money for a disco," I say. Rogarth doesn't invite me. He doesn't have the money for it either.

But my nice clothes improve my tips. In the afternoon the men come – to drink beer and eat *nyama choma*. They're all older than me, some of them quite old.

"Will you have dinner with me?" a tall, well-dressed man asks.

"My aunt won't allow me to be out in the evenings," I say and ask the lady at the cashier about the man.

"The tall one? He's always chasing the young girls. He's married with four children."

How am I going to move on in life? Now that I have a job that pays more, I would like a room of my own or maybe one I could share with a female friend. I hide my tips as savings towards a better future. But I haven't got enough to move away from Auntie, not if I want to pay for English lessons. They offer lessons every day at the K.N.C.U. building from 14.00 to 16.00, when the business is slow anyway. I ask the shopkeeper if he'll give me the time off.

"Of course," he says. But lessons will cost me my entire salary and then how am I to pay my rent? I am held captive by Auntie's watchful eyes.

12.

"Rachel, Rachel," Deborah calls out on the street. I am hurrying home, because it'll be dark soon. I stop. "Come down to the bar with me," she says. "Salama is there as well."

"O.K. then, but only for a moment," I say. Deborah is wearing her tight-fitting clothes, high heels and lots of lipstick. A man calls to her when we enter the bar, and she joins him immediately. Alwyn is sitting alone at another table.

"Where is Salama?" I ask.

"She's gone to the toilet," he says and buys me a soft drink. "I think you're a good girl," he says.

"I am a good girl," I say. What does he think of me?

"Running around Majengo like Deborah is a bad thing for a girl – it can only make you ill."

"I'm not like that. I don't run around," I say.

"I know. You're a natural girl from the village. I know lots of good men who would like to meet a good girl from the village – rich men."

"*Tsk*. I'm not for sale," I say.

"No, no, no – it's nothing like that. They're just men who would like the company of a sweet and natural girl; someone to talk to while they have dinner. There's nothing wicked in it."

"Just to have dinner with them?"

"Yes. You'd be picked up, fed well, driven home – no trouble at all."

"I can have corn porridge and bean sauce – why do I have to eat with those men?"

"They want to give you a present. They're good men – lots of them are looking for a good woman to share their lives with."

"What are you telling Rachel?" Salama asks, coming towards us.

"Me and Rachel are talking business," Alwyn says.

"Your business is not for Rachel," Salama says.

"I'm going home now," I say, because I don't want to upset Salama.

"Finish your Coke," Alwyn says. Salama sits down and lights one of his cigarettes. Two of the wicked girls sit at a table behind me. A man comes down the street and stops by their table.

"I need something," he says.

"You haven't got the money to pay for it," one of the girls says.

"I've got money," he says and tells her how much he's got.

"That's not enough," the girl says.

"We don't need a room," the man says. "Just round the back – quick. I need something now."

"You can't pump if you haven't got the money," the girl says.

"O.K., not pump then – just you help me out," the man says.

"Give me the money," she says. I can hear her getting up. She walks past us, disappearing with the man around a corner and into the darkness. Anna has told me that the cheapest of the *malaya* take their customers to the football stadium in Majengo, where there isn't a single blade of grass on the field, only dust. And then they do it right up against the wall. There are two sets of prices for the man, Anna tells me: the cheap one is for wearing a sock, the expensive is without it. Men always want to pump without it, and the cheap girls want to be paid the more expensive rate. They can get all sorts of diseases, of course, and get a bellyful of baby just for a few shillings. Not long after, the girl returns.

"*Haraka haraka,*" she says – quick, quick – to her friend and laughs. They're my age, selling themselves to market garbage. They're stupid. It's not normal. It's messed up. How can they do that to their own bodies?

"That's what life is like in Majengo if a girl hasn't got anyone to help her," Alwyn tells me.

"My life isn't like that; I've got work," I say.

"Yes," he says. "But does that give you enough to live for?"

"I manage," I say and, draining my Coke, get up. I don't thank him, not when he speaks to me like that. "I'll see you later," I tell Salama.

"Think about it," Alwyn says to my back. And I do think about it. If it's only having dinner with someone now and again – then I can do it. I can use my salary from the shop to pay for my English lessons. The presents from the dinner I could use as money to pay the rent. I don't need more new clothes or anything. I can get ahead in life. But I don't trust Alwyn after what Anna told me.

13.

In the afternoon men show up behind the shop. They're still quite young and not yet married, and they can afford to drink beer. And some of them like me as well. One of them, called Henry, asks if I'm going to the disco that Saturday at Moshi Hotel.

"How would your wife like it if I did?" I tease him, because I need to know if he's married.

"I'm not married yet," he says, laughing at me. And it's not like I don't want to go; it's not much fun being stuck at home. We don't have a radio, and I am sick and tired of Majengo. But I can't afford the entrance fee at Moshi Hotel, and I can't afford fizzy drinks either. I don't tell Henry that that's why I don't want to go, because talking about money like that is wrong, and besides, he sees where it is I'm working.

"My aunt doesn't like me being out late at night," I say.

"But I'll pick you up in my car, of course, and I'll pay for everything. And afterwards I'll drive you safe home."

"In that case I'd love to come," I say. "But I can't stay out late."

"No problem," Henry says, and we arrange for him to pick me up by the kiosk in Majengo, where I can wait outside with a fizzy drink – I can afford one. I look forward to it. Henry isn't too old. I think about where he might live, whether he makes good money, whether he's from a good family. I ask the lady at the bar.

"Henry?" she says. "He's married to the regional commissioner's niece."

"Really?" I say. A big scam. It makes me feel cold and sad inside. He's just trying to get a bit on the side. I don't want to be anyone's bit on the side. I tell Auntie that I am going to visit a friend. I sit outside the kiosk. He comes in his car. I go over and bend down to the window.

"But you have a wife," I say. "Why did you ask me out to Moshi Hotel?"

"Oh well, we were just going out for a bit of fun – a bit of dancing, a bit of beer."

"I'm not that kind of girl."

"Not what kind of girl? Don't you like dancing?"

"I'm not the kind of girl who fools around," I say.

"No, I know. We're not doing anything wicked."

"So we're just going to the disco to dance?"

"Yes," Henry says.

"But I have to be home early," I say.

"Don't worry, I'll get you home on time." And I do want to, because I've never been to a real disco – only one at the Y.M.C.A. in Arusha in the afternoon – a children's disco. So I get in the car. We drive. I can smell that he's had beer already. He's going towards Moshi Hotel, but then he drives to Liberty instead and parks there.

"Why do you take us here?" I ask.

"It's better than Moshi Hotel," he says. It's cheaper than Moshi Hotel. I know that from the young men I sell fizzy drinks to at the shop. Because Liberty doesn't have as good sound, doesn't have good lights and is a tougher place with more poor people, more drunkenness. But what can I say? We go inside, Henry pays. And it still looks great. There's good music here too, loud music. Some coloured lights. Lots of people partying. We find ourselves a table and Henry calls a waitress over.

"Two Safari," he says.

"No, I just want a fizzy drink," I say.

"You have to try a beer," he says.

"Let's dance," I say.

"Let's have a drink first," he says. I don't like it – Henry finishes his beer quickly and orders another. He tells me about big business he's going to do with the regional commissioner and how he's going to become very rich. It's obvious there are lots of wicked girls here. They wriggle up against the men. They leave with the men but not to go outside; they go in the other direction – further into the building. Henry puts his hand on my thigh and moves it about as if he were kneading dough for chapattis, and he doesn't have the first clue about how to do that.

"I need the toilet," I say and get up. On the way I look towards where the girls take the men. There's a table and the man who sits there has some keys; he takes their money. Behind him there's a corridor with doors along one side. Rooms for pumping in.

When I return, Henry's hand does as well.

"We're going to dance now," I say and get up. He has to, then, and the music is fast enough that he can't think his hands belong on my buttocks. But soon the slow music returns, and now my buttocks are like chapatti dough to his hands again. *Tsk.* We sit down again, and now he tries to kiss me – just like that, a married man.

"I have to go home now," I say.

"No, it's much too soon."

"I told you I had to be home early."

"Not yet," he says.

"Then I'll just walk," I say and get up, because I know all the shortcuts in Majengo and can easily avoid drunk people. Henry stays in his seat with his beer, looking at me with a smile. He sees himself as a big man and thinks I'm just playing hard to get, because who would ever want to walk out on him? I don't like people like that. I turn around and leave. He comes running after me.

"I'll drive you home," he says. In his car he puts his hand on my thigh. I push it away every time it gets too close to my fruit. In Majengo he pulls over next to one of the dirty bars. "We'll just get one last beer, before I'll take you home."

"I'm not going in there," I say. "It's full of *malaya*. We can go to Strangeways." It's the only borderline clean bar in Majengo.

"You're not that special," Henry says and gets out, slamming the door behind him, going over to sit down at one of the tables on the terrace. It is strange sitting alone in the car. People are looking. I have to get out. And the way home to our house, Saturday night in Majengo – it's dangerous, because there are drunk people everywhere. I go over and sit down at his table, and the bar mama brings us beers. I don't want any more – the first beer has already made me dizzy. Again, there's that hand on my thigh. I push it off.

"You crazy girl. It wouldn't hurt you to be a little friendly towards me, now that I've picked you up and paid for you at Liberty and bought you beers and everything – taken you home," Henry says – loud enough for everyone to hear it over the music.

"You're married. What is your hand doing on my thigh? Do you think I am chapatti dough?" Some wicked girls laugh nastily. They know exactly what he thinks.

"I need you very much," Henry says, as ingratiating as any drunk. It's embarrassing, because so many people here know my aunt; men who go to church also go to the bar. "You could be a bit more friendly towards me," he says. By friendly he means that we go over to the guesthouse and he gets one of the rooms for ten minutes and I let his pump vomit inside me. *Kuma mamayo* – your mother's cunt. I'm not going to do that. And it's dangerous.

"Stop that right now," I say. "You promised me . . ."

"You crazy bitch," Henry shouts and gets up. He tries to land a blow, but he's drunk, and I just manage to push back in my chair as the glasses of beer tumble and splinter against the floor. Henry himself almost falls over, but he manages to catch hold of the edge of the table and steady himself. "I could have had two girls for the money I've wasted on you tonight," he shouts. The bar mama comes out because she heard glasses and bottles splintering – it's very expensive. "The other girls aren't afraid of my black mamba," Henry says, spittle flying from his mouth.

"What are you doing?" the mama says angrily – she is a large lady. The wicked girls laugh nastily.

"His pump seems to be a bit too drunk right now," one of them says. I have pulled back from the table until I come up against the fence around the terrace.

"You're the worst sort of *malaya*," Henry shouts at me. "You tease, and you spend my money, and then you act all sanctimonious." What am I supposed to do? *Mama* doesn't do anything – maybe she knows that he's married to the regional commissioner's niece. He pushes the table aside, comes towards me. I'm crying now and want to climb the fence to run away, but my skirt is too tight for me to be able to lift my legs much. The girls are laughing at me.

"Henry!" Whose voice is that? "Come here. Let's have a beer together," the voice says. Alwyn – he appears behind *mama*, from inside the bar. Henry turns around.

"Alwyn," he says, sounding confused.

"You know you should always come to me if you're looking for a good time," Alwyn says. "Come on, let's get a beer. That girl's no good." And

Henry goes past Alwyn and into the bar. Alwyn waves me over while taking two steps away from the door. I go over to him. He hands me some money. "Get a taxi home," he says in a low voice.

"Thank you so much," I whisper.

"Run along – we'll talk later." And I hurry over to Strangeways where there are always taxis parked outside, and then home and to bed, but I just can't fall asleep. Do you always have to mingle with swine just to make a living? There has to be another way. Alwyn says we'll talk about it later. But I don't want to talk about the things he's thinking of. I carry money in my pocket, ready to pay him back as soon as I meet him.

14.

Anna wants to take me to the disco at Moshi Hotel. We have a little money, so we can afford to go. Anna tells Auntie.

"What do you want to go there for – only wicked people go," Auntie says.

"No," Anna says. "Moshi Hotel is for decent people with educations and proper jobs who you'd never meet in Majengo."

"You can meet people at church. There are many good men at our church," Auntie says.

"The church is full of poor people. Do you want me to live my life with a *shamba boy*?" Auntie doesn't say anything. She married a *shamba boy* herself – a field labourer who later became a drunkard.

"We're young," Anna says. "We want to have fun. To experience things. Do you want me to go to bars in Majengo? Or sit here and become an old woman who sells fish like you." Auntie starts crying.

"My only daughter ends up a mattress for all the men. A *malaya* at Moshi Hotel. Oh, God," she says, raising her arms and her eyes towards heaven.

"*Tsk*," Anna says. "You're my mother, and you think I would do that to my own body. You're mad." Anna spits out of the open door.

"Rachel isn't old enough to go to a disco," Auntie says.

"Yes, she is. We'll be home early, with the last *matatu*."

And we go. Rogarth is standing outside.

"What are you doing here, Rachel?" he says.

"I want to see the disco. What are you doing here?"

"Oh, I've got a bit of business here tonight – I'm meeting someone."

"Maybe I'll see you later," I say, and then we go inside. It's very expensive getting through the gate, but *ohhh* it's so nice. The music's good, the lights are great. And here are real *wabwana wakubwa*. Not little fishes like in Majengo – the men here don't drive their own cars, they have drivers for that. They have real suits from the West, nice shoes made of leather, smart watches. There are young boys and girls in nice clothes as well. I see Faizal standing behind a desk with machines for playing music and lots of L.P.s; he's looking very sharp in his shades. He must be very rich. There are beautiful girls around him, talking away. They wiggle their bottoms just that little bit more when they walk away, so he can see that everything is in perfect working order. I think he's very handsome. But how can I have a chance to speak to him when he's surrounded by so much beauty?

I look for Alwyn, because the money he lent me is ready in my pocket, but he isn't here.

A *bwana mkubwa* at the table next to ours signals a waitress. He orders beer for himself and a young man and two young women who are sitting at his table. Money is no object. But all the wa*bwana wakubwa* here are fat and old.

A single Coke is all I can afford, so I have to make sure to drink it slowly and make it last, because I don't want to sit here with nothing like a poor person – it would look wrong.

A young man comes over and asks me if I want to dance. Anna sends him away. We go out on the floor together, and I dance with her. Then another young man comes over and says that a *bwana mkubwa* wants to buy us a beer.

"*Tsk – toka*," Anna says – get lost. He leaves.

"Why are you angry?" I ask.

"That's how it starts," Anna says. "First they buy the girl a beer, then they want to pump."

"Really?" I say.

"Yes," Anna says. "A lot of the girls go out with just enough money to buy one beer and then they wait to catch a big fish and be wicked for money."

"Do they talk about money for . . . do they say it directly to the man?" I can't imagine it – talking to a man like that.

"Not to the man. The boy arranges it. He arranges it with the girl; how much soap-money she's going to need."

"Soap-money?"

"So she can wash afterwards," Anna says.

"Is it . . . a lot of money?"

"At Moshi Hotel – if you go with the right sort of *wabwana wakubwa* – it's more than a quarter of a month's wages." I don't ask any more questions. We dance again, but we have to catch the bus soon. Anna stops to talk to a friend, so I dance by myself, and I think Faizal has noticed me, so I dance very much to the beat.

Faizal comes over. Anna pushes a hip out and leaves her hand on it, standing with her back flexed so her *titi* poke out. He only has eyes for me:

"I've seen you at *mama mtilie*'s," Faizal says. "What's your name?"

"Rachel," I say.

"You dance very well," he says.

"We have to leave now if we want to catch our bus," Anna says. And we leave, and she is mad at me because I'm attractive, more so than she.

15.

After church Anna calls to a short, squat girl on the parking lot.

"This is Olivia – Deborah's sister," Anna says. Anna turns to Olivia: "Tell her what you told me."

"Deborah is a sinner," Olivia says. "She sometimes works for that guy Alwyn. When some *bwana mkubwa* wants a *malaya* but doesn't want to be seen at the bars, Alwyn can deliver the girl straight to him. Alwyn picks her up, drives her to some pre-arranged place – maybe a hotel or a guest-house – and then the *bwana mkubwa* comes and pumps the girl. The man has already paid Alwyn, who gives the girl her share. Alwyn is a pimp to the real *wabwana wakubwa*. It's the devil's work ."

"I know that Deborah is wicked," I tell Olivia.

"Salama does that work as well," Olivia says.

"I don't believe it," I say.

"Salama is just a young girl, but she has a good room, nice clothes, everything – how can that be if she doesn't do dirty deeds?" Olivia asks. I can't answer that.

Sunday afternoon Alwyn's car is parked outside Salama's house. I go over and knock on the door. Salama opens, wrapped in a *kanga*, comes outside and pulls the door to behind her. We say hello.

"Is Alwyn here?" I ask.

"What do you want with Alwyn?" she asks.

"I owe him some money." Alwyn's voice sounds from inside the room:

"You keep that money, Rachel – use it towards your English lessons."

I look at Salama and shake my head:

"No, I don't want his money." Salama sighs and opens the door, signalling for me to come in. Alwyn is in her bed with a sheet pulled up just enough to cover his pump.

"Here's your money," I say, holding it out.

"Keep it – it doesn't matter," he says with a nasty grin.

"No, I pay my debts," I say and put the money on the table, say goodbye and leave.

16.

Faizal shows up at *mama mtilie*'s on the Monday.

"You look very pretty today, Rachel," he says. That's because I have put my good skirt on. I ask the girls from the hairdresser's about Faizal.

"He's a Muslim from the coast like you," they say. I'm not a Muslim, but I don't tell them that. I can be a Muslim. On the Friday Faizal comes for lunch as well.

"Are you going to the disco tonight?" he asks.

"I can't," I say.

"It won't cost you anything, Rachel," he says. "I run the disco – you'll be let straight in, no entrance fee."

"But I have to go to work tomorrow morning."

"You can leave early," he says.

"How will they know that I know you . . . so they don't charge me at the door?"

"I'll tell the doorman who works for me that a beautiful girl called Rachel is coming and that he's to let her straight in."

"But I can't be out late – my aunt will be angry with me."

"You're an adult. You have a job – you should get to have some fun as well," Faizal says.

"Yes, but how am I going to get back to Majengo in the middle of the night after a disco?"

"I can have you taken home in a taxi," he says, as if money for a taxi just for me alone to Majengo is no matter.

"I can't," I say and go over to the desk. On the Saturday Faizal comes back when lunch is over. He sits down across from me while I eat leftovers at a table.

"If I don't like it here in Moshi any longer, I'll go to Arusha and play at Mount Meru," he says. The big hotel. I went there with my stepbrother Edward once when he was driving some tourists for his company. A very nice place, modern and European-looking.

"Maybe I'll take you with me," Faizal says and smiles. He gives me lots of tips. "I hope I'll see you tonight – the doorman knows to let you in," Faizal says. The tip is enough for Coke, and a *matatu* there and back. I go. An assistant takes care of the music for a bit, while Faizal pulls me into a dark corner. Oohhhh. His tongue in my mouth, he squeezes my *titi* through the fabric of my dress, I get very hot. Auntie scolds me when I get home late, but it doesn't work at all.

17.

On Rengua Road there's all sorts of gossip. Where can I go for a straight answer? I go to Roots Rock, which belongs to Marcus. You used to be able to have a tape recorded with all the good music in his shop. But that's all finished now, because the machines are bust. These days his girlfriend Claire uses the room to sell clothes. She's clever with business. She goes with her mother to the market in Kiborloni, where they buy the best of the European clothes and fix them up for to Claire sell to the wealthy people in *mtaa juu* – they don't want to be seen going through piles of clothes at the market in Kiborloni.

"Do you know that Alwyn with the car?" I ask her.

"I know who he is," Claire says.

"Is he . . . alright?" I ask.

"*Tsk* – he's no good," she says.

"But what does he do?"

"Wicked things," she says.

"What sort of things?"

"Dirty ones."

"But Salama – is she his girlfriend?" I ask.

"Girlfriend? He doesn't just have one girlfriend," Claire says and laughs nastily. I'm about to ask another question, but she cuts me off: "Alwyn is not a man a young girl can trust," she says. And then she refuses to say anything else. I wait until Rogarth passes, and then I ask him if he knows Alwyn.

"Alwyn is a thief of people's lives," Rogarth says and tells me that Alwyn sells girls to *wabwana wakubwa*. The girls are delivered straight to the hotel. "Salama does that work," he says.

"Salama? I thought she was a hostess at a restaurant – that's what she's told me," I say.

"She's the sort of hostess who pumps men for money. But not at the bar in Majengo. She's too expensive for that. Alwyn looks after her in return for some of the money. Even her child – I think it's Alwyn's."

"She says her child's father died in a traffic accident."

"Yes, because Alwyn won't acknowledge the child. He's got four children with different women, and now he's married to a *chagga* girl that he's pumped up as well," Rogarth says.

All the way through Majengo I take shortcuts to avoid bumping into Salama – I don't know what to say to her. I can't be in touch with that dirty world. There has to be another way in life.

18.

One Sunday after church I visit Faizal. I walk all the way from Majengo with butterflies in my stomach – slowly, so I won't sweat. We go to a kiosk, and Faizal buys us Cokes. He shows me where he lives, a room that he doesn't share with anyone. We are wicked in that room.

"Where have you been?" Auntie asks.

"At my friend's," I say.

"For such a long time? Weren't you supposed to do each other's hair?" Auntie asks – my hair has not been done.

"She had fallen ill, so I just sat with her and kept her company," I say. That night I lie on my stomach with my hand under me, rocking back and forth on the bean, that lovely place.

I manage to find ways to visit Faizal many times. One day I ask him:

"Do you know Alwyn – Salama's boyfriend?"

"Why do you want to know?" Faizal asks.

"Oh, only because he's always such a show-off," I say.

"He is," Faizal say. "Alwyn thinks he's a big man in Moshi, but Alwyn's father's the one with the money. A big *chagga* farmer on West Kilimanjaro; he's got dairy cattle and grows wheat for the brewery in Arusha. Alwyn's just a spoiled brat."

"But Alwyn has a car, doesn't he?"

"Yes, but the car is the only thing he's got left. You see, Alwyn went to the international school with all the *wazungu* kids. His father's so rich he sent Alwyn to Europe to study dairy – how to make cheese. But Alwyn didn't want to work in cheese. He came back with a huge stereo and played at Liberty. But his speakers broke down, and then he set up a recording shop instead, and then his decks broke down, and in the end it all came to nothing. Now you see Alwyn playing at Liberty some nights, but they're not Alwyn's decks – they belong to the owner, and the quality is very poor. And Alwyn's father doesn't want to help him anymore, because Alwyn is no good."

"How is he bad?"

"First he was *chagga*, then he went to the international school and behaved like a *wazungu* brat, always smoking *bhangi*. His hair turned into greasy sausages like Bob Marley's, and Alwyn thought he was a Rastafari. Now they've been cut off, but Alwyn's father has cut *him* off, so now Alwyn drives about in his car with his girls for sale and runs a lousy souvenir shop on Boma Road."

"Don't you think the shop makes any money?" I ask. Also because I'm thinking about learning English – a place like that with tourists would be a better place to work.

"There are very few tourists in Moshi. They only come when they're climbing the mountain. Maybe they'll stay one night in Moshi, and early the next morning they drive to Marangu. No time for souvenirs – they've bought those in Arusha on the way to Ngorongoro and Serengeti."

He's right. Moshi is nothing. The system with the tourists – I know it from my stepbrother. The German bosses taught him all the rules. Sometimes, at home, Edward would pretend he was a white boss to show us how the tourists must be treated: "The white people mustn't be allowed to roam the streets like wild animals in the national park, because if they do, the *mzungu* is the gazelle and the *mwafrika* is the lion," he says. "If the white people want to go somewhere, you go with them and look after them. And you never drive them to bad areas. They've come to see our nature and the African animals, and adorable children with chubby cheeks, not to see poor blacks."

19.

Salama shows up on the pavement outside the kiosk and buys a fizzy drink.

"Long time, no see," she says.

"Yes, I've been so busy with work," I say.

"Could you come over tonight? I need help fixing a top to make it fit." What do I say? "I'll pay you for the work," Salama says.

"No, you don't have to pay. I'll come," I say.

"I'll buy us supper, then," she says.

"But I don't get off until late – I'll have to walk back from your place in the dark."

"You can just stay the night," she says.

"O.K.," I say. I can't stand there and tell her no, I can't, because you're a dirty *malaya*.

First I hurry home and get my needles and thread and tell Auntie that I'm sleeping at a friend's.

"Are you sure?" Auntie asks. "You're not doing something . . . ungodly?"

"No, no," I say and show her my sewing things. "She has a top she wants me to sew, and she is going to pay me for it." Auntie says that it's O.K. then, and I hurry over to Salama's.

Once we've eaten, and I've sewn up her top perfectly, we lie in her wide bed and talk. There's a power cut. Salama smokes a cigarette, and the lit end is a firefly in the dark.

"Is it true . . ." I start then stop again. It's quiet for a while.

"Is what true?" Salama says.

"Is it true that . . . that Alwyn is the father of your son?" I ask – because I can't ask her about the other thing. Salama sighs:

"A man gets you pregnant, and then he just leaves. How can you prove that he's the father? And the courts will only help you if you pay the judge and the lawyer."

"But is it really Alwyn's?"

"Who knows?" Salama says. "I can point at the child and say: 'Look, that's Alwyn's mouth and nose and ears.' But is that proof? Alwyn will say: 'All the men in Moshi are father to that child, because they've all sown their seeds in your garden.'" Salama doesn't say anything while she smokes. Her voice is hard when she speaks again: "Now I tell myself that if my son is to meet a father, I don't want it to be a father like Alwyn."

20.

PAH – Auntie slaps my face. A disaster. It's my seventeenth birthday. I've been with Auntie for a year, and I tell her the news. Faizal has planted a seed inside me. Auntie fetches a stick and beats me. I howl until Anna comes running and stops her. I remember the reason; I demanded we use a sock every time, but the sock exploded because Faizal was so energetic inside me.

Right away Auntie goes to a respected *mzee* in Majengo, and he goes to Faizal and says he has to marry me. Faizal says no. But *mzee* knows that Faizal has an important uncle in Arusha. That uncle sees young people messing about as a sign of disrespect, and he is the biggest *bwana mkubwa* in Faizal's family. If the uncle says that Faizal is bad, the entire family will kick at Faizal like a mangy dog. *Mzee* explains it to Auntie:

"I told Faizal that if he doesn't marry Rachel, I'll go to his uncle and tell him everything. Now Faizal agrees." Auntie gives *mzee* a goat as a present for his help, but I must pay the money for the goat to Auntie. Auntie also writes to my father and tells him everything about what's going on with me. But my father doesn't read. When he gets a letter through the church's mailbox, he will carry it to the chaplain or the shopkeeper, who will then read out loud to him, and at the same time the news will spread all over the village: Rachel has been wicked.

The following week Faizal brings me to the local authorities, and we get official papers – I move into Faizal's room.

I still work every day at the kiosk, even though my baby bump will soon begin to show. I think that will be the end of my job, because the men won't see me as a gift to their eyes when they can see that another man has used me as field to plant his seed in. But my job disappears sooner than I had thought:

"My wife mustn't work as a slave in a shop," Faizal says, and so I have to leave it behind.

Now my only concern is being a good wife – sweet-tempered and obliging to my husband. I spend a lot of time in Faizal's room. He is the most important D.J. in town, but he doesn't have a single machine in his room so I can listen to music.

"It's better to have it locked up at Moshi Hotel," he says. "They have guards around the clock. If it were here it would only be stolen."

Soon I learn that it's all a lie – Faizal doesn't own the machines at the disco. He just plays the records – and even they don't belong to him. Some other man owns the decks and gets paid by Moshi Hotel – Faizal is only paid as a D.J.; it's not a lot of money. I don't reveal my new understanding to Faizal. It's too late to have second thoughts.

I manage the house while the baby grows inside me. I shop, I cook, I clean – I am a good wife to Faizal. Before I left the village, I had already been told everything about how to be a wife. I was taught to cook at home.

And when I started to have my monthly blood, I went through all the ceremonies. First I had to stay alone in a room at my grandmother's hut for three weeks without speaking to anyone. I thought a lot about life and who I am. I wove baskets and mats of palm leaves and felt very lonely. Then the grown women came and washed me and afterwards there was a three-day ceremony where all us young girls were instructed together. We were taught everything about how to behave towards your husband when you are married. Different grown women came and told us things like how to calm down your husband when he is angry. What we are told is very secret. We must never tell any man. But you are told how to apologize to a man, because it's not natural for a woman to apologize, but with a man you sometimes need to. We were of course also told everything about what to do when you're not clean, and how to tell a man. What it's like when you're having a baby. How relations are with your husband when you've given birth. All those questions were answered for us. How to interact with our neighbours and who to go to if our man doesn't behave himself.

It was my grandmother who was in charge – she watched the proceedings. Then a woman came who showed us how to make love with a man; how to touch him in different ways so that the man is happy and doesn't go to other women. What does he like? What are you supposed to say during and afterwards? How can you please him, and how can you be pleased yourself? In my tribe they don't cut girls, so the bean is still between the legs like it's supposed to be. The woman explained everything to us. How to dry out your fruit with herbs if your husband insists on it. She tells us exactly what to do to make the man think he is a big man and miraculous.

I do everything right, but Faizal is almost never at home.

"I have business to see to," he says. "How else will we live?"

What can I say to that?

21.

I have arranged with a neighbour who has a phone that she is to call one of Auntie's friends from church when I go into labour. The friend is a trained nurse and will come with Auntie and help. They've already explained everything to me.

My waters break and the labour pains quickly become very hard. The women manage to get here before the baby starts pressing me into a sea of pain that goes on for hours. I scream till I am hoarse. Finally they smile while I pant.

"The head is out," Auntie says.

"Push one more time," the nurse says. I push and scream. Auntie makes a long singing sound – the way women do back in the village when there's great rejoicing. Auntie's sound mingles with a new sort of screaming. The baby. The nurse holds up the baby – a little girl, so pretty. I'm going to call her Jasmina. I cry, I'm so happy. The baby is a lovely light brown, and her hair grows in the sweetest black spirals. Faizal comes in.

"She's pretty," he slurs. He was drinking all the time he was waiting outside. Maybe he's disappointed because it's a daughter. He goes out on the town to drink with his friends to celebrate the birth.

Auntie brings some small leather bags, about the size of a thumbnail, which she fastens with string around Jasmina's neck so no evil powers can harm her. In one of them is a small piece of the umbilical cord. It's meant to give her eternal strength and power, and ensure that she doesn't die. I powder the girl with Johnson's baby powder and wrap her in a *kanga* and cradle her against my breast. She sucks it greedily. Holding her close to me – it's the most beautiful feeling.

For a while everything is good, even though Faizal drinks a bit more than he should. I know everything about looking after babies from minding my younger siblings. But then Jasmina gets diarrhoea, and we almost don't have enough money to take her to the doctor. And I'd rather not spend my secret savings, because I want to use that for English lessons. I tell Faizal:

"How can we have money when you eat out all the time, even when I cook you good meals? That's wrong."

PAH - he hits me – right in the face."You set me up," he says. "How can I even know that it's my child? You've been with all the men in Majengo." He is the only man who has been with me – he saw the blood himself the first time we were wicked. But now he becomes very wrong. Drinking too much beer and coming home late, giving me too little money to shop for food. He beats me again. I have bruises on my face, because my Arabian blood makes me fair skinned. I have to stay indoors or everyone will see how we live. K.N.C.U.'s English course is about to start up again, and I tell Faizal that I want to attend.

"You're my wife. I provide for you – you don't need English."

"But it's good if I can learn. Then I can get a job in a shop later and make money for our family."

"Rachel – you can't do maths properly."

"I can do maths," I say. "I can do enough maths to work out that you're not rich because the machines at Moshi Hotel all belong to another man – you're just hired to operate them."

"Shut up," Faizal shouts and hits me again. Hard. The tears come. He hits many times. But he has understood the effect of bruises on my skin; if I have bruises I can't go outside and shop for our home, so now he only hits my body.

"You can't do this to me," I howl.

"I am the man of the house. I can do whatever I want," Faizal says. "Would you rather be a *malaya* for *wabwana wakubwa* like your friend Salama?"

I don't answer. Who can I turn to? Auntie already thinks that I am bad because I was wicked. And now I can't even be a good wife. They didn't tell me what to do when nothing works. Jasmina is three and a half months old, and it's my eighteenth birthday, but Faizal has forgotten everything about it. He comes home drunk late at night and snores.

The next day I take money from Faizal's pocket while he sleeps. I go to the bus station and start my journey towards Galambo with little Jasmina.

22.

Many hours later I get off the bus by the intersection on the main road and wait until there's a *matatu* towards Galambo. Some of the people in the bus know who my father is. They have heard that I've got married.

"I have come home to show him his grandchild," I say. And they believe me, because looking at my clothes I am rich compared to the villagers. I can afford to come by bus all the way from Moshi just to show off my baby.

Last time I saw my father was at Edward's funeral in Arusha – two years ago. I am afraid of what he'll say.

The landscape is familiar, and I can see my father's house; sticks and mud with a dirt floor and a tin roof made of twenty-litre oil drums that have been sliced open, tapped flat and used as overlapping roof tiles – it makes an awful noise during the long rains. There's no electricity. Water is fetched from the communal well which the authorities have had dug with funds from Europe. The toilet is a shed out back that stands on a concrete floor with a hole in the ground. From the time I started bleeding I also used it when I washed with a bucket of water, because inside the shed I was hidden from prying eyes.

We had five goats and three cows that I used to milk with my step-mother in the mornings. Our family drank the milk to keep our strength up. We also had cats to kill the rats that would otherwise eat our corn store.

When I was thirteen, when I had finished with school, I stayed at home and helped around the house and in the field. I was meant to help with the child minding, and cleaning, and washing, and cooking, and I had to fetch water and collect firewood, because charcoal is expensive. I had to walk a long way to collect firewood, because the village is large, and everyone is competing for it. And I also had to gather grass, and dry cornstalks, and leaves, and carry them home on my head so the cows would have something to eat.

From the bus stop I go to the house, which is surrounded by banana plants, coconut palms and a single mango tree. When my father opens the door, my eyes well up. The two years have carved new lines in his face.

"Has he shown you the door?" my father asks.

"No, he hit me, so I ran away from him." *PAH* – my father slaps me, but only once.

"I won't hit you hard," my father says, "because you're a grown woman now. But I'd really like to beat you till you break. You are a bad daughter."

"What was I meant to do?"

"When you can't be careful, the punishment is that you live as the stupid girl you are – lots of trouble. The man smacks you about a bit, and off you run. Who's going to pay for your food now?" he asks.

"I'll manage – I can work."

"And who's going to look after your daughter, then?" my stepmother asks from inside the house. I don't answer that. She knows – her and her two young daughters, just like I looked after them when they were small.

"Having a baby is expensive," she says. "You need special foods, medicine, clothes – lots of things."

"I'll make the money," I say. We have the large meal of the day in silence. Corn porridge and bean sauce. I tidy up with the girls.

"Tomorrow you go to the fields," my father tells me. He goes to visit someone. I look after Jasmina. My stepmother looks after her little girls and doesn't speak to me. Not long after Father returns, and we all settle down for the night.

My father and stepmother sleep in narrow net-beds. I lie on mats on the floor with little Jasmina and my stepsisters. My father only has me who has grown from his own seed. You can't plant more seeds in my stepmother – she is too old now. He has taken on my stepmother's children from her first marriage. But with Edward dead, my father faces the greatest catastrophe in his life – he's going to grow old surrounded only by women.

The two girls and Jasmina fall asleep right away, but I can't sleep with all the sounds of the night, which are so much more audible here than in Majengo. My half-empty belly rumbles while the mosquitoes buzz about closer and closer. I am afraid Jasmina will catch malaria – it's far more severe out here close to the coast, and sometimes medicine has no effect on it. My father grunts in his sleep while my stepmother breathes steadily. I can feel the wind through the thin walls. It sounds like spirits chasing each other through the huts.

23.

A whimper from Jasmina wakes me up. A ray of grey light is coming through the window. I gather my *kanga* around me and get up, going outside to breastfeed Jasmina. The air is cool, and the sun is still low on the horizon, shedding a gentle glow. Soon it'll be ablaze. My stepsisters get up. I hand Jasmina to one of them and hurry to the toilet. The stench is intense, and the flies are buzzing around me, landing on my face by my eyes and mouth. I brush them off with my hand. My stepmother is up now. She hands me the pail with a curt nod; I am to fetch water. I look towards Jasmina.

"Your sisters will look after her," my stepmother says. I quickly eat two small bananas, and start walking, meeting other women and girls also on their way to the well. We say good morning to each other. The road is pitted and uneven; the grass scorched and brown.

"*Shikamoo*," I say to the women who are older than me – I hold your feet.

"*Marahaba*," they answer – I am pleased. But I don't think they are pleased. My clothes are nice, I have lived in the city; they don't believe I would hold their feet. They are right. The older women are gaunt and gnarled-looking. Their *kangas* hang off them. It takes them twenty minutes to get to the well. I pass tracks from cattle that the village boys have brought to the watering trough and left to graze. I am overtaken by children who are about to be late for school – the school is in the next village. They're wearing white shirts and blue shorts or skirts. It is a three-mile walk, and they've probably not had anything but fruit for breakfast. I can smell the sea. Twenty women are queuing at the well. Other women are busy washing. When my pail is full, I twist an old *kanga* into a wreath which I put on my head. A woman helps me lift up the full pail, and then I walk homewards. It's hot now. Sweat is running down my face, and the *kanga* sticks to my skin. I am back in *malapa*. Soon my feet will crack at the edges.

When I return with the water, my father and stepmother are ready to go into the field. The cows have been milked, and the little girls have had runny corn porridge and milky tea, but the grown-ups eat only at night.

I put down the pail of water in the kitchen hut and tie Jasmina onto my back. I carry my hoe on my head and a *panga* in my hand and walk off after my father. He is a good man who often goes to work in the field. Most of the village women have to do all the field work themselves while the man sees himself as above the toils of the earth. We get to the field. The long rains haven't done much good, so the sweetcorn harvest is not going to be very good. Only the cassava has done alright, because it can survive anything. The soil has already been baked to a solid crust and must be hoed before vegetables can be planted. Those vegetables will then feed on water that must be fetched from the well several hundred metres away. My father grows sweetcorn, cassava, beans, rice, tomatoes, pumpkin, sweet potato and papaya. The sun is baking down. We hoe the ground. My stepmother looks tiny and gnarled. She has given birth to five children, but only two of them survive. I put Jasmina under a low lean-to made of palm leaves which my father has built under the largest papaya tree. If I were married here, this would be my life. At noon the sun makes my head pound. My arms and legs ache, and the soil is scorching my feet, which have worn shoes for too long. I get tired. I am not used to hard physical labour. And the food I eat here isn't as good as in the city. I am hungry. I feel dizzy, I have to slow down. But luckily my father stops us, and we sit down in the shade where Jasmina is dozing. My father cuts a papaya in half with his *panga* and divides it between us. We eat the juicy pulp. It helps. I breastfeed Jasmina.

"You must stay here," father says. "We will find you a good man."

But I know that when you've been wicked and you have a child, the only man who will take you is a weak man with bad habits, bad family and not enough land.

"No, I have a job in Moshi – I have to make something of my life."

"Make something of your life?" my father says. "You are ruining your life. You think the city is better than the village. And now you're too good for ordinary people. But the city is nothing but trouble."

"I can work for a *mama mtilie* in Moshi again. And if I can learn English, I can become a waitress at a nice place for tourists," I say.

"Those are dreams – not real life," my father says. My stepmother chimes in:

"Tell your husband you are sorry and stay with him."

"He beat me," I say. "He wouldn't give me money so I could take Jasmina to the doctor."

"These things happen when you don't treat your husband well and with respect – he becomes angry with you," my stepmother says.

"But I treated him well," I say.

"*Tsk*," my stepmother says.

"You friends have done well," my father says. "Zoinabo is married and has two young children. You could live like that as well."

"But I'm already married," I say.

"Either you make it work with your husband or you have to find someone else," he says.

"But if we separate, Faizal must pay for Jasmina," I say.

"*Tsk*," my father says. "And who is going to make him?"

"The law says he has to."

"Rachel," my father says, "don't talk like a stupid girl. He's not going to pay if you leave him. And you can't afford to go to court – it's very expensive."

I don't say anything. He is right.

We sit in the shade for a while, but soon we're working again. Sometime in the afternoon we go home.. I want to start making the large meal of the day in order to show that I am helpful.

"Where is the corn flour?" I ask my stepmother.

"There wasn't enough rain for the crops," she says. "We almost only have cassava."

"But we had corn porridge yesterday," I say.

"Your father didn't want to have cassava, because you had come home" she says, looking at me while I look away. Cassava always survives, but it is very low in nutrients and feels like concrete in your stomach. Yesterday my father told my stepmother to use corn flour and cook bean sauce to welcome me home even though I've been wicked. *Eeehhh*, I feel ashamed.

24.

The next morning I milk the cows with my stepmother while Jasmina hangs in a *kanga* milking me. The cows are skinny.

"You are a wicked girl," my stepmother says.

"Yes," I say. "It's sad that Edward died of illness and now you have to look at a wicked girl who isn't even your own daughter." She would have beaten me for those words if I wasn't a mother. She doesn't say anything else.

My father makes me gather dried corn stalks and leaves on his land, put them in bunches and carry them home to have as fodder for the cattle.

After work I stay by the house, because my stepmother has told everyone how wicked I am. Life here is so dull that my misfortune is a rare gift of gossip.

Zoinabo comes to visit to see Jasmina. She has a baby on her back and another by the hand. Zoinabo is my best friend from my time in the village. I can tell that she admires my clothes, but they're not what she asks about:

"How are things with your husband?"

"We are having a few problems," I say. "Maybe we'll divorce."

"No-one in the village has been divorced," she says. "The elders make sure people solve their troubles." I know that solution: You stay with your husband and grit your teeth when he beats you. Bad things happen in the village as well. It makes me upset. Zoinabo says:

"You should go to the witch doctor with a young cock and a bag of rice for the ceremony – he can get in touch with the spirits and change your husband. You can have a powder as well and put it in your husband's tea – it will make him affectionate towards you again." I say what my step-brother Edward used to say:

"If the witch doctor is so good at changing the future, then how come he's so poor? He can never do a ceremony without using a cock and a bag of rice. But does he give it back to you afterwards, even though you've paid money for the job as well? No, as soon as you leave, he sweeps the floor, picks up the rice, plucks the cock and cooks it for supper."

"Don't say that," Zoinabo says.

"Is your husband good to you? Does he make sure there's enough money for the family?" I ask.

"He's a good man," Zoinabo says, looking away. All the women work their own fields and sell their vegetables on the market to have their own money for medicine and other necessities for the family. The money is stashed away from the man – if he ever finds it, it'll make its way to the bar and go on drink.

"Does he help you in the field?" I ask to upset Zoinabo.

"A man's job isn't only in the field," she says.

"No, a man talks – that's his main job," I say.

"You'll never find a husband here if you talk bad," Zoinabo says. "They don't like girls who have been to the city and behave like they're special."

"*Tsk*," I say.

The next day I am back in the field. This time only with my stepmother. We weed and carry water. We spend the day in near silence while she waits for me to cave in before she does. I grit my teeth.

We walk home by the main road with the other women who have children on their backs and hoes in their hands. I have to go home and prepare the evening meal with my sisters. The sun is setting; the trees are black shadows against the orange sky, in the kitchen huts blazing fires are lit. The men are sitting beneath the big tree in the centre of the village. Some of them were there when I left for the field this morning. They're talking and drinking *mbege*. My father is sitting there. Zoinabo's husband is there as well. *Tsk* – none of the men have done any work today.

I am hit by malaria. I lie soaked in sweat with a pounding headache – for five days, the fever nearly kills me. When I wake up, I am too thin by far, and my eyes are red. How can you live like that? Jasmina learned to eat runny corn porridge while I was ill. They've fed her milk substitute. My *titi* have almost dried up. I stay home from the field and help my sisters with the housework. One of them is out gathering firewood in the bush while the other fetches water from the well. First I milk the cows. Then I take a coconut and split it in half with my *panga*. I pour the coconut milk into a little bowl and take a large flat basket, go outside and sit in the shade on a stool which has a serrated grating knife fixed to one side. I scrape the white coconut flesh against the knife to make a small pile of grated coconut in my basket. I go into the kitchen hut and start a fire between the three large stones on the dirt floor, cook a bit of water in a saucepan, add the grated coconut and stir to make it a stew. Once it's cooled off, I'll squeeze it, so the fluid will run down and mix with the coconut milk in the bowl. I'll use it later in the day to cook rice in.

One of my stepsisters returns, balancing a pail of water on her head.

She is tired from the walk, so I take the pail and pour the water into the earthenware jar which sits in a corner of the kitchen hut on a small wooden stand. I let the water run through a white cloth to skim off any dirt. I give the girls money to buy rice in the *duka*. That leaves me with just enough money for a bus ticket. And my secret savings for English lessons, which I've never told anyone about; I refuse to give up on my dream. I still feel a bit ill, so I lie down inside and relax for a while with Jasmina.

When my stepmother returns, she sees the rice I have bought.

"*Tsk*," she says. "You have developed grand habits in the city."

"The girls miss having rice," I say.

"Corn flour is cheaper," she says.

25.

Days go by. Then weeks. Three months. Sometimes I work in the field. Other days I tend to the house. I have got thin and my muscles have grown. My skin has become very dark from working in the sun. Jasmina has started crawling, and she has become very good at eating her porridge.

I am standing outside, pounding cassava roots in the large wooden mortar. I get into the rhythm and clap my hands every time the long pestle soars in the air. The mashed-up cassava roots are passed through a sieve to make flour, which is poured into boiling water. The porridge becomes so stiff that it's hard to stir with my flat spoon. I make a sauce with tomato, onion and chicken offal. I clean bowls for the food by rubbing them on the inside with hot ashes from the fire and rinsing them with water.

When I hear my father and stepmother come home, I quickly fill a mug with water and run out to give it to them.

Before the meal we wash our right hands in a bowl of warm water. I take a lump of cassava porridge, which I press into a ball in my hand before forming a hole through the middle with my thumb. Then I dip the ball in the sauce before eating it. Me and my sisters take turns at drinking water from an old tin. The only meal of the day.

"Don't get up," my father says when I want to get up to start tidying things away. The others clear up. I sit with my father without either of us saying anything while he smokes a cigarette of coarse tobacco rolled up in a scrap of newspaper. In the darkness I can't see the expression on his face.

"Go back to Moshi," my father says. "And then send us money to look after Jasmina."

"Yes, Father," I say. "Thank you."

"If you don't send money, then you're no longer my daughter."

"I'll send money," I say. Little Jasmina is done milking me. I leave her with my stepmother and go back to Auntie in Moshi.

26.

We're squatting outside their room in Majengo. I took the tray of rice from Anna right away to do the work of picking out any little stones. Anna has started plaiting her mother's hair. I have been here five minutes. Auntie Esther almost wouldn't speak to me; all she wanted to talk about was money:

"How are you going to earn a living? You can't stay here and not pay," she says.

"Maybe *mama mtilie* will give me my job back," I say.

"She is a Christian woman," Auntie says. "She won't want to have a dirty girl serving her customers."

"I am not dirty," I say.

"You're a wicked girl," Auntie says. We're sitting outside; everyone can hear her words. "Everyone is in trouble because of you. You're ruining my good name."

"Auntie has already asked *mama mtilie* if you could have the job back," Anna says, shaking her head. "The answer was no."

"And I fear the bad influence you will have on my daughter," Auntie says loudly. Anna doesn't say anything. What can I do? I need my family's help.

"I will be good," I say. "I have to work so that there'll be money for Jasmina."

"Yes," Auntie says. "You will be good, or else I'll kick you out, and you'll have to live as a beggar on the street." Auntie tells me to talk to the bad *mama mtilie* behind the Tanesco building on Rengua Road.

I do it and she gives me the job. It's only twenty metres from the kiosk and the good *mama mtilie*, but everything is different here. The food is not so good and much cheaper; the men are poorer, the pay is low and comes in dribs and drabs whenever *mama* sees fit. She doesn't pay for my transport, so now I have to walk morning and afternoon on my feet in the dust. I am afraid of pushing her, because there are lots of girls in Moshi with nothing to do.

"You have to do a good job," *mama* says. "Hurry up." I do things right, but everything is always wrong because I have sinned against the God's law. I have married a man who believes in Allah, who isn't real the way God is. Yes, this mama is a bride to Jesus on the cross as well. It's common for Christians and Muslims to marry here – it's not meant to cause trouble. But she thinks I'm satanic: first I get myself pregnant by a Muslim and then, when I've done the godless thing and got married at the registry office, I run away from the man. She keeps her stern eye on me at all times.

There are no *wabwana wakubwa* like at the good *mama mtilie*'s. The men who eat here don't have nice watches, smart clothes, good shoes. They may be lorry drivers, or mechanics, or junior clerks. But I've learned that what meets the eye doesn't tell the whole story. Faizal taught me that the man in the good clothes might well live in a bad room and own nothing but the shirt on his back. I should have had more sense back when I was at the kiosk and not have believed in dreams. Many of the poor men would have been better than Faizal.

Now I must save my money. No more shopping for clothes – I have to do something. I can't stay in this job long. The money isn't good, and I have to be able to send money home so Jasmina can be looked after properly. And I have to make something of my life – it's not good when other people control your future. I have to learn how to make my own way now. I want to take English lessons at the K.N.C.U. building by Clock Tower, but it's expensive. I have money saved, but should I spend it? On the street I meet Faizal.

"How is my daughter?" he asks. Does he think Jasmina is his daughter when he won't provide for her?

"I need money for Jasmina," I say. Faizal looks surprised.

"How can you expect to empty my wallet when you've run away from my house?" he asks.

"You beat me," I say. He won't meet my eyes.

"It wasn't so bad," he says.

"You wouldn't give me money for a doctor for Jasmina," I say.

"She wasn't that ill," Faizal says. *Tsk* – I miss the feeling we had in the beginning, but Faizal, him I don't miss.

"Goodbye," I say. He is surprised that I won't beg on my knees. Does he think my fruit only dreams of his pump? I can do better without him.

When I return home, Auntie scolds.

"If your husband wants to talk to you again, you have to be friendly to him. If he'll take you back, that's a good thing. You have to be humble towards him. He can take away the shame you have put on our family."

First I am evil, because I do this, and then when I do that, that's wrong too. What am I supposed to do in all this confusion? I can't live like this – I have to get away from Auntie.

Anna tells me that Auntie is arranging to marry Anna to a young man from church.

"Do you like him?" I ask.

"He has a good job as a bus driver," Anna says.

"But is he handsome?" I ask.

"*Tsk*," Anna says. "Faizal is handsome, but was he a good husband to you?" I don't say anything. "I just have to get out of Majengo and away from my mother. I don't care about handsome, as long as he works and treats me alright."

"Yes," I say.

27.

When the mama lets me off for the day, I go out on Rengua Road. I cross the street and sit down on one of the benches. Rogarth is there. He buys us fizzy drinks from the fridge on the pavement. Now I know what it is he does at Moshi Hotel: He is a dogsbody for *wabwana mkubwa* who want a girl but who don't want anyone to see them buying the fruit. Rogarth is nice – I like him. I need to be wicked with Rogarth, but he has no money. I must have a man with money so I can have Jasmina come back to me.

Lots of young girls work in the shops, cafés and bars, or hang about outside. Some of them don't need the money from their work because their parents are rich. But they all make themselves beautiful and wait for an important man who will like them and want to get married. In the village the parents would find him, but here, in the city, it's a jungle. A man can wear the best clothes with a good watch and still be as poor as a church mouse. I have tried it that way with Faizal – I don't believe in it. Now I have to help myself without knowing how.

On my way home I enter the K.N.C.U. building and sign up for an English course that has classes every day in the afternoon. I ought to send the money home to the village and Jasmina, but it costs me all of my secret savings which I've saved from back when I was at the shop and managed to keep hidden while I was with Faizal – no-one knows anything about it; not Faizal, not Auntie, not anyone.

"How can you pay for it?" Auntie asks.

"It's free for me – there's a European aid organization that pays the fee so that young girls can learn English, even though they haven't had much schooling."

"Ohhh, that's good," Auntie says. But it's a lie, and now I am very poor.

A few days later my course starts. It's very difficult and exciting to be back in school. The teacher writes on the blackboard – I copy it down carefully in my exercise book; it's difficult to write, but the teacher tells me I do well. We say the words in chorus, echoing the teacher as he points to each word with a pointer. In the evening I read the words till my eyes hurt, and I whisper the strange sounds to make them right inside my mouth.

28.

I need the money for Jasmina that I promised to send home to the village. There is no other way. That night I go to the kiosk in Majengo and sit down to meet Salama – I need a friend in this world. And I sit there to meet Alwyn. They don't come that day.

On the third night Alwyn's car comes down the street. I wave. He stops. Salama is in the car with him. She doesn't speak to me. Alwyn says:

"I heard you were back. How are you?"

"I'm good. But I need a better job," I say.

"Yes," Alwyn says. "You don't make real money with a *mama mtilie*." He hasn't switched the engine off. Salama still isn't talking to me – she only stares. She looks angry.

"I was wondering if perhaps you could help me?" I ask.

"I'll pick you up later," Alwyn says to Salama.

"Where are you going?" she asks.

"None of your business," he says. She stays in the car:

"If you're going to do business with Rachel, I'd better explain her everything, because she's just a stupid girl from the village," Salama says. Alwyn laughs.

"You're right about that," he says and tells me to get in the back. We drive off, away from Majengo, up past the Y.M.C.A. roundabout towards Shanty Town. The houses here are large, and clean, and nice. Alwyn stops at something called Uhuru Hotel. We sit down at a table in the garden. A girl comes over, and Alwyn orders Coke and food.

"You don't have to work for *mama mtilie*. You can work for me – it pays enough to live on and for your English lessons. You'll be like a friend to these men," he tells me.

"But . . ." I say.

"The deal is to have dinner – nothing dirty. I set it up and take you there. And I pay you. Anything else you decide to do is your own business." Alwyn tells me how much I'll get.

"That's not a lot of money," I say.

"It's dinner," Salama says. "If you want more money, you'll have to eat more than food." They laugh. I nod without saying anything.

29.

A couple of days later Alwyn stops by *mama mtilie*'s. He tells me to be ready on Thursday night – he'll pick me up at the kiosk. I am ready – my clothes and hair are very nice. A driver comes by with Alwyn in the car. Alwyn gets out:

"If you prove that you are right for the job, I can get you more work and your salary will grow," he says and points to the man behind the wheel – a big, bluish-black field labourer. "This is Tito," Alwyn says. "He'll drive you to the place." Tito looks like a criminal. He doesn't speak. He drives me to Newcastle Hotel and takes me to the roof terrace and introduces me to a man. We have dinner, we drink beer. I feel scared. After the restaurant we drive in a car with a chauffeur to the bar on Liberty's terrace. The man starts kneading my thigh like chapatti dough. He is already drunk. I don't think I can do it. I push off his hand.

"I'll be good to you," he says and goes back to his kneading.

"We said dinner," I said. "Nothing more."

"Don't worry," he says. "You'll get your soap-money."

"I don't want your soap-money. I'm not that kind of a girl," I say.

"What?" he says. "Do you think I pay to meet you just to have dinner?" He grabs my arm, holds me down. "That's how much I've paid Alwyn to meet a nice, clean girl." He names a figure four times higher than what I get. "But you think you're something special." I pull my arm away. Walk through the bar, out onto the street and into a taxi I can't afford. We drive to Majengo and Salama's house.

"But I had agreed with Alwyn to have dinner," I say, tears starting in my eyes.

"You're so stupid," Salama says. "Everyone pumps – then you get soap-money."

"But . . ."

"Do you really think you'd get soap-money without getting yourself dirty first? *Tsk*," Salama says.

"But . . ." I say.

"It's a job. Would you rather slave away at *mama mtilie*'s forever? First you have a couple of beers or a large Konyagi; it gets you a bit crazy – then the pumping isn't so bad. Just . . . think of something else."

"I don't know if I can," I say.

"It's not hard," Salama says. "Come. Let's go meet Alwyn – he's at Strangeways."

When we get there, I tell him what happened while I stare at the table. Alwyn goes very cold. He doesn't say anything. Then he leans forward and slaps me.

"*Tsk*," he says. "Stupid girl." I get up and go home. And I really need the money to send to Jasmina. And I need money for my own place away from Auntie and God. And I'll need to learn English for a long time before I can speak it properly.

30.

Rogarth comes and eats at *mama mtilie*'s. He gives me money so I can get fizzy drinks at the shop. "Sit down and have one with me," he says. I do it. He says:

"It's not good that you are seen with that Alwyn." Does Rogarth know anything about it? Moshi is too small a place – everyone keeps an eye on everyone else.

"What do you mean?" I ask. "I don't do anything with Alwyn."

"Alwyn can ruin you. His methods are dangerous," Rogarth says. I shrug.

"Faizal won't give me any money for my daughter," I say. "I have to get money somehow. Otherwise she'll starve back in the village. I have to do something."

"I know – but Alwyn isn't the only way," Rogarth says.

"I don't know any other way," I say.

"There's a good man, very rich," Rogarth says. "He works for Tanesco. He has seen you and would very much like to meet you. He needs female company, because his wife is ill – she is dying at K.C.M.C."

"Do you think I am that kind of girl?" I ask.

"It's nothing dirty," Rogarth says. "You'll meet him – he'll take you out for dinner. Nothing dirty."

"Everyone says that it's never anything dirty, but it was you who said that if a man buys you a beer, he thinks he's already paid for the fruit. I've seen it happen."

"He's not that kind of man. You would never see him in those places – in Majengo, Liberty. He is a nice, decent man with a family."

31.

Bwana Mbuya's driver picks me up at the Y.M.C.A., where no-one knows me. The car is a big new S.U.V. We have dinner at a nice little restaurant in Shanty Town – it's in a villa with a hedge all the way around it and a large iron gate minded by a guard in uniform. The house is surrounded by a lovely garden, and inside everything is beautiful and stylish. Very exclusive.

"I have never heard of this place," I say.

"You have to be a member to be allowed in," *bwana* Mbuya says.

We sit down and a waiter brings fizzy drinks for me and beer for *bwana* Mbuya. He asks where I'm from. I tell him I am from Galambo on the coast, not far from Tanga. "I am *mswahili*," I say, smiling.

"Are you a Muslim then as well?" he asks.

"*Kristo*," I say, because Mbuya is *chagga* so he must be Christian. Me, I can be either the one or the other. I know about Muslims from the village and from Faizal, and I know Christianity from going to church with Auntie every Sunday. Both faiths have a God you must believe in and humour. Keeping your legs shut till you are married and then obeying your husband when he tells you to spread them. How is that ever going to work when a man always wants you to spread them with no church around? *Bwana* Mbuya says: "My wife is very ill – she's been at the K.C.M.C. for a long time. She is dying, but very slowly."

"*Polo sana*," I say – I am very sorry to hear it.

"It's lovely to be in the company of a sweet girl again," Mbuya says. I don't know what to say. He is a lot older than me, a large man – calm and friendly. But still a man with a man's urges. He takes my hand. He has gold rings, a good watch, nice suit.

"A man needs a good woman," he says. He smells clean even though he is overweight. He signs to the waiter, and as he pays the bill, he sits back in his chair, and I can almost count the money in his wallet.

We meet again – more restaurants, good dinners. I kiss him with my tongue because I need him. He gives me lots of money.

"Get yourself a nice dress and have your hair done." Soon I am touching *bwana* Mbuya to make him go crazy for me. Finally I can send money to the village, because I've got enough dresses.

I tell *bwana* Mbuya about my dreams; that I take English lessons.

"That's good," he says. "It's important to learn things if you want to do well in life." Can I tell him that I have a child? No, I have to make sure he is so fond of me first that the child won't hold him back. I have to make sure I am a miracle to him, so that he'll go crazy, so that he forgets everything else. He has children himself. When we are married, we'll bring our families together. Oohh, I am nervous. A lot of people say that men just use young girls and then dump them. But he's not like that. He is good to me. I can hide my nervousness. His eyes only see the magic. And he loves it.

"I would like to take you to my house," he says. "But my children are there. You have to understand that . . ." I put my hand on his cheek.

"I understand. We'll just have to wait," I say, because while his wife is ill, it would be wrong for him to be seen with a new girl.

"We can meet in other places," *bwana* Mbuya says. Our place is at Mama Friend's Guesthouse in Soweto after dark – far from Majengo where I live and Shanty Town where he lives. The driver takes me there, and *bwana* Mbuya comes later. He brings socks with him that he wants me to put on for him – he looks after me. I make all the right sounds while he pumps me. But his stomach's so large that he can hardly get his pump inside me without breaking into a sweat from the exertion. So I'm on top. He does things no man would do. When I ride him, he pulls me forward so I sit on his face, and he sucks my bean in the most amazing way until his face shines with moisture.

That's how it starts.

"Is there anything I can do for you, Rachel?" he asks when I've washed him and am dressing him so he can leave.

"I still want to take English lessons on the days when you're too busy to see me. But it's difficult to afford with what I make from *mama mtilie*'s."

"You don't have to work anymore, Rachel. I'll help you."

"But I want to work," I say to show him that I am a good girl who is willing to work a lot. And perhaps when his wife dies . . . But *bwana* Mbuya could turn out wrong or disappear. I need my English lessons. I need independence.

32.

Bwana Mbuya has business in Arusha. He asks me to come for the weekend. I tell *mama mtilie* that I have to go to Galambo for two days because Jasmina is ill. Mbuya's driver picks me up outside the Y.M.C.A. and we drive.

"Going over to help Mbuya with his paperwork at the hotel?" the driver asks.

"Mind your own business," I say. He just laughs and turns on the radio. We drive all the way without a word passed between us, and he parks the car outside the big Mount Meru Hotel, where I have been before with my stepbrother Edward to pick up white tourists. The driver stops outside the entrance.

"This is it," he says. I stay in my seat. "He's in there," the driver adds. I can tell from his voice that he thinks it's funny.

"Give me the number of his room," I say.

"Oh, the number of his room," he says like he's forgotten that I need it. "406." I open the door and step outside without saying goodbye or anything. Slam the door and go into reception.

"I am meeting *bwana* Mbuya who is staying in room 406," I say. The receptionist calls the room, talks into the phone and then looks at me.

"You can go straight up," she says.

"Thank you," I say and wonder who she thinks I am. I take the lift – it makes my stomach full of butterflies. I walk on the deep-pile carpets down the corridor and knock on the door. Mbuya opens, wearing a handsome suit, pulls me into his arms and kisses me. I can taste that he's had a beer, but he isn't drunk or anything. The room is nice. He takes my bag from my hand and puts it on the floor.

"We're going downstairs to eat, Rachel," he says and takes my arm. We take the lift down and go into the hotel's restaurant – very luxurious. The places are set with two glasses, three forks, three knives and two spoons. The food is delicious, and there's always a plate under the plate your food is on. And the napkins aren't made of paper, they're of finely woven cotton – white as snow and newly ironed like the tablecloth. And the waiter wears a uniform. He pours fizzy drink into my glass as soon as it is half empty. After dinner we drink beer, and there's an orchestra playing European music, so we dance close.

"Let's go to our room," Mbuya says into my ear. We leave the dance floor and the bar and walk out through reception where a man greets Mbuya who introduces me: "Rachel is my secretary." He has to say that, after all, while his wife is still alive. I shake hands with the man and smile, and Mbuya talks to him for a while. Back in our room Mbuya says he has to make some phone calls about business.

"I'll just have a bath while you do that, darling," I say, because the bathroom is amazing. It has a bathtub and two sinks. There are two white dressing gowns, and we have three towels each. Never before have I tried showering with hot water – it keeps coming. When I am completely clean, Mbuya has finished talking. "Come and see, there are two sinks," I say. "We can both be out here at the same time brushing our teeth in our own sink." Mbuya comes out into the bathroom, but he has no time for sinks; he wants to taste my mouth right away. Soon we're lying down together, and I make sure I am on top of him with my fingers on the bean, because then I can even get a bit of pleasure from him if I close my eyes.

33.

A month later I move to K.N.C.U. Coffee House where I stay in a small room rented for me by *bwana* Mbuya. The room has a big and very good ghettoblaster, which is his as well. Auntie doesn't know anything about it – I still work for the bad *mama mtilie*. I have arranged with Salama, in return for a little money, that I live with her. If Auntie comes past and I'm not there, Salama always says that I'm having English lessons funded by a European aid organization. Auntie believes everything you tell her because she works all the time and doesn't hear much gossip and never goes to *mtaa juu*.

I go to Salama to give her a little money in return for the scam. I tell her about Mbuya.

"Awr, he's just using you."

"No," I say and tell her about the hotel room, the money for lessons, money for food, clothes, hairdressers, the fact that I don't even have to work. She sighs.

"Oh, you are lucky. It's good what you've done. I could do with meeting a man like that, instead of always having to run around. But you have to be careful. You never know . . . with men," Salama says.

Life is good. *Bwana* Mbuya only comes on some nights – the other nights are my time off. After a couple of weeks he goes away on business, and I go to Rogarth's room in Soweto and give him a present – a nice shirt that I have bought in Kiborloni and have sewn to make it fit his body perfectly. And it's a nice present and he has a lovely body and I get a good feeling in my body in his room. Not fat and sweaty like Mbuya. Wonderfully energetic and powerful to touch.

34.

"Ohhh, have you heard that Deborah was cut?" Salama asks when I meet her one day by Clock Tower roundabout.

"No, how . . . cut?"

"Three men; they used a broken bottle on her face, so she's had stitches on her nose and cheek – everything has been bandaged."

"But why?"

"A man stops her on the street one night. He shows her the money – enough for a quickie – and they go to the football stadium. Then two of the man's friends come – one of them has the bottle which he holds up to Deborah's face. He says he can smash it and cut her face. They all want to pump her and not pay. Deborah doesn't scream because she wants to live. But they've been drinking and are mean to her, so she makes a sound because of the pain, just once, and then the man smashes the bottle and pushes it into her face."

"That's terrible," I say.

"Yes – you need protection in Majengo," Salama says.

35.

A couple of nights a week *bwana* Mbuya comes to the hotel. These days we don't often go out to a restaurant to eat.

"I don't have much time," he says and undresses, pumps me and rushes out again. And he doesn't pay like he promised to so that I can make ends meet. I have spent the money on English lessons; I study very hard. And I need money for Jasmina. There's barely enough. In the end I have to say something, but I don't want him to know that I have a child yet.

"Ooh, I really could use a new dress, and my shoes are really worn as well," I say.

"Don't you have any of the money left that I gave you?"

"No, I spent it on paying for my English lessons," I say. *Bwana* Mbuya looks in his pocket and puts money on the table. I pick it up – there isn't very much.

"K.C.M.C. is expensive," he says. "Things will pick up when my wife dies." He makes a gesture round the room. "Paying for a hotel room for you is expensive as well," he says.

36.

Every Sunday I go to church with Auntie so no-one will suspect a thing. I meet the man Anna is marrying. He is not handsome, not charming, nothing special. I don't understand why she wants to be with him. Afterwards I visit Salama because we've agreed to do each other's hair.

"So, when are you moving into his house?" she asks with a smile when I step through her door.

"I don't know," I sigh. "His wife is still ill at the K.C.M.C."

"But his wife is dead!" Salama says.

"What?" I say. "Where did you hear that?"

"*Tsk*. You can go to the cemetery and see her tombstone."

"But he hasn't told me that. Are you sure?" I ask.

"He was at Strangeways yesterday, and another *bwana mkubwa* came over and offered his condolences on the death of his wife. She died a month ago."

"*Kuma mamayo*," I say – your mother's cunt. "He can't play me like that." But what can I do? I can tell people he sucks my bean like it was a boiled sweet. And that he whimpers like a baby when his pump pukes. Everyone will despise him, but at the same time, that will mean telling them that he's bought me.

"What should I do?" I ask.

"You have to tell him – that you know," Salama says. I sit down between her legs in the narrow entrance to her house, and Salama combs my hair and plaits it into lots of narrow cornrows across my scalp like I'm a village girl again, because he's meant to come tonight. And he was at Strangeways last night – he told me he was in Dar es Salaam on business for Tanesco until today.

When I have done Salama's hair, I go back to *mtaa juu* and into K.N.C.U. Coffee Hotel to the room he pays for where I have lived for nearly a month while the fat bastard went on about how his wife was ill and how she had to die before we could be together properly. Then she dies and I know nothing. He hasn't told me. I have to hear it from Salama and look like a fool.

What should I do now? What would be the right way to tell him? No-one told me anything about that back in the village when I was learning about how to be a woman. I shower, put on my best clothes – tight, pretty. I put coconut oil in my hair and rub vaseline into my arms, legs and face to make my skin shiny. All the things he likes, I want him to be reminded of them. I am going to have to be careful.

As soon as he gets here, he starts taking off his trousers so he can get his pump out and stick it into me. I have to say it:

"Your wife is dead."

"What?" he says – surprise on his face; he stops undressing.

"You told me that when she died, we could be together properly. No more secrecy at the hotel."

"But . . ." he says – one leg already out of his trousers, the other on its way out, but now he's not sure whether to take his trousers off or put them back on. He sits down heavily on the edge of the bed, so his large pouch hangs between his puny legs. "It's true," he says and pretends to be grieving. How can he be grieving when he's been pumping me while his wife was dying at the K.C.M.C.? And when he was telling me all the time how happy everything would be when she was gone and we were married and living together in his big house in Shanty Town which he had the driver take me past to show me the place that would be my home. "But we have to wait a little, Rachel. She was only just buried," he says.

"A whole month she's been dead, and you haven't said anything!" I shout.

"*Shh*," he says. His pump is hanging goofily in his underpants, almost hidden by his beer gut: "When things have settled down, I'll take you to my house."

"*Tsk*," I say. What can I do? I have to eat somehow. Where can I go? "How long will it be?" I ask.

"No more than a month. I love you – a lot," he says. Soon he comes over and kneels in front of me, holding my hips, lifting up my skirt, kissing my thighs – soon he is sucking at my bean. And the money is there in the morning as it should be, enough to send to my father to help him. There's money for my daughter to have proper clothes and food so she can become strong. I have taken a chance on *bwana* Mbuya. Perhaps I shouldn't have. I have to wait and see.

37.

There's a power cut. I am sitting at my window, staring into the dark – the headlights of a couple of cars cast brief light over buildings and people; Moshi has become a city of spirits. I miss Jasmina terribly. I try to smoke a cigarette from the pack that *bwana* Mbuya left behind, but it tastes bad. Everything is bad.

Why does that man want to be with me? It's strange. But not really all that strange, because I know why. I do the job well, because I don't have bad manners like a Majengo *malaya* or a city girl. The man sees me as the sweet girl from the village. Natural and erotic, helpful and without the filthy mouth. I make my *bwana mkubwa* forget that he is paying. Mbuya keeps me a secret and tells himself that he is looking after me because he is a good man – I am innocent and naïve and in need of his help.

When we were at Mount Meru Hotel in Arusha, Mbuya told people that I was his secretary. Back then I didn't understand that everyone knows what that means: a piece of meat for the man to play with until he gets bored with it and gets himself another.

You'll never see a man like Mbuya buy his girl at a bar in Majengo. He doesn't want to see himself as a man who pays for his pumping. He doesn't want other people to see him like that either. But he's worse than that. He has made me a *malaya* without making the transaction open. And he has made my life a prison – without him I have no home.

38.

The bells are almost done ringing by the time I get there – I didn't sleep well last night and almost couldn't drag myself out of bed this morning. The last people are on their way into the church, but Auntie is standing outside waiting for me.

"Are you going to church?" she asks.

"Yes, of course," I say.

"I hear bad things about you. If they're true, then the church is no place for you."

"What sort of bad things?" I ask and try to look innocent, but despite the sun my back feels cold.

"I can't bring myself to take those words into my mouth," Auntie says. "If it's true, you're damned."

"I don't know what it is you've heard. If you don't tell me, I can't say whether it's true or not."

"There was a letter for you from the village," Auntie says.

"Yes? Did you bring it?"

"No, I took it to where you live," Auntie says.

"At . . . Salama's?" I ask.

"Yes – at that terrible girl's. But I don't think you really live there. That's not what I hear."

"But I do live there – you can ask her yourself," I say.

"She tells nothing but lies. God has a special room in hell for liars," Auntie says and turns and starts walking towards the church. Then she stops and looks back to me. Anna isn't with her. Or perhaps she is already inside. And I don't want to ask about anything now – where is Anna? Has anything happened to her? If I don't go inside, it's like admitting my guilt. I follow Auntie. Just outside the door she stops and points to the pew at the very back.

"You sit here. And afterwards you'll leave right away. I don't want Anna's future in-laws to meet you before I know if the rumours are true or not."

I can't hear a word the chaplain says. How can I avoid being found out by Auntie?

After church I go straight to Salama's, even though I don't want to hear her questions about why I'm still at the hotel when the month *bwana* Mbuya said it would take has already been and gone.

"*Tsk*," Salama says. "I see him with another woman and ask people about it. That woman is from his village, from his dead wife's family; almost moved into his house already."

What about me – am I just a hole to piss into?

"Auntie says she delivered a letter for me."

"Oh yes," Salama says and gets it out. I open it at once. "Does it say how your daughter is doing?"

"Hang on," I say, because it's difficult for me to read. My stepmother writes from the village that Jasmina has had malaria. The doctor and the medicine were expensive, but my daughter is well again. My father had to sell a cow. They need money, otherwise they will have to sell . . . I have to spell it in my head. The cattle. Without money from me they will soon have to sell the cattle. My entire family will starve. And even if they do survive, selling the cattle would my break my father's heart. Never again would he be the man with the healthy herd who could walk through the village with his head held high. I have already shamed him with a grandchild who must live in his house while I am in Moshi and don't even have a husband. I start crying.

"But what's happened?" Salama asks. Between snivels, I tell her everything.

"*Pole sana,*" she says.

"Can you borrow me some money?" I ask.

"I hardly have any," she says.

"Could you try? I'd be very grateful."

"I'll see what I can do," she says. "Come back tomorrow."

39.

The next day Salama gives me the money, and I go straight to the bank and have a cheque made and send it to the village. I say nothing to *bwana* Mbuya, just give him the service he is used to. A couple of days later Auntie comes to pick me up when my workday in the kitchen ends. Her jaw is clenched, and she doesn't say anything but, "Come." I walk behind her to Majengo. We are out of *mtaa juu* and walking towards Coffee Curing. She stops under a tree. There's no-one about. She turns around. Before I've thought of anything to say, she has slapped me twice in the face. Her calloused fingers sting my cheek. I take a step back.

"I know everything now," she says. "You're a *malaya* at the hotel. I want you to get your things now and move back with me. I'm sending you back to the village so your father can take you in hand. You're bringing shame to your entire family." I shout:

"*Don't you tell me what to do. You know nothing.* I live at Salama's. I'm not a *malaya*. I'm not at any hotel. You know nothing." I turn around and walk away. At my hotel room I take all my things and get them together. The most important thing is the ghettoblaster – I can sell that for good money. I get all my possessions together in a suitcase. I have enough money to pay for a taxi so I can go to a cheap guesthouse in Majengo – he won't find me there.

They stop me in the lobby.

"Those are my things," I say.

"No, the ghettoblaster isn't yours. It belongs to the man who pays for the room."

"He's tricked me," I shout, but they don't care. They take the machine away from me. They lead me out the door and throw my suitcase after me, so that it opens and my clothes lie scattered in the dust. I am on the street with nothing but pennies and lies.

40.

"Two weeks. Three weeks, tops," Salama says. After that I'll have to pay what I owe for my share of the rent. And I owe her the money I sent to the village. "I told you to be careful with a *bwana mkubwa* like that – they promise you the world, but there's nothing but lies in their mouths." Salama's rent for the good room is expensive, and I only have my bad pay from the bad *mama mtilie*, and no money left for English lessons, which had really started going well because I had studied diligently all those nights at the hotel when Mbuya wasn't there.

"Come along," Salama says that night. Alwyn doesn't need her tonight, and she's going to the bars in Majengo to fish for a man to give her a little extra money.

"No, I don't want to," I say.

"You can just have a fizzy drink and maybe some meat to eat – you don't have to do it."

"Living like that doesn't work," I say.

"You know the work," Salama says angrily. "You've been a mattress for *bwana mkubwa* at K.N.C.U. for months. It's no different now – one man is just like another."

"You said you were a hostess at a restaurant," I said – close to tears.

"*Tsk*, you are dreaming, girl. You're no better than me," Salama says harshly.

"I'm not saying I am. I . . . just can't."

"You think you're better than me, but you're the stupidest kind of *malaya*: the one that doesn't even get paid." Drops of spit are flying from her mouth. "*Tsk*," she says, drying eyes that are wet with anger.

"No, no. I'm sorry," I say.

"You're a stupid girl," she says. "Three weeks, tops."

"Yes," I say. Three weeks – what am I to do?

"And now you have to leave the room," Salama says.

"But I thought you were going out?" I say.

"*Tsk*, you really can't fill in any of the blanks yourself, can you?" Salama says. "I need the room for my dirty work. If I have a room, I get a better price."

I get some clothes together and go down to the local tailor where we once rented a sewing machine to alter some clothes – me, Anna, Salama and Deborah. It's seems like a different life, but it was only two and a half years ago. I ask him if he can give me any work. The answer is no. I borrow his machine for a few hours and fix up my clothes. On my way back I meet Deborah. Her bandages are off. The bits of her cheek and nose were sewn up unevenly by the doctor and they've healed up in a strange way. Deborah's entire face now looks like a permanent accident. She is working again – she's very cheap now.

The next day I'm at the market at Kiborloni, but not to buy – I am selling my good clothes just to have something to eat.

41.

A white man comes with Marcus onto the terrace at *mama mtilie*'s. The white man looks at me while they go over to look at the food. He's wearing trainers, shorts, a worn T-shirt – but that doesn't mean anything, because all the *wazungu* are rich. He turns his head to look. I just go about doing my job. But I'm wearing my tight-fitting leopard-print skirt, and my T-shirt is tight so my *titis* are like naked. I look at him. I wonder how old he is. It's difficult to tell with white people – they all look the same. But Marcus is a good man and owns a shop nearby. His girlfriend Claire is always very stylish and sells clothes from their shop by Stereo Bar. The white man goes over and washes his hands while *mama mtilie* loads their food onto plates. The white man says something in English to Marcus, who calls to me to fetch two fizzy drinks from the shop. The white man says in English that I can take one for myself, I think.

"Get one for yourself as well, if you want to," Marcus says to me in Swahili.

"Thank you," I say. The white man pulls a lot of scrunched-up notes out of his pocket and hands one of them to me. I hurry to the shop and when I return they have been served. I go to their table with their drinks and the change. The white man looks at me. He says to Marcus in English that I was meant to buy one for myself as well.

"You were supposed to buy one for yourself as well," Marcus says in Swahili.

"I have bought it," I say. "But I'm saving it till after work." The money is in my pocket.

"She has kept the money for it," Marcus tells him in English.

"I don't mind," the white man says.

Marcus asks me to fetch some *pili-pili*, and I do. Even though the white man has rice, he tastes a bit of Marcus' corn porridge as well. Sometime later *mama* says that I should go and ask them if they need anything.

"Do you need anything? Is the food alright?" I ask.

"Yes, it's fine," Marcus says.

"*Nzuri sana*," the white man says.

"You speak Swahili," I say and can't help laughing.

"The *mzungu* has been here before," Marcus says.

"I don't speak very much," the white man says in Swahili. They have fish. Marcus has had the head while the *mzungu* has the tail.

"Which part of the fish is the tastiest?" Marcus asks, looking at me.

"It's all tasty," I say.

"No," Marcus says, "there has to be one part of the fish which tastes better than the other parts."

"No," I say, "because it's all the same fish."

"But what about you – isn't there a part of you that is just a little bit tastier than the rest?" Marcus asks. I hesitate a little.

"Yes," I say.

"Which bit is that then?" Marcus asks. I look away. Then I make a quick gesture towards my lap while I smile:

"This bit," I say. Marcus giggles, and the *mzungu* gives me a strange look, and then we all start laughing, and I turn around and walk away – slowly, so he can see everything I've got. I sit down at another table and look at the *mzungu*. He turns his head and looks me in the eye. I don't look away. He's thinking what men think.

They finish their food.

"Come," Marcus says. I go over to them. "What's your name?" he asks.

"Rachel," I say. The *mzungu* pays me for their food with a large banknote – I owe him a lot of change from that.

"Keep the change," he says in Swahili.

"Thank you," I say. First the fizzy drink and now the large tip. He's not old. And the money's there, even though his clothes are worn.

"How do you like my *mzungu*?" Marcus asks.

"I don't know," I say.

"Oh, come on," Marcus says. I look down.

"I like him," I say and turn around and walk away from the table.

"Enough!" the *mzungu* says in Swahili to Marcus, and they both laugh.

42.

Faizal hasn't discovered me yet. It's like the first time I came to Moshi Hotel; he is surrounded by girls who think he owns all the music machines and has big money. He is one big, hard lie.

"Four beers," Alwyn tells the waitress.

"I just want a fizzy drink," I say. The waitress looks over at me and then at Alwyn.

"Four beers," he repeats. He's the one paying, and he's the one who gets to decide. Salama is there as well, and Tito – Alwyn's big, blue-black right-hand man who drove me to Newcastle Hotel the first time I was to have dinner with a *bwana mkubwa*, the time I ended up running away. We're sitting at a table outside on the large, raised terrace. It's surrounded by lovely green plants, so you can't look in on the party when you're walking by on the street – but you can hear the music beckoning.

"Go over and dance with Salama," Alwyn says. We walk onto the dance floor. The men study us. I see Rogarth come onto the terrace with a *bwana mkubwa*. I haven't talked to Rogarth since things went wrong with *bwana* Mbuya, even though I know it wasn't his fault. But Rogarth is a dogsbody for the rich men – he can't help me.

There are *wazungu* men here as well; oldish and drunk – they work for

European aid projects in Moshi. Salama looks one of them in the eyes, and I can see him studying her body.

"Those *wazungu* are married," I say. "I've seen them in the market with their wives."

"Yes," Salama says. "But white women have no arse, and they dance like wooden logs. White men are always dreaming about the erotic girl from Africa."

"Just to use her for a single night – *tsk*," I say.

"Not always for a single night. Some *wazungu* divorce their wives when they get a taste of the black miracle. And then they marry the black girl and take her back with them to Europe," Salama says.

"They marry a girl they know is a *malaya*? That's not true," I say.

"They know nothing. You don't tell the *mzungu* that you want soap-money. You just tell him you work in an office. He'll give you presents automatically. You get to experience exciting things. And if he likes you, you can have it all."

"But not if you have a child as well," I say.

"It happened to a girl who had a child here in Moshi," Salama says. "She got married to a white man and now she is in Europe with her child."

"But those men are old."

"Old is good. Then they'll die, and you'll inherit everything." Salama is crazy. How can you be with an old man like that? There are four *wazungu* tourists at the bar – two men, two girls. They're wearing T-shirts with pictures of Kilimanjaro and have been badly sunburned – they've probably just come down from the top. All the *waafrika* are wearing good clothes – even the poor ones who come to the disco in their church clothes. But these *wazungu* have dirty boots on and wear worn trousers. I never did understand that – the white wealth is crazy. I know it very well – I haven't just seen it in the cinema, but with my own eyes. Edward gave me a trial at his work for two weeks just before he fell ill. He wanted to see if I could work there, because by then I had been at home long enough. The work was with a camping trip to Serengeti and Ngorongoro for *wazungu* from America. I was there as a waitress at the meals – helping the cooks with the prep, laying the tables, serving, washing up. You think your eyes are lying when you see it. The table is set with a white tablecloth, fine china. Each person gets several differently-shaped wine glasses and many knives and forks. For each course they use a new sort of knife and fork; in the middle of the bush, outdoors, while lions roar and buffalos grunt. It's true. A giant truck drives all their equipment and supplies. In the middle of the night I have to get up to prepare pancakes, omelettes, toast, coffee and freshly squeezed juice. When the white people have driven off to photograph the animals, we have to take the whole thing down again, move it and set it all up again somewhere else. You have tents that are showers with wooden floors. The water tank is on the lorry – it's put up on a stand during the day so the sun can heat the water for when the white people return and want to wash a little dust off. Eight *wazungu* are customers on the safari, but there are just as many of us working to make everything perfect for them. It was a very exciting life, but Edward died before he could get me into that sort of work.

Salama dances very naughtily, like her hips are on ball bearings, and now I can see that Faizal has spotted us. We're standing at the edge of the dance floor, and Rogarth comes over and says something to Salama but I can't hear what because of the music. Salama sends him over to talk to Alwyn. I watch how Rogarth goes over to Alwyn and then on to a *bwana mkubwa*, and finally back to us, whispering something in Salama's ear. She nods.

"I have to go," she says. "See you later." Rogarth escorts her out to the terrace and through the gate. Faizal is standing by the machines, staring at me. The *bwana mkubwa* Rogarth spoke to gets up and leaves. The soap-money has been agreed on, the pumping awaits at K.N.C.U. Hotel. *Ee-ehhh*, Faizal has left his machines and comes through the dancers towards me. He grabs my arm.

"What are you doing here?" he shouts.

"That's my business," I say.

"Those people you're with – they're *malaya*, thieves," he shouts, shaking my arm.

"*Tsk*," I say. "Don't tell me what to do."

"You're my wife," he says. "I don't want you to be like that."

"I'm only your wife if you pay for your daughter," I shout while I try to pull my arm out of his grasp. Faizal aims a punch at my face. I duck so his hand hits my ear – I go deaf, almost. People next to us have stopped dancing and stare at us. But the music and the lights continue.

"You're a bad husband," I shout, and Faizal raises his hand again. I duck, but the punch never comes. I look. Alwyn is there and has taken hold of Faizal's arm and speaks into his ear. Faizal lets go of me, turns around and leaves.

"A girl like you needs protection. There are all sorts of dangerous people here," Alwyn says.

"I have to leave," I say, "or I'll miss the last *matatu*."

"I'll take you home later," Alwyn says.

"But I have to go to work tomorrow morning," I say.

"Don't worry, we'll go soon," Alwyn says and leads me back to the table. "Drink your beer." I know I should go, because Alwyn has already paid my entrance fee and bought me a beer. So now he can start saying I owe him. I don't like it. Then I see that the *mzungu* from *mama mtilie*'s is at one of the tables talking to Rogarth, offering him a European cigarette. It looks like they know each other – perhaps from the international school? I empty my beer glass.

"No, I really have to go now," I say to Alwyn.

"O.K., I'll take you." He gets up. We leave the terrace without the *mzungu* seeing me. Alwyn drives us to Majengo.

"You know I can help you make good money," Alwyn says.

"Yes," I say. I know.

"All you have to do is say the word," Alwyn says. "I'll look after you."

"I'll think about it," I say. Alwyn is a bastard. He only wants to sell me as a *malaya* and take the lion's share of the profit. Alwyn stops his car outside Salama's house, turning off the engine.

"Thank you very much," I say and am about to open the car door.

"Wait," he says and puts his hand on my arm. "Come here – let me taste your mouth."

"What do you want to do that for?" I say.

"As a thank-you for driving you home."

"*Enough*!"

"Give me a taste – your mouth looks nice." I lean over and give him a quick kiss – I want to pull away, but he grabs on to my neck and pushes his tongue between my lips, and then he takes my breast with his other hand.

"You taste nice," he says and lets go of my breast, taking my hand and guiding it to his pump. "Do the job," he says. His pump feels hard through his trousers. I rub the fabric. Alwyn can help me – he's rich, he's got connections. He opens his trousers, and his pump springs out. I grab it and yank at it to make him finish quickly and tire.

"Go slowly," he says, so I have to do it slowly while he pulls at my nipples. He pulls a lever by his side and pushes the seat back as far as it can go. "Pull up your skirt so you can ride me." I let go of his pump.

"Do you have a sock?" I ask.

"A sock? Would you suck a sweet with the paper still on it?"

"I already have one child I can't afford."

"*Kulamba kono*," he says. "That won't get you pregnant." I twist myself out of his grasp.

"*Ah-ahhh*," I said. "I'm not doing that." Does he think I'll eat his ice cream cone in return for a little beer and a drive in his car? I push the door open and get out.

"You know the work well," Alwyn says. I am standing on the street.

"You're crazy."

"You'll eat up soon enough, little sister," he says and laughs. I slam the door shut and go to the room while the car starts behind me. Alwyn honks the horn three times – almost like he's laughing. I have a hard time getting my key into the lock. I'm shaking.

43.

"Can I have my salary?" I ask *mama mtilie*. "I really need the money."

"You'll have to wait a few more days – I don't have it right now," she says. What can I do?

Rogarth comes to have lunch.

"You look sad, Rachel. How are things?"

"Not good," I say.

"I'm sorry. What's wrong?"

"I need money."

"Yes, there's no money to be had," he says and stares into thin air. I want to ask him if he really knows the *mzungu* who was at Moshi Hotel Friday night, or if the *mzungu* was looking for a *mwafrika* girl to make him happy? I fetch salt for Rogarth. I like him – I wish he had just a little money, so we could be together. But I have to find a way to get Jasmina back. That's not going to happen with Rogarth – he's got nothing. Only what he can scrape together from one day to the next. I'm so afraid that I'm shivering. Almost all roads are closed to me. The English lessons are coming to an end, and the money's gone, and the chances of me getting any more for Jasmina are looking bleak. Then I'll have to be dirty all the time. Maybe I won't be able to do it.

Lunchtime is almost over when the *mzungu* shows up. He looks around while I quickly look down at myself. I am wearing black-and-white pinstriped gabardine trousers and a black T-shirt and *malapa*. I mustn't be sad when he's here. He has to see a lovely girl. I look up. He's standing there looking at me.

"How are you, sister?" he asks in Swahili, and I smile because I feel happy, but also a bit nervous because . . . how do I do this? He's thinking what men think, but is he thinking more than that?

I'm serving someone else as he sits down at Rogarth's table. Then I fetch the food for the *mzungu* – pilaf, which is the only thing left, except for corn porridge and bean sauce. I go over with his plate, focusing on looking confident and relaxed.

"Do you like him?" Rogarth asks and points to the *mzungu*.

"I might," I say and leave. Rogarth has finished and has to go. I walk behind the partition wall and fill my plate with corn porridge and bean sauce and a little pilaf – I eat at work now until I am completely stuffed, so I don't have to use my own money on food at night. I go to the large table in the shade of the tree and sit down. I concentrate on not looking at the *mzungu*. What should I say to him? He goes to the counter to pay. I don't turn around. He comes back, towards me – I can hear his steps on the ground. He puts a hand on the back of my chair, leans forward close to me.

"Why are you sitting over here, when I'm sitting over there?" he asks in Swahili.

"I don't know," I say. "I think I just wanted to sit alone."

"Do you mind if I sit down?" he asks.

"No."

"That's good," he says and sits down. "My name's Christian. What's yours?"

"Rachel."

"Rachel. Where do you live?" Christian asks.

"Down in Majengo." Maybe he doesn't know that it's a bad place.

"With your family?" he asks.

"With my aunt and her daughter." I don't know why I lie, but I think it sounds better that way.

"Do you dance?" he asks

"Yes," I say.

"Liberty – do you go there on weekends?"

"Is it that place on the other side of Clock Tower?" I ask.

"Yes," he says.

"I don't know," I say and wait for him to invite me. Ask me where I live, so he can pick me up. Oh, it has to work, so that I won't have to . . .

"I'm not really sure," he says. "Maybe I'm doing something in Arusha, so it might not be till Saturday that I go." Christian says goodbye and leaves. How can I go to Liberty both Friday and Saturday if he doesn't come? It's not possible without money. I have to be there. I have to sit at the bar on the terrace because there's no entrance fee there – only if you're going into the disco itself. But how can I sit there for two nights, making a Coke last? If Salama sees that I've bought a Coke, she'll be angry; all the money I haven't got, I already owe her.

44.

"I don't want you working here anymore. I want you to go right now," *mama mtilie* says the next morning.

"Why?" I ask.

"You're a dirty girl – a *malaya*. I don't want someone like that serving my guests," she says. How does she know?

"I'm not a *malaya* – never."

"Everyone knows what you did at K.N.C.U. Hotel – the entire street is talking about how dirty you are." Me? And what about Mbuya? Is he squeaky clean? He lied to me, used me, tricked me – but he's a *bwana mkubwa* with money, so everyone bows down before him as if he were God himself.

"I need my money – my salary," I say.

"Money? You get your money elsewhere."

"I'll tell the police."

"The police? They don't care about a little *malaya* like you."

"I'll go to the chaplain and tell him you steal my salary."

"Oh, stop it!" she says and gets out the money from her little box, throwing it on the ground. I pick it up. I leave before the tears come – I don't want her to see them. I go to Auntie at the market.

"Can I come and live with you for a while – I have lost my job," I say.

"You! I don't want you in my house. I am ashamed of being related to you. You're dirty, evil. I've heard everything about you. You're a *malaya*. Nothing more."

"I am not a *malaya*."

"Then what do you call spreading your legs for money?"

"I was with a man – we were together. But not for money."

"Do you think that a man wants a stupid girl like you? You're a *malaya* – if you didn't get paid for it, then you're more stupid than I thought." Everyone's looking at us.

"Yes," I say. "Perhaps I am stupid. But you're my mother's sister, and I really need your help so my life can become right again."

"I am glad my sister is with God," Auntie says. "She would die of shame, if she saw you now." She says that about my mother. *PAH* – I slap her in the face.

"*Shetani*," I say and spit on her, turning around and walking away.

"I'll write to your father," she shouts behind me.

She thinks it is God's work she's doing; it's Satan's.

45.

"I need that money, Rachel. I can't spare it," Salama says.

"But . . . I don't have it right now."

"It's Alwyn's money. He wants it now – or he'll beat me." Alwyn's?

"Why did you lend me Alwyn's money?" I ask.

"*Tsk*. You cried and begged me to lend you money so you can live without touching dirty pumps in Majengo. I have a rent to pay. I have my son at my mother's."

I don't say anything. Salama continues:

"How can I get money for them, and for myself and for you? Alwyn helped me. If I don't pay, I'll have to see Tito, and his beatings hurt like giving birth to a cow. And then I'd be out on the street right afterwards; anyone's always welcome on the street."

"But how can I . . . ? I can't get that money, I don't have anyone to go to," I say. What else can I say? No-one can help me.

"You haven't tried to get the money. You don't want to embrace your options, because everything has to be so clean for you, like you were the Virgin Mary. But you're not a virgin – you're just a stupid girl who gets pregnant with some poor church mouse the first time she's wicked. And afterwards you believe the empty words of some *bwana mkubwa*. And now you want to ruin me as well," Salama says.

"I promise I'll do . . . something," I say.

"What?" Salama says.

"I'll . . . I'll talk to Alwyn. Now. Tonight."

"Then get changed – get ready. Now. I'm meeting him at Strangeways in a bit. You come with me," Salama says and grabs her handbag.

"Yes," I say. Salama goes outside. I put on my tightest outfit, quickly. Dab some colour on my lips, coconut oil in my hair, vaseline on my skin. I go to the kiosk and buy two small bags of Konyagi with my very last money – I down them and wash them down with water. Then I go to Strangeways. Alwyn isn't there yet. Salama sits at a table, smoking. I sit down. She doesn't speak to me, doesn't look at me, just hands me the cigarette. We wait. Then Alwyn's car pulls up. He honks the horn.

"Come on," Salama says. We run over to the car. He has wound down the window. He's playing Zaire Rock. The engine's running. Alwyn looks at me.

"Shall we get going?" Salama says.

"I'll pick you up in a bit, Salama," Alwyn says. "Get in, Rachel. We're going for a little drive." I get into the car, shutting the door. Salama walks back towards the bar, but I catch a glimpse of her smile – it's nasty. I'm no better than her.

We drive for a while with only the sound of the music, which is good, but today it doesn't work. Alwyn stops in a dark alley. He pushes his seat back. I start pulling up my skirt.

"*Ah-ahhh*," he says, shaking his head. "*Kulambo kono*." I do it.

"Time for you to go to work," Alwyn says and starts the car. To Shanty Town – a large house. "I don't want to hear any nonsense," he says. "Salama is a Majengo *malaya* – dirty talk and bad manners. I don't want you to be like that. You'll be the innocent girl from the village. Natural and erotic and sweet. Never talk about money – ever. I'll fix it when I pick you up. In three hours." He grabs my neck, squeezes it and says: "No nonsense."

I get out, go over and knock on the door.

"*Hodi?*" I call

"*Karibu*," a voice says. A man opens the door. The man who is married to the regional commissioner's niece; Henry, who kneaded my thigh at Liberty, knocked over bottles in the bar in Majengo and ranted about his black mamba when I refused him. "This is a surprise," he says. "I thought I was getting a visit from Salama. A pleasant surprise." But there's nothing pleasant about it. He hits me, hard, several times while he does his business. Afterwards I take a shower, but he comes out and does it again, doggy-style, the rear-most way. That can never be washed off.

"He hit me," I tell Alwyn when I sit in the car.

"Yes, he's a bad man, but he's related to the regional commissioner, so he can do whatever he wants. And he pays well." Alwyn drives me back to Salama's room in Majengo.

"Do you want me to do anything for you?" I ask.

"Just get out," Alwyn says.

"What about my money?" I ask.

"The money's mine. You owe it," Alwyn says. I get out. He drives off. You can brush your teeth for as long as you can keep your arm going – it doesn't help.

46.

Anna is married now. I wasn't invited. One day I see her walking around town, shopping with her new mother-in-law. Anna looks away when she sees me. No-one can know she has a relative who is a *malaya*.

In the evenings, Tito looks after me. He doesn't have a car like Alwyn – he does everything by taxi.

A house in Shanty Town, a guesthouse in Soweto, a villa in Old Moshi. Fat, rich men. Is that a life? I am everything Alwyn tells me to be. The men pay their money to businessmen, the men who protect and escort the girl in this dangerous city. The erotic atmosphere arises between the man and the girl out of desire, and because the man is so big that it overpowers the little village girl and makes her dive into the man's arms. If I didn't want it, it would just be an evening of lovely company and conversation. The attraction is mutual, makes me dance and undress in front of the man. But why do I always love the man and want to have his pump enter every part of my body? A big deception, hypocrisy. But the money is there. For rent and food, to send home to the village and Jasmina, to pay the hairdresser, for a new dress and new shoes. For Coke with Konyagi. For good food. For soap so I can wash away the ugliness and relax in my room with Zaire Rock on Salama's tape recorder. I think about . . . I don't want to think.

47.

Saturday Alwyn says that I am going to Liberty with Tito.

"Why?"

"We're putting you on display," Alwyn says.

"At Liberty? That's a bad place," I say. Christian the *mzungu* can't see me like that.

"The men just have to see you there. You're not working – not until later. Salama will be there as well." What can I say?

We're sitting at Liberty; the sound is bad; the people are the bad sort. I dance with Salama for a while and then sit back down with Tito. There are fish in the sea here – *wabwana wakubwa* looking at girls. Who would they like to buy? Then I see a *mzungu* on the other side of the room? Is it Christian? White people are difficult to recognize. It is him! Because Marcus sits down at the same table. They talk and laugh. Christian signs to a waitress and buys beer for himself and Marcus. Christian isn't old like the white men who go out with young black girls just for the sake of pumping them. Christian is young. I'd like to talk to that *mzungu*, but how can I when I barely speak English? It's impossible. And Tito is watching me – what would he say if I made eyes at a white man? Salama is standing close to the *mzungu* on the edge of the dance floor, in a very small tight dress – she's rotating on the ball bearings in her hips. The *mzungu* says something to Marcus who shakes his head, waves her off. My *mzungu* doesn't want a *malaya* like that. He wants Rachel – I hope.

"I'm just going to the toilet," I tell Tito and go out and stand just inside the door to the ladies room with the door ajar. When I see him come out of the men's room, I go out at the same time and almost bump into him.

"Rachel," he says, sounding surprised.

"Christian. You came," I say, throwing my arms around his neck. He puts his arms tight around me. I press him close, so he can feel everything I've got. I smile. The music is loud. I try to explain that I'm here with a friend. Tito is waiting for me. I say I have to get back to my friend. But Christian comes with me – that's not good. He says hello to Tito who looks angry.

"You," he says. "You just want to use my girl."

"What?" Christian says.

"You just want to pump the black girl and then leave her," Tito says above the music.

"No," Christian says, putting his hand on Tito's shoulder, leaning forward so he can hear him: "You're quite wrong." Tito looks down on the white hand until Christian removes it.

"I am not wrong," Tito says. "You white people are bad: you use our girls and then don't care what happens to them."

"It's not like that," Christian says in Swahili and looks at me while he points across the room. "I'm sitting over there with Marcus – you can come say hello if you want to." Then he leaves. I want to, but what can I do? The evening's a disaster.

"You better be careful about these people," Tito says. "They promise the world, but it's all a lie." Salama comes over to us. She doesn't know I know the *mzungu* a little.

"Does he want Rachel?" she asks.

"White men are no good," Tito says. "They think the girl is for free. What did that *bwana* Marcus tell you?"

"*Tsk*," Salama says. "He said the *mzungu* already had a girl, that he doesn't want my sort of girl."

"What sort of girl does he have?" I ask. "I don't see any girl."

"I don't know," Salama says. Not long after the *mzungu* leaves with Marcus. He nods at me on the way out. I smile. Tito glares at me.

"I don't want you mixing with that *mzungu*," he says.

"No, no," I say.

48.

A new year, 1987; I should celebrate – I have become a complete *malaya*. Christian the *mzungu* has gone. I haven't seen him for weeks. I don't want to ask Rogarth about him – then he'll understand my plan to catch the white man. But Christian has probably gone home to the wonderful life in Europe. Rogarth likes me. But he is poor, so I have to live my dirty life to get my money for my own and Jasmina's survival.

"Tonight I'll drive you," Alwyn says. "Wait for me at Stereo Bar." I take a shower and get dressed up before I make my way – in no hurry, but leaving enough time to drink a Coke before he gets there.

I go over to have a look around at Roots Rock. Maybe Christian is there with Marcus. The recording shop is up and running again, there are new machines, plenty of L.P.s. It has to be the *mzungu* who owns it! Then he must still be in Tanzania. But he's not in the shop.

"Hello, Rachel," the voice behind me says. I turn around. He has come out of Stereo Bar.

"Christian!" I say.

"So, did you get in trouble with your boyfriend?" he asks in Swahili.

"He's not my boyfriend – just a friend."

"Then why was he so angry?" Christian asks, and because he's white I can't read the expression on his face.

"It's not like that," I say. "He's just trying to look after me."

"Do you want a Coke?" Christian asks. I nod and smile. We go down to the shop, and Christian buys two bottles from my old fridge on the pavement. We sit down on one of the benches.

"Your Swahili has improved," I say.

"It's waking up. When I lived here a year and a half ago, I spoke it well."

"You're speaking it well now," I say.

"Thank you," he says. "Why have you stopped working over there?" he asks and points at the bad *mama mtilie*'s behind the Tanesco building.

"I've got a better job," I say.

"Oh, doing what?" he asks.

"I am a hostess at a restaurant."

"Alright. Where?"

"Up in Shanty Town.

"Which one? I could come eat there," Christian says.

"No," I say, smiling at him. "Don't do that, because then I'd be working. Then we wouldn't be able to relax together. Do you live in Moshi?" I ask to change the subject.

"My family lives here," he says. "I think I'll probably stay on as well."

"That's good," I say.

"So what do you do when you're not working?" he asks.

"I used to take English lessons at the K.N.C.U., but now I can't afford them anymore because I have to send money home to my parents in the village." I say nothing about Jasmina.

"How much are English lessons?" he asks. I tell him.

"That's not so bad," he says. Maybe he'll help me. If he gives me the money, I could send some home to the village and still have enough money for food and rent while I get to know him. Then I don't have to be wicked every day. But I mustn't dream. Too many dreams make for one big disappointment.

"I'd like to see where you live," he says.

"No, no, you can't – my aunt is very strict. I'm looking for my own place, but I can't afford to because I'm trying to save up for lessons. But I'd like to find a room I can share with another girl. If I get one, you can come and visit."

"Christian," someone calls from a car. It's two *wazungu* women – one of them is young. Christian gets up. Just then I catch sight of Alwyn in his car. He honks his horn and waves at me. I get up.

"Do you know him?" Christian asks.

"Yes," I say. "It's my boss – he's giving me a lift to work." I look at the younger *wazungu* woman in the car. "Is that your girlfriend?" I ask. It's me he should love – it's important. That's the dream.

"No," he says. "It's just a girl I know." I don't believe him. But she looked as bitter as a lemon when she saw me with him. I am a lot more erotic than she is – I can love him, just once, and he'll have forgotten all about her. Alwyn honks his horn again.

"See you soon, I hope," Christian says.

"I'd like that, but I have to go now," I say and walk towards Alwyn's car and get in.

"What are you doing with that *mzungu*?" Alwyn asks.

"He likes me – maybe I am going to be with him," I say.

"No," Alwyn says. "You work for me."

"I decide if I want to work or not. I don't owe you anything."

"I've saved you from disaster. Do you want to be like Deborah?" Alwyn says.

"If the *mzungu* wants me, then I'll be with him. It's my chance," I say. Alwyn grabs me by the arm – hard. It hurts.

"You do as I say. If not, you'll have worse things happen to you than Deborah did." He lets go of my arm. Alwyn lives off my dirty job – he's trying to scare me.

"You can't sell me to all the *wabwana wakubwa* at a very high price if you've cut my face," I say.

"Maybe I can have Tito fix the *mzungu*," Alwyn says dreamily. "Do you know how Tito can wreck a man?" I don't say anything else. Tito looks very brutal. Alwyn takes me to the pumping. Picks me up after three hours and drives me back to Majengo. He hands me a little money and disappears. I go over to the kiosk. Order a Konyagi that I dilute with Coke. Sit down on the bench.

What should I do? Should I go to the police to stop Alwyn and Tito? Say that they threatened to cut me? The policeman will say: "I can't find the men you're talking about – they've disappeared. Maybe you can help me. If we meet later tonight, you can tell me more about them. Because right now, at the office, there's so much work to be done and I don't have much time." And then the policeman's help will have to be bought with my fruit. *Tsk.*

A young girl walks past the kiosk with her mother. The girl stares at me – my nice clothes. The mother looks straight ahead and won't dignify me with a look. The girl looks innocent as she pleads with her mother for a fizzy drink. Her mother says no, and they disappear into the dark. I want to crawl into that girl and run away from my life. I used to be like her. Not even three years ago. The girl looks over her shoulder at me. I see the dream in her eyes; she wants to be me. She doesn't know the price of nice clothes and money for fizzy drinks. You don't get a lot of chances in life. I have to take mine. Christian is my chance.

The Path of the Snake

I

Seven years I've spent in darkness. Pebbles, scraps, that's it. Enough to replace the worn-out shirt on my back and buy a little *bhangi* and *gongo* so I can escape into sleep – but only just. I sit in the shade under the lean-to and eat my wages: corn porridge and beans. The tin roof crackles in the scorching sun. I lie down on my back and close my eyes. How can it have been seven years? They stink like a dead dog on the roadside.

"Moses," my partner, Shirazi, says, handing me the cigarette he's rolled from a strip of newspaper.

I smoke slowly until the embers burn my lips. The coarse tobacco rasps my throat. I look out over the landscape. The mines are in the valley at the foot of the Blue Mountains southwest of Kilimanjaro. The ground is almost without vegetation – everywhere you look quartz and graphite dust glitters in the sunlight. We call it Zaire, named after the country where they dig for gold and diamonds and find great riches. Where we are, it's tanzanite stones that will give us fortunes to buy a heavenly life.

"Move it!" Hamza bellows – he's the boss' right-hand man. We're going into the pit. Shirazi ushers the workers towards the tunnel down to the shaft. I get up and put on my torch – adjusting it so the cone of light will be right. It's not a hard hat with a miner's lamp like the bosses have. We're dogs. We have bad Chinese torches with chrome shells that peel off in our dusty hair. We cut open car tyres, weave the torch into the strips, tie knots so we can stretch them around our skulls, with the lamp as a bump on the top.

I work for *mzee* Akrabi in a mine without a ladder. The poorest mines don't have ladders, because timber is expensive and has to be brought from far away. There's a rope tied at the top and crude steps carved into the wall of the narrow shaft. New workers get their hands cut up by the graphite dust on the rope, but with time they develop skin like the hoofs of a goat. Every metre and a half, you have a small platform where you can stand when the rubble bags are passed up to be emptied.

I climb down with Fillemon, who is the explosives expert. I've known him since we were children in Rongai.

Forty metres straight down the rope into the dark shaft until we reach the sedimentary quartz level. Onwards on hands and feet like monkeys through the tunnel: one metre high, two metres wide at best. The tunnels curve outwards and downwards in every direction; some of them are up to five hundred metres long. Above ground the plots lie cheek by jowl with only thirty metres between the shafts – below ground we move everywhere in our search for the seam of glasslike crystals towards the blue stone: tanzanite.

The tunnel is steep and filled with gravel. We move carefully, because if you're not careful, you may slip and fall twenty metres, and your body becomes a sack of bones.

We work at the bottom of the mine. The signs show that we are getting closer. The sedimentary level has lots of graphite, a sort of greasy coal that's used for pencils. And now the graphite is mixed with iron pyrites. Soon we hit the pocket of tanzanite. Fillemon points to where he wants the explosives to be buried in the rock. Shirazi and I start tapping out the holes; we use a hammer, a chisel and an iron rod. At *mzee*'s we don't have a pneumatic drill – everything is done by hand. It's not long before we're ready to blast.

"That's got it," Fillemon says. We cough and spit, because when you tap at the rock with a hammer and chisel, the graphite becomes a very fine dust which goes straight to your lungs. All day we swallow dust. Fillemon looks at me with the milky eye he got from a stone splinter that flew into it and ruined his sight. His good eye is almost red – inflamed by the dust, because we don't wear safety goggles; you can't get them out here. "Do we have any water?" he asks.

"*Nyoka,*" Shirazi shouts – snake; it's what we call the little boys because they can slither into even the smallest crack. It's the work of the snakes to fetch fresh water for us from above ground. The snakes cough as well; they're not fully grown, and the dust gets into the lungs and sows destruction.

A snake brings us a bottle. Fillemon crawls over to me. The ceiling is very low here. I take a gulp and hand him the bottle. He drinks and hands it to Shirazi. In a proper mine Fillemon would be paid in money, even when he didn't find stones, because he has the explosives expertise. But money is a big problem for *mzee* Akrabi. Only Hamza and the guard are paid proper wages, because they carry guns – *mzee* Akrabi has to ensure their loyalty until the day we harvest the fruit of the rock. Until that happens Fillemon's shirt is hanging in tatters from his back.

"We're ready to blast soon," he says and smiles.

"Good," I say and fetch the equipment. We stick small pegs of dynamite into the holes and connect them with fuses made from cordite, a smoke-free powder. At *mzee* Akrabi we use fuses; we can't afford detonators. When the fuse has been tied, we use a thin stick to gently push the explosives as far into the hole as possible so they can break the rock. We sweat profusely because the pit gets very hot when so many men are working in it. The dust works its way into our sweaty clothes and skin – we're grey-black ghosts.

I send Fillemon, Shirazi and the others back through the tunnel and call on the three snakes:

"You'll each light your fuse, and then you'll come back," I say. They each hold their own little torches because it takes a miracle from God to get three Tanzanian matches to light at the same time. They nod silently.

"We're ready, Moses," the biggest of them says. I light their little torches with my lighter.

"Count to thirty aloud before you light the fuses," I tell them. "Start now." While they count, I move away slowly, down the tunnel on all fours – you mustn't hurry, that leaves a bad impression. Blasting is the most dangerous part. The tunnel might collapse. The rock is solid almost everywhere; it holds tight to its fruit. But still, the roof may collapse, the floor can disappear underneath you – the tunnels of neighbouring mines cross over and under each other – everyone follows the same signs. *Eeehhh* – if we meet, death comes.

I make it around a corner to where Hamza is standing. He is the boss' henchman – always there when we blast. The three snakes crawl up to us. Just then we hear an ear-splitting, dull explosion, and a cloud of glittering dust rushes towards us. I tie my handkerchief over my mouth. We wait until the dust has settled, and then Hamza moves in. He must be the first man on the scene, ready to pick up any large stones at gunpoint, to defend *mzee* Akrabi's property. If we've hit the seam, us workers will get a share. First the large stones go to the owner, and then the workers come in teams and are allowed to take what we can carry from the gravel and pebbles that the explosion has loosened. We get what's on the ground. But even among the pebbles on the floor a man may find enough to buy himself a Land Rover or a Peugeot, houses, women, a new life. When we only find a little, we use the money on worn-out *malaya* in Mererani Township, *gongo* and potent *bhangi*, so we can forget the pit for a while. It's not unfair. I have no future in the village – all the good land is taken. The mine is my best chance. *Mzee* Akrabi is giving me that chance by feeding me while I work.

"Have we hit it?" Fillemon calls to Hamza.

"No!" Hamza shouts back. "Moses. Come." I crawl over. The explosion has left rubble and bits of rock everywhere.

"Do you see any stone?" I ask.

"No," Hamza says. "But we're close." The signs are good. The rubble on the floor of the tunnel must be filled into sacks and carried up to the surface where it will be carefully examined for tanzanite stones before it's tossed on the rubble heap.

"Do you want us to set up another blast?" I ask.

"No," Hamza says. "Today we'll load the sacks, and tomorrow we'll haul them up while your people try to knock their way through."

"Good," I say. The last bit before the seam you have to be careful; a great blast can blow the tanzanite stones to bits and then they're not worth much; it's better to proceed by hand.

The work is begun.

"You fill the sacks," I tell the workers. Many of them are only big boys. I am old down here, even though I'm only nineteen. I have a position of trust, experience, I call the shots. At first I was a snake – now I am the snakes' ruler.

"Do the job," I tell the snakes harshly. They have shovels with short handles because there's no room for proper-sized tools in the tunnel, but they need something so they don't have to load the sacks with their hands – it would take too long. I make Fillemon and Shirazi tap stones out of the floor with hammer and chisel and iron rods which they knock into the rock where the blast has loosened the rock. Yes, we do have a real pick, but can you swing it when the ceiling is only a metre high? They squat down and hack the tunnel wider and deeper. The cones of light from their torches jerk abruptly across the walls of the low tunnel – slivers of stone leap from the wall into their faces.

"*Tsk*, the air is bad," Shirazi says and pants loudly.

"The blast was a big one – it has eaten the oxygen," I say. The air deep into the tunnels is always thin, and the blast leaves extra poison in the air. In the beginning it's really nasty, but you get used to it.

"Maybe they've turned off the air," Fillemon says.

"I'll check," I say. Up on the ground there's a shed with a generator that runs a compressor – it pumps air into the mine through a black pipe. But the generator can run out of diesel, or the compressor can break down. We would never hear it if the pipe were to go quiet, because we're picking, and tapping, and scraping, and hauling sacks. The air that comes out of our lungs isn't the same as the air that comes into them. The used air is dangerous, like exhaust fumes from a car. When new air is pumped down, the bad air is pressed out, but if the compressor stops and the bad air hangs around . . . It happened to me once; the dizziness was my signal – I had to hurry before the air ran out. I was on my hands and knees, I was crawling on my stomach – three men passed out; five hundred metres was their eternity. I find the air pipe and feel it – nothing. Just then Hamza comes down. He's been up to speak to *mzee* – to tell him the results of today's blast.

"Right, Moses – that's enough for today," Hamza says. "Get them up."

"Has the compressor broken down?" I ask.

"You're all getting out now, so I stopped it," Hamza says.

"Don't stop it before we get out – we'll suffocate," I say.

"Stop complaining," he says and crawls towards the shaft. I call the others.

"He's a swine," Fillemon says.

"Yes," I say. We crawl over and climb up to eat. I'm on the rope right under Shirazi. Every time he moves a foot in the shaft, stone dust falls into my eyes. I have to get myself a hat with a shade to protect my eyes from fallout. But in the shaft I feel the air improving; richer and cooler. We only go up to take food in or let it out. We hardly urinate, because we sweat. And getting up takes a long time, so we squirt down here instead.

The air up here is heavy – we might have rain soon. Then we'll have to sleep in the pit because *mzee* Akrabi doesn't have any proper sheds – only a lean-to that lets the driving rain in. There's only a few of us that have blankets; most sleep in cement sacks made of paper. The nights can get chilly in Zaire.

Mzee Akrabi has already left, and Hamza is headed for his motorbike. He has locked the shed where the generator, compressor and explosives are. Then there's only the guard left.

"You must put the compressor back on," I shout at Hamza. "Otherwise we'll be choked in our sleep."

"Diesel should be used for finding stones – not for sleeping," Hamza says and gets on his motorbike. Now he'll drive five kilometres to Mererani

Township where he lives with a young local woman.

"*Tsk*," Fillemon. "Now he'll sleep warm, while we lie on hard rock."

When we've had our one meal of the day, we sit and share a cigarette in the growing darkness. We don't feel like climbing down into our cement sacks. I go over to the cook, and he lets me into his little shed, where I have a small bag with my few possessions. I have an extra shirt. I take it and go back, handing it to Fillemon.

"Take it," I say.

"Are you sure?" he asks.

"Do you think I want to work with a man who's as naked as a barbarian?" I say.

"Thanks," Fillemon says. "I won't forget it."

"You can tell that to your Maker when you meet Him: Moses once gave you a shirt."

"You can tell Him that yourself," Fillemon says.

"Nope, I'm not going up there," I say.

"Where are you going then?" he asks. I point to the ground:

"Moses is going to hell," I say. Fillemon grins:

"You got here early." We slap hands. I roll a new cigarette from a strip of newspaper – handing it to Shirazi who is sitting staring, dreamily, into the dusk.

"We're going to the sea," he says. "When we've picked the seam, I'm showing you the sea." He is *mswahili*. On the mountain we'd call him *mwarabu-coco* – half Arab, half black. The Arab bit is his father, who pumped a black woman. The family live in a village near Doda on the coast north of Tanga, where Shirazi's father works as a taxi driver.

I have never seen the sea – only a lake at a long distance when I left home to look for my fortune in Zaire – my family have too little land to live like people. I rode on the back of a lorry from Rongai on the other side of Kilimanjaro, on the eastern slopes. I could see the entire country beneath me; there was Lake Jipe on the borders of Kenya, and in the south was the water reservoir Nyamba ya Mungu.

"We can drive up to Mombasa," Shirazi says. "*Wahuuu* – the best discos with the nicest Kenyan girls."

"You've never been to Mombasa," I say.

"*Tsk*. I've heard about it," Shirazi says, spitting.

Five years ago, he heard it – before he even came here. Maybe his entire family is dead, his village washed away by the sea in an almighty storm. Maybe the rest of the world has gone; Zaire is all that exists – the dream of a blue stone.

Five years I have known Shirazi. He was given a job in my mine when he first came to Zaire; so scared even though he was strong. He came to me, apologetically, in the tunnel. "Excuse me, where's north?" he asked. I didn't understand. He said: "I have to know where Mecca is, so I can pray. It's Friday." I pointed at random – let him pray with his arse. Every Friday he asked, and I pointed. We became friends. These days I try to point him in the right direction.

Fillemon doesn't say anything. He doesn't believe in dreams of Mombasa. He has been here as long as I have. We were friends back in the village in Rongai. Our mothers dragged us to the same church, and we went to the same school. Yes, we can read. But what is there for us to read in Zaire? There are no books underground. Not even a headstone we can read, because the dead live under rubble; they don't use words.

A motorbike comes up. It's Jackson. He's wearing sunglasses, even though it's almost dark, but he wants to show his wealth while we go to him in our rags to sell scraps.

"Have you got anything?" he asks. Shirazi shows him the tiny stone he has carried in his mouth all day.

"Do you have *bhangi*?" I ask. Jackson stays on his motorbike. T-shirt, jeans, sneakers. Clean clothes – only a little dirty from the dust on the road. He leans forward, raises his sunglasses, and looks at the stone in Shirazi's hand.

"It's very small," he says. "I can give you three sticks."

"*Tsk*," I say. Jackson was a miner like us until a couple of years ago. But then they hit a good seam in his mine. These days he's a middleman. I once saved him from being pumped by six snakes who had forced him into the bottom of a mine tunnel. But these days the only law Jackson abides by is the law of money.

It happens to many miners after a few years. They hit a small profit and escape the pit – they feel that the darkness has become an evil spirit in their bodies, so they give up hope. Some become guards to the plot-owners, henchmen, drivers – regular salaries, better food. Others become middlemen, driving between Zaire and Mererani Township, buying the scraps we earn or steal, selling them to the buyers. It pays enough to live on but not enough for a house. And it tempts me, because the middlemen live in the light and the air – they sleep in beds, eat food that has meat in it, they don't cough, they can move on a motorbike, feel the wind, drive to Moshi and Arusha to party. They can be with a woman, forget the shuttered darkness. But I don't want to give up on the dream of the rich life.

Jackson has the three sticks of *bhangi* ready in his hand, and Shirazi is about to hand over the stone.

"Three sticks aren't enough," I say. Jackson turns his dark glasses on me.

"You can have more when you have a proper stone, Moses."

"It's not good that you cheat us," I say.

"The price is right. You can sell your boots – then I'll get you some good *gongo*," Jackson says and looks down at my boots; they're from the West, a strong house for my feet – the best thing I own.

"*Tsk*." I turn away and walk towards the shaft. Jackson has given up. A few good clothes and a motorbike aren't enough for a life. When I hit the great one, it'll be houses and cars for me. Motorbikes – maybe I'll have three. Then he can drive in the dust of Zaire while I pump nice ladies in Dar es Salaam.

We climb down the rope and lie down close to the shaft, so we can breathe. Before we go to sleep, we smoke a stick of *bhangi* from Arusha, very potent stuff. I share it with Shirazi and Fillemon while the others draw close. They haven't got any *bhangi*, but there's not much room, breathing alone will get you high. Everyone wants to forget the pit that is running away with our lives. But we don't sleep much – only a few hours. Why should we sleep? We're here to work. Down in the pit there's no day and night – only darkness and hope.

II

"You, stand at the end of the line," I tell a young man. "You, get up in the shaft," I tell another, who is strong.

"I don't want to be in the shaft," the strong one says. I slap his face, hard, my hand flat and fast.

"Do you want to eat?" I ask and look at him. He's about to answer, but his stomach answers for him. He goes to the rope and climbs to his spot. Working in the shaft is hard; you're given the fodder sacks full of rubble, hand them up to the next man – you constantly get sand in your eyes from the man above you. The sack is passed from hand to hand in the line up through the tunnel to the shaft to the light where other young men empty the rocks onto rubble heaps to be checked for little bits of tanzanite. The empty sacks go back down.

I crawl over to work with Fillemon, who is at the bottom of the tunnel, chipping away towards the seam . There's rubble everywhere. Soon we'll have to fill the sacks again. That presents us with a new problem. We're deep into the ground, close to the water table. The ground water starts to seep up through the bottom of the tunnel. The water is undrinkable – filled with disease. First it mixes with the dust and creates a greasy mud. But soon we're thigh-deep in water. We have no water pump, so if the tunnel is flooded, we'll have to abandon it.

"Shirazi, go up and tell *mzee* that the water is coming in fast," I say. I go back to the dry part of the tunnel and examine the pipe from the compressor.

It mustn't fall into the mud and clog up. I put my hand over the end of the pipe, feel the small pressure. Yes, air's still coming through. I pull it with me to get it closer to the men who are loading muddied rubble into sacks.

"We need sacks," Fillemon says. It's the work of the snakes to fetch them, but there are none here – they're all standing in the line. I crawl backwards to get the sacks. A large hand lifts me up and slams me into the wall while my entire body is hit by rubble, my ears deafened by the blast. I am wrapped in a thick cloud of dust – *eeehhh*, the greatest dread. A blast in the neighbouring mine. I see precisely nothing. Grit in my teeth, dust in my eyes. Sluggishly I move on my hands and knees, crawl – I have to get out before my lungs die. We never warn the neighbouring mines before we blast. I am crawling and coughing. I can see a little. It's clearing up now, and my torch is still shining from my head through the dust which swirls around me. I crawl on, spit, hold my T-shirt to my mouth, breathe, sit against the wall of the mine, shaking, while the dust settles around me. And now I see it – five metres along the tunnel, just where I was standing only a moment before: a wall of rubble and large pieces of rock. A minute ago the tunnel went on for another eight or ten metres. Now it's a wall. Everything has collapsed. Four men are inside that wall, or on the other side of it. The air pipe is lying under the collapsed rubble, but the pipe is made of plastic, made to transport water, not to carry rocks; it's been squashed by the weight and not a mouthful of fresh air will reach the people under the rocks. Suffocation. I grab my knife from my pocket and cut the pipe, so that air will not only come from the leaks in the faulty joints in the pipe but also to where I am going to be working. Hamza comes crawling towards me.

"It's a disaster," he says. "We were so close." Hamza only thinks about stones.

"Send people with spades and sacks – we have to get them out before they suffocate," I say. The blast has made my speaking voice sound hushed to my own ears.

"I have to go up and talk to *mzee*," Hamza says. "Maybe it's too dangerous to dig now."

"We have to try to get them out," I say.

"I have to talk to *mzee*," Hamza says. He's afraid. Four men may die – they may already be dead. The workers may get angry, dangerous. There's no police here, but if the story makes it to Arusha, they may send the army's special forces, the Field Force Unit, which could even shut down the entire area. We crawl back along the tunnel and come upon the workers who are moving sacks down the line. No-one's working.

"What's happened?" asks Shirazi, who is returning with empty sacks.

"A collapse," I say. "Four people are trapped." Everyone starts talking over each other.

"We're going back there to get them out," I say loudly. "We're saving our friends."

"Yes," people say and rush over to start digging. I follow Hamza. He starts climbing up the rope. He's wearing gloves. I don't need gloves.

Mzee Akrabi is standing at the top.

"The tunnel collapsed," Hamza says. "Four men were in there."

"But we can remove the rubble," I say. "It's loose. We can get to them and maybe we can save them." The tunnel is a tomb, but it may hold a real treasure.

"Then hurry down and dig," *mzee* Akrabi says. His hand is shaking as he lights his cigarette. He lets us dig for bodies in the hope of finding stones. The stones may be used for bribes so *mzee* doesn't get in trouble if the authorities hear about the dead workers.

I climb down and hurry back to the rubble wall. I get some men to shovel waste rocks away and others to fill sacks and yet others to haul the sacks away so we have room to work. I am digging alongside Shirazi. Fillemon is in there with his milky-white eye – maybe it's closed for good now. I shovel back rubble. For hours. Like a madman. To get to the trapped men before they suffocate, because perhaps the rubble is only a blockage in the

"Wait," I say. I drag the first body along the tunnel to the shaft. Hamza has lowered a rope for us. I tie the rope around a dead upper body and call to the people above. The body starts to rise in front of me and up the shaft, where it swings and bumps into the walls as it is pulled up. We move down to get the next body.

"What's that?" Shirazi asks and stops.

"Wait," I say and listen. I can hear hammering.

"It's further ahead," Shirazi says and crawls on. The sound becomes more noticeable.

"It's a neighbouring mine which has got close. Probably the people who blasted earlier," I say. Shirazi turns around, rushes past me, back. "What?" I say.

"It's dangerous," Shirazi says. "We have to talk to *mzee*." He disappears. Afraid. I crawl on. The last body is Fillemon's. The hammering continues, and I hear a crushing sound just across from me. The entire roof comes crashing down in front of me – an almighty noise. I cough and pull out my handkerchief. Through the dust I can see flickering torches shining towards me. The workers of the neighbouring mine.

"Madness," a man says above me.

"Our mine collapsed when you blasted," I say. A man appears in the opening with a gun in his hand and a hard hat with a good torch shining directly at me.

"Are you finding many stones?" he asks.

"No," I say. "The seam wasn't a rich one." I point to Fillemon. "I'm just working. Harvesting dead bodies."

"*Tsk*," the man says. "Get lost." And I pull Fillemon with me along the tunnel. He is my chicken and he can lay eggs. Really, he can. I tie the rope around him and take him up. Tomorrow we'll be sent down for the rubble. It'll be lifted up in sacks, and the sacks will have to be emptied, and all stones checked out under supervision. Maybe there is good tanzanite among them. I am not going to be here.

"We have to get them ready," *mzee* Akrabi says of the bodies. In his head are thoughts about the Field Force Unit. There's a risk the mine could be shut down. We have to bury the bodies, and it must be done right to avoid scaring the workers.

"I'll wash them," I say. The bodies are laid out under the lean-to. It's getting dark. I fetch water and a rag at the cook's. Go over, wipe their faces. Find my chicken. I open the milky-white eye and stick in my finger. Lodged between the eye and the skull is my stone. I dig it out of the eye cavity. "Thanks for your help, Fillemon," I whisper and put the stone in my boot, so I can feel it rubbing against my ankle – a nice sensation.

Mzee Akrabi has disappeared to speak to the owner of the mine we collided with. He is not a neighbour – our tunnels snake all over. On the surface, his pit is four hundred metres away. I go over to Shirazi.

"We're getting out of here," I whisper.

"Did you get the stone?" he whispers.

"Yes." We hurry out through the gate and off into the falling dusk. We're lucky: at the bumpy dirt road we can jump onto a tanker that has been to the mining area to sell clean drinking water.

III

We reach Mererani Township. It's dark now, but there's plenty of lights and life around here. The light reveals a disappointment, because our stone has a faint fracture line. It'll break in two when it's cut for a piece of jewellery. But it's too large to be sold on the street. We walk past little tables where Masaai are standing on one leg, leaning on the cattle-driving sticks with their red cloths wrapped around their bodies. They know their business, but you'll never see a Masaai climb into the pit – they can't live underground.

The ancients say that tanzanite was born out of fire. A lightning bolt started a steppe fire in the valley, and when the cowmen walked through the scorched countryside, they saw luminous blue stones on the ground which had never been seen before. The fire had brought out the particular colour of the stone. When you find the crystals, they can have many colours: grey, golden brown, purple, blue, green or a reddish lilac. The same stone can display several colours. But when you heat the stone over fire, the colour becomes a deep violet-blue that lasts forever and which women love. Only in this one place in the world can this stone be found.

We make it to the Indian's shop, Shah Jewellery. It's a small house and in front of it is the security guard – big arms and a gun in a holster under his jacket.

"Show me the stone," he says, because the very small stones can only be sold to middlemen on a motorbike. Shah only wants the larger stones or the perfect ones. I dig about in my boot, hold out the stone. "You wait here," the guard tells Shirazi and opens the door to me. First I stand in an antechamber with a secretary who's minding the phone – one of the first ones in Mererani Township. She is very plump and posh. Soon I am going to have a woman. She shows me into Shah's office, which has real furniture, Indian pictures on the walls and a sink in the corner. Shah is sitting behind his desk with his shining hair.

"Let me see," he says. I put the stone in front of him. He takes it up under the lamp, puts a magnifying glass in one eye and looks. Behind him is an advertisement poster: a white woman with smooth skin and shinning hair the colour of honey, and the jewellery – tanzanite. Yes, the stone makes a long journey from its pit. The beauty of her eyes is made wild by the thought of how much juice the negro has bled into the ground to dig the blue stone into the light so that it can shine on her pale throat.

"You can see that it's perfect," I say.

"I can see that it has a fracture line," Shah says. It's true. It will break during cutting, so it can only be used for small pieces of jewellery. There's a price per gram which decreases with each flaw the stone has.

"I can give you thirty per cent," Shah says.

"Fifty," I say. He puts down the stone on the table, raising his hands.

"Forty and not a penny more," he says.

"Alright," I say. Shah takes the stone, opens a drawer, counts out the money on the desk. I take it and he gets up and goes to the sink.

"Have fun," he says and turns the taps, but gets no water. He calls to the secretary: "Bring me some water."

"There is no water, Mr Shah," she says. I stop at the door.

"Those hands will never be clean," I say.

"Get out," Shah says. I laugh and leave. The money is like fire in my pocket. Now we're buying food and drinks. And women. We have the eternal problem. You have to hit the big seam, so that there's enough money to pay for the new life. I can steal a little, but it's only enough for a few days of pleasure, and then I have to go back to the pit, which is made even darker by my visit to the light.

"Let's go get a beer," I say.

"No," Shirazi says. "Let me get my half." I give it to him. He's a stupid boy, because he is too good. He'll stay at a guesthouse tonight and then get the bus to Arusha tomorrow to send the money to his father via the Bank of Tanzania.

"Safe trip," I say and head to the bar. Grilled meat and cold, bottled beer – *eeehhhh*, that's good. A made-up lady comes over to me, sits down at my table, putting her hand on my thigh close to the pump. She is old.

"You need company," she says.

"Yes, but not your kind," I say.

"*Tsk*," she says and gets up, walks away. Mererani Township has dirty *malaya* who have already been worn by many years of use in Arusha, and afterwards they come here to pump their way to hell. They see it clearly: How big is the car or motorbike? What are the clothes like? How fat is the wallet? They don't care about the pump; a small one is best, because they had enough of that a long time ago. And they're expensive. Everything is expensive in Mererani.

Little boys come into the bar to sell peanuts, single cigarettes, hard-boiled eggs – soon they'll end up as snakes in Zaire. If not their mothers and sisters will have to sell themselves to make money. I look at two men at the pool table. A dirty miner in grey-black clothes with red eyes and a fat man with a gold chain around his neck, wearing expensive clothes.

"These *malaya*," he says with a gesture towards the bar, "they're mattresses to all the miners. In Arusha I pumped the poshest women. A new one every night."

"*Eeehhhh*," the miner says, grinning.

"I bought a lovely house and my Land Rover and my motorbike, and every night I ate at the restaurant and went to the disco with a new woman – sometimes three in the same night."

"*Eeehhhh*," the miner says. He wishes it were him. I get up and go to their table. Look at their game, and at the fat man with the gold chain. He has made it big. Then you go straight to the hotel in Arusha. Buy cars and women. You have a party for many months. Every need you feel you try to sate with highs. It's like me in this bar. The great high is meant to erase the memory of the darkness in the pit. But the darkness always seeps through. The high can never be big enough. And all your money is spent on the high. The man at the table has come back to the darkness.

"Why have you come back to Mererani?" I ask.

"Before I was one of you," the man says, smiling. "Now I've bought my own mine. You can work for me . . ."

"*Tsk*," I say and turn away, going back to my own table. Working for a former miner is the worst sort of torture. He has already learned not to care about life.

A young woman comes into the bar. She's also working as a *malaya*, but is untrained. She does it because she is a mother who has no husband and no money for food.

"Come and sit down," I say.

"Yes, please," she says.

"Do you want to eat?" I ask.

"I'm not here to eat," she says, even though she's no doubt hungry. But she'd rather have money for her baby's food.

"I'm going to eat," I say. "And I want you to eat with me while we talk." I order more meat. We don't talk. She eats most of it.

"How much is the soap-money?" I ask. She names her figure. It's a little too high, but I can't argue. She has to make a living. We go to her room. Her baby is with a neighbour. The woman is young – not skilled in the satanic tricks of an Arusha *malaya*. When I'm inside her, it's almost like a sensation of warmth and pleasure.

The rain is tapping on the sheet metal of the roof; the woman is lying warm and calm against my body. A little light is seeping through the curtain and the grimy window. I was in a deep sleep after the pumping. My feeling is a good one. Last night I washed in a tub in the woman's room. Afterwards she washed my clothes in the same water. They're hanging, dry, on lines strung from the ceiling. She wakes up, and I pump her again, but now she's very distant in her behaviour towards me.

"You have to go," she says. "I have to pick up my child."

Yes, we have eaten and drunk together, and I've paid for the night, but you can see that I'm poor, so she's got no more time for me. To be honest my money is already running out.

"Goodbye," I say and leave. The rain outside has cleared the dust out of the air. I have regrets. How can I throw away my money on living flesh when I need it as a security? Tomorrow I may be so hungry that I will kill just for bread.

I walk on dirt roads between shops and bars. You don't see many women – they're out of sight in mud huts, doing their job. Mererani Township is a twenty-four business – the music is pounding from the bars. The town has everything we need, from dynamite to torch bulbs, *gongo* and sex. Two drunken miners are fighting in the mud outside a bar. They're all here: the stone merchants, people who run shops and bars and restaurants and guesthouses, the mechanic, the water salesman, the *malaya*; they milk me and live off the sweat of my back. I find the stone; yet out of everyone I am the one who has the least – *tsk*.

I go into a small eatery where a big mama sells tea and food. When I have eaten, I buy a few knick-knacks – painkillers, toothbrush, a bottle of Konyagi. Shirazi sends his money to his family, so I buy him cigarettes; they remind him of his uncle, who is a smuggler north of Tanga, sailing Kenyan cigarettes to Tanzania in his fishing boat. Later I go to the motorbike garages where the ground is black with oil. The middlemen are as abundant as flies in this area. The roads are hard on a motorbike, so they're always in need of a mechanic. I find Buxton, who used to work in the mines until he started shaking every time he had to go into the pit. These days he owns a shop and has grown long dreads. He is with a customer – a plump man who's standing next to a nice, big Yamaha, almost new. I sit down and wait.

"Give her a new dress," the man tells Buxton. The machine has been stolen – perhaps in Moshi, perhaps in Arusha. Now she needs a new look.

"How do you want her?" Buxton asks.

"I want her to be an ugly girl," the man says.

"But clever between the legs," Buxton says.

"*Eeehhhh*," the man says and sits down on the bench, while Buxton gets started on the job with a boy who helps him out. Off with the fuel tank, the seat, the mudguards, the side panels, the handlebars, headlights, number plates. I smoke a cigarette while Buxton grinds off the V.I.N. number and covers up the scars with solder which is sanded smooth.

I throw away the cigarette, and the boy picks it up and smokes the last bit until the ember is between his lips.

"Do you want me to give it a new V.I.N. number?" Buxton asks.

"Yes," the man says. If he's only going to use the motorbike in the area then the V.I.N. number is a waste because we have no police. But with a new V.I.N. number he can have it registered in Arusha. Buxton hammers in a new V.I.N. number. Paint on top. Now the former owner would never recognize his bike.

I can become a middleman like this man. If I find a good stone, I can buy a motorbike. Because the pit threatens to finish me. But the middleman never leaves Zaire. Yes, he lives a better life than I do and is one step higher on the stepladder to the good life. But he's standing still. The miner has a chance of climbing to the top, getting out, getting the heavenly life on earth.

"Happy?" Buxton asks. The man nods.

"But dirty her," he says. Buxton looks at the boy.

"You do it," Buxton says, and the boy gets up. He takes a plastic can of old engine oil and a rag and, squatting, rubs the thick oil onto every part of the bike. Then he picks up dust in his hands and throws it at the machine, rubbing it into the old engine oil. The motorbike has to be ugly so it won't attract thieves.

"Now I like it," the man says, pays and, getting on the bike, drives off. Buxton comes over to me. We slap hands.

"How are things with you?" I ask. Buxton holds out his hands. They're no longer shaking.

"Poor, but calm," he says, smiling sadly. I hand him the money I owe him from one time when I was in trouble – it's important to have friends when hunger is at the door. Buxton nods and stuffs the banknotes into his pocket. I hand the boy a little money.

"Run down and get us three Cokes," I say, and off he runs. "Where does the boy come from?" I ask.

"His mother sells vegetables around here," Buxton says.

"His father?" I ask.

"Gone." It's common enough. The local women move in with the local upper class; middlemen, guards, drivers, henchmen. The man makes the money, the woman provides for him and has his children. The marriage is unofficial – it's not about love, but about survival. Often the man has a family somewhere else in the country, and he has never told the woman the truth about where he is from. The day the man makes it big, he's gone. The name the woman knows is false. The authorities can't help her. She can never find him again. The only thing he has left her is their children. The boys can become new snakes in Zaire; the girls can sell themselves.

We all use false names. Now that Fillemon is dead, I am the only person in all of Zaire who knows my village and the name that is written in the parish register. You call "Moses", and I respond. If Moses gets in trouble, he'll vanish into thin air.

The boy returns with our soft drinks. Perhaps it was his mother I pumped last night.

IV

Back in the pit at *mzee* Akrabi's. We blast. Nothing. Climb out.

"Did you get it?" they call from the top. We don't answer. Climb all the way out into the light. Now the workers are almost silent. I shake my head. Snakes look at me with empty eyes. Hamza is angry – the mine is making no money. *Mzee* is having financial difficulties. The next morning disaster strikes. Three Land Rovers full of men from Field Force Unit drive up to the mine. The story of the collapse of the mine has made it to Arusha. *Mzee* Akrabi talks to them with Hamza standing by. But *mzee* has no money for bribes, so they stuff him into the car and drive off. We workers stand on the square looking at Hamza, who comes back towards us.

"They're taking *mzee* to Arusha. There is to be an inquiry into the accident," Hamza says. If Akrabi can't get the money for greasing the military as well as the court, they'll lock him up, and the mine will be shut down.

"But we can go on digging – see if we hit on something," I say.

"There's no more money," Hamza says.

"What about food?" my friend Shirazi says. You need a friend here when madness lurks.

"I have to talk to *mzee* first," Hamza says. The workers move in closer.

He goes over to lock the shed with the generator and compressor, diesel cans, explosives, charcoal and food. He wants to go to his motorbike – get away. He has a gun. But we are sixty workers and snakes. He can have no more than seven bullets in his magazine and one in the chamber.

"We have worked," I say. "We must be fed." If he doesn't give me food, I have to take it myself – that's only fair.

Hamza looks at the cook.

"Cook for them," he says. "Take it from the shed."

"There's not a lot of food left," the cook says as he starts to get his things together and carry them out.

"You cook the food there is," Hamza says. The workers pull in under the shade of the lean-to. That's all we're going to get from Hamza – he's just a hand with a gun, no brains. He locks up the shed. He drives off. What valuables are there? The generator and the compressor – but we can't move them without a vehicle, and we can't sell them to other mine owners, because the mine owners stick together against us workers.

The cook is standing next to the shed, cooking our food in pans over a coal fire. *Ugali na maharage*; corn porridge and beans. The *ugali* we have in Zaire is cheap – the yellow kind. Nothing is removed from the corn. The entire grain is ground in the mill to make it like pig swill. You don't eat it for the taste – you eat it to fill your stomach. But the miners aren't vegetarian. The beans, they're old with holes made by *dudus*. That means that the beetle is inside the bean, lives inside it, adds flavour to it. If we're lucky, it's a real sauce made with tomato and onion. And we can drink tea with milk and cane sugar to boost our energy. But we're often not lucky. Sometimes all we can have is old water, dirty, full of disease.

Us workers know it: if *mzee* hasn't got money, then we'll starve. We pretend we don't know. For now we're free until our sentence is passed. We go to the nearest kiosk between the mines – a simple wooden shack where you can buy tea and biscuits, painkillers, single cigarettes, batteries if you have a radio, knick-knacks. We meet workers from the other mines.

Some of them have earned a few scraps, have been to Mererano Township to spend money the night before. Jackson is there with his sunglasses and motorbike.

"I pumped a nice girl yesterday – young, her papaya all new," he says.

"There are no nice girls in Mererani," I say, even though I ought to be careful. We are poor now and need all the help we can get. And Jackson has money to spend. But I am angry – I keep at it: "You pumped an old mama, already worn out as a *malaya* in Arusha."

"No, she was nice," Jackson says, but he doesn't attack me because everyone knows that Shirazi is my friend, and he is strong.

"Perhaps it was your mother you pumped – she was that old," I say.

"Watch it," Jackson says. "My mother is a good woman."

"You haven't seen your mother for years – who knows how good she is?" I ask. Jackson smiles at me:

"You have killed so many snakes, Moses. I look forward to seeing you starve." He walks off. *Eeehhhh*, always so sure of himself.

"Is there work?" Shirazi asks the people from the other mines. His answer is a no.

The next day *mzee* comes back with two men in a large Land Rover. The men are for his protection. Hamza comes with them on his motorbike.

"I haven't got any more money for the running of the mine," *mzee* says. Everything has been spent on greasing the authorities, so he can go out into the world a free man. "I have to get the money first, then I'll come back and re-open it. But you're welcome to stay on," he says with a gesture towards the lean-to, the shed. Hamza wants a couple of workers help him lift the generator and compressor out of the shed and into the Land Rover. But the cook has told us: there's no more food. Hamza has to pay in cash for the help. He doesn't choose me and Shirazi, because we have made too many demands, and I am connected to the collapse. I was running the job – now the accident is my fault.

"How long will it be?" I ask *mzee*.

"I don't know," he says and leaves Hamza and the guard to protect the mine so we can't steal the fruits of the earth. Why must it be protected when he has left with the valuables? Does *mzee* Akrabi think we can dig for stones without food or water? Without air from the compressor? Forty metres below ground and four hundred metres into a tunnel? Does he think we can steal stones that haven't even been found yet? Madness.

We are never paid in money, and now there's no food, no water, no nothing. We borrow from each other. We can sell little stones to the middlemen, and at the Indian shops in Mererani we can barter scraps for food. But we have no little stones. In the morning all us workers go to the next mine, queuing at the gates to ask for work. The guard comes out. He has a whip and a stick. He picks some and the rest he shoos away. If we don't hop it fast enough, we get a taste of his stick. Shirazi is desperate with hunger. We sift through the rubble, and stones, and dust that have been carried up from the mines. We have a frame made of four boards with metal mosquito netting stretched between them. Shovel rubble onto it and then sieve away the dust. Afterwards we sit and examine the stones that are left. We have to find the tanzanite that wasn't seen, before we faint. I think about my mother, sitting with her tray of woven palm leaves, cleaning stones out of the rice. She cooks it for me, and I am full. The cook leaves *mzee* Akrabi's mine to go and work for someone else. What is a cook to do when there's no more food to cook?

Three days come and go, and we haven't found anything. We need water. It's hot. Tall, thin dust devils move restlessly across the landscape in the afternoon heat. The water in the wells in Mererani Township is bad; we can bathe in it, but we don't bathe. You can drink it and shit like an explosion. In Zaire there are no wells, because the groundwater is full of disease. The drinking water is transported here, sometimes in tankers, but more frequently in old twenty-litre cooking-oil containers strapped to a donkey. It's very expensive and we have no money. There are so many young men now without a job. Ready to pounce. When we don't have food or water, things get dangerous around here.

We return to *mzee* Akrabi's mine to sleep. There's a three-metre-high fence made of sheet metal and wooden boards around the mine. The gate is locked.

"*Askari*?" I call, because the guard is usually right inside the gate.

"Get lost," someone says inside. It's Hamza.

"It's Shirazi and Moses," Shirazi calls. "We're coming back to sleep."

"I don't want you here," Hamza says – closer to the gate now. He's afraid. If *mzee* Akrabi doesn't come back, then Hamza is without a salary like us. The guard must have left because there's no food.

"But *mzee* said we could stay here until he came back," Shirazi says.

"No," Hamza says. "You can sleep in a disused mine."

"Then let us in to get our blankets," I say.

"I don't want any nonsense," Hamza says, now right behind the gate.

"We just want our blankets, so we don't fall ill," I say. Hamza is fiddling with the lock now. It's dusk now, but the first thing we see is the gun in his hand. He pulls back a few steps as we come through the gate.

"Close the door behind you," Hamza says. I do it.

"I'll get the blankets," Shirazi says and goes towards the shaft, dragging his feet. He is tired with hunger. I am tired too.

Hamza sits down on a knocked-over oil barrel by the gate and looks at me, his gun resting in his lap. I squat on the ground and get the tobacco pouch out of my pocket, starting to roll a cigarette.

"*Eeehhhh*," I say. "It's hard when the owners just run away and leave us here in the dust."

"*Eeehhhh*," Hamza says, because we're almost the same now, except for the gun.

"If we don't find work within two days, we'll have to run home to our mothers," I say. Hamza grins.

"I thought you were good at stealing, Moses," he says. I grin back at him

"Yes, I'm good," I say. "But there's nothing to steal here."

"*Tsk*," Hamza says. "Life is one big problem." I put my roll-up between my lips and pat my pockets.

"Do you have a light?" I ask.

"Yes," Hamza says, because he's always dying to show that he has that special kind of lighter from America which runs on petrol: a Zippo. I get up and walk towards him. It's almost dark now. I lean forward with my hands on my knees. Hamza has his gun resting on one thigh and his Zippo in the other hand. He opens the lighter and lights it with one hand. He holds it towards my cigarette, and he looks at the flame as I move my cigarette towards it. And as I do, I move my right hand away from my knee and move my hidden knife up and straight into Hamza's neck where I pull it through things inside to destroy him. Yes, I think he likes to have things stuck into him. Hamza opens his eyes wide, blood sprays everywhere. He doesn't even manage to curl his finger around the trigger of the gun. Only a gurgling sound from his neck and he keels over. Dead.

"Yes, Hamza," I say. "Life is one big problem. Now you don't have any more problems." I go over and slam the padlock shut so no-one can come through the gate. The banknotes are in Hamza's pocket. Is there a stone? I search along his gums, under his tongue. Nothing. Open his trousers, grabbing his pump to see if he hides a stone. But Hamza is one of the sons of Allah – cut. I only find the stench of dirt. I make do with the money, it's fine for saving our lives for a few days. I hear steps behind me. Shirazi.

"What have you done?" he asks.

"Got us some money," I say and search Hamza's motorbike. It's locked with a hefty chain, and I didn't find any keys in his pockets. They must be hidden somewhere, and it's completely dark now, so I can't look for them. We have no torches that work. I don't have the tools to open the chain and not enough strength to drag the machine three kilometres to my friend Buxton's. But we'll have to drag Hamza.

"Can't we just leave him?" Shirazi whispers in the dark.

"No," I say. "We have to be careful while we are starving." We drag the body through a hole in the fence and up the hill. The sky is overcast, the night is without stars. For seven years I have breathed the dust constantly. My lungs are clogged, my breathing heavy. We finally make it to one of the disused mineshafts – I have worked in it and know its depth; we let the body fall. No-one will look into it; there's no shortage of people in Africa.

Shirazi has sat down on the ground. The tiredness. Tomorrow the sun will rise and burn us to twigs.

"We have to go," I say and pull him up by the hand. We go down to *mzee* Akrabi's mine and sleep for a few hours. I wake up Shirazi in the dark because we have to go before it's light. Slowly we totter up the bumpy dirt road towards Mererani Township. It takes a long time, and before long the sun comes up. The flies are everywhere. Always. The flies are thirsty and land on moisture – the eyes, the mouth. We get there. Right away we look for a donkey with water tanks. The man gives us clean water in return for a banknote. We drink it carefully, so we won't be sick.

We go to a *mama mtilie* – a cook who has a street kitchen under a tree. We eat well and rest in the shade most of the day. Then we buy food and drink. And have nice strong tea with lots of sugar. We have to get back to Zaire; the money is almost spent, and we have to find work before we starve.

On our way up the sloping hill we are overtaken by middlemen on motorbikes. They're going in the opposite direction. Tonight they can lie down in a bed, perhaps even with a woman.

An old man comes, pulling a donkey. It's laden with empty vegetable baskets and water containers.

"*Shikamoo mzee*," we say respectfully – I hold your feet. The rest of the world can buy the vegetables from a woman with beautiful curves, but no woman will go near Zaire – not even in daylight.

Messages are written with white paint on the large rocks on the roadside. *Mungu Mkubwa* – God is great. *Mungu Yupo* – God exists. The final message is written in black – someone has tried to rub it off with sand and gravel:

Mungu Kufa – God is dead. From the top of the hill we can see the mining area in the dusk. It sprawls across a three-kilometre stretch of a valley in the Merelani Hills. The mines are owned by small operators – many of them are tanzanite sellers who invest the profit in the mining industry. Everything is run on a tight budget. There are about 150 small mines here – the oldest are at the bottom of the valley, where the distance to the sedimentary layer is at its shortest. The newer ones are on the hillsides – you have to dig further before they reach the quartz-filled rock. There's almost no vegetation here, only a few crippled bushes and hedges, and otherwise just rubble heaps and wooden sheds. I see very few people, even though they are here in their thousands – they are underground. How can I start in another mine after seven years? I have worked in six different mines already. Every time an owner runs out of money, I have to get myself another place. And if I am starting in a new mine, I'll have to dig the shaft first: forty metres straight down – the winnings are hidden by tons of stone. By the time I reach them, I'll be worn out already. I may as well be dead.

V

Mzee Akrabi doesn't show up the next few days, days which Hamza spends rotting in his pit while we live on the last of our money. We run out. Go about everywhere and ask: "Have you got work?" The answer is no. There are already too many hands in Zaire. If we sift rubble heaps in the sun, we'll dry out like twigs. And we can't work when it's cool; in the evening we can't see the difference between a worthless crystal and the valuable stones. The torch's batteries have died. Jackson drives up and stops in front of us.

"Is *mzee* Akrabi not back yet?" he asks. If he were, would we be standing here? "Hmmm," he says. "Maybe you should go down to the other end."

"Why?" I ask. We've already been to the other end of the valley – no work to be had there either.

"Will you sell me your boots now?"

"Why?" I ask again. Maybe he has heard something?

"*Tsk*," Jackson says. "That's what I get for being friendly. Two more days and you'll give me those boots for a glass of water."

"Friends help each other," Shirazi says.

"They're starting a new mine tomorrow. That's what I've heard." Jackson starts the motorbike again – shoots off towards Mererani: light, food, women, beer. We drink our last gulp of water, climb down into a deserted mine with the other hopeless. It's hard to sleep without *bhangi* when hunger is gnawing at your guts.

The next morning we're up before the sun. We find the place. It's marked out with sticks and string. There are a lot of men and snakes standing about. "They need a hundred," someone says. "They have plenty of money," another one says. I have heard it all before. In the beginning you get tea with milk and sugar, but before long there's nothing but rotten water.

There is no shade. We sit on the ground. I look at my boots – I am almost ready to say goodbye to them when a new Land Cruiser appears at the top of the hill, followed by a large Isuzu lorry loaded with timber, and a Land Rover. We all follow the motorcade with our eyes. Is it coming here? So much timber; enough for several hundred metres of ladders – madness. They must be very rich. They do come here. We get up, dust ourselves down. Stand by and watch. They pull into the square. Men get out.

"*Wowowo*," Shirazi says in a low voice; billowing arse. But it's not just her arse. Out of the Land Cruiser comes a giant lump of blubber wearing a dress. You almost can't believe there's a woman inside it. She is a teeming mass; her dress is stretched so tight it's close to bursting. Three families might have lunch under her arse – if it rained they'd still be dry.

The men erect tall sticks; they attach a tarpaulin to them. Underneath they place a sturdy easy chair which the mama sits down in. A man comes towards us.

"Get in line," he says. We slop over – not much pushing and shoving here, because everyone can see who the strong ones are. I am at the front of the line, right behind Shirazi. We approach the tarpaulin.

"Go in front of me," Shirazi says and moves me ahead of him. He doesn't like talking to important people. After what seems like a long time we stand before the mama. She's talking to the man who is standing next to her, asking people what their skills are. They are miners. They're skilled at picking stones apart. The mama hires the people who look strong and fit. We're not fit; we're hungry and thirsty. We need a yes. I look at the timber. I greet them politely when we reach the mama, point to Shirazi and say:

"We are carpenters and can work with explosives." I have never nailed two pieces of timber together in my life.

"Could you build a fence?" the man asks.

"Yes. We have built many fences. We could also construct sturdy ladders for the shaft." He points us towards the herd of workers that have been employed. Suddenly everyone in the queue has become a carpenter, but now it's too late. Right away we're put to work unloading the lorry. There are almost-finished walls and floors and roof plates for a small house and for a shed. A man from west Kilimanjaro is there.

"*Shikamoo mzee*," I say respectfully. "We can help you." He tells us everything we must do. We leap about despite our thirst – it's too important right now. The shed must be for the generator and the compressor. But the house? The man grins at me.

"You're not carpenters," he says.

"We're no way near as good as you," I say. "We'd very much like to learn from you. Are you going to be working here?"

"No," he says. "My job is to build houses. I'm just here to put up the house and the shed they bought from me." Shirazi rolls a cigarette from the last tobacco we have and offers it to the man. He shakes his head and takes out a complete pack of cigarettes, Embassy. He holds them out to us and smiles.

"Do you know how to build a fence?" he asks. What can we say? We don't say anything.

"Alright," he says and starts explaining. Everything: how to dig and anchor holes for the posts, how to make lap joints and butt joints to attach the rails, how to mount cross braces. He is a great worker, very friendly. I ask him:

"What is the house for?"

"The mama wants to live in it," the man says.

"No," Shirazi says and laughs, shaking his head. The man nods.

"Really?" I say. The first woman in Zaire; *mama* Bomani. The man tells us that the right-hand man who hired us is the mama's nephew, Makamba. And then there are two guards who have *pangas* and long sticks. A cook has started working. We're going to be fed. The same pigswill as always, but there's enough of it, the water is good. And we have tea with milk and sugar. Oohhh, it's good. That night the Land Cruiser drives away with the fat mama. The house isn't finished, so the carpenter stays the night – we can ask him about all the tricks with timber. The right-hand man stays on site as well – Makamba, but the workers have already named him *bwana* Nine-Millimetre after the gun in the holster under his jacket.

The next few days we work on the house and start on the fence, while the others hack, tap and blast their way into the rocky ground. The house is finished, and the good worker leaves. And *mama* Bomani arrives – she stays in the house that night – a woman in Zaire.

Me and Shirazi build the fence – we're given other young men who work for us. The fence goes all the way around the property and ends in a large gate with a padlock – no-one can see what we're doing. Security for everyone. At the same time others are working on the shaft – soon they'll need ladders.

I make ladders from unplaned boards, knocked together with nails. Shirazi works with me. Every four or five metres down the steep shaft there is a notch to give the ladder something to rest on; the next ladder continues on another of the four sides of the shaft, further down into the dark. The ladder has to be very sturdy. I know the drill – I have been up and down that kind of ladder often enough. The workers must form a line on it and pass along the sacks of rubble. We hack a deep, narrow hole into the wall of the shaft next to the ladder and hammer a pointed piece of timber into the wall; the timber is then nailed to the ladder to stop it from vibrating. At a right angle from the ladder we place boards at regular intervals to make sure the ladder is firmly fixed.

At first the shaft is two metres wide. Before it's reached the fifteen-metre mark, it will have narrowed down to a mere one by one metre. We also help by lifting a number of rubble sacks up the new ladder. There's not that many of us yet. Only when we reach the quartz layer will our numbers increase – perhaps to as many as two hundred men.

Already at thirty-five metres the first signs of the seam appear – there's marks of the blue stone and other less valuable crystals. We dig and blast our way onwards and downwards – following the poor, glasslike crystals, watching the development of their colour and hoping to hit the jackpot. *Mama* and Makamba demand a lot, but conditions are good. We blast with Semtex and detonators. We're given enough food.

Me and Shirazi climb up in the evening to sit for a while before going to sleep. It's very late. It's quiet – the generator has been switched off. A paraffin lamp shines behind the curtain in the mama's house, and bats are flying through the air. Shirazi is lying on his back, staring at the sky as we share a stick of *bhangi*. We're close to the fence – it keeps the light of the moon out, meaning the guard can't see us. The door of the house opens, and *mama* steps onto the veranda.

"Makamba?" she calls into the dark. Shirazi shifts uneasily.

"Shhh," I whisper. "She can't see us."

"Where are you, Makamba?" she calls again.

"Here," he shouts from the gate where he's standing, chatting with the guard.

"Come here, will you?" she says and leaves the door open when she goes back into the house. I hide the lit end of the cigarette with my hand as Makamba crosses the square, goes into the house and shuts the door. Not long after, the paraffin lamp is put out behind the curtain. I thought he always slept in the back of the Land Cruiser.

"*Shingingi kabisa*," Shirazi says, spitting. She is the fat old woman who sleeps with the young man. I grin noiselessly in the dark.

"Yes, Makamba decides everywhere but inside that house – he's the one who's got the dirty job in there."

We climb into the pit. I take my blanket, crawl away from the others a bit and lie down in the dust. My eyes are shut, but the image is alive. I open my trousers; I pump.

The systems differ. At the mama's the promise is that all finds are divided with half going to the mama and her henchmen; the rest split between the workers. You can take days off if you want, but if you're not here when a find is made, you don't get a cut. We work two long shifts – from 6.00 to 6.00 – twelve long hours. A hundred men in the pit at a time. A large shed has been put up for us to sleep in when we get off our shifts. I am woken up by lots of shouting.

"The generator's stopped," Makamba shouts. He prods us with his foot. "You have to go down."

"It's not our shift," I mutter. When the generator's not working, the compressor is dead – there's no air in the mine.

"You have to go down and get them out," Makamba says. I get up and stand in front of him. He tries to look strong. Other people are shouting down into the pit: "Come up, come up. Pass it on – the generator's bust." But no-one goes down. And no-one comes up. Only a couple of little boys – snakes who have been down to bring water and are coming back with empty cans. Last night we blasted a lot, so today everyone is gathered at the very bottom of the mine, filling rubble into sacks.

"*Tsk*," I say and go over to the shed with the generator and compressor.

"You have to go down," Makamba tells Shirazi, who looks at me. I shake my head and continue walking. We're not going down. In the noise from the hacking in the mine you can't hear that the air pipe has gone quiet. The air is always thin and bad, so you're used to feeling sick. It's normal.

Suleimani, the mechanic, sweats profusely as he pulls the generator's starter cord over and over. He sees me coming.

"There's diesel in the tank," he says.

"What about the fuel line for the engine?" I ask.

"It's clean – I have checked," he says.

"The filter?" I ask. He takes a screwdriver and tries feverishly to open it. I look towards the shaft. No-one's coming. No, we won't run down to them. Other rescue teams have tried it in the past, and we know how it goes. At first you feel your heart beat very hard, you can't breathe, you get dizzy, you feel like your body is weak. And when your brain doesn't get any oxygen, your thoughts are foggy – you can't reach an understanding of the situation: that you must turn around – get out. Soon you pass out and then you're dead.

Something happens; the first of the workers come up and get out of the shaft, very tired – some of them are retching. We count. All in all seventy-six come up. Twenty-four are missing, if there really were a hundred. After twenty minutes Suleimani gets the machine to work. It has to run for a while so the fresh air can push the bad air out of the mine.

Mama is hiding in her house. Makamba is very nervous – keeping his hand on his gun the whole time. When the story reaches Arusha, it'll create great concern with the authorities. They'll send Field Force Unit and shut all the mines; *mama* will go to prison.

"Right," I say and point at some of the men. "We're going down now." I go first, and then Shirazi. About a hundred metres along the tunnel, we find the first ones. Fainted but alive. The men start dragging them towards the shaft where there's more air and where they wake up. The air in the tunnel is terrible. I am dizzy but continue crawling. A dead body. No, there's a pulse. I pull him along, but then start being sick. Shirazi appears behind me. "Let go of him and crawl back to the air," Shirazi says.

"We'll pull him with us," I say and spit, collapsing on the mine floor. Shirazi slaps my face – *PAH, PAH*. It wakes me up a little, and we each take an arm, pulling the man with us. The air improves. We reach the shaft. Slowly the man comes to, and we tie the rope around him so he can be lifted up. For a while we stand under the shaft and gather strength before the climb back into the pit. By now the compressor has pumped air in. At the bottom of the mine we find them. Fourteen dead. We drag them to the shaft, pull them up with ropes. Start digging holes for them. Suleimani is nowhere to be seen – afraid of the revenge from the dead men's mates, because even though he isn't a real mechanic, the compressor and generator are still his responsibility. *Mama* has driven off in her car. Makamba is made dangerous by fear.

The next day the mine is at a standstill. But no authorities appear. When the mine is running, we can die of suffocation. Now we can die of hunger.

Mama Bomani must have greased the right *wabwana wakubwa* in a very thorough way, because the authorities don't appear at all. After three days she returns with a new mechanic, and work resumes.

VI

A year with the fat mama.

Two hundred metres into the new tunnel. Nothing. The cone of light from the torch on my head glides through the clouds of dust towards the narrow crack in the rock which the explosion has created. I lean in and my torch scrapes against the top of the crack, which is full of gravel and stones. I scoop it out with my hands until I can't reach further in because my upper body is too wide. The signs are dubious – we should examine them before we continue in that direction. I turn around and the light from my torch glides over Shirazi. Makamba is there – the mama's henchman.

"Send in a snake," he says.

"That crack isn't safe," I say. "The roof isn't stable – it might collapse." The experienced snakes have moved back – working busily at filling sacks of rubble, dragging them off, handing them up the ladder. If I call to them, they won't hear me. They'll be deaf until I beat them and they hear themselves scream.

"The new one," Makamba says, looking at me lazily.

"You – snake?" I shout over my shoulder. "The new boy, where is he?" The other snakes hear me in the tunnel behind me. They shout.

"You – new boy. You have to go to the front and do your job." They almost push him towards us. He doesn't know anything, is very small, just a child.

"Come," I say and hold out a hand. He is silent, attentive, comes towards me. I point to the crack. "You must climb in there and – all the gravel and pebbles, you just push it out so we can clear it away – to see if the seam is there." He nods without saying anything. Shirazi comes over with a rope which he starts tying around the boy's waist.

"You push it back with your hands, and then you use your feet to push it further back where we can get to it," I explain. He nods, looks down on the rope around his waist but is too afraid to ask.

"Sometimes it's hard to crawl backwards if there isn't a lot of room and too much gravel, and then we have the rope so we can pull you out," I say. He nods. There's a new torch on his head, *mama*'s big investment in her new worker. He doesn't need it, because he doesn't know how the sedimentary layer is supposed to look to point us towards richness. He must dig first – later a wise snake must go in to look.

"Right. Off you go," I say and pat his back. He climbs in and starts pushing gravel and pebbles out. "Easy does it," I say, my upper body leaning into the crack, scooping out the gravel so it lands on the floor of the tunnel. An experienced snake has come over and is busy loading it into sacks. He doesn't look up at me. We all understand the risk, except for the boy inside the crack, who uses his feet to push out the gravel so I can reach it.

"That's good," I say. "How far does the crack continue?"

"Far," he says. "I can get further in." He climbs back in. Makamba is squatting, looking at the gravel. Should I send another boy to check on the structure of the rock – is it porous or solid? Could it collapse? The rope moves slowly up from the floor as the boy climbs into the crack. Makamba doesn't care if it's porous. Either I send one boy or I send another; it's all the same to him. I have other things on my mind. One side of my stomach hurts round the back – two days now, even though I've eaten.

The boy is only a couple of metres into the rock, but digging the gravel away is hard work. He only has a chisel with which to loosen it. Once it's loose, he must push it backwards with his hands, push himself further back over the gravel so he can push it even further back with his hands. Then he has to crawl over the gravel again until his feet can push it so far out of the crack that we can reach it and scoop it out, and he can move forward and continue digging. His skin will be cut everywhere, and his eyes filled with dust. Very hard to breathe in there – that's another reason why they use boys, not men. Boys can handle it better. They think that only other people can die.

A sound comes out of the crack: a crushing noise, the rolling of the gravel.

"*Pull!*" I shout to Shirazi. He braces his bodyweight against the rope while I push my upper body into the crack, reaching forward, fumbling for the rope. My hand touches the gravel – feels the rope, which comes out of the gravel taut. Too much resistance. There are more people behind me now, pulling.

"Can you reach him?" Shirazi shouts. My hands tear stones and gravel aside – I have to get to his feet, they could be lodged against the sides of the cracks and then we can't pull him out. The rope is trembling slightly in the flickering light from my torch. It's not moving. My hands are digging. Ohhh, a small tremor.

"Now," I shout. Shirazi shouts:

"*Pull, rest, pull, rest . . .*" One jerk at a time, the gravel is shifted. I dig into it, feel a shoe, an ankle – it's turned the right way around. The boy is so new to Zaire that he's still wearing his church-going shoes that he had on when he fled his home to look for riches. Through the pebbles I find the other foot. There – I yank it away from the wall, have the boy's legs between my hands, and the rope jerks him towards me. I crab backwards, the boy's legs leave the crack – all grey-black with dirt. I grab onto them and lower him to the floor, wiping the dirt from his face. All the light cones are directed at him. One eye is open, full of sand, empty of life. I slap the face – his head jerks spastically. I bend down, hold his nose, blowing into him so his chest rises. It doesn't work. I pound his chest, blow into him – many times.

"Quiet," I say. Lean my head down to the boy's mouth and listen, but it's difficult to hear anything because of the sound from the plastic pipe bringing us air from the compressor. No heartbeat.

"*Ameshakufa*," Makamba says – he is dead. Small tuts of disapproval come from the workers. "Move it," Makamba says. The others slink away, resume their work of filling sacks, handing them up the shaft on the ladders. Shirazi removes the rope from the boy's waist, rolling it up. I am silent – sitting, holding my side. The pain is growing in there; not because of the boy's death – it was his time – but some things inside my body have turned bad.

"Put the boy into the bad tunnel," Makamba says to me. "At the bottom of it." He's talking about the tunnel we dug a long time ago which had no signs of the seam.

"Do you want me to do it?" Shirazi asks.

"No, I'll do it," I say, lifting up the boy. "Make way," I say, and Makamba turns around, walking in front of me, shouting to the others:

"Move over. Stand back." I follow him, hunched over, the boy slung over my shoulder. The others have pressed themselves into the niches in the tunnel so that I can squeeze past with him. In the light of their torches I can see that my hands are bleeding from having dug my way through to the body. No-one says anything. There's only the sound of our movements in the dark. The flickering light on the rock walls. Makamba stops.

"Put him at the bottom," he says. And I crawl into the dead tunnel, putting the boy at the bottom. Quickly I search his pockets – nothing. Pull off his church shoes and tuck them away inside my shirt – they can buy the love of a snake. I fold his hands on his stomach so the boy looks at peace.

"If You're there," I say quietly into the dark, "this one is one of Yours."

I grab onto my one side at the back; an intense pain – radiating down towards my pump, so fierce that it bends me double. Almost at once it's over again.

I hurry back past Makamba, then stop and turn towards him:

"Everyone must be out before you blast," I say because that's the rule at a funeral.

"Yes, yes," he says. I return to my work. Makamba is going to get the explosives ready at the bottom of the dead shaft. When it's a funeral he'll use the cheap dynamite with only one fuse. Everyone will be sent up the ladder except for the one who will light the fuse and then run like a rabbit. We'll stand on the ground above while it's happening. We workers don't want any more burials above ground, because the grave is never deep enough – hyenas, jackals and vultures can smell the rotting dead bodies from miles away and see the grave as their own personal restaurant.

I ask the others on my way back: "Did anyone know him? Where did he come from? Did he know anyone else in Zaire?" But no-one knows the dead boy.

"He had run away from home," one of the snakes says.

"Where was that?" I ask, even though I know it doesn't matter – I don't really care either.

"Somewhere in Arusha," the snake says.

"His father beat him too often," another snake says.

"Now Zaire has beaten him," a third snake says.

"Zaire beats harder than any father," the other one says. I crawl on. Back to my work. A stab in my stomach. My face crumples. Everything in my body is working, there's nothing to see, but over and over the pain comes in waves, making me writhe. It's not hunger. An evil spirit from the dark.

"Is it bad?" Shirazi asks.

"Yes," I say. We work. Sometime later Makamba shouts that we have to get out. He is ready to blast the snake's grave. We crawl along the tunnels. Climb out into the light. It hurts our eyes. No sunglasses; I have to shade my eyes with my hand – sit quietly and get used to it, otherwise I can't see where I put my feet. Slowly shapes appear – the wooden house with *mama* Bomani sitting on the veranda, fat as ever. The others come up and sit down on the ground.

"What are you doing up here?" the mama says angrily.

"Makamba is about to blast," I say.

"Blast? He hasn't told me he was going to blast!" I get up and walk towards her. I don't want to talk about it loudly. Her eyes are almost drowned in fat, but they're burning at me.

"It's a funeral," I say so that no-one else can hear.

"A funeral?" *mama* says.

"The new snake – he was crushed."

"*Tsk*," she says. "Can it not wait till you come up to eat?" I shrug and go back, sitting down next to Shirazi. I don't want to explain to her that the work comes to a halt if there's a dead man who hasn't been tightly wrapped in rubble. Then we all think too much about the risk – no-one dares do anything that might go wrong. Once he's buried, he rests in dignity – we can all move on. Shirazi hands me one of his rollies.

"*Tsk*," he says, spitting. "We all wait to die, while she is so fat it would take an entire afternoon to locate her arsehole."

"Unless you used your nose," I say. The pain in my stomach comes suddenly. I bend double, tears springing from my eyes.

"That's not good," Shirazi says. "You need tea and medicine."

"I haven't got any money." You can't ask *mama* Bomani for anything, so we wait until Makamba is around. Shirazi goes over and tells him:

"Moses' stomach hurts. He needs medicine for the pain and tea with sugar and milk."

"You want tea?" Makamba says. "Then find some stones to buy tea with." Shirazi comes back to me:

"I've got a little money," he says and pulls me up. We pick our way to the shop. The pain has gone now. Shirazi orders tea and buys tablets from the shopkeeper and gives them to me without saying anything. He turns on his radio, which he got from an Indian in Mererani in return for a nice stone – he loves that radio. Whenever we have a break, he holds the radio up to his ear. But he doesn't play it loudly, because batteries are expensive. I sit close to Shirazi, who is my protection. A lot of people feel animosity towards me because I am almost like a boss, only without the gun. When I first came to Zaire, I was beaten a lot and was used – I don't want to have that happen again. We drink tea with workers from the neighbouring mine. We are all slaves – not competitors.

"Will we see you soon below?" I ask.

"If you follow the signs this way all the way down – then we can meet here, below the kiosk," one of them says. We laugh together.

"Then they can shoot each other," I say, because it's the henchmen that go first after an explosion – carrying their guns.

"That would be good," Shirazi says. "Then we could harvest the big stones ourselves."

We go back to the mine. The batteries in my torch are dead. What good will it do us to hit the seam if we can't see it? We can't use paraffin lamps in the pit because the flame eats the air we live on. Shirazi goes over and asks Makamba for new batteries.

"You can use the batteries from your radio – I'm not giving you more," Makamba says. Shirazi returns.

"*Basha*," he says, spitting. Makamba sleeps in the house with his aunt. Every night she makes him suck her bean. He is his own aunt's *malaya*. We have to put our batteries in the sun to have them suck a bit more strength from it.

Everyone goes down – hacking, blasting, dragging; following the seam that killed the snake. It hits me – the pain; I am rolling around on the rubble. I am sick. Oohhh, the snakes watch me coldly; they know I'll use their lives in the hunt for the stone – it's a pleasure for them to watch me suffer. If I had been on the ladder in the shaft . . . I would have fallen. The end.

The crystals peter out, come to nothing, without giving us the blue fruit. Work is over for today. We climb out to be fed. The mama has been out today – to the market on Arusha Road to shop. Chicken, onions, tomatoes, spices, bananas, potatoes, cabbage – all the good things. How do I know? The cook prepares her food. The smell of fried chicken is an evil spice in the pigswill in my mouth.

The man who runs the neighbouring mine has come to visit the mama. The name is Savio; a big, young man – Indian. The workers say he treats them well, almost like people. Savio sits on the veranda and speaks to *mama* Bomani. I can't hear them; yet the topic is as clear as anything. The question all bosses ask: How do we squeeze that last drop out of the worker?

Savio leaves. The other shift hasn't been sent down yet. Makamba calls us to the house. The mama is standing on her fat legs on the veranda. We're one hundred and eighty men, including the snakes.

"I can't afford to feed you any longer, not when you don't find any stones," the mama says. Doesn't she understand that the time is right? – the earth has been fed by the dead snake. But *mama* Bomani gets into her car, driving off to Arusha.

We slaves have to borrow from each other, build up debts without any hope of an income. Maybe the mama hasn't run out of money, but she is putting pressure on us – we starve and go thirsty when there's no work.

She never starves. She wants more from us. She wants stones. When she harvests, we get a bit too. How can we rebel when we're already working for no pay, only food? Can we stop working? She's already done that for us; sitting in her villa in Arusha, eating her meat.

In the night the pain comes terribly. Shirazi runs around, getting *bhangi* for me to smoke, but it only takes the top off the pain.

"You need a doctor," Shirazi says.

"There are no doctors in Mererani Township," I say.

"You need a hospital," Shirazi says. It's true, but where is the money to come from? And will it help? The evil spirit is eating me. In the morning I give Shirazi my last little stone. He goes right out and sells it. I am lying in the shade of the fence, resting. Shirazi returns and puts the money in my hand.

"Thank you," I say. "Now I just have to find someone who can take me to Moshi or Arusha – it'll be fine."

"You don't have enough money. You need money for the doctor," Shirazi says. "I'll sell my radio."

"It's a risk – it might not help me."

"It's only a radio," he says. "I know someone who wants to buy it." Shirazi – he'll give me a chance to cheat death. He takes the radio out of its plastic bag, cleans the dust off, tunes it to make it nice for the sale. I look down – my nice boots. Will I need those in the realm of the spirits?

"See if you can find Jackson," I say.

"Do you think he will take you?" Shirazi asks, spitting.

"The boots," I say. Shirazi goes off. He is gone a long time. So many idle hands around me – snakes' and the other workers'. My job is to put them to work. If need be, I must beat them. And here I am unable to run. Only their fear of Shirazi keeps them away.

Finally I hear a motorbike coming towards the mine. Shirazi on the back of Jackson's Yamaha 250cc. Jackson is wearing strong jeans, a great Bob Marley T-shirt and hides his eyes behind sunglasses. But his shoes are bad. I sit up – have to control the cramps so Jackson doesn't see how ill I am.

"The boots are very worn," Jackson says. But he's come – he wants them. I don't say anything.

"Let me try them on," he says. The cramp attacks just as I am about to unlace them. Shirazi helps me. Jackson puts them on.

"I haven't got money right now," he says.

"Don't be like that," Shirazi says.

"It's true," Jackson says. "I've only got a little, for petrol. I am going to Moshi to see my family."

"If you're going to Moshi in Moses' boots, you must pay for them," Shirazi says. Jackson shakes his head.

"You'll have to wait until next week."

"Then you must take Moses to the hospital in return for the boots," Shirazi says.

"*Tsk*," Jackson says, shaking his head. "I've already helped you so many times. I showed you the work at the mama."

"There is no work," I say. Shirazi stands very close to Jackson.

"Take them off," Shirazi says. But Jackson wants those boots. And he's going to Moshi anyway, so I may as well go with him. Shirazi drags me to the motorbike and loads me onto the back.

"You stink," Jackson says. Yes, the stench of old sweat, and my clothes full of salt and dirt. Jackson drives. The air is amazingly clean and fresh; I have my handkerchief away from my mouth and tied around my hair. I sit calmly on the back of the motorbike – relaxed so the cramp won't attack me from behind. The rough treads of the back tyre reach into the dust; the engine, the chain, the wheel – the machine tearing away from Zaire to a world where people live in the light that is cutting into my eyes. I mustn't think like the little middleman – I have to be tough; must wait for the big one. The evil inside me – what can it be? Perhaps I am dying already.

From far away I see the airport terminal at Kilimanjaro International

Airport. *Ohhh*, a screeching rumble when we approach it; a giant aeroplane soars to the sky. "It's going to Europe and America with white tourists," Jackson shouts – he thinks he knows everything. We hit the tarmac at the airport slip road – so smooth and good – just as the plane passes over Kibo so the white people can look into the crater on Africa's roof. When I left home, my older brother was a carrier for the tourists – the barefoot negro who carries the white man's food and drink so the white man can enjoy the view and take photographs to show people at home how clever he was to go all the way to the top himself. So what? Perhaps my brother is dead now. I'd like to see him, my mother, my sisters. But how can I return to the village with empty hands after eight years? We reach Arusha Road, the market on the intersection. *Ahhh*, the girls, the women – so many of them. Their eyes tempt with all sorts of secrets. Rounded bottoms, full thighs, pert breasts; all of them different and all of them nice. They sell fruit and vegetables. If only I could hold a girl in my arms. But I have to wait for the big win – if I live that long.

Entering Moshi. So green, large trees, nice houses, people everywhere, cars, bikes – it's a feast to my eyes. I think of Rongai, which is even greener than Moshi. Plenty of fresh water, mango trees, banana trees, cattle for milking, chickens, beans, sweetcorn. An abundance of everything. If you own land.

Jackson lets me off by the bridge over Karanga River. I buy a piece of soap in a kiosk. Go up along the river. A lady is on her way home from the market with her baby on her back. I greet her.

"Are there crocodiles in the river?" I ask.

"No, it's not dangerous," she says. I find a hidden place. Wash myself and my clothes, which I then put out to dry on a large stone in the river. Two white children appear on the slope. I turn my back to them and squat down. What are they doing here? They sit down and light cigarettes. The river is where they hide from their teacher.

When my clothes are dry, I go to the K.C.M.C. hospital. I arrive in the late afternoon, and they won't let me into the waiting room for the night. Not far away is a shed – I can spend the night there in return for a few coins. The next morning I am up early and am already queuing when they open the doors. I sit in the waiting room all morning before I am shown in to see a doctor. I find the money in my pocket and pay for the examination. He asks. I tell him about the pain, point to where it hurts, tell him about how it comes over me.

A *mzungu* woman comes into the room. She is fair-skinned like an angel with long legs like a Masaai. The woman is wearing a white doctor's coat and greets the greedy doctor in English.

"You must drink plenty of water," the doctor tells me.

"Water?" I say. "Why?"

"Your kidneys have shrunk," he says.

"Kidneys?" I say.

"Do you drink very little water?"

"Good water is expensive," I say. "The cheap water can ruin your stomach. But I do drink water."

"Enough to make you pee many times a day?" he asks.

"No, I don't pee. Very little pee. Mostly I sweat."

He explains that the water I drink moves through my kidneys, and there is a poison in my body which is transported out of my body when I pee. If I don't pee, the poison stays in my kidneys and grows to become stones. Now I must drink like an elephant to dissolve the poisonous stones and pee them out.

"If the pains continue and you get a fever, you must come back – then we'll have to cut you," he says. Come back? If I have to pay for the cutting as well, I'll have to starve so much that I'll already be dead. "Do you have money?" he asks.

"More money?" I ask.

"No, not for me. But so you can stay in Moshi for a few days. Drink water all the time."

"I can stay until the day after tomorrow," I say.

"Lots of water," the doctor tells me again. "Done." He claps his hands and leans back in his chair. I stay in my seat.

"You can go now," he says.

"What about *injection*?" I ask. I am ill. I need treatment.

"Injections don't help against stones in your kidneys," the doctor says. *Tsk*, he is a doctor. He is supposed to help the sick, but he wouldn't touch me until he had the money in his hand, and now he wants to save money by not giving me an injection. He won't even give me any pills. It's a total scam.

The white woman asks the doctor something in English which I don't understand. The doctor shrugs and shakes his head as he answers. The white woman says something else and smiles. The doctor looks at me:

"She is going to give you injection," he says, getting up and walking away. She comes over to me.

"I am going to make injection on you," she says in hopeless Swahili. Her scent around me is like a very special flower. She finds the needle and makes it ready. Ahhh, the white angel has sent the greedy *bwana mkubwa* away – now she is fixing me. Very good injection, right into my arm. I can feel it getting better already.

"Thank you very much, *mama*," I say. She calls for a black nurse to translate what she tells me:

"You must drink a lot of water. Every day enough to make you pee at least three times – then the injection will work forever," the black nurse tells me.

"Do I need more injection or tablets?"

"No," she says. "It's a brand-new kind of injection from America."

"Ahhhh, America," I say, nodding at them both. The *mzungu* woman smiles. America has all the best things: Donna Summer, Marlboro, good medicine. The black nurse makes sure I get clean water to drink. She gives me a can. I can get as much water as I want from a particular tap where the water has been cleansed in a scientific way. I drink water. My stomach is like a balloon. I piss like an elephant. In six hours I can be at home in Rongai. My mother and my siblings. After eight years I can come home. I would be greeted by my mother's tears. They have almost nothing. They would have to share that nothing with me. Above all they have disappointments and problems. They would share those with me as well. And I would have to go to Fillemon's mother and tell her: first your son lost an eye. Then he died under rubble. He was lifted out of the ground and buried in such a shallow grave that he ended up as a meal for the wild animals.

I sleep in the shed. Continue drinking. I buy cans and fill them with water. I drag water with me into the bus. I arrive in Mererani with twenty litres of clean water and get a lift to Zaire.

"I have to drink more water," I tell Shirazi.

"Water?" he says. "We haven't even got food to eat." *Mama* Bomani hasn't returned yet. The mine is at a standstill. The guards by the house and the gate don't know anything.

I drink water and piss on the rubble heap. Injection from America works perfectly – no more stabbing pains. The boss from the neighbouring mine comes driving in his Land Rover. I run over to his car:

"*Bwana* Savio, do you have work for me?" I shout. He slows down.

"Who are you?" he asks through the open window.

"I have worked in the mines for eight years," I say. "My name is Moses. I know all the methods."

"Moses? I've heard of you," he says.

"Have you heard that I was good?"

"People around you die," he says.

"No, no," I say.

"Get lost," he says and drives off.

In the evening we climb down the ladder with the other workers to sleep in the warmth.

"Come with me," I whisper to Shirazi. He doesn't ask questions. Follows me into a barren tunnel where the air is thin – we need privacy. We only have the faint light from the dying batteries in our torches. The bottle I bought in Moshi is sitting behind my belt. I pull it out.

"*Ehhh*," Shirazi says. I hand it to him. He drinks. "*Tembo*," he says – elephant – and drinks again. We share it. We smoke a stick of *bhangi*. We get high. A snake joins us – he wants to smoke as well. Shirazi hands him the stick.

"Do you want to taste the *gongo*?" I ask.

"Yes," the snake says.

"Do you think he's up to it?" Shirazi asks.

"I'm up to it," the snake says. He takes a gulp.

"Have another taste," I say. Because I want him high. My body is good now – the evil stones are being flushed out with piss.

"*Tembo*," the snake says. I hand him the stick. Shirazi looks at me; I raise my eyebrows and nod. We empty the bottle with the snake. He is high now, dizzy, tired. Shirazi grabs hold of the snake from behind with an arm tight around his neck.

"If you scream, I'll break your neck," he says and flips the snake over so he is on his stomach. The snake is breathing quickly with fear, but his voice is quiet. In the dense darkness it might as well be a girl. I pull off her trousers and spread the girl's legs; spit and push my pump into her, pumping her hard – *ehhh*, I am a big machine inside the tight papaya. I spray into it. We change places so Shirazi can pump her as well. We're done. Now she can go back to being a snake.

VII

Mama Bomani and Makamba return after four days. Work is resumed. Night and day. Finally it looks right – it can't fail. We're almost there. We're ready to blast again. Everyone has been sent up because there's a risk of the mine collapsing. I am to start the explosion with Shirazi. There are little bits of Semtex inside the holes we've made in the rock. We're lucky that we don't have to use fuses. We have detonators; we run the cables along the tunnel, around a corner and onwards. You have to be at least eighty metres from the blast and then you find cover. If you're unlucky, the mine collapses on you. Dead. I squeeze into a niche. I have stuffed rags into my ears, tied a handkerchief over my mouth. Then I nod at Shirazi and gather the cables around the battery. A big boom – the air pressure – the dust billowing towards us. We shut our eyes. Wait. It sings in our heads. Makamba comes with a big lamp. We have picks, spades with short handles, hammers and chisels. Makamba climbs in and sits with his back against the wall while the dust subsides; he has his 9mm in his hand, hanging at his side, but ready. He looks at the loose rocks, the rock wall. The seam. We've seen it as well. Makamba doesn't want me here. When the seam is discovered, you have to be careful – everyone goes mad.

"You go up and tell *mama* that we've hit it," he tells me. I don't budge. He lifts his hand a little – nine millimetres. "Now," he says. I turn around and crawl back along the tunnel, arrive at the ladder and start climbing towards the light, which is fading fast. It's late in the day. The others see me, shout to me.

"Did you get it?"

"Yes," I shout back. I reach the top, get out of the shaft and out from under the lean-to. *Mama* is sitting hunched over, tense in her chair on the veranda.

"We hit it," I say. Strange that a mountain of lard like that can leap from her chair like a young gazelle. Greed changes everything. This is a dangerous place tonight. People are going to die, but who? Is it me? It's better if it's someone else. The mama is on her way to the shaft, almost flying. Close to the shaft now.

"Move, move," she shouts. In the faint light I see her pushing the workers aside. "Moses, you go first and light the way for me." I quickly climb some way down the ladder. She wants me below her, so I don't get dust on her from the ladder's steps. She turns and steps out on the ladder. I see the wooden beams that come out of the black, flowered nylon dress – her legs. The cloth is stretched so tightly over the fat that it's ready to burst. Her legs fumble against each step of the ladder; she finds sure footing and moves her arms one at a time. She starts moving the next foot. Everyone is silent. In one hand she holds a torch – the cone of light flutters in the shaft; she doesn't want to ruin her Arusha hair with a hard hat or rubber bands around her head. The ladder is made from unplaned timber, and the steps are set far apart to save on wood; they're worn smooth and shiny by hands and feet – after a blast they're always covered by a fine layer of stone dust which makes them even more slippery. I hear her panting; her body is heavy with food and drink earned off our sweat. An arse so big and fat I can hardly see anything else. I am moving down again to find a niche to stand in. After fifteen metres of vertical descent the shaft is only one by one metres. It has to be narrow so we don't have to carry too much rubble up in feeding sacks. And we are thin – us and the ladder, we don't need much space. *Mama* groans. First I feel the drop on my upturned face – her sweat. And then the cone of light which turns and swings madly, flying past me – she's dropped the torch. "Light!" she yells. The idiots above don't think; they shine a light down for her. I have turned my lamp off.

"Moses?" she shouts. Now I want to see, so I turn on the lamp, shining it at her.

"What?" I say.

"Ohhhh," she says – can the voice of such a big sow really be so small? One tree trunk is hanging flopping about under her skirt, she can't find the next step – it's too far down because she's using her arms to cling on rather than to lower herself down. You have to hang by your arms while your leg searches for the next step. But her arms are tired – their muscles are only used to carrying their own lard. I shine my light straight up between her legs, but I can't see any knickers – those legs are so fat that fat's all you see – if there are any knickers, they're trapped in a prison of it. I squeeze myself all the way into the niche. "Aaaiiiiiiii . . ." And she slips; flies towards me, a flaccid, screaming lump. I make myself flat. Right in front of me I see a leg flail towards a step and be caught by it but . . . CRRUUUUUGN – a snap of bone, a twist of the leg and it's pulled away from the ladder once more. Her dress skims over my face; a smell of perfume and sweat. And her body keeps falling. Until the bottom, twenty metres below. The sound of the impact, dull. They scream and shout from above ground – then start to climb down. I hurry to the bottom, quick as a squirrel. She is unconscious but breathing in small gasps; one of her legs is twisted under her at a strange angle. But she's not dead. The body has bumped against the ladder and the walls of the shaft on her way down, and it has broken her fall – all that fat was like a mattress for her to land on. I shine the light of my torch on her, while the others approach from upstairs. I kick her – no reaction.

"Is she dead?" one of the snakes asks. I lift her dress, saying:

"There's her big fat papaya, in there." I grab onto her knickers and tear them off. You can barely see her hole for all the rolls of fat on her thighs. I spread her thighs – one of them is bent the wrong way because the bone is broken inside it. With my hands I take the fabric at the neckline of her dress and rip it away from her body. The workers are standing above me on the ladder and around me. I grab a snake by the neck, staring at him so my torch blinds him. "You run down the tunnel and tell Makamba that *mama* has fallen. Go." A slap over the neck – he runs off with his head down.

"I think she's still breathing," someone says.

"I don't care," I say. More people approach from above. Many torches shine on *mama* Bomani's fat body – those big balloon tits. I lean forward and slap her face. A sound comes out of her throat.

"Is she alive?" someone asks. Now I can hear them come back through the tunnel: Makamba, Shirazi and the snake.

"She's still warm," I say, pulling down my trousers, squatting down, leaning in over the enormous body.

"Stop that, or I'll shoot!" Makamba shouts behind me. I turn my head and look at him. He's holding up the 9mm. I've got much more than nine millimetres. I look around at the others. Everyone is looking with empty eyes at Makamba. Behind him I see Shirazi. He is holding up his pick with both hands, spitting.

"You won't shoot," I say, because I can see it. If he shoots, he's a dead man.

"But is she still alive?" the snake asks.

"She's unconscious," I say, "but she can still feel my love." I start pumping inside her, spitting in her face, slapping her. She moans and a spasm moves through her body. "Yes," I say, pumping quickly. "Moses is giving you satisfaction." A short, scrawny guy has sat down next to the mama's face – he is kneading her tits. He takes his pump in his hand and slaps it against her mouth.

"My turn," he says and pushes me off. I get up to let him get at her. I button my trousers while the guy pumps inside her, and I look at Makamba. He has put his 9mm away – he knows Shirazi is standing behind him with his pick.

"She's taking that to hell with her," I say.

"Our love," says the scrawny guy, who is still pumping her. I grab Makamba by the arm.

"You too, *basha*," I say. There are more than forty workers here with torches. Many of them are shining on Makamba. He has his 9mm in his pocket – that's all. Everyone is waiting to see what he will do. They have hammers, picks, their bare hands.

"I don't want to touch her," he says.

"You must touch her tonight like you do every night," I say.

"Pump her," someone says. They start shouting. "Pump her, pump her." It becomes a chorus. I hold up my hand and they become hushed.

"You'll pump her, or we'll give you a onceover with our picks." The scrawny guy has got up to make room for him. Makamba is shaking. Shirazi has his pick ready. I reach into Makamba's trousers; I can feel the stones in his pocket. He has already got his share of the tanzanite seam. I let him keep it so that he too will be a thief. I take his gun away. "Now," I say, tearing at his belt.

"I can't," Makamba says – tears running down his face. "She's my aunt." But I know: the man's pump will always stand as a weapon against destruction. I pull down his trousers, and every lamp shines at his pump – it's ready. He must do it. He gets down on his knees, thrusts into her, quickly – that's him done for. A guy starts pissing on the mama. The scrawny guy has a shovel in his hand – he goes over, raising it.

"*Shetani!*" he says. Satan. And he hacks his shovel into *mama*'s throat; a big gash, red blood pumping out – in spurts, running over the black skin, into the rubble, into the dust, fertilizing the earth so blue stones can grow. More people piss on the body. The snake I sent for Makamba is pulling at my arm.

"Won't they be able to see that we have . . . done things to her?" he asks.

"Won't who see?" the scrawny guy asks.

"The police," the snake says.

"The police don't come here," the scrawny guy says.

"Who is she going to complain to in hell?" I ask. "Satan?"

"But God can see us," the snake says.

"God's eye doesn't reach Zaire." I turn away from the sow, diving into the tunnel, Shirazi right behind me. The gun is in my hand. I am going to harvest.

Ramadan Express

"You've grown a beard, Sharif," my uncle says when I get out of the taxi in front of his villa on Kilimanjaro Road. "Going to be a mullah, are you?" He comes towards me, grinning.

"It's the fashion," I say. "In Dubai."

"And you're well?" he asks, embracing me, kissing my cheeks. "Your mother? Your father?

I tell him everyone in Mwanza is well.

"Come and have some tea," he says. I travelled from Dar es Salaam to Mwanza as a passenger on one of the company's four lorries, in order to have meetings and to see my parents. The plan was to get a flight back to Dar, but Air Tanzania is grounded; there's no foreign currency with which to buy fuel for the planes. So I've come to Moshi by bus to see my uncle.

We sit on mats on the veranda and are served tea by the cook, Abdullahi, who gives me a wide smile. I lived with uncle the first two years I was at the international school – until my brothers could afford the boarding fee.

"Do you know that Christian is back in town?" Uncle asks.

"Yes. He came by the office in Dar a couple of months ago when I wasn't there," I say.

"He's been asking after you," Uncle says. I don't say anything. Christian and I were friends at school. We played football. "He's going about on a motorbike with a black girl on the back," Uncle says.

"I haven't got time for his nonsense," I say. It's easy being white. You don't have to live with the consequences. When Christian has ruined something for someone in Tanzania he can go home to Denmark.

Everyone leaves Tanzania. Wealthy Africans and Indians send their children to the West to study – they never come back.

We're Arabs. East Africa has had connections with the Arabian Peninsula and the Persian Gulf for a thousand years and has created the Swahili culture – the language is full of Arabic words. My parents emigrated away from the poverty in Yemen when they were young – in 1955. Tanzania was a British colony and full of opportunities for trade, especially inland where the Indians didn't offer much competition. I grew up in Mwanza on Lake Victoria. We're eleven children, all of us with Tanzanian passports, but three of my brothers work in Saudi Arabia or the United Arab Emirates. My uncle in Moshi is Orthodox but in the Tanzanian way – laid back, not strict. He goes to the mosque, yes – but only on Fridays. He drinks alcohol. I respect him – he's my uncle.

Last lorry to Dar before the long rains leaves tomorrow night," Uncle says. "Then you'll be home in time for Ramadan."

"That's good," I say.

I get up early and wash, pray and talk to Abdullahi while I have breakfast – getting the news about his wife and children. Afterwards I go up to Kijito and say hello to *mama* Hussein who was my houseboss when I first became a boarder. The pupils have already gone up to the school by the time I arrive. *Mama* is in the sickbay for the boarders, which is also placed in Kijito.

"My boy," she says, hugging me tight – then holding me out at arm's length. "You've become a man," she says. She questions me about Dubai, about Dar, about my plans for the future. I ask her about her family, her health, her work. We have tea. "Do you know that the Danish boy, Christian – he's come back to Moshi?"

"I had heard that," I say.

"When the European children come back here after they've finished school; *tsk* – I don't like it," *mama* says.

"No," I say.

"They're chasing the dream of a life that no longer exists. They should stay where they belong – get to know it, get qualifications. Then they can return when they have something to offer."

"Maybe they shouldn't return at all," I say.

"Maybe not," *mama* says.

"What does he do – Christian?" I ask.

"Ahr, *tsk* – he's running around with a poor girl, setting up small nightclubs in town."

"With local people?"

"Yes. They'll eat him for breakfast the day they feel like it."

"Yes," I say.

When I return there's a motorbike in the drive. A man gets up from the veranda. Christian.

"Sharif," he says and comes towards me with his hand held out. I look at the infidel hand. Shake it.

"Have you come down to visit your father?" I ask.

"I live here," Christian says. "With my girlfriend, not far from here."

"Your girlfriend?" I say.

"Rachel, that's her name. A girl from the coast near Tanga."

"But what are you doing in Moshi?" I ask.

"I run a disco at Golden Shower Restaurant. You could come by tomorrow night. We could have a few beers," he says.

"I don't drink," I say.

"Have you stopped drinking?"

"I never did drink."

"You weren't above having a beer or two when you lived in Moshi," he says.

"I was young then – I didn't know what I was doing."

"But here at your uncle's – on Sundays men used to sit on the veranda and drink Konyagi and chew khat and play cards," he says.

"That's my uncle's choice. I'm not my uncle."

"Then have a soft drink. But come – I've got all the good music," Christian says.

"You can't be serious," I say.

"Can't be serious about what?"

"A disco. Adults don't do discos."

"Adults?" Christian says.

"Yes," I say. "We're supposed to be adults."

"There's no rush, is there?" he says.

"Life isn't all fun and games. It's serious," I say.

"You're the one who's serious," Christian says. "Life doesn't care one way or another."

"You're living a godless life with that . . . girl," I say.

"You bet I am, Sharif."

"That's why you're lost," I say. Christian shakes his head.

"Diana told me you'd got like that, but I didn't believe her," he says and walks towards the motorbike, kick-starts it and drives off. Good.

My uncle carries the shotgun out of the house and hands it to the driver, Yasir, who puts it behind the driver's seat in the cabin. Uncle returns to the house where he's standing on the patio with his hands at his waist, looking at the lorry and trailer, and towards the sky, which will be getting dark soon.

"It's ruining my digestion," Uncle says in Arabic.

"That we're bringing the shotgun with us?" I ask.

"The haulage company is a plant. We've tilled the earth, sown our seed. We've watered it and cultivated it. And all the barbarians want is to tear up our plant by the roots and eat it." My uncle spits at the gravel in front of the patio and the well-kept flowerbeds.

I am standing next to my half-cousin Qasim, who is a driver's assistant. Qasim is smoking a cigarette. Abdullahi comes out with a small wooden box packed with food and thermoses for the trip. Abdullahi is a mulatto – half Arab, half Negro. But a first-generation blend, not *mswahili*. Abdullahi is Orthodox. All afternoon he has been frying chapattis for our journey. His chapattis are perfect; flour, oil and water are kneaded so perfectly that the bread separates into the thinnest flakes when you tear off a piece.

"May Allah protect you," he says, and I swing myself into the cabin. Yasir turns on the engine, and the articulated lorry slowly jerks into life. We roll heavily down the cactus-framed drive and out through the iron gates into the early evening. The articulated lorry is overloaded. Four axles let the valuable tyres grind against the gravel until Yasir guides the wheel round in a sweeping motion, and the lorry swings out onto the middle of Kilimanjaro Road's patchy tarmac.

"May Allah protect you," Abdullahi shouts, waving as he closes the gate to Uncle's property so that it blends once more into rest of the fence, which is topped by three rows of barbed wire.

Yasir is an experienced driver and very solid even though he is *mswahili*. Qasim is his helper. Something inside Qasim is not quite right – you can't trust him. He left school because he never really went. Yes, he's part of the family, but his father has got him together with a local woman – a Christian. No thought of marriage or order. Qasim will run after any girl. He drinks beer when he can get it. I know he's even eaten pork because he wanted to try it. In the last year we've lost two drivers to the disease. A lorry driver makes good money. He is away from his wife for a long time, and he's lonely. Maybe he doesn't have the strength to sleep alone. He catches the disease and carries it around the main roads of Tanzania like freight.

But Qasim is family. You can't live without a family. Then you're just floating about, disconnected from all order. Families are falling apart in Tanzania – there's no work to be had in the rural areas, so the multigenerational families are split up. The young people come to the cities; ignorant illiterates with hunger in their bodies. That tidal wave will knock over any man who stands alone. But family and the community at the mosque and your neighbourhood, they can keep you safe. And Tanzania is full of opportunities if you work hard.

I look forward to getting home to my older brother in the Arab quarter in Dar es Salaam – the harbour of peace. To sit and talk with my sister-in-law, drinking tea, playing with the children. And I'm in love with a girl from Dar. Very much in love. Fadhila. She's studying to be a nurse in Saudi Arabia, and at the same time she's improving her Arabic so she can teach girls when she returns home.

Eighteen months ago I started noticing her in the neighbourhood. I found out that she was helping out at the office of her father's electricians – she took orders, did the bookkeeping, minded the phone. I saw her whenever there was a do at the mosque. I asked my friends who she was. But how could I speak to her? I looked around my older brother's flat. There were a few electrical sockets that had to be changed or fixed – they were loose, and it was dangerous for the children. I told my brother that. He smiled.

"Will you take care of it for me?" he asked.

"Yes, I'll make sure it's fixed," I said.

"I think you'll go to Najib Quhtan al-Shaabi," he said – the full name. And then he winked at me, starting to laugh. My face went red.

"Yes," I said.

My heart was pounding when I stepped into the shop and greeted her. She was wearing her veil high on her head, and it was a little bit see-through. I could see how her hair was twisted into a series of dark plaits that were fastened at the nape. She let her veil slip a bit further back. For me? I rested my arms on the tall counter and leaned my body across the desk a little as she turned to take some papers. Her pretty, slender feet in sandals. When I saw feet, I thought of ankles, and when I saw hands, I thought of arms. And when I saw her neck . . . I thought. Is that wrong? She is young, unmarried and the little fine hairs hang like misty tracks in front of her ears and on her upper lip. She looked at me and looked down, straightening her veil. I stood up – her father came in from the back of the shop.

"Ahh, Sharif," he said and shook hands. "Good to see you. How can we help?"

I said that it was good to see him and asked after his family and everything. We agreed about the job.

"You'll have to come and eat with us. I'll talk to my wife, and then I'll let you know when to come."

"I'd like that very much," I said.

"Fadhila will be going to Saudi to study very soon, after all," he said.

"Really? Congratulations," I said and smiled, feeling sad. She smiled as well and looked straight at me. We said goodbye. I talked to my older brother, my sister-in-law. Our families are in touch.

Yasir is keeping the articulated lorry in the middle of the road so the wheels won't tip into the holes at the sides where the tarmac has broken up after being undermined by water during the rains. The deep ditches along the road are never cleared of mud and can't carry the water away quickly enough during the monsoon. The scent of the acacia trees by the side of the road comes into the cabin as we slowly roll round the Y.M.C.A. roundabout and out onto the main road towards Road Junction. On our left the dark ridge of the mountain looks like a beached draught animal, and on our right the plain spreads out underneath the scattered clouds that catch the last rays of the sun and give off a glow the colour of cigarette filters.

Before Fadhila left, our families were on a picnic together in the park by Gymkhana Club. I strolled with Fadhila on the green grass, down towards the beach.

"Let's walk by the water," she said, and we crossed Ocean Road. Fadhila looked over her shoulder. The others couldn't see us.

"Now we're all alone," I said. Fadhila smiled and looked down. We were walking on the firm sand by the edge of the sea.

"I want to get my feet wet," she said and took off her sandals, holding them in her hand, lifting her *hijab* up a little and letting her feet be licked by the breaking waves. I took my sandals off as well, looking at her.

"I am going to miss you, Fadhila," I said. Fadhila smiled at me but quickly looked down. We were standing a metre from each other. She didn't say anything. She looked at her toes and at the hem of her *hijab* which had got wet. "I look forward to when you return," I said.

"I do too, Sharif," she said without looking up. And then she held out her hand, taking mine, and smiled a little smile, and then we started walking together at the water's edge, saying nothing, and her hand was soft and light. In the end I had to speak:

"What I want is to give you a good home. I'll look after you, Fadhila."

"I know you will," she said. I was going crazy. I wanted to kiss her so badly.

I too went abroad. Six months in Dubai to learn about computers. On a scholarship because we're Yemenites, Arabic-speaking Muslims. Yes, Arabic countries make a point of keeping close connections with their Muslim brothers in East Africa. I stayed with my brother in the Arab Quarter and worked as a taxi driver at night. The centre of Dubai – a shining pearl. Broad boulevards with uncracked tarmac, the cars brand new, buildings of steel and glass and smooth concrete, beautifully ornamented mosques made of sandstone, the lawns in the parks like green rugs, the abundance in the shops – like in a Hollywood film but with more style. No rubbish, no dirt, no beggars, no power cuts, no lack of anything. A society with a respect for religion. The freedom to pray without anyone shouting at you. And wealth. People behaving in very civilized ways; none of the wild stupidity of Africa. But expensive. A very expensive place. And far too many Westerners.

After the heat of the day, the temperature of the road has dropped so much that Yasir can increase his speed to sixty-five kilometres an hour. He has to be careful about the tyres because when the articulated trailer is heavily loaded, warm tarmac can eat the rubber and make it stick to the road in two black tracks. Getting new tyres can take months. But we have to get on because by morning we have to be on the tarmac road north of Dar es Salaam. If the sun rises too far, the heat will soon become so stifling that the treads will melt off the tyres under the weight of the articulated trailer and its load of corn flour, coffee beans, cooking oil, potatoes and plantain.

I researched the market in Dubai. We can import only slightly used equipment – computers, printers, photocopiers, telephones, fax machines – and then sell them in Tanzania. If we can get an import licence. The haulage business is a good one, but we need more, and I would like to build a business in Dar.

Politically it's still difficult to run a business in Tanzania. You can't let your business get too big or get too high a profile in other people's eyes. Then you'll be under pressure from politicians and high-ranking officials who can't be overtly involved in business – it'll ruin their careers – but still want a slice of the cake, some greasing of the palm in return for leaving you alone – there's still a lot of African socialism in the political system. But in a city like Dar you can hide. A small concern here, another there, with different names – different owners on paper. It does fine.

Fadhila is in Saudi Arabia for another four months. I have to talk more to my sister-in-law. She can advise me on everything. How do I go about it? What will matter to Fadhila, to her father, to my own family? But I've got an education, my family is a good one, I've got businesses, stability. It'll be fine. It has to be.

Yes, I've had girlfriends before – not many, but some, particularly when I was at school in Moshi. But it's different now. Fadhila. I want to marry her, have children, have a life. When the day comes when I ask her to take off her clothes – no other man will have seen her body, touched it, kissed it, possessed it.

The sun has gone completely now and only makes its presence felt by a faint purplish sheen on the horizon. At Road Junction, shortly before Himo, we turn right on the road towards Tanga and Dar and stop at the last petrol station before the tarmac ends and four hundred kilometres of maltreated dirt road begins. If we're lucky, a road scraper will have pulled its steel blade across the road to even out the deepest cracks and fill the holes. Yasir fills the tank with diesel while Qasim washes the front window and headlights, making the dead insects land in a moist dust-crusted strip on the bumper. I wash as best I can in the toilet and carry my prayer rug to the edge of the concrete patio surrounding the petrol station. With a little help from the stars I can turn to the north and then a little bit east – Mecca.

"Aren't you going to pray?" I say to Qasim.

"It's my job to guard the lorry," he says.

"You could pray next to the lorry, or on top of it," I say.

"I haven't brought my rug," he says. I drop the subject. Yasir comes over to us. We stand outside the cabin, hurriedly gulping down a little bit of food and tea – it's hard to eat when you're driving on the dust road.

It is fully dark by the time we roll out of the petrol station, only to be stopped immediately at the first road block. Yasir gets out of the cabin and talks to the military men, discreetly handing them the money that will allow us to move on. Otherwise they could delay our transport by refusing to recognize our paperwork. They could make us empty the articulated trailer of goods so they could search its every nook and cranny. The night could end with the cargo on the road where the plantains and potatoes would be made dirty by the dust and start disintegrating as soon as the sun rose. No violence or threats – just a lot of trouble, because everyone needs money to live on. When we pay, it's easy. We save our cargo, we stay on time. Now we can only be stopped by thieves who have placed felled trees across the road. But that almost never happens, and we have a shotgun behind the front seats. Or we could be stopped a large animal on the road. If you hit a goat, you have to just to drive on, otherwise a crowd can gather around the lorry, and you can become stranded in endless negotiations that culminate in your having to pay through your nose for the animal. A cow is enough to crush your bonnet even at low speeds.

We're driving again – now on the ravaged dirt road. Our speed is low, and Yasir is keeping his eyes glued to the front window as he steers us away from the worst potholes. But they're everywhere, and the cabin tips violently on its shock absorbers.

"Check the cargo," he tells Qasim, who opens the passenger door and nimbly swings out so he can climb onto the articulated trailer while the fine red dust rises the ground in a constant cloud. Qasim loosens the tarpaulin and climbs in with his torch to check if the cargo has moved around. Afterwards he climbs up the stepladder on the back of the cabin and looks ahead while he whoops.

"*Tsk*," Yasir says. "He is a stupid boy."

Luck is on our side. During the rain the waters carve deep furrows through the road, but they have been evened out.

Qasim comes down again. Road Junction disappears further behind us. We're driving parallel to the railway that the Germans built using Indian labour, because back then the negroes didn't understand the concept of money. Everything was a trade-off – they didn't want to work in return for paper and round bits of metal. The Indians knew about money and trade. They knew so much about it that after the railway was completed they set up *dukas* – little shops – all over the country. It beat being a coolie in India. The negroes learned to understand money, because now money could give them access to all the exciting items in the Indians' shops. But the Indians have always kept the blacks at arm's length. They don't want to mix blood with black people. And the Indians kept each other at arm's length too, dividing into groups of Sikhs, Portuguese-speaking Catholics from Goa, Sunni Muslims, Shia Muslims, Hindus with the caste system. Little groups. And they have each kept their cultures alive through their mutual distrust and hatred. There is no mixing between the different Indian communities – no-one speaks to anyone from another group. Each one gets its wives from India – new blood for the exiles. Or they send the Marriage File around to similar little communities in East Africa. Their doors are locked, because all Indians view their own peculiar culture as perfect. That's why everyone hates them. No-one wants what they have. On Sundays the Indians in Dar drive out to Oyster Bay – men, women and children. They sit in their little groups, go about on the beach, stand about. They try to stare right across the ocean to the lost land. I think: just start swimming. But they don't want to go to India. They all work to get their children to the West – America, Britain, Canada. Africa is only a stopover.

The white people aren't hated – all Africans want what the white people have. It's very appealing: car, fridge, radio – the negro turns a button and sound gushes out; is that paradise? But the white people have lies built in to their lives. They go out and use other people's countries until they go home again. They don't belong here. A white man in Tanzania – even one that was born here – will always keep his European citizenship. He's not dedicated.

I am looking forward to going home. To walking on the pier, looking at the yachts from Zanzibar. The smell of the sea. I live with my oldest brother's family in the Arabian Quarter between the city centre and Kariakoo, close to the mosque. There are many Arabic-speaking people there, and at home we speak only Arabic so the children pick it up. My job is mostly with the haulage company, and I am starting a computer shop. I play old-boys football twice a week in the Gymkhana Club; I participate in the social work set up by the mosque. But mostly I just work hard.

In a few days Ramadan will start. It'll be difficult in Dar es Salaam. The population is a mixture of many religions, so I have to keep the businesses going while I am fasting. The worst thing is when you have to go out to customers; you can easily become trapped in traffic under the burning sun for an hour and a half. You become parched.

I started fasting when I was six or seven years old; it was like a competition between the children over who could go the longest – I may have fasted five days during Ramadan that first year – the next year it was ten days. Children who didn't fast were bullied by the others at the Muslim school. They were weak. I snuck out to the toilet during the day and had a little water. And the Prophet's piercing eyes came right through the roof and saw me. And when I went back to the classroom, I thought everyone could see it – how bloated I was with illegal water – the shame spun around in my veins. I had failed. I was worse than the infidels because I had violated the inviolable. Sometimes my mother would insist that I drink a large glass of water when I came home from school. I cried, dizzy with thirst, because I didn't want to drink it. "Fasting isn't for children, Sharif," my mother said. "It says so in the Koran."

"I am not a child," I said, pushing the glass away so violently that she dropped it on the floor and – plagued by thirst herself – could feel the water splash coolly over her feet.

"Are you a man then, blubbing like a girl?" she asked.

"I don't want to break the fast. It's shameful," I howled.

"You're going to drink a glass of water right now. And if you don't stop crying, you'll get another glass to replace all those tears, because if you don't you'll end up a dry boy and get ill."

"I don't want to," I said.

"I'm telling your father," she said – her hand raised. And I drank the water. A glass and a half of it – the half glass was for my tears. I remember the year when she stopped offering me water after school. I was sitting in the kitchen waiting for the glass – it didn't come. One day I drank so much water in the bathroom that I was sick. She didn't say anything when I came out. But her eyes.

We fasted at boarding school as well. *Mama* Hussein organized it for us; we were woken up at five – well before sunrise – so we would have time to eat and drink. She taught us how. Fruit and vegetables are good, much better than water, because the moisture is locked inside complex carbohydrates that are slowly processed by the stomach and so it continues to be released for a long time. Tea and coffee are diuretics – a bad idea. After lessons when the others went off for lunch, it was time for us to lie down on our beds, to rest. Afterwards we could wash our faces, rinse out our mouth but spit out all the water again – not a drop was allowed to run down – the dryness in the throat must be preserved. I thought a lot about who I was. I thought that that was the whole point; contemplating your religion, your relationship with Allah, asking questions. Back then I did. Not everyone sees it like that. These days my questions are a personal matter, private and only for me. In the mosque in Kariakoo there's no room for questions – only for answers.

At school I was the top scorer on the football team. I had to play – during the fast as well. Sweat would gush from me until I ran dry; I saw spots – was dehydrated, dizzy. One day I fainted during the second half. I came to on my bed. *Mama* Williams was sitting there with a glass of water. She lifted up my head.

"You're allowed to drink when you're ill," she said. Gently I pushed her hand away.

"I know who I am," I said.

"Are you being arrogant?" she asked.

"It's my own fault," I said. She waited. I said: "Playing football – it's ambition." She left. Was it ambition? Or just a game? The girls on the side, watching, cheering? Katja – my first love. I was lying there, waiting for sunset. At half past six dinner was served to the Orthodox. And it was a feast, sharing. Every night was a great joy.

Not all the Muslims at school fasted. Nowhere near. I knew Hadija all the way back from school in Mwanza. She didn't fast. I asked why?

"I had an ulcer once. I'm not allowed to fast," she said. "It's dangerous for me."

"When did you have an ulcer?" I asked.

"In the Greek school in Arusha; it was stressful for me to be away from home and live in the dormitory. It made me ill," Hadija said. I don't know whether to believe her. All sorts of excuses are used. Some people say that they can't fast because they travel. Travellers are not required to fast. Every day they travel from Kijito up to school and back again. Others claim that they don't fast because they're staying among strangers at the boarding school. According to the Book one must keep the customs of strangers when visiting their countries, so as not to cause offence. All the excuses are lies to mask laziness. We're not visiting a foreign country; almost half the population of Tanzania is Muslim, even though there are more on the coast than inland. It's our country as much as it is anyone's.

And yes, it's hard when you live among Christians, Hindus and Sikhs. Our everyday life is not designed to accommodate fasting. You have to keep up with your obligations to both the school and Allah. A hard discipline. It's almost impossible to learn if you haven't done it since you were a child.

"I need tea," Yasir says, because we're on the stretch when the road is almost perfect. Qasim pours it. Lights a cigarette for Yasir. We drink the tea, and I look at the solid wall of darkness standing before the headlights of the lorry. We have opened the windows to let in some air, and I can see the vaulting sky that surrounds us with stars all the way down to the ground where unbroken darkness marks the horizon. The smell of baked dust fills the cabin, and the light sweeps across the grey-green shrubs on the side of the road. Qasim finds a brown paper bag of khat leaves which Yasir starts chewing so he can stay awake all night. Our bodies are thrown around in the cabin when we suddenly swerve.

The dust seeps into our skin, nose, eyes, clothes. We sit in a daze.

"Sharif. Sharif." Qasim is shaking me. I must have slept. The air is cool and clear. I open my eyes. Raindrops on the front window. The wind is hurling past us.

"It's too soon," I say. The rains aren't due to start for another few weeks at least.

"It's bad," Yasir says. The drops fall one at a time, heavily. There's lightning. And the skies open. We drive into a wall of water which makes the road liquid. Yasir lowers his speed and leans forward to see through the pulsating windscreen wipers – every hole is invisible, filled with water. The articulated lorry is overloaded. If we get stuck, we're really stuck. The road shines boiling and black in the light from the headlights. The road is made soggy by the masses of water. I lean forward and squint. Something matte black on the road ahead.

"Tree," I shout and grab the dashboard. Yasir gears down, brakes. We're at a standstill twenty metres from the tree trunk.

"Lock the door," Yasir tells Qasim.

"The wind may have knocked it over," I say, while Yasir looks to the sides.

"Only one way to find out: Go over and see whether the tree has broken or been felled," Yasir says.

Qasim doesn't say anything; the job will fall to him. The tree trunk stretches right across the road from the shrubs on one side to the ditch on the other. It's a young tree, full of leaves and branches which are still juicy – just fallen. But was it felled?.

"What do you think?" I ask.

"The trunk isn't thick," Qasim says.

"I'll try to go over it," Yasir says. He puts the lorry in gear, starts it slowly and increases speed. The tree gets bigger the closer we get. "*Tsk*," Yasir says and brakes. We stop four metres from the tree. We're never going to get over it. Qasim opens the door on his side, and the lights in the cabin switch on. "Close the door," Yasir says sharply. He doesn't switch off the engine. Qasim closes the door again. We sit in darkness.

"Why do you want me to close it?" Qasim asks.

"I don't want them to be able to see in," Yasir says.

"Who?" Qasim says.

"There might be robbers out there," Yasir says. To the left of the road there are scattered trees and to the right is the ditch, full of water.

"Shall we turn around then?" Qasim asks.

"The road's too narrow," Yasir says and takes the shotgun from behind the front seat, checking that it's loaded. He reaches his hand up to the ceiling and moves the switch on the light so it doesn't turn on when the door is opened. We all peer through the windows, but there's nothing to be seen but darkness and pouring rain, trees that sway in the wind.

"How do we do this?" I ask. Qasim reaches across me and honks the horn. Yasir slaps away his arm.

"Don't do that," Yasir says.

"We need help," Qasim says.

"There is no help," Yasir says. "There is only us." He looks at Qasim. "Take the *panga* and the torch and go over to see if the tree has broken or was felled, and shout back to us. I'm ready with the gun if anyone comes." Qasim doesn't say anything. He takes the torch from the glove compartment and the *panga* from under the seat. Opens the door and jumps out, while Yasir roots around in the glove compartment and gets more shells ready. Qasim's shirt is first mottled and then completely dark with water as he walks past the headlights to the roadside and the roots of the tree. Yasir rolls down his windows a little so we can hear. Qasim shines his torch into the roadside and turns around to us.

"The tree was felled by people," he shouts.

"Robbers," Yasir mutters. The darkness behind Qasim shifts; a young man with his hand raised high. In his hand a *panga* which he hacks into Qasim's shoulder by the neck. Qasim screams and falls to his knees, while the torch flies from his hand. The man is gone. We can't see anyone else in the dark. The blood spouts in a jet from Qasim's neck and is beaten to the ground by the rain, mixing with the mud. Qasim grabs his throat and tries to get up. "Take the gun," Yasir says, handing it to me, giving me the shells and looking out while he feverishly rolls down the side window. Rain whips into the cabin. The torch is on the muddy road, shining faintly. "Sharif," Yasir says as he takes the *panga* from under his own seat. He grabs my shoulder and shakes me; looks at me with his eyes wide open. "You stay in here, ready to fire," he says.

"Yes," I say.

"And you will fire."

"Yes."

"As soon as you see anything." He opens his door, steps down, and I see a *panga* come rushing down towards him from the side.

"Yasir," I shout as his arm is struck by the blade. He screams, and I throw myself over towards the wheel and see the man a metre from Yasir, his *panga* ready to strike again. And I shoot – the man's head jerks back, red, without features; he falls, loose-limbed on the muddy road; a young farmer. A ragged shirt, worn trousers, car-tyre sandals. Yasir grabs his right arm, and I can see the blood seeping out between his fingers. I stare out into the darkness by the side of the articulated trailer and ahead to the lit-up sodden road where Qasim is lying, blood pumping from the wound in his neck. The tree trunk lies there, with slick leaves trembling under the raindrops. Qasim's face is resting in the sludge.

"Qasim," I shout.

"He's dead," Yasir says.

"Do you think they'll be back?" I ask.

"They'll be back," Yasir says. "Maybe they've already cut the tarpaulin open at the back of the trailer and are taking our cargo right now."

"Maybe there were only two of them, and the other one is afraid of our gun now," I say

"There's only two of us as well," Yasir says. He's standing looking at his blood-soaked shirtsleeve. I pull the used shell out of the shotgun, put a new one in, take a few in my hand and tuck them into the pocket of Yasir's trousers. "What are you doing?" he asks.

"See if anyone comes back," I say and put the gun on the floor of the cabin, where I can grab it quickly. I tear off one sleeve of my shirt at the shoulder. "Let go of your arm and pick up our *panga*," I say. He does it. I tie my shirtsleeve tightly around the bleeding gash in his arm. I pick up the gun and hand it to him while I take the *panga* from his good hand. Yasir's eyes look sunken. "Go and stand in the light with the gun while I move the tree trunk," I say.

"You can't move it," Yasir says and looks at the ground, shaking his head slowly.

"Go on," I say. He gets out and stands with the gun right between the lorry and the tree – looking around. I run past Qasim and pick up the torch – it's still working. With the *panga* and the torch in my hands I light my way as I go behind the cabin to open the toolbox which sits welded onto the lorry body. The water running down my face tastes acidic and salty. My clothes are clinging to my body. I grab the rope and run back to the tree, secure it and go back to the hook below the bumper. My chin is shaking. I swallow. Grit my teeth. Tighten the knot. Yasir roars. He's standing with the gun raised, roaring. There's no-one to be seen except for the bodies. I hop into the cabin and reverse slowly. The rope is stretched and the tree trunk shifts. I pull it slowly backwards, so it'll lie parallel to the road. I can sense the back of the articulated trailer turning behind me – a couple of more metres and it will end up in the ditch. The front wheels start spinning in the mud. No traction.

"Stop," Yasir shouts. Otherwise the tyres will only sink further into the sodden ground. The tree is still blocking the road. I sob involuntarily and slam my hands into the wheel. I dig my nails into my palms. Open the door and leap out. Now the farmer's body is lying within the cones of the headlights – the face is blackish-red and pale white from brains or bone. Little tremors go through the body. Yasir sees it.

"Should I shoot him?" he asks.

"I don't know," I say. Yasir stares at the front wheels, which have ground themselves more than a hand span into the mud. Little rivulets are running around towards the ditch. The patterns on the tyres are worn.

"We're never getting out of here," he says. I put a hand on his neck.

"Be alert," I say.

"Yes," he says, standing up, looking around at the curtain of rain which is pouring down around us. I leap up to the toolbox and grab the spade. Behind the front tyres I dig out trenches for the wheels to drive up. But they must be lined so the tyres have something to grab onto. I grab my *panga* and go to the side of the road. I hack at the shrubs, tearing grass and branches loose with my hands while I stare into the dark and my arms shake. I carry the lot to the trenches, which have already filled up with water. I push branches and grass down behind the wheels, but the streams of water that are coming over the road take them with it, making them float, sail away.

"The load is heavy. We need more traction," Yasir says.

"*What do you want me to do?*" I scream.

"Get into the trailer and grab some sacks," he shouts. I don't say anything, just climb into the trailer, loosening the tarpaulin, sticking in my head and shining the faint light of my torch; no-one has cut their way through to the cargo. My stomach is a knot. I climb under the tarpaulin and over lumpy sacks of potatoes while the rain beats against the canvas. Out again. Down. My heart is racing as I go to the side of the road and hack more branches from the shrubs. A thin screech is coming from my throat when I breathe, and my eyes burn from staring out into the darkness. I go back, fall to my knees in the mud, packing branches into the trenches, folding the sacks and putting them on top like tracks over the first two metres behind the front tyres. I build a way out of the mire. I sit up. Look at Yasir, the tree trunk, Qasim's dead body, the faceless man. I climb into the cabin, getting the lorry in gear, pressing down the clutch – carefully. The wheels catch, the cabin rises a little, but I feel spinning, declutch; the lorry tips forward once more into the holes. I try going forwards, but now the wheels won't catch. I can't bear it. I know I should get out, try something different. It's unbearable. Yasir is standing there shouting, waving his arms, wanting me to stop. I turn the steering wheel a little, putting it into reverse and giving it full throttle – the wheels spin, I let go. Turn the other way, giving it full throttle. Lift. It shifts. The cabin rises, the wheels catch, the lorry and trailer are moving. My bladder lets go. Warm liquid runs down my legs as the rope tightens and the tree trunk shifts. I brake. I'm not going to end up in the ditch. Neutral gear. The tree is lying where we can pass it.

"Are you ready?" I shout out to Yasir. He turns and looks at me with empty eyes. I grab the *panga* and jump out in the mud – urine mixing with the water in my shoes. I run over to the tree where I hack the rope in two so I don't have to waste time untying the knot.

"Keep watch," I shout. He turns around and watches. I can smell myself, but the rain is washing me. I run over and untie the knot on the bumper, quickly rolling up the rope, throwing it into the cabin. I go over to Yasir. "We're going," I say.

"What about Qasim?" he asks. I grab the gun to take it from him, but he won't let go.

"No," Yasir says. I let go.

"What are you going to do?" I ask. Yasir doesn't say anything. He turns and goes the few steps over to the farmer's body, which is lying quietly in the mud. Yasir raises the gun and fires – the body jerks. I turn my back before Yasir can look at me. I leap into the cabin and get behind the steering wheel, shutting the door.

"We're going," I shout. Yasir walks slowly to the passenger side. Puts the gun on the floor of the cabin. Gets in. "Hurry up," I say. He sits down heavily and shuts the door, panting, looking straight ahead.

"What about Qasim?" he says.

"Qasim is dead," I say and get the lorry into gear.

Security Guard – Helsinki

Today's lecture is over – I missed it. I am sitting in a café with a ciggy and a paper. It's winter. A security guard at the port was killed by a lorry full of stolen video recorders. This morning the ambulance crew had to wrench him from the tarmac. The heat of his body had made the ice melt. Later the water froze.

I am going to work. Five days a week I sharpen skates at an ice rink from 16.00 till 22.00. I don't know how to skate.

Helsinki is white. Snow and skin. University stinks. Philosophy. Kant, Hegel, Schopenhauer. Great thoughts, ideas – but the world . . . no, not the world, *man* – we're the same. Man is neither good nor bad – he's an opportunist.

It's not like I once thought: that I was carving a new path through life, doing something real. I am walking in someone else's footsteps. I am not shining. I am casting a shadow. Why? An action cannot be wholly good. Utopias are utopias. Humanists who yell at everyone that they must behave, that if they did the world would be beautiful at long last. Fascists in disguise. The philosophers. Humbug. I still have to eat, shit, sleep. Reading is nothing compared to experiencing. Words are the dust with which our flesh will mix. And deep inside me is my reptilian brain. It only cares about three things: sex, food, power.

We are different; what is good to one man constitutes the destruction of another. No "One Love" paradise on earth, no Zion. Only Babylon. Terror; dread – it's growing out of my head. My dreads are returning. I cut them off four months ago because I suddenly had problems. Last summer they were fine – I was playing golf, and I was the "Lion of Zion". A couple of girls showed an interest. A drunk person came over and grabbed on to one of the long ones. "Is that real hair? Or did you have it made somewhere?" I said: "It's real." He said: "How do you get it like that?" – not in a polite way. I said: "It just grows. I leave it alone." That's what I did. Left it alone. Those sausages of hair that got too big, I just pulled them apart. Otherwise the hair will start pulling at the skin on your skull – it can most likely pull off your skull. In the late summer I got scalp plague; had to cut off everything because it was bleeding. I had sores and scars. It was probably just dandruff and dirt. It was a warm summer. I played golf and drank a lot of beer. It's not very good for you. A shower won't wash your head if you're getting fat and drinking beer and have chemicals gushing out of your skin. You shouldn't pretend to be dread if you're drinking. It's a part of the basic philosophy. And it makes sense: what comes in must come out. I picked up the dreads I had cut off and wove them into a short rope. Cut back on the drinking. Now my dreads are coming back. The terror must come from inside my head until I have made myself three metres worth of rope. Enough for hanging myself. If I sprog up before the rope is long enough, I'll tie it round a branch and a car tyre; a swing for my offspring. A child – what for? – negating the terror, or passing it on – to make it be relived? Or I could swing in the rope myself. Dreadlock.

The police say to the paper that the Russian mafia is active in the Helsinki ports. I leaf back to the job ads. Security guard; you must be eighteen and have a clean rap sheet – those are the requirements. I am a 23-year-old saint. I apply for the job.

"You put a hat over that hair of yours," Haiko, the boss, tells me.

"Got it," I say. The first week is introduction. I catch a thief on my third day. One of the older guys is showing me the ropes. He is very nice – simple, but civilized. We get a call on the radio. He has to go. The guard service is constantly understaffed because of people falling ill or just not showing up, going away. My mentor has to go on call on another route; he is a foreman and must fill gaps in the rota. We've been out once together; now I get my first trip alone. I am called on the radio: the alarm's gone off in Hakkaniiemen Elantor – an old department store two kilometres from the city centre. Three floors of food, clothes, furniture, everything. I drive out there. My headlights sweep across the snow and blind me. At the head office they have a machine with buttons and bulbs – a sort of fuse box – and it shows where in the building the alarm was activated. I get there, let myself in through the back door in the basement and open the alarm box. I call them over the radio and ask:

"So, what does it say?"

"Right," Haiko says. "A window on the second floor and a motion sensor in the hunting department on the third floor."

"Hunting department," I say. "Lovely."

"Try pressing the buttons first," he says, because the alarms are often due to a fault in the system. I press the buttons.

"Anything?" I say into my walkie-talkie.

"It doesn't beep now," he says. "But you're going to have to do a round and check everything's O.K."

"O.K.," I say, switching on my torch. If the thief has closed the window after he got in, then the alarm isn't active any longer. And I'm sure the motion sensors can be bypassed. How the hell do I get to the hunting department? Do I even want to go? I don't know this place. On the second floor I wander around looking for an open window. My torch sweeps the place – fuck, this is creepy. O.K., there – a broken window. Maybe someone threw a stone through it, or the windowpane just lost its will to live. I go to the third floor. Weapons, they said. I call over the radio. "Broken window on the second floor."

"Alright, leave the radio on. Can you see if anything's missing?"

"I have no idea," I say. How the hell can I know?

"O.K., hold on. We're going to have to call an experienced guard. The police are on their way. We're going to have to be thorough."

I wait. Let the cone of light sweep the place and walk towards the till to shine the torch down behind it; up comes a guy of about sixteen, short and thin with a black balaclava. I'm terrified. He's almost sobbing. I realize I'm wearing sunglasses. I take them off.

"Good evening," I say.

"Can't you just let me go?" he says.

"Shit, I can't let you go. You should have got out sooner, because the police are on their way, and you've broken that bloody window. You should have made yourself known sooner," I say.

"But I'm sorry I did it," he says.

"Yes. What do we do?" I ask, as I hear police sirens outside the building. My walkie-talkie bleeps. "Hang on," I say, listening. I turn it off and look at the kid: "Alright then. There's someone here now – you're just going to have to come out with me."

"Can't you just say you saw someone run out?" the kid whimpers.

"Look," I say and let my arms fall to my sides. "If it were up to me ... But they're going to search the place with dogs, in case there are more of you. Those dogs, I tell you, they've got teeth." I put the walkie-talkie back on. "I've got the guy. I'm going to try to find my way out." The kid comes with me. We get lost. "Are you known around here?" I ask.

"Er, yes," he says.

"Lead the way," I say.

"You're the security guard," he says. Haiko's voice scratches through the radio.

"Jarno! Where are you?"

"I'm damned if I know," I say into it. "We're trying to find our way to the basement. I haven't got the keys to the front door." We're on the second floor. The kid points to the broken window, saying:

"I could climb down from there ... ? I could disappear over the roof."

"No, that won't wash. They're down there, ready. They know you're here – I can't lose this job. I would have let you go, but ...

We're standing across from each other in the dark department store. He's probably thinking about running away, hiding. But then there are the dogs. He's still got his balaclava on.

"Take your hat off," I say. He does it. He's just a boy. Sixteen years old, dressed in black, spotty. He's done it all; he's seen the films. But he's scared now. I feel sorry for him. We finally find the way out; I put an arm around the kid's shoulder. Open the door. There's a policeman with a gun.

"Hey, John Wayne," I say. "It's just a boy who's . . . you know." I shrug. Another policeman cuffs the boy, and I have to go to the station with them to give my statement. I repeat it: "Hey, you know, the boy. Come on. He's just a child."

"He's a criminal," the policeman says. I drive over to an office building – find a bottle of wine. Yes, of course I'm shocked. A little boy. He was standing in the hunting department, waiting for the heavy-duty security guard – instead he got Michael Jackson with dreadlocks. We'll both have fond memories.

Safely home, I read through the guard's manual, which describes how the job is to be done. I want to know what to do if I run into something. It says that guards must drive down to check on the stationary guards at the entrance to the harbour – if there's enough time. I'm lonely. Perhaps it would earn me a cup of coffee, a ciggy, a late-night chat.

The night is white; everything is lit by street lights and reflections from newly fallen snow and the glass facades of the office buildings. In Stoman's I steal mirrored sunglasses with a Dixie flag on each lens; a red background, the blue X in the middle with a white rim and embellished with white stars. Stars sweep through my eyeballs. I drive an Opel Ascona through the night, listening to a great *dub*. I perfect skidding wide around the corners on the icy roads. I have heaps of keys, a torchlight, a walkie-talkie, a uniform. I go to work at 16.00 and continue till 8.00 the next morning. The law says you can't work more than eight hours a day.

Whatever. If you work for two hours, you can get away with resting for an hour – it depends on how serious you are about it and how clever. I have lectures at university, so I have to sleep occasionally. If you do the job by the book, you'll never make it – it's not doable. Minimum wage. I go everywhere in Helsinki, including the harbours. Stockman, the large abattoirs, the American Embassy, the State Radio, the Finnair offices. My work can be monitored; I have a key that I stick into time clocks that are placed here and there around the site. The clock is a round metal box with a keyhole. My key is supposed to be turned within certain timeframes, and my clocking in is registered inside the time clock as a cut in a roll of paper.

In most buildings there are two staircases – the front and the back ones. I am supposed to go between the two so that I am physically moving through each and every floor, and at either side I am to stick in my key and turn. Everyone just goes up one staircase and down the other, turning the key in the time clock on the way because, really, who cares? The truth will come out if anyone ever examines the time markings on the paper rolls; the floors are never checked.

The guard service hires a Negro. I smile when I see him. He doesn't smile. He looks at my sunglasses.

"Do you know what that means?" he asks in Finnish without the slightest trace of an accent.

"Means?" I say.

"The flags on your glasses," he says. I do know: red is blood, blue is longing, and the stars are the dream of Zion.

"No," I say.

"It's a Dixie flag – the Confederate battle flag from the American Civil War. The Confederates fought for the preservation of slavery," he says.

"Yes," I say. "They won."

"What do you mean?" he asks.

"*Tsk*," I say and go to the coffee machine. I fill my mug and go down to the car. Pseudo-black.

Hotels – they're fine by me. I can eat. That's fantastic. Go into the kitchen. There's no-one at night. It's the same in the kitchens in the large companies; food galore. I take whatever I like; get my fingers into the big bosses' food. I am careful. Wash my hands first, so my germs don't make them ill. Whole boards of directors could get ill from the lobster the next day if I get sloppy. It's a war. I know the companies that have good kitchens, and I visit them three times a night. The first time there might be someone working late, so I do what I have to – I check them out. I'm in charge – twenty-three years old and covered in beer-spots. I even boss the boss around if he's there:

"Who are you?"

"I'm the boss."

"O.K., let's see some I.D. – your card."

And in the middle of the night I get the munchies; I have to be smart about it. Because I've got these keys, and the time at which I turn them is registered and randomly checked, and if something goes wrong, someone will certainly look into it. If I take fifteen minutes and eat myself a nice dinner with wine and everything, I'll be in the shit. Yes, it'd be my own company that would be checking me and they're not strict, but there are limits. I have three minutes to eat in this office building, and then I can go to the hotel, see what they've got – half a lasagne would do the job, even if it is cold; there's never enough time to heat the food. I eat as I go. The plate – I toss it into the night.

The shops – I'm fair. I don't take very much at all. Things go missing, sure. Sunglasses, food, clothes, shoes, golf balls. It just ends up in the stolen-items statistics – they don't do an inventory of the stock every morning. Morals? They're a pastime for people who can afford them. I enjoy life's simpler pleasures. Try this pinstriped shirt – it suits Jarno.

University? No, I don't do that much. Morose, tacit Finns, unapproachable girls.

It's thawing even though it's the middle of winter. I'm parked at the airport, watching the planes take off – their lights sailing towards the night sky.

The work. Supermarkets. Veg and meat packed in plastic foam and cling film. There's no other difference between Africa and Europe. A thousand years of evolution – vacuum-packed meat. Tarmac on the streets, and street lamps, and sewers, and central heating. Fragile. White people are always working. Black people sit down and talk. It's dark when I go to work – dark when I get off in the morning. Tarmac. Cold counters. Street lamps. I drive the car back. Walk home on the sludgy pavements. Sunday morning. It's my birthday. Twenty-four years. The air is crisp and cold. The flagstones are perfectly aligned to each other in an unbroken line, and the facades of the housing-association blocks are flat and void of expression. People hurry past each other without looking at anything, other than the window dressings. Cars are driving with studded tyres even though the snow has gone. I kick at some sand that is lying on the pavement – pointless after the thaw. Drink a cup of coffee. Listen to the neighbours having a row. Then they start laughing, then they copulate. Jesus.

The entrance to the harbour. There's a small wooden cabin with light, and heating, and coffee, and a girl is sitting in one of them. Laina. I'm interested in that girl. Yes, she does look a little mousy – thoughtful, raw; mousy straight hair framing her pale forehead. Finnish; that slightly Mongoloid thing about the eyes, the Nordic frost. She's perhaps five years older than me. But once she smiles – pure poison. I make a habit of driving down to her, asking if she's alright. Grabbing a cup of coffee, trying to make her laugh. I tell her about my childhood in Tanzania, which I left four years ago.

I tell her about pigs:

"There's this village not far from us where they have pigs running free. Dark pigs, otherwise they would burn. One day my dad drives through the village and hits a pig. It's dead on the spot. He stops – you should never stop; you'll pay through your nose for it. But he's white, so he thinks people are full of the milk of human kindness. He's made to pay through his nose but is quite pleased with the pig, which we have for dinner. We hear about the same thing happening to other white people. It turns out that the boys in the village listen out for cars; if the person driving is white, the boys will whip around, trying to catch a pig each. They'll lie flat on the stomachs between the shrubs by the roadside, holding their pigs by the hind legs. When the white man's car is very close they'll let go – the pig will squeal and dash across the road. Sometimes it gets hit. It's good business."

I tell her about the time my mother went to her driving test in Morongoro, but I tell the story like it had happened to myself:

"You had to bring your own car. The driving examiner directs me to a shop where we buy a huge sack of rice. Then we drive over to the man's house, drag the sack inside, and then return to the police station. And then he tells me I've passed."

I tell her about corruption:

"My father's tailor in Msumbe has a list with the price of all government officials in Tanzania from office clerks to schoolteachers, mayors, government officials, all the way up to ministers and even the president himself. Next to each of them there's a number, except for the president."

"After all, he can't be bought," Laina says.

"He can, but the tailor doesn't know his price," I say and look into Laina's grey eyes; a windswept tundra. I tell her all sorts of things just to see her smile. On the way back I have to stop on the pier, turn off the engine and switch off the headlights, so I can sort my flustered self out.

The next night I am there again.

"Any problems?" I ask.

"As a matter of fact there was one guy who's been giving me a bit of bother," Laina says. "I think he's drunk. He's the boss at the meat factory."

"Bothering you how?"

"You know. He's been around several times, trying to say something clever."

"O.K. – I'll stay," I say.

"What about your schedule?" she asks. "I could just call you if I had any trouble."

"I'll just have a cup of coffee," I say and offer her a cigarette. We sit, smoke. A Merc comes out from the enclosed area.

"That's him," she says. We get up and go to the window, where there's a desk that controls the gate. The man in the car can see me through the window. She opens the gate, he raises his hand, drives off.

"Oh, didn't have anything clever to say this time," she says. We hear a metallic sound.

"What was that?" I ask.

"Did he hit something?" she asks. We go out. My car is parked right there.

"He winged it," I say.

"Drunken idiot," she says.

"Shit. I'm going to have to report it," I say.

"Sure, report him," Laina says. It's not a big scratch. If I don't report it, it'll be put down as something I did. "I've got his name and number plate," she says. We go inside, light cigarettes. I call it in.

"We'll notify the police," they say. Alright then. Catch the bugger. I want things straight. I put out my ciggy. Get up. Go towards the door. Grab the handle.

"See you," I say. She takes hold of my arm. I turn around. She lets go.

"I'm glad you came," she says, looking down at the floor.

"Yes," I say. "Well then . . ." I go out. Damn. I get into the car, turn on my *dub*, drive off. There's something black at the roadside – is it . . . ? I break, reverse. A car tyre. I get out and get it vertical. Almost no wear. In South Africa traitors against the A.N.C. had a car tyre put round their necks, and were doused with petrol, set alight – a burning necklace; an ornament. I throw the car tyre into the boot to take it home. I may need it.

The next day foreman Haiko comes over to me when I report to work:

"Your eyes look like piss holes in a snow dune," he says.

"Thanks."

"And what were you doing on the harbour at that time of night?"

"Using the toilet," I say.

"Denting the car, more like," he says.

"No, I didn't. He . . . there was this person; the boss at the meat factory. I've got his name, and I called it in last night. He should have been picked up by the police."

"No, the police haven't been," Haiko says. "And the boss says he hasn't done anything."

"You can ask the security guard by the gate. This guy was the only one there last night. It can't have been anyone else. It's clear as day. We heard the collision. We saw him drive off."

"What were you doing there at the harbour?" Haiko asks.

"Security guards are supposed to look in on the guards on the harbour," I say.

"What do you mean – supposed? I'm not paying for you to get your leg over," Haiko says.

"It's part of the job that the mobile guards must drop in on the stationary guards," I say.

"That's not your job," he says.

"It says so in the manual," I say and go to a desk where there's a copy of it. I find the manual and show it to Haiko. His lips move as he reads.

"I did not know that," he says.

"I'm just doing my job," I say. Nothing happens to the meat boss, who has hired the guard service and pays our wages. But nothing more is said about the dent. And the girl is alluring. Maybe I shouldn't hang myself in the rope I am making from my hair after all – maybe it's meant to carry a car tyre.

I ask Laina to a bar. She drinks. A lot. She tells me she comes from somewhere up north. A long way up north.

"The nearest bus stop was thirty kilometres away," she says.

"Let's go," I say.

"I'm not going to sleep with you," she says when we've got outside.

"No, but let me walk you home," I say. She's sick all over a dirty snow dune.

"I've got a bit of a problem with alcohol," she says.

"Alright," I say.

"And what's wrong with you then?" she asks.

"I'm a white negro."

"I can live with that," she says.

"Why do you drink?" I ask.

"I'll never tell you – can you live with that?" She flashes her poison smile at me. I don't answer. Outside her front door I light a cigarette and put my hands in my pockets.

"Aren't you even going to try?" she says.

"Not today," I say.

"That's probably because I was sick," she says. I shrug.

"See you then," I say without going anywhere.

"Will you come have coffee with me at work?" she asks.

"If you want," I say.

"I want," she says. I turn and walk with my shoulders around my ears. Home. Staring at the ceiling.

The next night I am knackered. I don't go down to see Laina even though I want to. I'm too tired to speak. It's not like I visit her every night – maybe I should wait a few days. The same problem as always. At the boarding school in Tanzania I was the disc jockey at all the parties; then I didn't have to dance or talk to the girls. I don't know how to say it.

The phone rings. The alarm says it's 12.00. Night or day? Day behind the blinds. I've slept for four hours, I'm completely done in after my fourteen-hour shift.

"Yes?" I say. It's the police:

"Did you notice anything strange at Finnair Headquarters? When did you do your round of the building?"

"It's in my report," I say. "As usual: 22.00, 1.00 and 4.00."

"Did you notice any broken windows?"

"No, of course not. What's the problem?"

"I can't tell you right now."

"Then what? Do you want me to come down?"

"Yes, I do." He hangs up. So that's how it is. But why does he want me to come over? Wake up in the middle of my night and go out into the snow. I take a bus, go over to the Finnair head office. They take me up to the fourth floor. We go about fifty metres into it, down a lot of corridors, past a lot of offices. The policeman opens a door into a corridor:

"Do you smell anything?" he asks.

"No, I smoke," I say. There's a strange smell.

"O.K. When did you pass here?" And I think: I've never opened that door in my life. I've only been up and down the stairs.

"What time does it say in my report? It must have been around four," I say.

"You didn't see anything strange, did you?"

"No." He goes down the hall ahead of me, and the smell gets stronger. We turn into a big office. Damn me if the thieves haven't blown up the safe, and of course – as I've done my duty – it must have been after 4.00

when I most certainly did my duty, because the cleaners came in at 6.00 and found this mess.

The people from my company open all the time clocks, take out all the paper rounds, check the lot. Finnair has one of those office buildings where I just whip up and down the stairs, turning my key as I go. I never wander any of the floors. Of course they'll see that the times where the key has been turned in the time clocks don't fit with my having walked through the floors. Just up and down. But is the guard company going to tell the police that they've messed up? Then the company would get a bad name. And do the police want them to get a bad name? Then the police would have to work harder. And I can always explain to the police that the job simply can't be done. Shit. I've been given a work book which details each place I have to check on my route, complete with a drawing of the building's layout. I haven't read it even though I've done this job for six months. I have to know that on the fourth floor there's this bloody safe which I absolutely must check three times every sodding night. No-one has told me. No-one else knows. No-one reads the manuals. That's how it is.

"Go home and sleep," Haiko says. "So you're ready for tonight."

"O.K.," I say and leave. They're not going to fire me. I've done my job – what they've hired me to do. No-one's said it. I'm one of the good guys. There are guys at work who are on the booze and out of their heads.

Back home I brew a pot of coffee. It's too late to go to sleep – I'm going to get back out soon anyway. I'll have to sleep in the car or on the sofa in a warehouse. Something. Someone's ringing the doorbell. Laina is outside the door when I open. I am struck dumb. She points past me.

"In?" she asks.

"Yes, come in," I say.

"It's nice here," she says. Yes, I've gone out of my way to pretend. I offer her some coffee. She sits at my dining table, smoking. My philosophy books are under a thin coat of dust. They're no help now.

"So," Laina says. "What is it you really do, then?" I get up. Go to the bedroom. Come back.

"Do you see this?" I say, holding it out to her.

"It's a rope," she says.

"Made from my hair," I say.

"Really?"

"Yes – when it's long enough, I'll hang myself with it," I say.

"You still have a bit of time left, Jarno," she says.

"Yes."

"You could take up drinking," she says.

"If I have a child before it's long enough, I'll make a swing – you know, one of those with a car tyre in it."

"Instead of hanging yourself?"

"Yes," I say.

"Alright – now I know."

"I'm serious," I say.

"Yes, but it's pathetic," Laina says.

"It's something I feel very strongly," I say.

"Feelings are potent shit," she says. "It doesn't mean that they're real."

"I like you," I say.

"Potent shit," she says.

O.K. International

I am called to the E.R. to translate; none of the doctors speaks Spanish, and they're standing with a loud-mouthed, dehydrated middle-aged Latina who is bleeding from uneven rows of tiny stabs all over her head, wrists and ankles. Oozing pus; the edges of the sores were broken open not too long ago.

"What happened to you?" I ask her in Spanish.

"My boyfriend crucified me," she says. I look at her questioningly. She sneers, saying: "Barbed wire, over our bed. And he injected me with rat poison." She is bent double by stomach cramps, tries to be sick, but nothing comes up. "I'm dying," she says. "You have to change my blood."

"Why?" I ask.

"So I can live," she says.

"Why did he do it?"

"He says the Virgin Mary should learn to take it like a man."

"A man?" I ask.

"My husband's name is Jesús," she says. "I have to make more money."

"How can you make any money when you're strapped down?" I ask.

"He was going to get some men in," she says.

"How long ago was that?" I ask, holding her thin arm, the skin thick from old puncture marks.

"Two days," she says. "My daughter found me."

"Your daughter," I say, swallowing – looking away from her eyes. My daughter died three months ago, when she was born. "But when did he inject the rat poison?" I ask.

"Two days ago – he didn't use enough," the woman says.

"We're going to give you a drip with salt and sugar in it," I explain. "And then we'll look at your blood and see what we can find. A nurse will be with you to clean your wounds."

"Sure. Are you from Cuba?" she asks – that's what my accent sounds like.

"No," I say. "Tanzania in East Africa, but I went to university in Cuba.

"You're not a doctor," she says, looking at my white coat.

"I work in the lab," I say. "But there's no-one here today who speaks Spanish. No-one but me." Just then a policeman comes – he's a Latino.

"Charo, what happened?" he says.

"Jesús is a devil," the woman says.

I speak to the doctor – explain what the woman said. I could be that doctor. Three and a half years I've been in America, working at the University Hospital in Chicago as a lab assistant because the authorities won't recognize my medical degree from Cuba. America has an embargo against Cuba, so I had to retake all my exams in English in America. It's a good job all the medical terms are in Latin. I started by taking a lab exam, so I could have something to live on. Retaking my medical degree while working full-time has been a huge undertaking, and taking the exams was expensive. It's only now I've got a job as junior doctor in a paediatric ward that I can specialize. I am due to start in two weeks.

I take the lift to the lab. We cater for the E.R. and the surgical unit. The blood work is pretty much automated. Once I've started the machines I sit down in a chair. Exhausted. I lost my baby. I didn't miscarry, I gave birth to her – and she was strangled by her own umbilical cord. I need a cigarette, badly.

My doctor has advised me to lose weight. The fat is lodged around the organs in my abdominal cavity, pressing down on everything – leaving no room. These days I spend an hour in the T.V. room at home every night sweating on the StairMaster and the exercise bike, watching my shows. Have I waited too long? All that time spent on education, new exams in the U.S., certification. Have I got too old to have children? Or have I got too fat from all that American food? I'm a doctor – I ought to know better. But it's hard. I'm not from around here. I was a Tanzanian. Now I float about in empty space. I speak Swahili, French, English, Spanish, Latin. My family's blood travels the world.

The tox screen shows no rat poison. Only a low blood count, and traces of heroin, alcohol, marijuana, nicotine, caffeine – the usual. I get up from my chair in the lab and tidy my desk. Hand in the woman's blood work and pass the case over to the doctor on night duty, Miss Huáng, before going to the parking lot. I am driving Albert's car, because it has a tape recorder. A marine Pontiac Firebird. He bought it for a thousand dollars and it's got enormously wide Firebird tyres. It's ridiculous because it costs a fortune to drive, but it was the sort of car he always dreamt of having when he was a boy in Dar es Salaam and saw the American films.

Albert is a computer programmer for a Chicago bank. He's at a conference in New York and won't be home until tomorrow. I'm thinking about going over to my mother's, but I'm tired. As I leave Chicago I go into a mall and buy a cassette of Elvis and a packet of cigarettes. I've developed a thing for Elvis. Albert only has funk in the car.

I go back on the freeway and turn east towards the state line to Indiana; we live on the first floor in a house with four flats in the good end of Gary where Michael Jackson was born. In Gary the rent is cheaper than closer to Chicago. We have a bathtub, and air conditioning, and a waste disposal, and we have a large T.V., and a computer, and two cars. Our building is mixed – whites, Asians and Latinos. We're the first blacks. It helped when we told the others that we were from Africa – not Americans.

I drive past tall housing estates on the outskirts of Chicago; black projects. People here live like poor Africans do. The girls become mothers while they're still only children themselves, and the men shirk the responsibility. Their children grow up and repeat the pattern. It's hard for them to get on in life.

In my family we have fought our way forward for generations. My paternal grandfather was educated by the German missionaries in the Usambara Mountains in northern Tanzania. They sent him to the mission school in Dar es Salaam before the First World War so he could become a teacher. And here I am now, well on my way to getting a career as a doctor, an American passport. This is how long it takes to create a good life.

On the freeway I can see across town. America isn't a great melting pot. We don't mix. Chicago is divided into areas: blacks, poor whites, rich whites, Latin Americans, Chinese – the divisions are starker than in Dar es Salaam. I am in disguise – a black in America. Everyone thinks I descend from slaves, am rooted in African-American culture. They have a preconceived opinion of who I am. I don't want to be like that.

When I arrived from Cuba I visited a black church in Chicago; full of slave-souls demanding special treatment because their ancestors were given a raw deal. Black Americans think that the world owes them wealth in return for their boo-boo. Every time the wound heals, they peel off the scabs and howl that they're bleeding. Everything is someone else's fault.

Traffic on the freeway is heavy, even though it's late. The three inner lanes are packed and move slowly. I get into lane four, checking my speedometer; a hundred and twenty kilometres an hour. Elvis is singing in the cabin.

Not long after I arrived in America I found work as a lab assistant at the University Hospital in Chicago. I lived with my mother and her husband in a mixed neighbourhood – there were Latinos and people from the East. I bought an old Chevrolet and was happy; a Tanzanian woman with a car of her own is a miracle from God. I wore rhinestone-studded sunglasses. No-one could see that I was African – a first-generation immigrant. But I made a big deal out of telling people. Black Americans call themselves African-Americans. They're not African. I am. They use the past as a safety blanket; whingeing about having been cheated. It's not pleasant to be considered one of them. Who do they think sold their ancestors to the slave merchants? Their black brothers. Get over it. They got out of Africa and have 125 years head start as free people in America. They were born with a starting point that I've spent all my life trying to get to. Get that finger out and press Start. Or kiss my black Tanzanian arse and congratulate me as I climb ahead of you on the ladder.

At a social event at the university I met a female Tanzanian road engineer. She recommended a mixed church in the suburbs where there are more Tanzanians. I met them. They study, work, live in trailer parks, fight tooth and nail – upwards and onwards. We all say we'll go home one day, give something back to Tanzania. But will we? Nothing works in Africa, corruption permeates everything. America is good. If you work hard you can create something lasting here. People are responsible for their actions – people have rights, security. When you have children they can go to proper schools if they're good enough– not only if their parents are corrupt. In Africa you can fight like a beast and still starve. I love Tanzania. But I have to save myself first – myself and my family. There's no room for compassion. Love just isn't enough.

Through church I met Albert, who is from Dar es Salaam as well. We started going out. We got married. I got pregnant.

A red Mazda is growing inside my rear-view mirror and is about to pass me in lane five – the one furthest out. I keep an eye on it. He's speeding. Probably about 150 an hour. Something's not right. What? A Ford is stopped a bit further ahead in lane five – congestion – while the inner lanes snail ahead. The man in the Mazda overtakes me. He approaches the motionless Ford, sees it too late. I look at the Mazda; his brakes are squealing; he tries to pull to the right, into lane four, into my lane. There isn't time. The front of the Mazda slams into the right-hand corner of the Ford's trunk. The Mazda rises diagonally into the air, lands again, starts sailing to the right, pulling the Ford with it into my lane with a screech of metal and brakes. A Toyota in front of me only just manages to squeeze past. And ahead of me the Mazda scoots into my lane while its bumper pulls the Ford with it, and my foot is raised above the brake as they slide into an inverted V in front of me and let go of each other, and a small gap opens, and I'm standing on the accelerator, heading for the opening, smashing between them, hitting both of them with my front wings and pushing them aside until they spin, and I'm through, and everything goes quiet. To my left lane five is one big concertina crash. In my rear-view mirror I see the Mazda sail into a car in lane three without a sound. A slow dance; no sound – screeching steel, splintering glass, squealing brakes – but nothing. I'm driving. Through my side window I can see cars slam into the Mazda from behind, and the entire road is whirling around like a storming sea of silent destruction. Around me the freeway is almost empty – everyone is stranded back there in the accident. My hands are clutching the steering wheel, and it's only now that I notice that one of my wheels must have been knocked crooked; a shrill, scraping noise comes through – the stench of burned metal that makes the sweat gush forth under my arms and from my palms. I slow down. I haven't got insurance; when you're a foreigner, insurance is expensive – it costs more than the car. I look around, see an exit a bit further ahead, and carefully pull to the right. Intense stench. Is the car bursting into flames? I go onto the slip-road and enter an industrial zone. I take the first right; a shopping area – Foot Locker, Burger King, Safeway, Kmart. I stop at the kerb next to a payphone. There's no-one in sight. My head hurts. I feel my temples. No blood. Maybe I hit it against the window. Slowly I get out, tottering. Steady myself with a hand on the car. Stand still. Everything's in working order. I go to the payphone and look back. Both sides of the front chassis are bent down and have ground against the tyres. I am holding the phone in my hand but have to go back to get my coins, which are in a bowl between the seats, ready for the toll booths on the interstate. I fumble about in my bag. Albert has given me the number of the hotel in New York where he's staying during the conference. I call; am put through to his room. No-one answers. The wheel looks wonky. I call my mother. Tears well up in my eyes. The phone goes on ringing.

"Yes?" Mum's voice says.

"Mum," I say in a voice I don't even recognize.

"Yes? What's happened?" Mum's voice says, and I don't recognize that either. I look towards the car.

"Mum, I was in a car accident, and . . ." Two police cars without sirens or blinkers drive up over the kerb and stop on the lawn in front of the payphone. A black policeman comes out of one of them, moving both hands to rest on the roof of the car – he's holding a gun.

"Are you alright, Shakila?" Mum asks into my ear, while a white policeman with mirror sunglasses gets out from the passenger side of the other car. They're wearing black uniforms, newly ironed blue shirts; from their belts hang instruments that can destroy people.

"*Get down on the ground*," the black policeman yells. I am standing without being able to move; staring at the gun as the white one comes towards me.

"Mum," I say into the phone.

"*Shakila?*" Mum screams.

"Get down on the ground, ma'am. Now," the black man yells again, and I let go of the phone and raise my arms while the phone dangles on its wire, swinging against my thigh – I hear Mum calling my name, her voice thin and metallic.

The white guy with the mirrored sunglasses has come up to me and takes my one arm, guiding it behind my back. Metal against my wrist.

"You're under arrest for leaving a crime scene," he says, pulling down my other arm. Handcuffs. It's like a film. He grabs my arm and walks me to the back of one of the police cars. Opens the doors with his free hand. "Watch your head," he says, raising his hand to guide me as I get in. I sit behind a metal grille – awkwardly, with my hands behind my back. I stare into the back of the driver's head; it's brown – maybe he's a Latino, maybe he's Asian. He's wearing a flat cap. He doesn't turn around. This is serious. I force myself not to cry – I don't want them to see that.

The black policeman is standing outside his car, speaking into his police radio.

"We have apprehended the hit-and-run driver in the dark blue Pontiac," he says. Hit-and-run driver. That's all I hear, because the white policeman gets in and closes the door. He looks at me quickly, and through the grille I see my face reflected twice in his glasses – dark and anonymous. Then he looks ahead. We drive. I turn and look back at my car. My things are in there, my handbag with my driver's licence and papers. No-one says anything. The car drives a couple of blocks and comes to a stop in front of a police station. A concrete block – it might as well be a warehouse. The white policeman pulls me out of the car, leads me through the door, down a corridor. I see out of the corner of my eye that he takes off his sunglasses as we walk – it makes me feel oddly relieved. There's lino flooring, white plasterboard walls, institutional furniture – it's like a hospital, only more scruffy. He opens the door to a small room which has a table and three chairs. Nothing on the walls. Bare concrete floor. Fluorescent tubes behind a grate in the ceiling. I can see the darkening sky through the bars of a narrow window high on the wall just under the ceiling. The police officer guides me to the single chair on the far side of the room. The table looks like the one I used to use at the university in Dar es Salaam, except for the metal bar that comes out from one side of the table. The officer undoes one side of the handcuffs.

"Sit down, ma'am," he says. I sit down. He's holding on to the empty side of the handcuffs, my other arm is free. "Give me your other arm," he says as he puts the handcuffs through the metal bar on the table and back around my other wrist. I look at him. He's not as young as he was. Slim, freshly shaved; grey close-cropped hair. His eyes are green.

"Why am I here?" I ask.

"You're suspected of leaving a crime scene," he says, standing up, going to the door. "Someone will come down to interrogate you," he says and leaves. That's all I'm told. I look at my watch. It's 6.30 in the evening. I'm alone. I try to reach my trouser pocket, remember that the cigarettes were on the backseat of the car.

What's going to happen? What could happen? Do you have to be American to have the right to a lawyer? What are my rights? They weren't read to me when I was arrested. Or were they? Perhaps my arrest is illegal. I am cuffed to a table. If I hadn't gone in to buy that Elvis tape, this wouldn't have happened.

A black officer comes in with a notepad and a pen – I think he's the one who pointed his gun at me. I am black. He is blacker. What does that mean? He's an American. The white officer – is he different? Is there a good-cop–bad-cop thing going on? Which colour is the good cop? The black officer sits down on one of the two chairs. They're not bolted down.

"What's your name?" he asks.

"Shakila Smith," I say. Smith is my mother's slave name from Jamaica. Her ancestors were African slaves who worked on the sugar plantations owned by white English aristocrats – my mother has some white blood as well. I've taken the name to be anonymous in America.

"Where are you from?" the officer asks.

"I was born in London, but I am a Tanzanian citizen – it's in East Africa. I live in Gary, Indiana," I say and give him the address. He's from Africa as well, but it was a long time ago.

"Do you have a residence permit?" he asks.

"Yes," I say.

"Why are you in the United States?" he asks.

"I . . ." I start but come to a halt. How can I explain? In order to have a better life – I can't say that. I breathe in: "My mother's an American," I say. "I've moved here to be closer to her."

"What do you do for a living?" he asks, looking at me searchingly.

"I have a green card and work as a lab assistant at Chicago University Hospital. My papers are in my handbag," I say.

"Tell me what happened," he says.

"I got scared," I say. "I just kept driving."

"Just tell me what happened. In your own words, right from the beginning."

I tell him about the Mazda which hadn't seen the congestion in lane five. How I slipped between the two cars.

"It wasn't my fault," I say. "I'm sorry I didn't stop, but I got scared. I didn't know what to do." He writes something down on his pad. Should I tell him I was calling the police when they arrived? Can they contact the phone company and check which numbers I was pressing on the payphone?

"Thank you," he says and gets up and leaves. Now what? The door is locked. I'm afraid that I'll need to pee – what do I do then? My tongue sticks to the roof of my mouth. The air is very dry. I think about my father. He's getting old. I haven't seen him in seven years, and we don't speak often. When my mother left Tanzania he remarried, and I was sent to a boarding school from Year One so the new wife wouldn't have to be reminded of my existence. After seven years in Arusha I went on to the international school in Moshi, full of the children of diplomats and corporates. I stayed there until I was ready to go to university, when I moved in with my father and stepmother in Dar es Salaam. That didn't work out well. My father let my stepmother run the house, and she favoured her own little bastards. O.K., Dad – you let her make you weak. You let me down. You're going to die lonely. But you made sure I got an education. You got me out of Tanzania. Thanks for everything.

I look at my watch. It's been an hour. I don't need to pee, but I am parched.

The white police officer comes through the door with pad and pen.

"My name's McAllan," he says, sitting down.

"O.K.," I say.

"Tanzania," he says. "How did you end up in the States?"

"Why?" I ask.

"Please just answer the questions," he says.

"My mother lives here," I say, shrugging.

"Yes, but you come from Africa," he says, twirling his pen in his hands. "What does your father do?"

"My father? Why do you want to know?"

"Answer the questions, please," he says. I take a deep breath:

"My father is a black Tanzanian who came to England in the late 1950s when Tanzania was still a British protectorate to study gynaecology. In London he met a black nurse from Jamaica – my mother. They got married, and she had me. When he had finished his education we went to Tanzania. All three of us – it had become independent by then, and my father became the first Tanzanian professor of gynaecology at the university in Dar es Salaam." McAllan doesn't write a single thing on his notepad.

I think about Mum. She says that back then everyone believed in socialism and that *mwalimu* Nyerere would build up Tanzania and make it a good nation. Dreams and ineptitude. It all became a disaster.

"But your mother lives here," McAllan says.

"My parents divorced when I was six. My mother wasn't allowed to take us out of Tanzania. She didn't have any means of providing for us either. So she went home to Jamaica and became a nurse at a hospital," I say.

"Why did they divorce?" McAllan asks.

"Does it really matter?" I ask. The black officer comes in through the door, and McAllan turns towards him. They divorced because my mother couldn't live as a Tanzanian woman and submit to my father. That's the reason she had left Jamaica as a young woman to live in Britain. At least that's how she tells the story.

The black officer puts two cups of coffee on the table in front of us. The white officer looks into the cups and then up at me.

"He's sure you take it black," he says. The black one smiles wryly.

"She'll take it black, because black's what I got," he says.

"Do you want me to uncuff one of your hands?" McAllan says.

"*Tsk*," I say, looking at the wall where there's nothing to look at.

"Black obviously isn't her thing," McAllan tells the black guy.

"It's a matter of thirst. She'll drink it," the black guy says and goes out the door.

"I don't drink coffee," I say.

"No, no," McAllan says and pulls a packet of cigarettes out of his pocket, lighting one. "Tell me about life in Africa."

"I don't have anything else to tell you," I say. He blows out smoke, sighing.

"Look. We were just kidding. It's been a long day. We're not racist – that would be too easy. And too absurd," he says.

"Keep talking if you like the sound of your own voice so much," I say.

"Are you a racist?" he asks.

"Why would that be too easy?" I ask.

"What?" McAllan asks.

"Being a racist."

"Because everyone is, given half a chance. Even me. Even you. The racist reaction comes first."

"How?" I ask.

"A white man pushes you in a diner, making you spill down your front, and he continues without apologizing – you think: Can't that white bastard see where he's going? Or a black man pushes me – I think: Can't that black-ass monkey see where he's going? The man is an inattentive asshole in both cases, but we choose to put his actions down to a malice stemming from his race. It's in our D.N.A. We're all tribal warriors. I am from the white tribe; you're from the black."

"Right," I say. "But I'm cuffed to a table, and you're walking about free."

McAllan nods and drinks his coffee. He winces before ashing his cigarette in the coffee. He still hasn't written anything on his pad. He gets up, leans forward, uncuffs me, removes the cuffs, looks at his watch. "I'm going out to see how things are moving along. In the meantime you can try to forgive me."

"You could leave your cigarettes," I say. He turns, looks at me, leaves the packet and the lighter on the table and goes out. I light one, sucking at it. I am parched. Drink some of the black coffee, which is lukewarm and tastes of dust.

McAllan returns.

"We're interviewing a number of witnesses to the accident," he says.

"Is there anything I should be doing?" I ask.

"What do you mean?" he asks.

"In relation to the accident?" I ask.

"Right now, you and me – we just talk. Your mother left," he says.

"Yes, my mother left," I say.

"A free woman," he says.

"Yes," I say. "I didn't see her for another thirteen years."

McAllan makes a long, low whistle.

"Some years later Mum met a black American man at the hospital in Kingston – he was selling medical supplies in the Caribbean. They were married; she returned with him to America and found work at a hospital in Chicago."

"And you were walking around in Africa?" McAllan says.

"Yes."

"Why Cuba?" McAllan says.

"Cuba?" I say.

"You studied in Cuba," he says. I look at him. He shrugs. I haven't said anything about Cuba. He must have been into some database. The American authorities must have registered the four times I travelled from Cuba via Mexico to the U.S. while I was a student to visit Mum and Granny in Chicago; maybe he's read that I tried to break the embargo by smuggling a bottle of Havana Rum into the States to give to my grandmother. By then Mum had got her own old mother to Chicago from Jamaica. I was twenty the first time I met my grandmother. She was a lovely old woman who spoke just like Bob Marley. She died about six months ago.

"Why do you want to know about Cuba?" I ask.

"Well, it's . . . we have to pass the time until the witnesses have been interviewed and forensics are done with the freeway," he says, adding: "I'm Irish myself. Colin McAllan – my great-grandparents came to Albany as children on the run during the famine in Ireland."

"First I went to university in Tanzania, but it didn't work out, and then I went to Cuba," I say, letting my cigarette butt fall into his cup, where the lit end hisses and dies.

"Why didn't it work out in Tanzania?" McAllan asks.

"My father had left his position as professor at the university and had founded a private hospital, even though that really oughtn't be possible under African socialism. But my father was the personal physician to all the big shots in government, so he was off-limits and made good money." I don't say anything about how my father needed the money to put me and my little brother through the international school and give us a proper education. "My father's former colleagues were envious of his success, which meant that I was forever failing exams and was harassed as a revenge on my father."

"So you left college in Africa?" McAllan says.

"Yes."

"African socialism. Is that like a kind of communism?" he asks.

"Yes," I say. "It's not working either."

"Corrupt like in Mexico?" he asks.

"Or Cuba," I say.

"Why did you go to Cuba then?"

"My father got me a scholarship at the university in Camagüey."

"How do you do that?" McAllan asks.

"You give the Cuban ambassador a hernia operation and a lovely summer house on the coast in Tanzania."

"Corruption," McAllan says.

"Yes," I say. I assisted my father during that surgery; I did that in all my holidays, starting when I was thirteen. Blood doesn't bother me. I drink from the lukewarm coffee, even though it tastes of dust.

"How was Cuba?" he asks.

"I liked it," I say. "I learned to speak Spanish, to drink rum. I lived in a room with students from Angola, the Soviet Union, Venezuela, Jamaica. We had fun."

"And after college you came to America," McAllan says.

"Yes," I say.

"Because your mother had got her citizenship?" he asks. I look at him. Does he understand that America is harvesting my brain, which was grown in the Third World? I am a gift – ready to carve into American children who are collapsing under the weight of their own fat. Does he understand how wrong that is?

"My mother had got her citizenship, yes," I say.

"And your little brother?" he asks. The database has told him about my little brother.

"He arrived four years ago and went straight into the military," I say.

"Cannon fodder for Uncle Sam," McAllan says. I don't say anything, but he's right. If you go into the military, your ass automatically gets an American citizenship after five years. If – after five years – you've still got an ass, that is.

"He's standing in South Korea by the demilitarized zone, staring north," I say. McAllan nods and gets up.

"I'll be right back," he says and leaves, closing the door behind him. The black officer comes in with my handbag in his hand, putting it on the table. They've taken it from the car. He looks at my hands, which are in my lap – uncuffed. He doesn't mention it.

"We know it's not your fault," he says. "We've got three independent witness statements which all confirm that it was the driver of the red

Mazda who caused the accident. The technical examinations at the crime scene also show that you braked as hard as you could."

"Are you sure?" I ask. Because I can't remember braking, only that I went for the gap between the cars. Out of there.

"Yes," he says. I sigh. He tells me that they'll send the police report to me by post. That I can file a civil lawsuit against the driver in the red Mazda. That I must pick up my car within twenty-four hours or it'll be seized and impounded and then I'll have to pay to have it returned to me.

"O.K.," I say.

"You're free to go," he says. I get up carefully, taking my handbag from the table.

"Thank you," I say, standing still, staring at his uniform, his skin. I realize he scares me more than the white officer – the police in Tanzania have a reputation for being heavy-handed.

"It's this way," he says, holding the door open, pointing down the hall. I walk on past him, under the fluorescent tubes. I am incapable of stopping to ask if I can use their phone. I look for McAllan, but he's nowhere to be seen. I pass the desk and leave the station. It's dark. The air is cold and clear. I find a bus stop, get on a bus, but it goes the wrong way, and I get off. I study the bus timetables, but can't understand them. I look in my handbag. The cigarettes and my lighter are there. I realize I don't have any cash. I'm standing on a street with dark office buildings. There are no taxis here. It's late. There's almost no traffic. No shops and no A.T.M.s. I think I know which way to go. I start walking. It's like in Africa; the night is dark and there are no pavements, just hard soil and tufts of grass. Behind me the bus stop is lit up. I stop and look into the darkness. Turn. Go back to the small circle of light at the bus stop. And I start sobbing. First I try swallowing it, but it keeps welling up. I sob violently, and snivel – bawl. I think I might be pregnant again. And I've just landed a job as a junior doctor at the paediatric ward – exactly what I wanted – I'm due to start in two weeks. My shoulders shake. I am all alone, hiding my head in my hands, crying. I have to stop. What am I crying about? My father who might die without seeing me again? The car I've wrecked? My daughter? If I am made in God's image, then who is God? If God has power, then it's like my power. No more, no less. Then God is small.

A car comes driving slowly and stops at the bus stop. The sound of the electric window in the passenger side being rolled down. I stand up.

"Are you alright, honey?" a woman's voice asks – I can hear that she's black.

"I was in a car accident," I say, raising my face from my hands. I can't see her inside the dark car.

"Oh," she says and opens the passenger door from inside, turning on the cabin light. "What happened to you?" she asks.

"I'm alright," I say, going to the door, leaning down. She's fat, with purple eyeshadow, pink trackies, burgundy satin shirt and straight hair in an updo.

"Are you sure, honey?" she asks. "Do you need to go to the E.R.?"

"I'm a doctor."

"You can't stand around here," the woman says. "Where are you going?"

"I don't know."

"But where are you from?" she asks.

"Tanzania."

"Is that close?" she asks.

"I'm from Africa," I say.

"Aren't we all, honey?" she says, patting the passenger seat lightly, fat fingers wearing gold rings with coloured rhinestones. I get in. She looks me in the eyes. "But where can I take you?"

"I'd like to go home," I say and give her my mother's address – it's only a couple of miles away. The backseat of her car is loaded with shopping bags. "I'm Shakila," I say.

"Sheona," she says and reaches a hand into one of the bags. "Have a Coke," she says, handing me the can, which has dewdrops on the side. I dry my eyes. We smile at each other. I drink the cool, sweet liquid. It's strange not being behind the wheel myself. We've turned down a street I recognize. I look out of the window, and we're driving smoothly past shopping malls, auto shops, liquor stores, junk-food restaurants, workout palaces, cinemas, estate agents', strip clubs, churches. I force myself to speak:

"I was in a car accident," I say. "The police let me go, but I didn't have money for the bus and there was no A.T.M." She shakes her head:

"*Tsk,*" she says, almost like an African. "Was it bad?" she asks.

"They cuffed me in a room, and let me wait, and interrogated me, and insulted me. I didn't like it," I say.

"Never you mind the police – they're afraid of us," she says.

"Us black people?" I ask. She laughs:

"Us women. We're walking around free, like horses that have escaped their paddocks."

Nyumba ya Mungu

We sleep in because I arrived late last night, and we were up until 3.00. But we're not hungover: we didn't drink. Tonight we're going to a party at some of Sigve's friends'. I don't know if her husband, Tore, will be there.

The cook serves us brunch – he's made pancakes.

"Wouldn't it be nice to go for a proper drive?" Sigve asks.

"If you like."

"How about that lake you were talking about?"

"Nyumba ya Mungu?"

"Yes – I'd like to see some water."

"Then we'd have to go now – it's a long way around."

"I'll make us a packed lunch," she says and gets up from the table. I look at her pale Norwegian legs. Sigve is an anaesthetics nurse at K.C.M.C., Kilimanjaro Christian Medical Centre. Pale legs. They're calling to me. I light a cigarette and brew my second cup of Africafé.

"Erm . . ." she says, standing by the worktop. "Could you ask the cook to make a lot of ice cubes? I promised to bring some tonight." The cook looks at me questioningly – he likes the fact that I speak the language like a native despite being white; but he wonders at the fact that Sigve's husband is nowhere to be seen while I am here.

"No problem," I tell him in Swahili and get a heavy pan from the cupboard myself.

"O.K.," Sigve says. "I've got a bigger pan than that."

"No, it has to have a heavy base, otherwise it'll bulge – the water expands when it freezes."

"You know everything, Mick," she says, laughing. I fill the pan with water and make room for it in the freezer while I think about the party tonight; her friends, it's the first time I'm meeting them. Many of them know her doctor husband, who's now living at Uhuru Hostel. I'll be coming through the door with a lump of ice which I'll smash against the bathroom floor, loading the pieces into the bathtub with its cans of Carlsberg, its bottles of tonic; I will show my customary energy while swallowing my own spit.

At 13.00 we're off. I've talked her into putting on full-length trousers, because the sun bites even harder when it's reflected from the surface of the water. She's got a crash helmet on, and in my rear-view mirror I can see how her blonde ponytail flutters like a banner behind us.

I ought to be at the garage in Arusha; fault-finding – the electrical system in a Range Rover belonging to an English safari company that's due to have guests down on Monday. The air conditioning in the car only works when its long lights are on, and none of my boys are any good with electrics. I'll have to do it Sunday night. That's how I met Sigve and her husband. The cylinder head gasket of their Nissan Patrol was falling apart, and the husband wasn't sure it would hold up for the drive to Chuni Motor in Moshi. It was late in the day – I was going up to my mum at the lodge to eat. "I've had you recommended," he said. "They call you the Wizard." I didn't feel like staying late – flattery or not. Mostly I live off repairing and rebuilding cars for the safari companies, as well as purchasing wrecks, doing them up and selling them on. I have a professional relationship with Chuni – I don't want to steal his customers.

My first glimpse of Sigve was of her long, pale legs as she got out of the car. Then the rest of her followed.

"They tell me you can mate a totalled Land Rover with a wrecked motorbike and produce something that will actually drive," the man said. She was leaning against the open door of the Nissan behind him. I wished I could do more than that. She smiled at me. He looked to be about ten years older than her. She looked to be about my age. As always in Africa when white people meet, I was told a lot in the hour it took me to fix their car: he's a doctor, she's an anaesthetics nurse – they'd arrived in Tanzania six months previously from Norway. Married, no children yet. During her training Sigve had spent two months in Moshi in an internship at the K.C.M.C. She had fallen in love with the country.

"I spent most of my time giving saline injections to the patients," she said.

"Why?" I asked with my upper body under the bonnet.

"Tanzanians love *injection* – they get better right away," she said. I turned:

"I feel the same way," I said, winking at her. "And I go to the witch doctor, just to be on the safe side."

Right outside Moshi we pass the exit to Majengo – I wonder if that's where Sigve's husband finds his *malaya*. He'll learn, but not yet.

On our left the cap of Kilimanjaro is shrouded in clouds. We drive out to Road Junction and take the road south towards Tanga and Dar es Salaam. We pass several dried-up riverbeds. The motorbike trundles nicely across the tarmac. It's a Saturday and the traffic isn't dense. A few buses and gargantuan Isuzu lorries rumble down the road – with their rounded forms like old, showy American cars. The engine is imported from Japan, but the body and cargo hold are made in Tanzania. They use metal plates that are much too thick, which makes the vehicle top heavy, so it's always unstable on the road when they're driving with full loads – and they always do. Many of the lorries have been bent out of shape in traffic accidents, so they crab across the road spewing black diesel fumes – the engines are never checked. When you overtake one they speed up, even if there's oncoming traffic; it's the victory of the fittest. The motorbike is a 350cc Bultaco – a Spanish engine; it's geared for climbing but still has nice acceleration, so we're fine – I don't want to go too fast when she's with me.

A few days after I had patched up their cylinder head gasket, I called a doctor I know at the K.C.M.C. and got him to give me her duty rota. I went there. Bumped into her in the hall. Told her one of my lads was in with a crushed leg – a chain had broken in the hoisting apparatus; an engine block had crashed down – I was coming to visit. In reality I had just found Ngana in a room; he was a casual labourer at a mobile sawmill on West Kilimanjaro and had had a cypress tumble down onto his leg. I gave my doctor friend some money so the boy would get proper treatment. I visited him often. Always when Sigve was working. The next time I came the doctor had just cut his leg off under the knee because it had got infected and was rotting.

"Too bad about the leg," I said.

"They cut it off with a special chainsaw," the boy said excitedly. "The white lady gave me a special painkiller. I could hear the saw go into my leg, but no pain."

I found the man who makes prosthetic limbs. He came into the room – looked at the stump.

"I can give you a leg of steel and plastic," the man said.

"Will I be able to play football then?" the boy asked.

"Yes, it's a very good leg. You can play football like a dream."

"Good. Because I was never any good at football," Ngana said and laughed.

"Enough!" I said.

"But we have to wait," the man said. "The wound must heal first."

I thought about whether Ngana could become a mechanic or a driver – if he would be able to press down a clutch with a prosthetic leg. Perhaps I could get him a job.

Ngana looked expectantly at me. I sat down on a chair with my back to the other beds and leaned forward.

"Do you get enough to eat?" I asked, because the boy looked famished.

"The food is no good," he said. No, you can die from malnutrition at K.C.M.C.

"You can have someone buy you some food in the staff canteen," I said and pulled out some money from the front pocket of my shirt, handing him the banknotes. He took hold of them with his fingers. I didn't let go. "Don't give them to your mother when she gets here," I said.

"My mother is dead," he said.

"*Pole*," I said and let go of the money. "What happened to her?"

"She was on the back of a lorry with timber, and the timber shifted. She was squashed – *kwisha*," – done for.

"*Pole*," I said.

"I've had it with timber," Ngana said. "It's tried to kill my entire family."

"And your father?"

"He won't come," Ngana said. "Not unless you tell him I've got money." He smiled

The wheels spin beneath us. The short rains have started ever so slightly – the bushes are sprouting. We'll soon reach the first hills of the North Pare Mountains, spottily bathed in shade from the cotton clouds in the sky. The hills rise from the near-flat plain, gnarly and covered in shrubs, studded with boulders. At Kifaru the dry landscape is replaced by a brief stretch of swamp next to the road, with small bushy palm trees and reeds.

"Why does it look like that?" Sigve calls.

"It's the groundwater – it surfaces here," I shout.

We reach Mwanga where I stop at an Agip, filling up the tank. She hands me a tube of sunscreen, holding up her ponytail while I do the back of her neck.

Along the river – lots of giant mango trees and coconut palms, which are really quite rare in this part of the country. After the village, the sisal plantations spread out across the softly curved countryside at the foot of the mountains. Sisal as far as the eye can see. Exports have collapsed – the western markets have been taken over by polyester fibres. People fell the five-metre-tall seedpods that stick out at the middle of the sisal plant –

they're as thick as an arm and are used for firewood and as a building material.

The nurses at K.C.M.C. were my accomplices, even though they didn't know it. It was surprisingly simple. Tore watched the smooth rhythms of their sluggishly billowing walks. The curves under their flimsy white cotton uniforms, their close proximity in the operating theatre; the scent of coconut oil, Vaseline, fresh sweat. The glitter of the eyes above the surgical masks when his scalpel drew blood.

I met Sigve one day when I was visiting Ngana. She was looking tired.

"Do you want to go for a smoke?" she asked, gesturing towards the K.C.M.C. inner courtyard, which is encircled by the external galleries of the floors.

"Let's," I said. We stood by the low wall facing the yard. She offered me a Marlboro. I lit hers. She didn't say anything.

"So how do you feel about it?" I asked.

"Well," she said, shrugging.

"Are you both happy to be here?" I asked – I didn't want to have to mention her husband, but I didn't have any connection with Sigve. At all. I didn't know if I could have one. She leant against the low wall.

"I don't know what he gets up to," she said. "He's never at home anymore."

"But . . ." I said and took the plunge. "Have you been married a long time?"

"No, we went out for about a year and were married right before we came here."

"And no children?" I asked, even though I knew they didn't have any.

"No, not yet," she said and threw her cigarette aside, stepping on it. She turned her head to me, speaking quickly: "I think he's chasing after some of the local women." I looked at her, but now she was looking away, wouldn't meet my eyes.

I didn't say anything.

"Tore has always been a very . . . controlled man," Sigve said into the air. "Almost too controlled. But now . . ." She started rooting in her pockets, almost fidgety. I handed her one of my cigarettes, lit it for her – we were standing very close and the sunlight came down like a pillar in the inner yard.

"Away from Europe," I said, "there's no-one to watch him."

"No-one but me," Sigve said.

"Yes," I said.

"Do you do it as well?" Sigve asked.

"What?"

"Chase after women?"

"The only woman I'm chasing is you," I said. She sucked the cigarette hard, squinting – then turned and walked away. I didn't know what that meant.

We pass through Kindoroko and reach the sign:

TANESCO-PANGANI HYDRO SYSTEMS, NYUMBA YA MUNGU, DAM & POWER STATION.

Turn right on the gravel road and go west; the rusty red dust comes up in clouds from our wheels. We immediately pass the railroad at Moshi, and the country lies before us in a series of long, low peaks and troughs, stretching west all the way to the Blue Mountains south of T.P.C., the sugar plantation. Bush and unkempt state-run sisal plantations. The road rises slowly and for a long time; we meet several herders with their cattle, so relaxed in the afternoon heat that the animals rub their flanks against our legs as we pass through their warm, tangy smell. When we reach the top, we can see the large pane of water stretching north some way below us. I stop the motorbike; we drink water from our bottles and smoke cigarettes.

"Why is it called Nyumba ya Mungu?" she asks. I explain that before they built the dam there was a large rock which came out of the water by a curve in the river – it looked like a throne carved by human hands. The locals called it *Kiti ya Mungu* – the Seat of God. The river was dammed, the water rose, and these days God's Seat is underwater.

"So they called the lake *Nyumba ya Mungu* – House of God," I say and check the cooler bag where we keep our food and drink. It's strapped on safely, and the cooler bricks are still frozen. We don't know the first thing about fish, but we mean to buy some. We set off again, driving down the faint slope towards God's House. Soon we reach a metal bar blocking the road by a solitary guard's shed – the local police station. I explain to the man that we're just going to Spillway to buy some fish at the lake, and that we'll go back via T.P.C. It's fine.

As soon as we're out of sight of the police station, Sigve asks me to pull over. She needs to pee. I look around.

"Do you see anyone?" she asks.

"No, you're all clear." She squats behind a bush by the roadside. She pees. The sound seems intense under open skies.

"I am leaky," she says.

"You're lovely," I say.

"Even when I am peeing?"

"Everything going that way is something I am particularly fond of at the moment."

"Only at the moment?"

"There were a couple of things earlier," I say and smile. She doesn't say anything. I would like to say something else, but I don't know what. The sound stops.

"Are you trying to tell me to give you a golden shower?" she asks, pulling up her trousers.

"Always," I say. She comes over and stands next to me – putting her hand in my back pocket. Fishing villages are dotted along the edges of the artificial lake – the hydroelectric dam is at the southern end. I've been here before and start to tell her about the lake; that the Germans started building the dam in 1961, and that it was inaugurated by the president,

Mwalimu Nyerere in 1964 – the dam provides some of the electricity for Moshi but not very much, because there isn't enough water in the dry season. The lake is immense – we can't see the northernmost end from where we are. The landscape here only has gentle contours, and in many places the water's so shallow it's more of a wetland reservation.

The rumours about Sigve's husband started to spread amongst the nurses on the surgical ward – soon they reached Sigve; I could see it in her face when I was visiting Ngana – the boy from West Kilimanjaro. For many European men it's just a question of time. Their brains start adapting to the situation – to the extent that they're capable of understanding it. Their values can't hold up to the pressure. Young black beauties offering themselves up, being miraculous in bed; slaving like mad to earn their ticket out of Africa.

We drive through a village made of sticks, mud and reeds. Small, barely dressed children run around between the huts, and a mangy dog on three legs stumbles along the road. We drive all the way down and turn at the fenced-in power plant at the foot of the tall, German-built stone and concrete dam that spans the river. There's nothing much to look at here, except for Ruvu River, which twists away on the far side of the power plant.

"What does it say?" Sigve shouts, and I stop in front of the sign:

WARNING. THE ROAD ALONG THE CREST OF THE DAM IS EXTREMELY DANGEROUS BEING ON A VERY HIGH EMBANKMENT. ALL TRAFFIC VEHICULAR AND PEDESTRIAN CROSSING THE DAM DO SO ENTIRELY AT THEIR OWN RISK. SPEED LIMIT 5 M.P.H.

The road is wide and good, flanked by two solid stone walls. On the far side we stop before the control post, greet the uniformed guard and his assistant politely and ask if we can have a look around. We can; we're just not allowed to take any pictures, the guard solemnly explains. I have to put my name down in the tatty notebook which is used to register passers-by: name, job, address, licence registration number. They glance furtively at Sigve – she is very beautiful. The water level is low; calcareous deposits on the dam's walls reveal how high it comes during the long rains. The dam's mechanisms are invisible; the canals are under the surface of the water and the turbines are placed inside Tanesco's fenced-off area below. On the other side of the power plant the water quietly runs back into the river and continues towards Pangani. The guard's assistant raises the black-and-white-striped bar for us, and we go left just after the dam to see Evil Spring – a small waterhole about half a metre deep where the water sizzles up from the ground – boiling hot in the mornings, but at this time of day just hot. The women come here to wash their clothes, but right now there isn't anyone here. We get off, watch the bubbles rising from the muddy bottom, dip our hands in the water. I drive us slowly to the mud-filled quarry and stop some way from the edge – there's a drop of fifteen metres to the surface of the water. The Germans got their building materials for the dam by blasting their way deep into the rock until the groundwater rose up from deep below.

"Can you swim in it?" she asks.

"Yes," I say. "But there are crocodiles."

"In there?" She peers down into the greenish pool , encircled by steep rock walls except for a single opening, which – today – connects the quarry with the river beyond the dam. The reptiles are out of sight. Later in the day the fishermen will paddle their narrow wooden boats into the quarry, because it teems with large fish, and they often come up to the surface where the water has more oxygen.

"Yes, there, and in the river, and all over the lake – lots of crocodiles," I say. We roll back towards Evil Spring. Even though this river doesn't dry out, the surrounding landscape is parched and the vegetation singed; there's rocks and sand right under the thin, barren soil. A mother has just arrived at the spring with her two children and is washing her clothes with energetic movements in a blue plastic bucket. She gets up when she hears us – her top must be in the tub as well because her breasts poke out, large and dark brown, from her upper body. The children shout "*mzungu*", I shout "*mwafrika*", the woman laughs and waves; her breasts wobble gorgeously, and Sigve waves back. The wild people of Africa, I think; they can feed the starving.

I made enquiries about Sigve's husband in Moshi. Asked the mechanics at Chuni Motors if they had seen him in town. They told me he went to Golden Shower – a restaurant with a disco just east of Moshi. I asked if he had a lady friend. Yes, they thought he had a friend there – tall girl. "White?" I asked. "Black," they said.

I'm not a racist: colour, religion – it's all one to me. I've lived here all my life. I get it. White love thinks it's all about emotions. Black love is survival. You're poor and lacking in skills, in options – what can you do? You have a body – you use it. Survival is an emotion like any other.

Back on the gravel road we continue to Spillway – a fishing village named after the place where the lake overflows when the long rains bring more water than the power plant can handle. The flow bypasses the dam and rejoins the river on the other side.. In Spillway we find a kiosk that sells lukewarm soft drinks. Sigve talks to the children even though she barely speaks a word of Swahili. There are too many of them for us to be able to buy them soft drinks – the kiosk doesn't have enough. Instead we buy boiled sweets, and they stare at us as we sit there eating our packed lunches. They touch Sigve's long hair; blonde and moist in the parts that have been under the crash helmet, the ponytail is crisp with dust. And then they laugh when Sigve smokes a cigarette and blows smoke rings – more than thirty children of all ages stand around her, their mouths open, talking excitedly. When she puts it out, they call for more, so she has to light another one. "I'm getting light-headed," she says eventually and stubs it out in the dust, then curtseys to all the children.

There are no fish, and one of the boys explains to me that the fish aren't landed until two in the evening – translated into European terms that's 20.00, because in Swahili 0.00 is the same as our 18.00, and you count upwards from there.

African lambs and sheep with short fleeces, fat tails and floppy ears roam the village; and there are chickens, one or two scrawny dogs and ducks, which are quite rare elsewhere. The houses are made of sticks with mud slapped between them; the walls are pale because the earth is sandy and salty. The roofs are thatched with reeds from the lake.

I look at my watch – it's already 15.20. "We have to get a move on," I tell Sigve. I can't remember how long it takes to drive round the west of the lake back to Moshi. The children run after us, waving and shouting as we drive off. Down to the edge of the water, passing the overflow, which was also built by the Germans, with concrete walls as tall as a man and a concrete bottom – the whole thing as wide as a runway. It serves that first, brief stretch of the mouth of the canal, so that sudden floods won't wash away the soil and threaten the village downstream. If we made the trip during the long rains, it would be difficult to drive on to T.P.C. along this route; the road would be sodden and the tyres would sink in.

Not far from Spillway the road splits in two – I take the left fork, because the sandy trail looks like it's used more often; the right one most likely leads to the lake. Shortly after we meet a donkey-drawn cart full of logs. "I'm just going to ask him something," I tell Sigve and turn off the engine. I'm glad she doesn't understand Swahili – particularly not when it's spoken as quickly as this. The man explains the route to me; I should have gone right – he explains how to go on from there as well. I give him some cigarettes. "He says the route to the right is better at the moment," I tell her, taking us back to the fork in the road and choosing the right road.

I went out with local girls when I was at the international school in Moshi – culturally they were half-breeds like me. A Goan – a closet-Catholic; a Brit who had grown up in Tanga who died of confusion, stupidity and an overdose of heroin cut with fertilizer, so that blood poured from her eyes, her nose and her ears. And Shakila, whose father dealt with the Cuban ambassador's hernia and got him a cheap summer house at Pangani so Shakila could get a full scholarship to the university in

Camagüey, Cuba. They've all gone now; the States, Canada, and six foot under. They're not coming back. What would they do here? Nothing works; corruption, nepotism. I've gone away once – to Germany. But I couldn't live with the stiffness of it. Europeans are so cold. No-one speaks to anyone unless it's about work. They only live in their brains; they can't laugh before they've considered whether the timing is appropriate. The country is ugly.

The pylons bring the juice to Moshi – we follow them over the bumpy dirt road at a distance from the edge of the lake. The road leads away from the pylons and down through another fishing village – Ngorika – after which it continues along the edge of the water, and I can see a large shallow area full of wading birds. People fish from narrow boats – two or three men in each. Along the edge of the water there are steep rocky inclines down to the lake, interchanging with a scorched grass-like plant which is just beginning to put out green shoots and will be flooded when the lake rises during the rains. This time of year the Maasai use it as pasture for their herds of donkeys, sheep, goats and zebu cattle.

I was visiting Ngana at K.C.M.C. Nothing happened. I was worried they'd send him home soon. I didn't want to make the decision for Sigve. I didn't want to be instrumental in it either. I didn't know what to do. One morning I drove some tourists to Marangu as a favour to my big brother. I let them off outside the entrance to Kilimanjaro National Park and drove to Moshi and up to K.C.M.C., hoping that Sigve would be on duty. First I went to see Ngana, but his bed was empty.

"Where's Ngana?" I asked a nurse I had previously given a little money to ensure that the boy would be given a fair treatment.

"Nothing's wrong," she said. "He's trying on his new leg."

"Do you know if Sigve's here?" I asked.

"You can wait for her here," the nurse said.

"No, I have to go soon," I said. "Is she working today?"

"Yes. She's in the building to the left out back."

"Alright, cheers." I went down the stairs and outside. To the left there's a one-storey building. There are no signs telling you what's inside. I opened the door and entered an antechamber empty of people, reeking of disinfectants, pus and human effluvia. I went over and pushed open the two swing doors; stepped inside. I was in the mouth of hell. Living dead everywhere. The stench was staggering. The long room was poorly lit, but I could see Sigve. She was standing further in with her back to me, leaning in over one of the beds standing close to the walls at the side of the room – some of them containing both a woman and her child. I knew what it was. The death room. The illness is a taboo – shameful. The families keep their afflicted hidden from the outside world. Only people with money can be treated at a hospital. The poor people in the villages stay in their huts, hidden from their neighbours' eyes. The families say that it's a case of rampant malaria.

"You, *mzungu*," a rattling voice next to me said. I looked; an emaciated Rasta whose dreads were like a matte-black halo around his bony head. "Let me have a cigarette," he said in English. I went over to him, taking the packet out of my pocket, shaking out a few ciggies for him.

"*Tsk*," I said. "A bad place, this."

"Babylon. Aids. The message is hidden," he said. I looked at him questioningly. He looked back, feverish, sunken eyes surrounded by bone-dry skin: "*A-I-D-S*," he said, marking the pauses between the letters. "African International Death Star." He laughed briefly – his head falling back on his pillow, and he smiled; his skull seemed about to come out through his mouth.

"How long have you been here?" I asked.

"I'm going home soon," he said – I didn't know whether he meant home to the village. Or home.

"Can you travel?" I asked.

"I can't afford to die at K.C.M.C. I have to get to the village before my last breath."

"Does it matter where you die?" I asked.

"In the village they'll stuff me in the ground. A bus ticket is cheap. Once I'm dead, the price for a ticket goes up."

"Yes," I said.

"My wife can't afford that," he said. "They'll burn me in the K.C.M.C. oven. *Tsk*. That's dirty, that is."

"What will you do?" I asked.

"My son's coming to pick me up."

"Mick?"

I turned. Sigve was coming towards me. I went to meet her. She took my arm, turned me, led me through the swing doors – the mouth of hell – through the antechamber and out into the light. I wanted to hug her, but she was at work – had to be seen as a professional. It was mostly for my own sake. I needed to hold her. She stopped:

"I need a cigarette, Mick." I lit one and handed it to her. She took a deep puff, exhaled, took another deep puff and handed it back to me.

"Tough place," I said. "Can anything be done for them?"

"Saline injections," Sigve said.

"That's not a lot."

"It keeps them calm. And me." I didn't say anything. Smoked in silence for a while. Said:

"Yes."

"Have you seen the boy?" she asked.

"He's gone, trying on his new leg," I said.

"I know he's from West Kilimanjaro," Sigve said.

"I'm busted," I said.

"Where do you know him from?" she asked.

"From here," I said, making a gesture. "K.C.M.C."

"How?" she asked.

"I found him up there, and we agreed on the story about my work.

Otherwise there'd be no explanation for my coming to K.C.M.C. all the time," I said.

"Mick," Sigve said. She took a quick step towards me, and rising to her toes, putting her hand on my shoulder, kissed me on the cheek.

"Is there anything I can do for you?" I asked. She shook her head. Then she turned her back to me and went back in – through the mouth of hell.

I stop at a deep, dried-out ravine to assess how to force it. Sigve gets off. "It's too steep," she says, smiling, and starts jumping downwards through rocks and hard bits of earth. Her thighs flex against the fabric of her trousers – dust in the pale blonde hairs on the back of her upper arms. She's with me. Once she's up on the other side, I let go of the clutch and stand on the footrests as I guide the motorbike carefully to the bottom, adding gas in a low gear and leaning over the tank so I don't crash backwards as the deep treads of the back tyre delve into the soil, the chain pulls the wheel and the machine carries me up. Sigve applauds. "I'm glad we didn't get here till now," she says.

"Why's that?" I ask.

"The air is comfortable, and we can see the sunset." I don't tell her that once the sun has set we won't be able to see anything.

"Yes, it'll be quite something," I say, kissing her; her dusty lips and her warm, moist mouth.

We drive for a long time, steadily on along the lake, from one village to the next. The water stretches on and on to the north. Far to the north the clouds around Kibo are spreading, and I can see its snow-capped crown. The sun no longer burns quite so hot, and the evaporation from the rainforest on the mountain can't keep up with the clouds anymore. But the distance is so great that Kilimanjaro seems misty, as if behind a thin veil; the dust particles in the air don't disappear until the rains really start. Here and there the edge of the lake is covered in fields of reeds. I go as fast as I dare, without Sigve reacting. When I was younger, I used to race; I've got thirteen broken bones to show for it.

The road takes us through another village. IsLAm guEsthousE, it says in large, clumsy letters on a painted sign on one of the huts – upper- and lowercase letters in a jumble, the way most Tanzanians write. Small covered windows in the bumpy mud wall, its lime and plaster finishes peeling under the thatched roof. "Did you see that?" she says behind me. I saw it.

"What?" I say. What am I thinking? We're in the middle of nowhere. The sun is setting. I can easily be up all night fixing a motorbike or crashing for a few hours anywhere, speaking to people, eating crappy *ugali*, drinking lake water, shitting between bushes. But she . . . I shiver; my infatuation with her makes me reckless; there's no doubt in her mind that I will get us home to her little Europe before nightfall.

"It looked so sad, that guesthouse," she says – am I detecting the first traces of uncertainty in her voice? "Why do you think it was called Islam?" she asks above the roar of the engine.

"I think some of the fishermen came here from the coast when the lake was made. So they're proper Swahili people, Muslims. You can see that their features are different – their skin is fairer; Arab blood."

"We could always stay there if we can't make it home," she says.

"Oh, but we'll soon be at T.P.C.," I say with more certainty than I feel. Maybe she's adventurous, but that yearning can soon be sated by a rock-hard kapok mattress in Islam Guesthouse while the bedbugs feast on our blood.

It's already 17.30, and shafts of sunlight are kicking through the clouds like angels' legs. A flock of herons, a few marabou storks; the purity of the light because the sun is reflected by the large surface of the lake. There's no end to the House of God. Boys play football on the shore in front of the villages. The coolness of the late afternoon. Women washing their clothes at the water's edge, and girls helping to spread the colourful clothes out to dry on the sparse grass beyond the shore. .

*

I don't know what happened between them, but one day Sigve was in Arusha – in the middle of the yard at the garage, with the sun burning high above her – and asked if I wanted to go out for dinner. Our relationship began then.

"Look," Sigve shouts from the back of the motorbike, pointing towards the Blue Mountains, where the light from the setting sun comes through the clouds, warm, soft and golden, and I don't want to tell her how late we're running. The edge of the lake disappears for a bit and we're back in rocky terrain; the road rises and falls steeply through dried-out ravines, carved when the rains flush in swelling streams up and down from the lake. I stop to consider how to force them – we don't have time for her to get off and walk. The Blue Mountains are coming closer, but it's 17.45, and she doesn't like it when I go too fast. We still haven't reached the northernmost side of the lake, but here and there the rocky landscape gives way to lakeside plains where the road is nice and smooth without too much loose sand, and I can step on it.

"There are people there," Sigve shouts, waving her arm towards the water. I've seen them – a crowd of children and grown-ups gathered together.

"It's getting dark," I shout. "I don't think we have time to stop and ask for fish." She squeezes my shoulder in reluctant acceptance. "Alright," I shout, "But only for a minute." She squeezes my shoulder again and laughs, I think, as we race off the road and across a flat stretch of dry lakebed. Not far from us, young men jump out of two fishing boats and dive under the surface. We stop behind the group at the water's edge, and immediately the children surround us. They point to the outline of Africa that's tattooed on my upper arm, chatter and smile. All the grown-ups keep looking out towards the lake. They're strangely quiet. I stop the motor and can't see any fishing baskets. An elderly man in a baseball cap comes towards us. I greet him. When I ask how he is, he simply shakes his head and doesn't answer. The children are standing close and fall quiet.

"We're on our way to Moshi and wanted to know if there were any fish we could buy," I say in Swahili.

"There are no fish yet." He sees my surprise at his strange behaviour. "It's a boy – he's drowned," he says.

"No . . ." I say. Sigve squeezes my shoulder.

"What's he saying?" she asks.

"*Pole sana,*" I say to him and turn to Sigve. I tell her in English that a boy has drowned – they're diving to find his body.

"No," Sigve says and falls quiet. Then she swallows. "Is there anything we can do to help?" she asks, and her voice is thick. I turn all the way round to face her. Her eyes are moist. She looks at the man.

"No," I say. "We have to go."

"But . . . should we give them money . . . for the funeral?"

"This is not the time," I say and turn back. The man is standing in the same place, looking ahead with a vacant expression. I say goodbye to him. He says goodbye to me. I flip out the kick-starter. He tells the children to stand back, and I feel Sigve's arms tighten around my middle – she's leaning her entire body into mine. I drive off, quickly back to the road, which soon veers away from the northerly end of the lake and becomes a twisty, dusty, bumpy track. It's a good job we're not in a car and they had already found the body. We would have been asked to drive them to K.C.M.C. Then you have to. You can't not do it. Wrapped in a blanket on the backseat with the father and another male relative from the village. The hospital can't help the drowned person, but the family get a death certificate, they do something – you need that.

It's 18.10. There are many hawthorns. We can't have a puncture. The sun sets behind the Blue Mountains; the clouds are lit from below – orangey-yellow and purple. They don't grow many things here; the earth's too salty; just a little sweetcorn. The layer of dust on the road gets thicker, the rocks fewer and further between. We meet the odd minibus with large open-weave baskets strapped to the back – going out for fish; they whirl up dust from the road, and the cloud hangs thick and unmoving overhead so that I'm blinded and have to slow down.

The Blue Mountains really are blue in the dusk, and I know it upsets her that she's sitting alone behind me and we can't really talk. I don't know if I should say anything, and wonder if she'll mention the party soon. It's getting late and we have to go home and shower first – her hair has to dry. She squeezes my body and leans her face closer to my ear – the wind whips her hair into the back of my neck.

"I can't go to that party," she says. "They'll just ask what we've been doing today." She's been looking forward to that party – it's at her friends' place. The first time she has a chance to show me off: the Tanzanian Austrian. We didn't drink last night so that we'd be ready for tonight. Sigve's husband, Tore, has been called to a meeting at the project office in Dar es Salaam next week; the Scandinavian countries don't look on polygamy abroad with a fond eye. I've been told they might send him home. He might be there tonight.

"We'll just say that we were at T.P.C., swimming at a friend of mine's," I say.

"No," she says and is silent before adding: "If we skip dinner, they will have had a bit to drink . . . if we come later?" We'll do that, I think – that much is certain.

"That's what we'll do, then," I say.

Finally we reach a peeling, battered metal sign that says T.P.C. and Arusha Chini. We're in the southern part of the sugar plantation, which they don't use, because the soil is too salty – like most of the earth around Nyumba ya Mungu. The road is covered in a thick layer of fine dust which comes up around us and seeps in everywhere. We pass a large grey village of mud houses with thatched roofs. There's no light here, because they haven't got electricity in the village. We're some distance from the lake – what can they be living on? The plants by the roadside are singed with drought and seem crippled by the saline-rich soil. It's getting dark now.

It's 18.30 and I am relieved when we encounter the pylons, and the track twists along under them, and I know that they lead into Moshi. I have my lights on, and slipping in the dust is easy – if it had rained we would be driving in something like soap now. We follow the road through scattered clusters of houses for a long time without reaching T.P.C. Having moved west since we left the lake, we're now going north. The Blue Mountains are too big by far; we are too close to them and that has to mean that we're still a long way south of the sugar factory, which is more than half an hour's drive from Moshi in the dark. We pass a large bridge across a river – on the far side there's a control post with a bar across the road. I stop, greet the guard, tell him where we've been, where we're going. Here it's the Mbuguni River, which feeds Nyumba ya Mungu and is used for irrigation at T.P.C. – it's only on the other side of the dam that it becomes Ruvu River. I turn my head, and ask over my shoulder:

"Are you alright, Sigve?"

"Yes," she says.

"We'll be at T.P.C. soon."

"Yes," she says – that's all. And I accelerate. The road is better. The smell of molasses is in the air – we're close. Finally, not long after the bridge, we pass fields of sugar cane on both sides of the road. We pass a series of farm labourers' houses; little brick buildings with tin roofs. And then we reach Langasani; electric lighting in the houses, tarmac, the odd street light, and after a couple of speed bumps we have reached the workers' canteen. I stop outside the entrance. Turn my head.

"Shall we eat here?" I ask. "We won't make it in time for dinner anyway if we're going to shower first."

"Alright," Sigve shouts above the roar of the engine. I can't get a feel for her mood; I turn off the engine. She gets off. I lock the motorbike onto a railing with my chain. We stand there, looking at each other, something unspoken between us.

"Come," I say, taking her hand. We go in through the canteen and out the back, where there's a bar, a man barbecuing meat, tables and chairs under the trees.

"Just order something for me," Sigve says and sits down at a table. I go over to the waitress and order cola, fried meat, grilled plantains, rice and tomato sauce. I promise her a bit more money if she can make it snappy. We sit down, waiting for our food.

"We just have to be quick about the shower and then go," Sigve says.

"We have to remember the ice," I say. She leans forward, taking the cigarette from my fingers. Takes a puff. Hands it back. I lean forward towards her as well.

"Are you O.K. about it?" she asks. About what? That we're going to a party at her friends' house? That her husband might be there?

"Yes," I say.

"What if . . . ?" Sigve starts but stops.

"I'm with you," I say. "I'm happy." She grabs my hand on the tabletop. The waitress approaches with our plates.

"Good," she says. We eat while scrawny cats circle under the table. When we've finished, Sigve pours a little bit of cola onto the ground. She's seen me do it once with a beer.

"Have you become African?" I ask, smiling. She gives me a look.

"Sometimes I drink with my ancestors," she says. "Like you. There." She puts down the bottle. I nod at her. We get up from our table, and the cats leap at our leftovers.

"My thighs are buzzing," Sigve says when we get back on the motorbike. We drive past the administration office and the lit-up factory itself; a narrow dark chimney spews out sticky black smoke from the ovens where they burn the dried-out pressed sugar canes to produce electricity. The steam from the turbines comes from a wider, silver chimney. Now we're on T.P.C.'s good tarmac into Moshi. The railway tracks to the factory run parallel to the road , and I see a diesel train with a single light snailing its way towards us, pulling carriage after carriage loaded with sugar cane. The factory operates 24/7. Here and there in the fields, light is thrown up to the night sky; they're the places where the trains are loaded, even at night. The stars are out. Bats scurry past in the glare of my headlight. We're hit by sprays of water from sprinklers in the field by the side of the road. In the north-eastern corner of the sky, the moon comes out of the earth, full and red.

"We're going to a party to dance," Sigve shouts. She speaks so suddenly that . . . I don't quite know how to react. I have stopped thinking about her, because I feel her all the time. I don't say anything. "So the dead child will go to heaven," she shouts.

"Yeah," I shout. The dead child is in the House of God. Isn't that heaven?

After twenty kilometres of sugar cane we reach the outskirts of Moshi. Once this was all fields, but the population is growing, the city is spreading. We pass through Swahili Town, the inner city, and drive to Shanty Town, stopping in front of the house.

"You first," I say when we go inside. Sigve pulls off her clothes and throws them in the hall before going to the bathroom. Luckily there's water. In the meantime I find the pan with the lump of ice, get it out and load it into a woven shopping basket. I also find my clean clothes. The shower stops.

"It's all yours," Sigve calls – I go there. She stands naked, drying her back. I kiss one of her breasts. She laughs. I step into the shower. When I come out, Sigve is dressed in a light, white dress with silver threads sewn into the ribbed fabric; it makes her tanned skin glow. We take Sigve's car to the party.

There's a power cut. The house is dark except for a paraffin lamp on the concrete decking outside the front door, left there to attract insects. We go in and walk carefully down the hall towards the faint mumbling in the sitting room. They have lit candles.

"Sigve," a child's voice shouts – a little girl comes running and hugs Sigve's legs.

"Hi, darling," Sigve says. And here's the hostess – she's Australian.

"We're all outside looking at the stars. Grab yourself a drink," she says.

"Where do you want the ice?" I ask. She points towards the bathroom, where I find the bathtub full of cans of imported Carlsberg and bottles of Tanzanian tonic. There's already plenty of ice to cool things down, so I just put the lump in the tub and go to the car with the empty basket, light a cigarette, stand there smoking. I don't really feel like givng an account of myself to a load of aid-trippers with bleeding hearts. I go through the house. Out on the veranda, down the steps into the garden. Everyone is blurred except for Sigve, whose dress is glinting white in the starlight. I go to her. The Australian host starts questioning me: a white man born in Tanzania? A rare species.

The host's two children are running around between the guests, offering snacks; peanuts and thin flakes of coconut – oven-roasted with salt. It's a very white party, except for a couple of local doctors and a single Indian.

A couple come walking across the lawn and are lit up briefly by a passing car. Tore and a black woman.

"Hello, everyone," he says to no-one in particular. People nod and mutter. Everyone is oddly quiet – perhaps because it's dark and there's no music. Tore shakes hands with a couple of the black doctors and introduces the woman: Tunu. She is tall and slender, probably Maasai. Tore speaks to the doctors about the power supply for the operating theatre – something about a defective generator. Tunu is standing some distance behind him. She probably knows none of the people here. She's waiting. No-one can match an African who's waiting. A hundred years? It's nothing. These white people can never unsettle her. She's on a mission. She wants to climb the ladder. Maybe Tore is looking for the exotic in her. Maybe I'm looking for the same in Sigve. I go over to Tunu and introduce myself in English. She is beautiful, well-dressed; her eyes are hard. Maybe she's a lady of the night. I ask what she wants to drink. Beer. I fetch one, pour it, handing her the glass. Then I speak in Swahili:

"Let's wash away the tiredness," I say. She lights up.

"You're totally Swahili," she says and laughs.

"Yes," I say. "Born in Arusha."

"I'm from Arusha Chini," she says.

"I've been there hunting, with Maasai," I say.

"Really?" she says, laughing.

"Yes," I say.

"Do you know my friend?" Tunu says, nodding at Tore.

"I know who he is," I say. "I'm with his wife."

"Really?" she says, laughing. "Who is his wife?"

"The one with the long blonde hair," I say with a head movement towards Sigve, who is talking to the children. Sigve looks up at me. I smile at her. She looks down at the children and then up at me again. I can't read her eyes.

"She looks lovely," Tunu says.

"When you take her husband, I have to step in so the lady doesn't get lonely," I say. Sigve's husband has got himself a drink and comes over. Nods at me. I nod back.

"So, do you two know each other?" he asks.

"No, but Mick is from Arusha," Tunu says. "He's with your wife."

"Yes," Tore says. "I know." I can see that Sigve is watching us. But she doesn't come over. Tunu hands Tore her beer glass.

"Hold that for me," she says and goes up the steps and into the house. I smoke my cigarette. Tore takes a deep breath. Holds it in for a while before saying:

"You have to treat her well."

"I do," I say. A middle-aged white woman comes towards us. She is a Dutch doctor – also at K.C.M.C.

"How can you bring her here?" the woman hisses. Tore turns towards her slowly.

"You've been here seven years, haven't you?" he asks.

"Yes," the woman says.

"Have you never had sex with a black person?" he asks.

"No," she says.

"That tells me what kind of a racist you are," Tore says, turning away from her – back to me.

"And what kind would that be?" the woman asks.

"The inexperienced kind," Tore says, looking me in the eyes, smiling faintly. The woman snorts and leaves. I look at Tore. Standing tall. Now I can see why Sigve married him. Maybe Tore is wrong about who Tunu is and what it is she wants. Or maybe I'm wrong about his motives. Maybe Tunu is exactly what he wants. Right then the music starts. Light comes rolling out over us from the house. The power is back. Tunu returns. Tore hands her the glass of beer.

"Erm," he says. "I just have to talk to Sigve. About how we're going to do this," he says.

"Alright," I say.

"I'll be right back," he says to Tunu.

"Good," she says. He goes towards Sigve.

"Where did you meet?" I ask.

"At Golden Shower Restaurant," Tunu says.

"And then you became an item," I say.

"An item?" Tunu says. "He wants to marry me," she says.

"You're kidding?" I say

"*Haki ya Mungu*," she says – I swear to God. "He's rented a house and has moved me in. That leaves the wife free for you."

"Well – that's very efficient," I say.

"Yes. I have to think about my child's future."

"Does he know you have a child?"

"Not yet," Tunu says.

"Do you love him?" I ask.

"Of course," she says. "He wants to be with a woman who knows something he doesn't understand."

"Do you know many things?" I ask.

"I know everything," she says.

"How do you know?"

"My experience."

"Your own life?" I ask.

"Yes."

"Everything?" I ask.

"Everything that matters," she answers.

"I have to go to the white lady now," I say.

"Yes," Tunu says. "Don't stand here with me. You already know too much." I approach Sigve. She says something to Tore. He answers, she laughs a little. It all happens in Norwegian.

"Mick," she says. I go all the way over to her.

"Yes," I say.

"There's no problem," she says. "Everything's fine."

"Absolutely," I say.

"Alright then," Tore says. "I'll talk to you later," he says, leaning forward, kissing Sigve's cheek. I take her arm. They're playing ABBA on the stereo. Music for old people. I can't dance. I lead Sigve into the house, onto the floor, take her in my arms, give it my best shot. We dance for a long time. Drink more beer. Dance close.

"Let's go home," Sigve says. "Before we get too tired." We go over and say goodbye to our hosts. Tore and Tunu have left. I can drive even when I'm drunk, but I know that Sigve dislikes it, so we leave the car. The scent of the flowering flame trees soars towards us. The security guard lets us through the gate. Behind the villas dogs howl at each other. We walk through the darkness.